I0637279

RUNNING WILD PRESS

SHORT STORY ANTHOLOGY

VOLUME 8

RUNNING WILD

Running Wild Press Short Story Anthology, Volume 8
Text copyright © 2025 remains with authors
Edited by Benjamin White

Published in North America and Europe by Running Wild Press. Visit Running
Wild Press at www.runningwildpress.com. Educators, librarians, book clubs
(as well as the eternally curious), go to www.runningwildpress.com.

Paperback ISBN: 978-1-960018-81-6
eBook ISBN: 978-1-960018-80-9

CONTENTS

In Memory of
Nathaniel Farcas

THE STORY

NATHANIEL FARCAS

The question of why he was drawn to the house was one that he could not answer, but since there was no one around to ask it, he felt that it was irrelevant, and so continued his ambling walk up the driveway. The season was turning to fall, and the leaves were turning to gold and red, crunching beneath his shoes with every step he took; a brisk breeze nipped at his skin and the air smelled of rain.

Stark against a cloudless blue sky loomed a house that looked as if its owners had left hundreds of years ago, and perhaps smashed it with a bulldozer a few times on their way out. The windows were cracked and caked with a thick layer of grime, the walls had gaping holes with only spider webs to fill the gaps, and the door hung crooked on its hinges. The paint might once have been a lovely cream color, but was now a faded, filthy gray. Still he went on.

He reached the porch, where the stairs were slanted and the wood was rotted through, and with great care, he tiptoed across the fragile boards and swung the door open. It creaked, and groaned, and then detached from its rusty hinges and clat-

1

tered to the ground. For a minute, he puzzled over how to reattach it, then gave up, and stepped into the house, instinctively reaching to shut the door behind him before remembering there was none.

Inside it was well-lit by sunlight shining through the walls, and that was about all it had going for it. The hallway that stretched in front of him looked ready to collapse at any moment; the bookshelves on the side had fallen apart, and novels and knickknacks lay scattered on the floor; an incredible amount of dust covered seemingly every surface, causing clouds of it to rise into the air whenever the man even shifted.

He kept his footsteps light and careful, creeping through a doorway on the right. This room had been a kitchen once, but now shards of the tile floor lay askew, and the few appliances still standing on the counters had rusted beyond recognition. He stood, and shut his eyes, and squeezed them tight until all the light was blocked out, and focused; when he opened them again, he had been transported to another world. The counters were polished and shining, and the coffee machine whirred softly as it brewed fresh coffee.

Through the large open windows he could see the trees waving, stirred by a gentle breeze, and a tire swing hanging from a thick branch swinging back and forth like a pendulum. Somewhere there were voices—cheerful, bright voices, voices of happy children and loving parents. He tried hard to make out what they were saying, but it escaped him. Then he blinked and all of it vanished, and once again the windows were shattered, the swing was long gone, and the coffee maker was indistinguishable from the other lumps of old metal.

He let out a breath and moved from the kitchen, down the hallway and into the living room, where the smell of mold was so potent he could taste it, thick and bitter on his tongue, clogging his nose and lungs and making his eyes sting. Ruined fabric hung from the skeleton of an ancient couch, and an array of blackened, torn magazines were strewn across the rotting rug. They sunk beneath his feet as he walked to an old fireplace and knelt before it, peering at the remnants of ashes that had once been a crackling fire, keeping the house warm in the coldest autumn, bathing the room in soft golden light. He blinked, and it changed in an instant; he was hit by a wave of heat that warmed his skin and sent a bead of sweat down the back of his neck, and when he opened his eyes he saw the ashes had become a fire again, and he watched as flickering blue danced among the red and orange, and though the silhouette was soon stuck in his vision, he did not look away.

Again, he heard voices calling out—they seemed closer now, but the words still managed to slip from his grasp. He rose to his feet and turned, surveying the room. The couch was plush and the fabric was a pleasant pale blue; brightly colored magazines were neatly stacked on a coffee table, displaying smiling people with flashy clothes; the carpet beneath him was soft and clean. He could detect the faint scent of flowers. As he stood in that sunlit room, a voice rang out clear as day, loud against the crackling of the fire and the muffled chirping of birds outside—a child's voice—"Mommy! Come look! The big planes are here again!"

He spun to look out the window, but as he did he shut his eyes for just a fraction of a second, and he found himself looking through the spaces between jagged shards of grimy glass as the smell of mold once again overwhelmed him. For a moment he was discouraged, lowering his head and letting out a weary sigh, as if the weight of the world had been placed on his shoulders and he was just now coming to realize it. Then he lifted his chin, and left the room with renewed determination. With a sense of purpose, he marched up the stairs, barely noticing as one of the steps gave way beneath him and his foot nearly sunk into the rotten, mushy wood. The house creaked and groaned like a wounded beast; still he continued his journey until he reached the first room on the upper floor, and then he froze, struck by a shocking revelation—now he did not even have to close his eyes, for the house changed before him.

He had only a moment to take in the dilapidated bedroom before it was suddenly flushed with color. A bookshelf filled with thick, well-worn books stood against the wall; a large, neatly made bed sat in the corner of the room; most fascinating to him were the picture frames hung with care on every wall. Eyes wide with awe, he inspected each photograph closely, as if expecting to find a secret hidden in the portraits. They were pictures of a family, it seemed. They had been taken in various places—a beach with the wide blue ocean behind it, a snowy mountaintop, a little cafe—but the consistent factor was the two mothers with their three children, and they were all always smiling, always laughing, always utterly happy; even just a photograph, a moment frozen in time, seemed to radiate a feeling of joy and love. He felt himself smile looking at them, though he did not realize he was crying until he felt a tear roll down his cheek.

A child's voice again, not the same child he had heard before, and so sudden it startled him—"Mommy! Mama! Look at them! It's the big airplanes! They're here again!"

"I see them," a woman said, but it was a stark contrast to the child's cheerful tone. She sounded apprehensive. Scared even.

"They're getting closer to us!" another child shouted out.

"We—"

Before the woman could finish her sentence, the world changed before him, and, as the walls began to crumble, he left the room with haste. He was impatient now—he was close to the end of something, he knew. It was a feeling deep in his bones, beating in his chest, pounding behind his forehead. He was not sure if it was a good or bad feeling, but his curiosity itched at him, so with bated breath, he crossed the hall, each footstep creaking loudly in the silence, and stepped into the other room. His room. Or rather, the room he shared with his siblings.

* * *

Everything was untouched, exactly as he remembered it. The bunk beds had been sloppily made by him and his siblings and then fixed by one of his mothers earlier that morning; his favorite stuffed animal, a small, worn yellow duck, lay against his pillow; there were candy wrappers in the trash can, evidence of the chocolate they had devoured the night before. Three backpacks sat in a row, hanging half-open, filled with folders and textbooks and crumpled papers. It was all lit by soft sunlight, all warm and bright, all peaceful, and yet—something was wrong.

Something was out of place.

"We have to get to the basement," he heard his mama say, as if she were standing right behind him. "Quickly."

"Come on," his mommy said.

And then there was a great roar, like a giant lion ready to devour the town, and then there was nothing, and he stood in his room and wept and watched as it fell apart, except could he really call it falling apart when it had been that way for hundreds of years? And no matter what he did, no matter how much he cried, nothing would bring it back. Nothing would bring his family back, or the rest of the population, for that matter. The only sign of life now was the forests, the hardy trees still stubbornly determined to grow, popping out of the dry barren earth and forever reaching towards the sky—perhaps it was easier for them since there were no humans left to destroy them, he thought.

No humans left to destroy the world.

And so the question of why he had returned to the house after so long was one that he could not answer, but since there was no one left to ask it, he felt that it was irrelevant, and so he climbed onto the roof and sat and watched the golden-red sun rise over the horizon.

There were many questions, in fact, that he could not answer, and he pondered them in the back of his mind as his body began to crumble. He knew that he was not real, that he had died a very long time ago, and yet here he was, breathing and feeling and seeing. He existed just long enough for him to see his home, just once more. But now his muscles were disintegrating, his bones turning to dust, and soon he would be gone again, and still there was so much he did not understand, so many things he never got to do. He thought perhaps it didn't matter, though, because he was content.

Not happy, but content, and that would have to be enough.

A ROYAL PAIN IN THE EAR

LAUREN LANG

The highest room in the tallest tower of Wray Castle was the darkest, coldest, dankest place in the kingdom. It always smelled slightly of wet stone because even on the warmest day, the moisture never quite fully evaporated from the granite blocks the structure was made of. That may have been because the only window in the room faced north, and very little sunlight came in. The tiny bit of sunshine that did manage to make its way toward the room's interior was blocked by a pair of thick velvet curtains that were almost always drawn closed. The window coverings only let through tiny pinpricks of light where the moths had eaten through the once luxurious fabric. The curtains were necessary because one of the panes of leaded glass had broken where a bird struck it, and the wind whistled freely through the hole.

The rest of the room's contents were just as worn. The straw in the sagging mattress frequently poked through the threadbare sheets. A rectangular desk sat against one circular wall, its two good legs desperately trying to keep it standing. There was a single stool that, like the desk, wobbled and had been worn smooth from years of use. The only candle balanced precariously on top of the desk and was burned down to a mere nub. Even the rats avoided the top floor of the tallest tower as there was little there to justify their climb.

The room would have felt like a dungeon if not for the colorful costumes and props strewn carelessly across the floor. However, the room's only occupant, the famous court jester Charlamade, didn't mind his living quarters. After all, his life was one drawn-out joke, and he was the punchline. The fact he was assigned the shabbiest room in the castle was just the latest farce.

Charlamade frequently tripped over his juggling balls and marottes in the dim light and incorporated his various mishaps and injuries into his comedy. Reenactments of his clumsiness had helped make him famous, so he saw no reason to change his living habits now. Thus, the bureau, with its doors hanging half off the hinges, remained dusty and unused, much to the palace maid's dismay.

The maids were forbidden from entering the room to tidy up and only allowed to deliver meals on the rare occasion Charlamade was awake and dressed in time for breakfast. To their collective horror, the jester slept in the nude, so they quickly learned not to come in without knocking, lest they be offered a show they didn't care to see.

However, Matilda was in such a rush to wake the jester on this particular morning that she failed to remember her manners. She unceremoniously burst into Charlamade's room, red in the face and panting with exhaustion after running the tower's many stone stairs. She soon found herself blushing for another reason as she discovered the jester standing in the middle of the room practicing his juggling while clad in only a poofy pair of yellow velvet pants.

Charlamade, startled by the sudden interruption, missed

catching one of the balls, which quickly came down and hit him square in the nose.

"Ow!" Charlamade exclaimed as he grabbed his smarting face.

"I'm sorry!" Matilda cried. She whirled away from the half-dressed jester to offer him some privacy, but didn't leave. The message she was sent to convey was too important. She had to tell the jester his services were unexpectedly needed, no matter how angry or embarrassed he may be.

"What's the meaning of this?" Charlamade yelled, his voice coming out nasally and distorted through his hands.

"The Queen has an earache!" Matilda exclaimed as if those were the most important words she had ever uttered.

"And?"

"Well," Matilda stuttered, still speaking to the wall, "she has called for you to fix it."

"I'm not a doctor. I believe the treatment of physical ailments falls to the court physician."

"He's already been. It's no use. The Queen is miserable. She wants to hear your jokes. She thinks listening to them is the only thing that will take her pain away."

Charlamade sighed heavily, "And I suppose there's nothing that will dissuade her?"

"No. She's demanding you."

"Tell the court I'll be down as soon as I'm dressed," Charlamade said.

"But what will you do if you can't stop the pain?"

"Well, I guess I won't have to climb stairs for a few weeks," he said, his tone brightening at the thought, "The dungeons are in the cellar. Going down stairs is so much less work than climbing them."

Matilda let out a nervous giggle, afraid that the jester may not be joking. The Queen was notoriously ill-tempered, and her mood this morning was especially foul.

"Well, get moving, girl!" Charlamade shouted, prompting Matilda into action. She raced down the stairs and across the castle, where the court crier waited anxiously to announce the jester's arrival.

Charlamade took his time selecting a shirt and shoes from the pile of discarded clothing on the floor. He theorized that none of his typical tricks would work considering the severity of the situation. He needed something genuinely unexpected for an emergency of this magnitude.

He dug through the pile, picking up and throwing aside item after item until he came to the bottom of the heap. There, he discovered a plain white linen tunic he rarely ever wore and an almost brand-new pair of brown leather boots.

Getting an idea, he stripped off his gaudy yellow pants and found the brown leather trousers he wore only when he didn't want to be recognized at court. Between his clothing and his lack of makeup, he could easily pass for a commoner, which he often did when he wanted to enjoy a pint in peace at the pub outside the castle walls.

Slowly, Charlamade got dressed, gathering his courage as he donned his clothing. He headed down the stairs, hugging the shadows to avoid being seen by palace staff and passing guards. His movements were as precise and practiced as his juggling, and he made it to the throne room without incident.

There, he presented himself to the guards standing outside the closed, large mahogany double doors with a dramatic flourish and, in a loud voice, demanded to see the Queen.

"I would like an audience with her majesty! An audience with her majesty, I say!"

The startled guards stared at Charlamade as if he had grown a second head. Surprised by his sudden appearance and clever disguise, they failed to react immediately, giving the jester the time he needed to make a second appeal.

"Are you deaf? I demand to speak to the Queen!" Charlamade shouted so loudly that he was sure to be heard, even through the closed doors.

The noise startled the guards out of their stupor, and they rushed forward, grabbing his arms and dragging him backward and away from the throne room.

"Unhand me, you unwashed riffraff!" Charlamade yelled, "You cannot keep me from my monarch. I am her majesty's subject, and I have the right to speak to her! She has a problem, and I am the only one who can solve it for her!"

The guards grumbled and tightened their grip, dragging Charlamade across the cobblestone floor more roughly.

"Your majesty! Does your earache prevent you from hearing me?" Charlamade's voice was nearly hysterical as he screamed, "I beg of you, I am but a humble man, but I have brought you the cure!"

The doors to the throne room opened, and the guards at Charlamade's side paused. The court crier emerged. He was easily recognized in his deep red coat with gold trim, white breaches, and distinctive black tricorn hat. He approached the guards, whispering furiously in one man's ear. The soldiers released Charlamade, who promptly fell hard on his bottom. He winced as the crier stared at him, unamused.

"The Queen will see you now," the crier said sternly, "But I warn you, you'll pay for the offense with your life if you anger her."

"I shall not disappoint my monarch!" Charlamade proclaimed dramatically, picking himself up off the ground and dusting off his dirty trousers.

The crier did not look convinced, but he led Charlamade into the throne room anyway. The room was full of nervous looking nobles, who whispered amongst themselves as the disguised jester entered.

"A supplicant to see her majesty!" the crier announced as Charlamade paced down the long red carpet leading to the Queen's dais and threw himself to his knees in front of the monarch. He cast his eyes down at the rug and kept them there, staring intently at the lint on the pile like it was the most interesting thing he had ever seen.

"Who dares cause such a commotion in my court?" the Queen demanded in an icy tone.

"I am but a humble servant of the crown come to relieve her majesty's pain," Charlamade said, allowing a slight quiver to enter his voice. It wasn't entirely an act. He knew he was taking a considerable gamble presenting himself this way, and her majesty would not look kindly on his performance if she did see the humor in it.

"And what remedy do you offer?" she demanded.

"Why, laughter, your majesty. It is the best medicine."

"I have a court jester to entertain me," she said.

Out of the corner of his eye, Charlamade caught sight of the Queen raising her hand towards the guards. One flick of her wrist, and he would be headed to the executioner.

"But where he is?" Charlamade asked, risking a glance up at the monarch.

She looked older than her 45 years today, her face wrinkled in pain. She was rubbing the right side of her head, making the gold and diamond studded crown she wore list to the left.

"I don't see him here," the jester continued. "Allow me to act in his absence."

"Go ahead, *make me laugh*," the Queen said, her tone growing colder and more threatening by the second, "What do you propose to do? Juggle? Act? Maybe you'll *mime* something for us." She said, gesturing to the assembled nobles behind Charlamade.

"Oh, nothing so elaborate as that," Charlamade assured her. "Your majesty, all I ask is that you smile down upon me."

The jester could feel the tension in the room growing. The nervous whispering stopped, and the crowd went deathly still.

"And what have you done to deserve that?" the Queen asked, her lips twisting into the beginning of an angry smirk, "Nothing! Guards, take him away!" she yelled. "To the executioner with this one!"

And then, it happened. As her majesty pronounced the death sentence, her face upturned into a full-on evil grin.

"Oh! Oh!" She exclaimed suddenly, grabbing the side of her face with her hand. "My ear! My ear just popped!"

"Your majesty?" Charlamade asked.

"The pain is gone!"

The Queen let out a relieved moan as the rest of the court stared wide-eyed. Finally, someone in the back let out a nervous titter, and the tension in the room broke. The entire court erupted in laughter. The Queen's face relaxed, and even she joined in with a few hearty guffaws before composing herself and raising her hand for quiet.

The laughter died away, its passing marked by a few chuckles that quickly turned to coughs. Charlamade waited anxiously for the Queen to speak.

"Well, you've solved my problem. What reward do you seek?" the monarch asked, "Perhaps a job might be in order. My jester is still absent, and his tardiness has not gone unnoticed."

"Is he?" Charlamade said, the question hanging heavily in the air. "If your majesty were to look again, you might find him."

The Queen scanned the throne room, searching the crowd for a face she recognized.

"Your Majesty," Charlamade said, calling the Queen's attention back to him, "perhaps I would be easier to recognize if you had my juggling balls brought down. There is a maid who was watching me practice with them this morning. In fact, she assisted one of the balls in finding my face. I nearly had my nose knocked right off, but seeing as it is still firmly attached, I'm sure I could attempt the trick again."

The Queen stared at Charlamade through narrowed eyes, finally emitting a small chortle.

"I may have underestimated your skills, jester. Yes, let's see what other tricks you have up your sleeves. Go get your toys."

"I live to serve, your majesty," Charlamade said, bowing to her majesty before turning to leave the throne room. The Queen stopped him before he could fully rotate away from her.

"Oh, and jester," she said casually, "I wish to keep you closer. Have the maids move your things to a new room nearer to the rest of the court. I wish to keep my eye on you, funny man."

Charlamade just smiled and bowed again before leaving. He kept the smile plastered on his face as he climbed the long flight of stone stairs up to the highest room in the tallest tower for the last time.

UPROOTED

JON FAIN

The cops came the second hour, in separate cars. One of them pulled up at the end of the driveway where Matt's stepmother sat at a table under a red and white striped beach umbrella with what she'd called "the good stuff." The other cop parked out on the street, got out of his cruiser, and crossed the front lawn.

"I've got compost older than this guy," Matt's father said.

His table had a dozen pairs of old shoes on it: boots, loafers, and three pairs of slippers with dirty fleece lining, including a left one without a mate. One of the early birds to the yard sale had bought some wing-tips that looked like elf shoes, turned up at the toes. Putting them out with all the rest of the stuff that morning, Matt thought, *Who buys used shoes? They look like someone else's feet.*

The kid cop was one of those beefy broad-shouldered ones, with a harsh haircut. He glanced at the tables as he walked past old radios, dishes, bottles, souvenir spoons, brash-colored women's clothing, and what was left of Matt's old comics and stamp collections that somehow had never gotten tossed.

"You call?"

"They tried to steal," Matt's father said, "but I wouldn't let them get away with it!"

About twenty minutes earlier, he'd challenged a woman he saw picking the price sticker off a refrigerator ice maker. It was still in the box, never used. He wanted eighty bucks for it. He'd been in a sour mood all morning, which was more like the father Matt remembered—a serious guy who took the wrong things seriously—and less like the jokey guy he'd been during parts of Matt's visit.

His phone pulsed again. Nothing in the photos he'd gotten looked great. Work-wise, Matt had one of those jobs, responsible for everything, but reliant on others to make things happen. That was especially the case here, scouting locations when he couldn't be there.

The second cop, done for the moment with Maureen, came toward them, up the driveway.

When Matt was a kid, they had three police in town, none of them women. Although he hadn't seen her since high school, she still gave off the energy of one of those crazy terriers that dig rats out of their holes. She had the same intense blue eyes too.

"You can't be selling your old prescriptions, Gordon," Nancy Joy said.

"They're not mine," said Matt's father.

No, his were brand new pills Matt had picked up for him from CVS the day before. While he said they hadn't helped with the pain, they did have him hustling to the toilet. Sometimes, it's the side effects they end up marketing. Someday, Matt might be doing location work on TV ads for Blohopoo.

"Hey, Biscuit," Nancy Joy said to him. "Heard you went Hollywood."

"I guess you could say that."

"I guess there's hope for little fat kids everywhere."

Nancy had short hair like her younger cop associate and looked fit in her tight uniform. Her father Ernie had been a town cop, too; the Chief, in fact.

The cops were bad for business. Everyone was driving by, not stopping. The only current customer was a kid who'd discovered the old comics, and was going through the boxes, carefully setting some of them in a pile on the table.

"Mikey still around?" Matt asked.

"No... like you, she left." Nancy Joy smiled at his reaction. "He goes by Michele now."

Matt tried to imagine Mikey Joy as a woman. Matt had lived long enough in LA not to be surprised by much, but Mikey Joy?

When he was eleven, he'd get off the bus and run for his house because Nancy Joy—two years older than Matt and her brother Mikey—would be after him. She'd run him down, throw him into the brush and go for his nascent nuts. One time she made him touch her newly sprouted tits; over her shirt, but still. Nancy Joy bullied him until he gained fifty pounds one summer and got bigger than she was. That fall, she stopped bothering with the bus too, getting picked up in the morning by older guys in hot cars.

At the end of the driveway, under her beach umbrella, Matt's stepmother Maureen yelled something he missed. He remembered his first night back, when going down ahead of him to the bedroom in the basement, she whirled and glared at him—

"If you two think I'm not entitled to some of your old man's money, think again!"

Now, from down the driveway she shouted, "What's your objection to people being kept alive by modern medicine? Longer lines at the movies?"

* * *

Matt had not seen his sister Sunny since she'd come out to California and stayed with him for a week when she was eighteen. It had been almost five years since they'd talked. Now she was thirty-two, working an insurance admin job she hated, and involved—as he would find out, in more detail than he cared to —with a married man who had set her up in a house on Salisbury Beach, near where she and Matt had grown up in Massachusetts.

"How'd you find me?" he said.

"It wasn't hard," Sunny said. "You've lived where you have for a long time and still have a landline. Oh, and nice to hear your voice, too."

He knew it had to be something serious if she'd bothered to track him down. Their father was dying of cancer; she was blunt about it. Bladder, spread from there. She thought Matt should come see him. Talking about their father and the fate that awaited him got her upset. As she alternated talking and crying, Matt felt forced to listen.

She blamed some things; at GE, Gordon had spent time working on projects in nuclear subs and nuclear power plants. No doubt that had planted some cancer seeds. Or who knew? Diet, bad genes, lawn chemicals, power line proximity. Take your pick.

Matt had been long detached from his family, so had minimal interest in cause, effect, or any other contributor. He wasn't proud of the recognition, but that's what came to the top, like a film on the surface of the situation.

He wondered at one point if his father had any money, and if, in spite of the devolved connections, Matt might be eligible for some.

When she gathered herself, Sunny said, in a conversation

lull free of his evasions, "Sounds like you need more practice thinking about someone other than yourself."

He didn't commit to anything before he hung up. He had moved and stayed away—well, something like that has many seeds too. But by the end of her subsequent calls that came over the next week, when he heard more than he cared to about his sister's issues, along with a brief by-the-way comment about the bitter nursing home passing of their grandmother, Matt got betrayed by some imaginary, better idea of himself, which took over just long enough for him to agree to it. That and a possible inheritance, hopefully less imaginary. The production company he'd been with for the last three years had dangled an ownership stake, but he needed at least $250K to make that happen, and he was well short.

That first morning of his return, he lay in the basement bedroom his father put in originally for Grandma Selkirk, and listened to the birds, the footsteps on the floor above him, and the cars passing by the house. Earlier, he'd heard over-wrought peepers down at the pond. He remembered as a kid pounding sticks into the muck to make smothered creatures scatter. Wasn't June too late for them?

In summer, kids would get fishing line caught in the branches of submerged trees uprooted on the shore and fallen into the water. In winter, the pond froze fast because it was so shallow. Growing up, Matt wanted to be in one of the houses down closer to the pond. It wasn't like the rest of the neighborhood was that welcoming though. He just wanted to be out of his house, the family he was stuck with.

It smelled of mildew in the damp basement. The bedroom looked smaller, although he didn't think that could be the case. The walls had been cheap wood paneling back then, but now were painted off-white. The single bed had been replaced by a queen.

Whenever his mother was gone, the first time when he was eight, and Sunny was two, his father's mother would arrive. Grandma Selkirk drank Tab, smoked Virginia Slims, wore silk blouses with pearls, and had a box of peach Kleenex on every flat surface. The peach smell mingled with lilacs, lavender, whatever it was. The first two times Matt had to give up his bedroom for her. Eventually, his father hired a contractor to create the space in the basement.

Matt thought about texting his girlfriend, but it was too early. After being together four years, more or less, he was moving into her place in Long Beach. Donner, a graphic artist with a ten-year old daughter, had finally decided it was okay. Her family had been slow to come around to her living with another white guy.

If he was being honest, it hadn't been any newfound compassion that had brought him to his childhood home, nor was it any pipedream of buying into the production company. Matt had come because of Donner. She was the only one to whom he'd told his true full story. Before that, Matt would reduce it to a tale of abandonment, saved for women he was trying to sleep with. Donner told him if he didn't go and see his father he would always regret it; she doubled down, by hinting his moving in couldn't happen until he went.

Arriving in Boston, it was a foggy, rainy evening, 55 degrees. The passengers mixed groans and laughs when the pilot announced it. Typical New England June gloom. Matt had been back—without going home—a few times over the years as the region became more open and generous to film productions, but always in the summer. Now, the next morning, it had stopped raining, but remained gray. He went upstairs, opened the door into the kitchen where Maureen sat at the large center island, drinking coffee and reading a magazine.

"Boy, can really hear you coming," his stepmother said.

He still hadn't seen his father. When Matt arrived the night before, a couple hours later than planned, Maureen, she of the carrot-colored hair and face riven with wrinkles like tributaries, was the only one up. She was somebody who didn't hold back. Matt, who travelled so much he'd grown numb to it, didn't think anyone should expect anything else but delays, fuck-ups, and variable plans. He supposed that she was right, that he should have called about running late; he decided he had been wrong, letting Sunny convince him to stay at the house.

Matt heard someone in the hall, the laundry area, near the back door. He went and saw Sunny yanking a ball of mingled clothing from the dryer. A sheet was twisted around everything and she fought to get it loose. She swore and started to put some of the wet stuff back in.

Matt gave his little sister the once-over—not so little now. She'd grown broad in the hips, full in the face. Her blonde hair had dulled. She gave off the faint echo of their mother.

"I can't take Dad to his appointment today," she said, looking over at him, then stood up.

"Hello to you too."

"Oh, hey, yeah," she said, and they came together in a brief clinch.

"It will give you some time with him," she said into his ear.

Matt had expected something like this, but not so soon. He tried to think of an excuse, but what else was he going to do? Although he wouldn't have minded driving around Hapford some, see how much it had changed, or more likely, not.

He let his sister go past with an armful of the old man's boxers. "Lots of leaks," she said over her shoulder, as Matt followed. "Oh hey, Dad...did you see Matt?" she added, "Matt is here!"

Gordon stood at the island across from where Maureen sat.

He looked more hunched over than he was when Matt was a kid, but he straightened up as Matt and Sunny came into the kitchen. The kids in the neighborhood called his father "Abe," as in Lincoln, because he was tall and had a big head. Tommy Cramer would come up to Matt at the school bus stop and throw pennies at him. "Ask your dad to autograph them!" he'd shout, while Mikey and Nancy Joy and other kids laughed.

The two men caught each other's glance and the older one let his slide off first. It surprised Matt that his father didn't look worse. Sunny had made Gordon's fate sound bad, and now he thought it might have been a ploy to get him there.

His father drove to the appointment, but agreed after a mild argument with Sunny to let Matt drive back. He played the same AM news station on the radio that Matt had heard as a kid. "Traffic and weather together on the threes." He had heard it the summer after his senior year in high school, when he got a job at GE, part of the plant complex janitorial crew, where Gordon worked as a mechanical engineer. They rode back and forth to Lynn together for the three months he lasted as a jerkoff janitor's gofer, until he got enough for a one-way plane ticket to California.

After a patch of awkward silence and weather comments, Matt began to get the first of the day's texts, and he alternated responding to them and looking out the window. He hadn't been lying to Sunny in the times they'd talked before he agreed to come; it really wasn't a good time, work-wise, with a new production starting. The director wanted some location shots of the neighborhood he'd grown up in outside of Chicago, and beyond that there were the two dozen trailer rentals, the Teamster contract, and the usual dozen or so other things needing Matt's input, like negotiating with the businesses where they wanted to shoot, where they would park trucks and equipment, and determining noise levels at various times of the day. He had sent Lauren and Skip ahead, but he was due in Winnetka, Illinois as soon as possible. His plan was three nights, tops.

He didn't see much of Hapford before they got on the highway. Another rain shower started, and traffic slowed. The stretch they traveled was built up with company headquarters and other commercial developments, but nothing like LA, and neither was the traffic, which was almost quaint compared to the six lane, hours-long clogs Matt had grown used to.

He snuck looks at his father during the stop-and-go. His clothes were loose on him. He seemed to have a bluish hue to the whites of his eyes. Matt wondered about the bruises on the backs of the older man's hands. Now that he was paying more attention, his father was more ravaged than he'd first thought.

It wasn't just a doctor's appointment; his father was also getting an infusion. They waited in a crowded room among like-looking pairs of a patient and a family member; some people waited in wheelchairs, some people wore head scarves. Gordon's hair had stayed dark unless he was dying it, and he still had good coverage up top.

Matt hadn't planned to go in with him, but when the nurse came into the waiting room to call out his father's name, Matt stood automatically when she asked if he was coming too.

The middle-aged doctor was sharp-eyed, trim like a greyhound, with a firm handshake. Matt let him and his father talk. The doctor had a laptop that he used to direct the interview and take notes. The nurse who'd brought them into the exam room had taken vitals and that's what they started with.

"I think souls go into the Earth," Matt's father said at one point. "Like nutrients for the soil."

"Uh-huh," the doctor said, tapping on his keyboard.

"It's either that or we're all like pigs and chickens in a factory farm...when we get 'harvested' then you know, these aliens, whoever they are, they gather up our souls to snack on."

The doctor gave what Matt thought at first was the standard face reserved for the offspring of doddering old fools. But Gordon winked at Matt, and the doctor smiled and shook his head. Matt got that this was some sort of regular routine between them.

He lost track of what the doctor said next; something about a recommended treatment or procedure "because you're not letting us take the bladder." His father had always been Joe Serious. Matt thought having cancer would make him—anyone—more so. *Is he joking about death?* Matt had put his father out of his mind for a long time; now, questions about who he might be—who he had come to be—threatened to pop up.

The infusion room was on the other end of the building, one floor down. When Gordon was called, Matt followed before being asked. A short walk down a hall brought them into a larger room, with numbered areas along the walls, and a nurses' station in the center. One of them farther down called out to Gordon and waved for them to come all the way to the end.

Matt tried not to linger his look on any of the other patients as he passed, out of respect for their privacy. They were all in their big leather chairs, some alone, some with a companion. He saw more than one person huddled under a blanket. TVs ran softly. Tubes were attached to arms. A couple of the areas had their curtains fully drawn.

The nurse and Gordon joked a bit, and then she took another batch of vitals, and left. Matt started to get a flurry of new texts on his phone.

"That's Co-Pilot Karen," his father said about the attending nurse. "Her husband flies his own plane, and they go places on weekends."

The doctor had said this infusion would be the last, and

then his father would get something else going forward. Matt assumed Sunny and Maureen knew all the details.

"Hey, Gordon!" called a young guy in light green scrubs as he passed by.

"That's Chemo Sabe. The mixologist."

Gordon still had a penchant for giving names. His daughter had been named Abigail but her blonde hair glowed like sunshine, so Sunny it was. Matt remembered the guy who showed up at all the father and son activities, touch football, Little League, Cub Scout pinewood derby, even though he didn't have kids. Matt's father came to hardly any either, but he saw enough to dub the other man, "Jose Swervo." Although Matt at age eight didn't get it, he knew it was a slam.

"Did you know the kids used to call you Abe?" he asked.

"Did you know they used to call you Biscuit?"

Matt had been the fattest kid in elementary school. He got the nickname in 2nd grade, when he started eating all the lunches that his classmates didn't want. His record was eight plates of cheese ravioli. Plus, his own. The only time he regretted it was the day he had too many of the little biscuits that sat on top of the individual chicken pot pies the kids got. He thought the custodian that came with a mop and bucket was going to make him clean up the puke.

The infusion nurse returned. It turned out that Matt's father had a port for the chemo inserted in his upper chest.

Another text came into Matt's phone. He had too many things happening in Chicago. Now the director wanted a local crew brought in to do establishing shots with the movie principals, and Lauren and Skip were freaking out about the extra tasks.

"I've got to make some calls," he said.

"I'll be here."

Gordon watched as Co-Pilot Karen attached a bag filled

with blue liquid to the stand. She punched some buttons on the display, and it began its regimented drip. She patted him on the arm.

"Okay Gordon... you're up and running, I'll come around."

For the first time that day, Matt recognized his father, as the older man stared at the blue medicine being dispensed. Not that out-of-place jokey guy. Jose Serious was back, fallen back within himself.

* * *

The first time his mother disappeared, his father came into Matt's room the next morning, before he went to work. It was so early, the sun hadn't come up.

A couple of days later, his father sat him down and said how his mother was going to be gone for a while. This time, next time, each time—Matt hoped that his father would tell him something important. But he never did. Not even about the thing that mattered. He never explained why his mother kept going away. Or coming back, for that matter—until she didn't.

Before his mother, Annie, began going off to wherever, she'd show up sometimes at the end of the school day in her black Accord. She'd take Matt along to the grocery, or other places to shop, or to the small restaurant in the next town over, where they had his favorite—chicken tenders and fries. The spring, into summer, after second grade, they'd drive to the coast, usually Plum Island, or Gloucester. In Gloucester, Annie knew a group of artists. Matt wandered around by the water, climbed around on the rocks, and looked at tidal pools while she was in their studio.

When Sunny was born, their outings together stopped.

Grandma Selkirk came every time his mother left, because Matt's father traveled a lot. She and her sharp scents and sharper opinions. She cooked like a distracted drunk, which was what she turned out to be, those glasses of iced Tab fortified by the regular contributions of Mr. Boston 100 proof. She took his side against his father when he didn't want to get his hair cut, but was otherwise unsupportive through the years. "Speak up for yourself!" his grandmother said all the time, because he was a quiet kid. "Silence is unacceptable!"

Another thing she told him: "Your father rode a motorcycle up from Key West to Connecticut to see her. Don't you ever be that stupid."

Matt supposed once, in a more generous mood than usual, that maybe it was such a love for his wife that allowed Gordon to let her go like he did.

Less than a week after he turned twelve, with no cake or anything—he never would get a birthday party as a kid—when Annie left this time, he went for long bike rides. He'd plot revenge against all of them through the miles: his family, teachers, the kids who made fun of him, called him Biscuit. He lost weight that summer, and although it wouldn't be permanent, it brought a brief interlude of discovering he could accomplish hard things.

His father still took lots of business trips, but whenever he was around, Matt had to deal with him spewing random, platitude-filled advice. Other times, Gordon's anger popped; he told Matt how dumb he was when he got bad grades, how difficult life would be if he didn't lose weight. That was one reason why after his mother left for what turned out to be for good he went feral. When he started to show he would do just about anything, his neighborhood peers and pests Mikey Joy and Tommy Cramer let him hang out with them for a change. They broke into a small colony of homes on the biggest pond in the town. They threw M-80s onto the roof of where they went to elementary school. Mikey told them no matter what they did, if

27

they got caught nothing would happen because his father was the Chief.

Then came the building of the fort. A spit of land like a pocket peninsula, with two separate stands of white pines, extended from the Cramer's back yard into the pond. The five-sided structure was built from the ground up. Matt had helped with the wood; Tommy told him to sneak behind people's houses or into their garages and steal it, and he did. He also gathered whatever scrap was at his house, and then when they started on a second floor, he took one of his father's stepladders and brought that to help build and provide access to it.

After the structure was up, Tommy told him to get lost any time he came down. Mikey Joy would just laugh, and if kids from other parts of town were there they would chase him away. Matt would sneak back and hear them behind the blanket they had pulled across the entrance. He stayed nearby, kicking at dirt, picking up a rock or a branch to throw into the pond. It reminded him of the times he'd gone with his mother to Gloucester and he'd had to stay outside, climbing on rocks and looking into tidal pools.

Matt went back up to the hospital's main floor, looked out the large windows at the parking lot for the emergency room. An ambulance came in, red lights whirling. He didn't hear any sirens.

The traffic out beyond the hospital on 128 had thinned. The rain had stopped, but it was still gray-skied. Farther out, he could see the parking lot of the shopping mall.

It had been near the mall that he'd gotten dropped off after a second ride, hitch-hiking away from home when he was fourteen, freezing in the middle of December, two days after Tommy Cramer drowned, when he got afraid Chief Joy or another cop was going to come for him. But his thinking he could get to the Berkshires by lunchtime turned out to be stupid. He'd spent an hour warming up in the mall, and then managed to hitch back home before dinner. It was a school day so no one asked him where he'd been.

Likewise, his father had yet to ask him how he was, what he was doing, his job, anything about his life in California. No question as to what he's been up to for all the years. Maybe Sunny had filled him in, but he doubted it. She hadn't seemed that interested either during the course of their phone calls, talking mostly about her troubles.

A few years before he heard from his sister, Matt had started to believe he would be getting a different call from his past, from a woman claiming to be his mother. It was less wishful thinking than a regular reverie. She would have seen his name in a credit crawl. Arnold Schwarzenegger was Governor, so anything was possible.

He would finally agree to meet the maybe-mother, choose a sushi place he liked in Santa Monica. They would make the standard jokes about eating bait. She would look older of course, but like he remembered. She would ask that he call her Annie.

He still isn't sure she is who she says she is. But then she'd talk about their trips to the Busy Bee the next town over, for his favorite meal. And she'd drop in the same complaints she'd had about her husband, like, "Your father can't turn on a light without worrying about how much it costs" and "He'd rather live with your grandmother anyway."

After, they'd walk in the park ignoring the convention of homeless people, and on the path overlooking the ocean, stand at the fence and look at the Pier, all lit up.

Now, looking out the hospital window, upstairs from where his father was being infused, Matt imagined a new chapter.

He and Sunny are at the house, sitting on chairs on the old flagstone patio that's scarred with stains and lichen. Through the trees at the back of the yard, they can see a sparkle on the surface of the pond that he used to have dreams about, until he didn't. His phone would go off, and for once when he pulls it out his pocket, it's not about work.

"Here." Matt would hand it to his sister. "It's your mother."

* * *

Twenty minutes after the cops left the yard sale, three hours before Matt's scheduled flight to Chicago, Sunny—whose idea the thing had been, the thing being the whole thing, him being there, not just the yard sale—finally arrived. She was pissed off that there was so much stuff left, that they hadn't sold more.

"I think we need to keep everything out later than one o'clock," she said. "Unless some fairy godmother shows up and buys everything."

It hadn't taken him the full 72 hours he'd been home to realize that the yard sale wasn't strictly about down-sizing—his father and stepmother needed the cash. Gordon had insurance, but Matt had overheard enough inside conversations to glean that it wasn't paying for everything. He didn't have anything to offer them; the best he could do would be not to ask *them* for money—or scope out if any would be coming to him—as had been his half-assed and unlikely-anyways plan.

The night before, after a dinner of takeout pizza, pasta, and salad that Matt had treated everyone to, and after Sunny had made him agree before she left for Salisbury that he'd get up early and move everything out from the garage into the driveway for the yard sale, he went into the living room.

"Check out Maureen," Matt's father said, laughing.

Although there was no music playing, his orange-haired wife danced in front of the fireplace, rocking her hips, arms twisting over her head. She flapped her fingers, her hands up high, like she was playing castanets. When Matt saw the way Gordon looked at his wife, he recognized how disconnected to all of it he was. He felt like an intruder, a ghost that had come back to haunt the wrong house.

Maureen worked on a pair of women who were looking through clothing and bedding. Another two cars pulled up on the street. Sunny went over to Gordon and moved slowly with him toward the house. Matt could hear his father telling the story of the cops. He wondered how long it would take Gordon to come up with a nickname for the young one.

The kid who'd been the only potential customer while the cops were there continued taking comics out of the box and adding them to his stack. Matt walked over.

"Find some good ones?"

An index card that Sunny had prepared, folded like a table place setting, listed all the comics as $.25 each. Five for a dollar. Matt knew they were worth more than that. Probably more than a never-used, still-in-the-box icemaker for a refrigerator. But even if Sunny's wish came true and everything sold, the proceeds wouldn't add up to a decent tip for Chemo Sabe.

"My Dad says I should...ask them less, make them cheaper," the boy said.

"Dads say a lot of things," Matt said.

Sunny had gotten Gordon back into the house. Dropped back into this world after so long, Matt had no clue about what his own father was thinking, just like always. Whether Gordon having his long-gone son around even mattered.

"Just take them," he said.

The kid's face brightened with surprise, then he collected his chosen comics and ran off. Farther down, the original road had been extended into an overly-wide sub-division. It had just been woods, with a footpath to the pond, wide enough to bring a rowboat or canoe in. The kid ran toward one of the newer houses.

More people arrived to catch the end of the yard sale. Maureen waved to get his attention. *Fuck it*, Matt thought, *I'm leaving*. He needed to see what he had to see before he did.

He walked down through the back yard that looked like no one was caring for; his father had been obsessed with it when they were kids. Now it was loaded with dandelions, moss, and other weeds, patches of brown dirt, and rotting stumps of long-gone trees.

He went onto the road, and stopped at the first house he came to, where the Cramers had lived. It didn't look like anyone was home, no car in the driveway. It had been painted yellow when Matt was a kid; now it was gray, with black shutters, white trim. He remembered seeing black-haired Mrs. Cramer standing and looking out the window in the living room. He'd been in the house only once, for a birthday party for Tommy when they were in first grade.

He went into whoever's yard it was now, and then along the side of the house, toward the pond, water sparkling in the midday sunlight. It was formally named Mill Pond, but most called it Low Pond, because it wasn't very deep, no more than six feet anywhere, and most places closer to three.

Matt used to dream about the pond, but that stopped soon after he arrived in California. In those dreams, the recurring one anyway, he'd walk into the water, then fall forward and float on top of it face down, before jumping up, splashing, standing in the shallows, where even as a kid it only came up to his waist.

Because Tommy and Mikey didn't want him around when they were playing in the fort, Matt used to sneak down through the woods behind his house, and go through a dense patch of small pines and undergrowth to reach the pond, at the place where the old mill had been, and there was a cracked but functional dam.

The time that sparked his dreams, one mid-December Saturday late afternoon, already growing dark, Matt went his usual route to try to spy on the other kids. As he reached the pond he heard voices. Mikey and Tommy had extended their bullying the previous fall beyond their small neighborhood to the freshmen football team. Since they were two of the better, popular players, they had plenty of help going after Matt in the locker room and on the practice field, where his position was tackling dummy. He waited to hear if maybe there were a lot of kids there; it would be like walking into a trap.

He recognized Mikey's voice. The other he assumed was Tommy's, but it sounded different. Just the two of them, not in the fort, near the water.

Matt crouched below the dam, near where the spillover dropped to join a stream that wound its way into the woods. The ice never formed close to the dam, especially this early in the winter; a semi-circle of open water stayed of variable size.

When he heard splashing, he realized somebody was in the water.

He stepped out of his hiding place in the thick bushes.

Mikey stood on the shore. His pants and coat were dark-stained, wet up to his waist. He was big for a ninth grader, already six feet tall, so he could have gone anywhere in the pond and it wouldn't have been over his head. He heard Matt come up behind him and turned. Then he looked back at where the splashing had started again.

Sometimes it was better not to see things, but Matt knew he had to help. He couldn't swim though; he was scared of being in the water. It was one more thing the other kids made fun of.

Mikey stopped staring at him, but he still didn't move.

Mikey was the one who should have gone in there, gone back. Tommy was his best friend, wasn't he?

Matt turned and worked his way back through the tangled brush, emerging near the corner of his yard where he'd entered. He went up the slope to the back door of his house, into the hall, past the washer and dryer, and into the kitchen.

Grandma Selkirk sat at the kitchen table, a cigarette fuming in the large palm tree shaped ashtray, a souvenir from Key West that Matt's father had gotten when he was stationed there in the Navy. Next to it was the blue and white ceramic tea mug that she sipped from in the winter months, the seasonally appropriate vodka vehicle, the tall glasses of Tab waiting for warmer weather.

"What got up your kilt?" his grandmother said. "It's not time for supper yet, big boy."

She'd seen him coming up through the big picture window that overlooked the back yard, from her perch at the kitchen island, where she settled at 3pm every afternoon. A small TV on the counter played a game show.

"Go tell your sister to send her little friend home, she's got to come down and do the ironing," said Grandma Selkirk, flicking ash. "Mozambique!" she said to the TV. "Idiot."

Matt went upstairs. His bedroom was at the front of the house at the top of the stairs. Sunny's was at the back, next to their parents'—Gordon's alone by then. His sister's door was closed, and he could hear voices, but didn't knock.

His sister yelled at him from where she was playing on the floor with Barbies, toy horses, and coloring books and crayons, with Lilly Joy, who was Sunny's age and at the time her best friend. Lilly was one of those kids who had to wear eyeglasses absurdly young, and their pink-colored frames made her look like a startled bug when Matt surprised them coming in. He went to the window.

That's where he was ten minutes later as a police car, with lights spinning, but no sound, and then a fire truck, came down the hill on the side street, toward the pond that most called Low, because it was so shallow. Always safe, until it wasn't.

* * *

At the back of the old Cramer house, Matt went out onto the spit of land that extended from the yard. The fort had been taken down, and so had most of the trees that Mikey and Tommy had hammered the boards into.

They had been on the too-thin early winter ice and broken through. The story was that Tommy got his foot caught in a nest of sunken branches that had fallen into the pond and drifted to the dam over the years. He fell face forward and couldn't twist or raise out his head. His heavy winter coat got saturated and held him down. Mikey had gone in but couldn't pull him free. He ran to get help, but when it came it was too late.

Matt sometimes thought over the years that he had seen Tommy's body, but if so, it was only a coat floating on top of the water. There were too many half-assed amateur psychiatrists who thought the wrongs that had been done to a person, bad things that had happened, bad things they had seen—the *trauma*—collected to form and develop who they were. Matt believed that people who survived shaped—and saved —themselves.

"Hey! Biscuit!"

Startled, Matt saw Nancy Joy, without her hat, coming from where she'd parked her cruiser on the street. The equipment and weapons hanging off her duty belt made metallic and rattling sounds as she walked.

"Got a call there was some big guy in their back yard," she said. "And it's just you."

Matt waved, took a step, and his left foot landed on a tree root exposed above the ground. He stumbled, staggered, and his ankle twisted. He toppled to the ground.

"Oh, for Christ sake!" said Nancy Joy.

Matt got up, but couldn't put any weight on his foot, had trouble standing, hopped a bit before letting himself drop down.

"I need this like a second asshole," Nancy Joy said.

She got under one of his arms and lifted and while she wasn't as strong as Matt hoped, they managed to move up and across the old Cramer back yard.

"Don't be a wiseass and grab a tit," she said.

He saw a woman with dark hair looking at them out her glass slider at them, and Matt thought for an instant it was Tommy's Mom, still living there, but the family had moved out less than a year after their son's drowning.

Nancy Joy said she'd give him a ride up the hill, because he clearly wouldn't make it. He was able to start putting weight on his left leg and foot, and by the time they reached the cruiser, was feeling more hopeful that he hadn't hurt himself badly.

"Nice car," Matt said, trying to stay on whatever passed for her good side.

"We've got an anti-terrorist, anti-bomb vehicle, fully loaded," she said.

Matt didn't know what to say to that. As he finished easing himself into the back seat, a call came in on the radio.

"Sergeant Joy...we just got a call from a resident over in West Hapford. Says there's a human torso on the side of the road. Over."

"No shit," Nancy Joy said. "No *shit*."

She punched in some sort of code on the rig in the front

seat, glanced at the video monitor that took up the passenger side. She called back and said she was on her way. The cruiser shot forward and flung Matt against the back seat. As they whipped past his old house at the top of the hill and through the stop sign onto the main road, Nancy Joy snapped on the blue lights and siren.

"Hang tight!" she said.

It was kind of crazy she didn't let him out, but he wasn't surprised. Her father, the Chief, used to take kids for rides in his cruiser all the time. Matt saw familiar fields, stone walls, and houses flash by as they sped across town.

When they arrived, another two cruisers were already there, including the one with the young cop who'd been at the yard sale.

"Hang tight!" Sergeant Nancy Joy said again, getting out of the cruiser, putting her hat on.

She walked over to where the other cops were standing by the side of the road. The radio in the front seat snapped and crackled with activity; other towns were sending cops too. A state police cruiser pulled up behind where Nancy Joy had parked. Matt hoped the Statie who glared at him sitting there in the back seat as he strode past didn't jump to any conclusions.

Cars traveling on the road slowed from both directions, as drivers tried to glimpse what was going on. It was a stretch of road that Matt had ridden his bike on countless times, or on the bus to high school, which was only a mile or so away. He took out his phone, to see if his flight to Chicago was still on schedule, and when he saw it was, started looking at a flight to change it to. He was never going to make it now.

He looked over at the expanding crime scene. If someone dumped a body, and he was right here, he could be sitting on something big. True crime shows were hot. Maybe he could work something out with his bosses; he put down his phone and tried to see what was happening, thinking to get out and get closer, but Nancy Joy was coming back.

"Fucking bullshit!" she said as she got in. She tossed her hat on the seat beside her.

"What's going on?"

"It's a brisket!" she said, put the still-running cruiser in gear, pulled off the side of the road and away.

Matt thought Nancy Joy said, "Biscuit," like she'd been doing all morning.

For a dazed moment, he thought she was bringing him to the station. Finally, he was going to have to confess he didn't do anything to help Tommy Cramer. She'd caught him earlier at the scene of the crime.

"Fucking kids," Nancy Joy said.

She drove fast, but not as fast as before. Matt wondered if Nancy Joy was crazy enough to give him a high-speed, lights-flashing run to the airport in time to make his flight. Become an accessory to his escape.

"Were you joking about Mikey?"

She looked at him in her mirror with a hint of the same smirk she used when she bullied him growing up.

"What do you think?"

What do I think?

Matt thought he was in a poorly directed, miscast mess of an unnecessary sequel. But the locations were true.

"Where's she at now?" he asked, though couldn't imagine any of them anywhere but in deeply rooted memories and dreams.

OPEN HOUSE

ELIZABETH S. DEVECCHI

Sam exited the car, brushing at the creases in her blouse. At least her skirt was mostly wrinkle-free, the front anyway. The back had been sweat-glued to the driver's seat for half an hour, thanks to the air-conditioner's untimely death five minutes into the drive. She'd longed to trade the hot breath panting at her from the vents for some fresh air, but kept the windows up to preserve her coiffed hair. This was her first open house. The office would send someone to check in on her. She wanted to look professional.

Translucent spots bloomed on both sides of her blouse, threatening to join forces.

I should've brought an extra shirt. Next time I'll bring an extra shirt.

The thought was followed by the voice in her head that enjoyed picking at the scab-like edges of her short-comings.

Like there'll be a next time.

It was *his* voice. The latest in a chorus of abuse.

How stupid are you? There's a fucking heat wave. Useless bitch.

Her lips pressed together like opposing forces locked in combat. She reached into the car to gather her purse, a transistor radio, and a platter of cookies.

"I've got this. I can do this. I am a strong independent woman." The line from the internet secret-to-success site sounded hollow from her lips.

Fake it till you take it.

The misquoted expression pushed a smile to her face. This was the voice of a friend. And, despite having the vocal texture of a gravel driveway, it calmed her. The raspy voice of lifetime-chain-smoker, Mrs. Turner, always did.

Mrs. Turner was the first neighbor she met after she and Jimmy moved into their little yellow house with its adorable white window boxes. The ones Sam tried planting a million different kinds of flowers in, to no avail. It was Mrs. Turner who finally told her that she'd have to strip the old toxic paint off those boxes if she ever wanted anything to grow in them. It seems a thing can look absolutely precious, and still be seeping poison.

They met a week after the move when Mrs. Turner's terrier, Teddy, had dug under the fence and up through Sam's flower garden while she weeded. Thankfully, Jimmy was at work. He despised dogs.

"Oh, thank goodness you found him, *cara,*" said Mrs. Turner when she'd opened the door to Sam holding the squirming escapee. "Such a naughty boy. Such a *birichino.*"

Then, Mrs. Claudia Turner had apologized for English not being *the mother tongue.*

"Mr. Turner, he was a soldier, a handsome, *bellissimo* soldier. He scoop me up from my mountains, my beautiful *Alpi,* and bring me here. He is with our beautiful children, with God now. I stay here and bring flowers."

It was Mrs. Turner who said she thought *Sa-man-ta* (her

pronunciation of Samantha), would be good at "selling the houses, like on the HGTV."

When she said it, Sam blushed and dismissed the notion. But, a seed had been planted. The day she mentioned it to Jimmy, he laughed until he could barely breathe. When she asked if she could borrow some money for a course and the licensing exam, the laughter stopped. It wasn't the first time he'd raised a hand to her, but one of the more memorable ones.

She flinched at the memory.

It was Mrs. Turner who gave her the money, though Sam had protested.

"My money, I spend how I desire," she said, pushing the wrinkled white envelope into Sam's hand. "The flowers for my loves, I buy every week. The *biscottini* for Teddy, maybe I should buy less." Both women looked at the plump pup and smiled.

"After this, there is plenty. Please."

In the end, a tearful Sam accepted and vowed to pay back every penny, plus interest, when the commissions started rolling in.

Now, here she was in front of her first listing, an abandoned fixer-upper. Any commission would be small, her cut microscopic. But, as Mrs. Turner said when she heard about it, "you gotta start at somewhere."

And, *somewhere* for Sam was this little white Cape Cod with faded red shutters.

It needed fresh paint, and the lawn was mostly weeds. The previous owners had disappeared, left it in disarray. But, it had its charm.

Sam entered the foyer. Each step shot waves of doubt up through her bones and echoes down the hall. She wandered into the kitchen, and set the radio and the cookies on the aqua-blue laminate counter dominating the space. Someone had started to clean. The chrome countertop trim was polished, the floor swept, and a hint of lemon lingered in the thick stale air. But, whoever had been here had not finished. A dirty yellow dust rag lay on the floor.

Sam chewed the inside of her lip. She didn't have cleaning products with her. She was told to do a walk-thru, stage furniture and personal items to make the house look spacious and lived-in. Then she was to neatly arrange spec sheets and set out treats for the open house so she could greet potential buyers and charm them into making an offer. Her broker hadn't mentioned anything about cleaning.

Ha! I'll bet it was the first thing he said, dumb bitch.

"Go away," she ordered the voice, fists clenched, recalling his sneer when she'd left the house.

No way you don't screw this up, dumb bitch. And, that old hag down the street is even dumber for giving you money.

That had pissed him off something awful. Sam worried he would march down to Mrs. Turner's house to *give her a piece of his mind.* In the end, he gave that piece, plus others, to Sam.

She reached over and switched on the transistor radio, another gift from Mrs. Turner, fiddling with it until she captured her favorite channel, a local station that played hits from the 70s on up. The news wrapped up, and Phil Collins' "Take Me Home" filled the air, lightening her mood.

She ventured through the house. Things weren't as bad as she first thought. Of course. Her mind always raced to the worst possible scenario. Mrs. Turner once asked if Sam got tired always being so pessimistic. Coming from a woman who had lost her entire family, the question had put things into perspective. She had given Sam the radio because "music make the brain happy."

Aside from some dusty surfaces and the occasional dead fly or beetle, the house seemed in good shape. It needed some

TLC, but Sam could imagine a young family making a loving home here, the kind she dreamed of. She sighed and continued her tour, fingers laced at the front of her waist.

When she opened the linen closet in the very tiny, very pink powder room, her face brightened.

"Cleaning supplies," she announced, mentally flipping the bird at *his* voice.

She set to work tidying to the beat of Madness's "Our House."

Toward the back of the house, Sam found the door to the main bedroom. She opened it and her heart rocketed into her throat when a thin gray cat with white paws shot out and dashed between her feet. It turned the corner toward the kitchen.

"Kitty, kitty," she called, following the feline. "How the hell did you get in here?"

The cat was perched on top of the old refrigerator.

"Poor thing. Who locked you in here?"

Sam plugged the sink drain and opened the faucet to let water accumulate in the basin. The cat hopped down.

"You must be thirsty. Here you are." She stepped away to give some space.

The cat inched over to the sink. It eyed her, hesitant to take more than a couple licks. Then, thirst took over, and it plopped its front paws into the basin, drinking without so much as a glance. After lapping up its fill, the cat sat cleaning its soaked paws.

"You look like you're wearing socks."

The animal paused to observe the paw it was grooming. Sam gave a startled laugh.

"May I pet you?" She took a step forward and paused.

The cat didn't run, so she approached and gently scratched

behind its ears, something her new friend seemed to enjoy. Its gentle purring vibrated against her fingertips.

"Sorry I don't have any food," she said.

The cat looked over at the tray of cookies.

"I don't think cookies are good for cats."

It continued to stare.

Sam reached under the Saran wrap covering the cookies and broke off a small piece. She held it out, and the cat devoured it.

"I can't give you anymore. After the open house, maybe I can take you to my friend to find you something better to eat."

The cat hopped off the counter and trotted down the hallway.

"Wait," said Sam. "You can't be in here for the open house."

She followed, trying to think of a way to lure the cat into the garage. It slipped into the main bedroom. When Sam entered, the cat looked back, meowed, then ducked behind a closet door, ajar at the far end of the room.

"Come on, kitty. I don't have time for this."

A dead cockroach, legs in the air on the dusty red oak floor, caught her eye. She winced. Its body poked out from under a rusted bed frame topped with a mattress resembling an ancient treasure map, its landscape painted in dark sprawling stains. She stepped into the closet, straining to see, kissing for the cat. Sour, dust-filled air assaulted her sinuses.

Before she could reach for the chain hanging from the light fixture above, the door slammed shut and darkness swallowed her.

Stupid bitch, even a mangy cat's smarter'n you!

Sam squinted, her eyelids damming up tears. She waved her hand, searching for the chain that would bring light. The tinny voice of a weatherman, reminding his listeners to wear sunscreen, sounded in the distance. Then, purring from somewhere in the darkness. Purring that grew louder until it had all but drowned out the radio. *Something else is in here.* The thought overwhelmed her. *Nothing in here besides your fat ass and a goddam sock-wearing cat!* Callous laughter ricocheted in her skull.

She searched the air with both hands until something tickled the backs of her fingers, sending a tingle down her arm. *The chain!* She grabbed it and gave a decisive yank. Light exploded, as if she'd lit a tray of flash powder. Then, the room went black.

When she squeezed her eyes shut, an after-image like the negative of a photograph appeared. In the image, the cat, now dark gray with black paws, stared from the far corner, head slightly tilted.

Something soft brushed her calf. Sam reached down and felt the cat lean into her.

"Did that scare you?" Her voice squeaked past quivering lips. "It sure scared me."

The cat reached its front paws onto her knee, the tips of needle-sharp claws prodded and retreated. She scooped the feline up and reached to where she'd seen the door, feeling for the knob. When she opened it, natural light flooded in.

"Oh, thank goodness," she said, stepping out and pulling the door shut behind her. "Let's not go back in there."

* * *

"Mamma! You found Socks!"

A wiry little girl with pigtails the color of roasted chestnuts, and a towheaded boy perhaps a few years older ran over and hugged her legs. The boy took a step back and stretched his arms up towards the cat ... Socks.

The stiflingly hot room shimmered like a desert road. Sam handed the cat to the boy and reached for something to steady herself, finding a sturdy piece of furniture next to her.

Was this dresser here?

Her thoughts skittered like roaches from the light. The more she tried to orient herself, the more confusion nipped at the edges of her mind.

Someone had staged the room as perfectly as any she'd seen in *Home and Garden*. The old dingy mattress was now concealed by a rose-print bedspread and set against a dark wooden headboard that curved back to kiss the wall. Velvety pink and green pillows lined the top of the bed, leaning against a mound of larger pillows dressed in matching rose-print shams.

Sam's temples pulsed. She did not remember seeing the nightstands or the Tiffany lamp centered on each. Her free hand floated to her forehead, the other stayed firmly clamped around the lip of polished oak where the top of the bureau sat above the drawers. The children stared with expressions of concern.

"Mamma is having an episode. Get Daddy." The boy released the cat and waved the girl toward the door. She hesitated, then rushed out. He grabbed a pillow from the bed, and helped Sam ease down to the floor, sliding it neatly under her head.

"It's ok, Mamma. Daddy's coming."

Sam's breaths sputtered in panicked gulps. The boy watched with piercing green eyes. Socks lay against her shoulder.

"It's ok, Mamma."

An inky black tide swept her away. The faint sound of Boston's "Let Me Take You Home Tonight" reached out to escort her.

When she regained consciousness, Sam was tucked under the bedspread. She tensed and lifted the covers, relieved to find clean white cotton sheets beneath her. The air had cooled and smelled of springtime. Someone had arranged a bouquet of wildflowers in a pink vase on the night table next to her. Leaning against the vase, a piece of construction paper, unevenly folded into a card.

She reached for the card. On its face, a child's rendering of the sun shining over a field of flowers. Inside, large orange crayon letters spelled out "GET WEL SEWWN MAMMA, LUV ME (IZZY) AND WILL."

"AND DADDY" was added below in green crayon next to a smiley face. Below that in blue, "AND SOKS."

Sam grinned despite herself.

The door knob rattled, reminding her of the present situation. Which was what, exactly? Had she fallen and bumped her head? Was this a dream, a hallucination. Or ... was she in the wrong house? No, she remembered following the cat into this room.

Something stirred at the end of the bed. As if summoned by her thought, Socks the cat stood and stretched. The door creaked open. Both Sam and Socks directed their attention to the man who peeked in.

"Oh, good. You're awake, sweetie." He sauntered in. Sam shrank back, her amber eyes fixed on the man.

He was handsome, in a sitcom-dad kind of way, bookish and not at all intimidating. She studied him, her panic ebbing before his soft presence. He was quite the opposite of Jimmy, who had swept her off her feet with his rakish good looks, and devil-be-damned attitude.

"I brought the cookies you made this morning." He held up a plate.

The plastic wrap was gone, but Sam recognized the plate

she brought for the open house. The cookie with the missing bit she'd given the cat peeked up over the edge. She opened her mouth, then realized she didn't know what to say.

Excuse me, sir. I have no idea who you and those adorable children are? I was kidnapped and brought here by the cat, Socks? Actually, this is probably a dream and I am lying on a dirty closet floor with a lump on my head?

She closed her mouth and decided to enjoy this pleasant dream while she waited to wake up, or for someone to find her and call an ambulance.

"How are you feeling, my love?" The man sat on the edge of the bed and extended the plate.

Sam reached out and took a cookie. It felt so real. She held it up, watching tiny crumbs make their way to the bedspread.

"Don't worry. Just relax and enjoy your cookie." He reached a hand toward her cheek.

She flinched.

He frowned. "Did you have that nightmare ... with the awful man, again?"

He set the plate down, took her free hand in both of his, and brought it to his lips. When he lay a soft kiss on Sam's palm, warmth spread through her. She shifted her gaze to his. He held it with his gentle green eyes, a more mature version of the ones that belonged to the towheaded boy. She didn't flinch this time, but her face burned with embarrassment and guilt.

"Jimmy." She had not meant to say the name out loud.

The man smiled. "Yes, honey?"

Her mouth curled into a crooked grin. Somehow her traumatized brain had turned Jimmy from ... the man he was, into this knightly specimen. *Just how hard did I hit my head?*

"Want me to help you up? I made dinner. You were sleeping, so the kids and I ate. I'll warm a plate and help you to the table if you'd like. Or, I can bring your plate here, but you know how messy my spaghetti is." He paused, perhaps waiting for her expression to reflect that she did, in fact, know how messy his spaghetti was.

"I want to get up," she said, half worried that speaking to the apparition would break the spell. "I'm feeling better. I want to get up." Her voice was shaky, almost fuzzy, like a radio host when the channel isn't quite centered.

Sam set down the cookie and let Jimmy help her sit straighter. He took a step back and she swung her legs around. When she noticed she was wearing a sheer silk nighty, she yanked a corner of the spread up in front of her.

"Would you like your robe?"

She nodded. He walked to an armchair in the corner of the room and gathered something from the seat. When he returned, he draped a long white robe over her shoulders. She slipped her arms into the sleeves, secured the front, and stood.

Dark spots peppered her vision. The room swayed like a dinghy in the swells. She reached out to grab onto something. Jimmy, *new* Jimmy, caught her, but not before her hand sent the vase of flowers crashing to the floor. Water and glass pelted her bare feet, and flower petals rode fresh rivulets across the floor. Tears gathered, waiting for the voice, *his* voice, to set them free.

Are you ok, sweetie? Don't worry, I'll clean up. Let's get you back into bed.

She looked up at the man. Had he spoken those words aloud? He was positioning her on the bed, plumping pillows, but paused when he saw her staring. He leaned down to kiss her. She did not flinch or pull away. Instead, she leaned into his embrace and sank comfortably into the dream, allowing it to claim her.

When she awoke, the kids were in the room, quietly observing. Was there a subtle change in their expressions, like they'd been caught in a moment of mischief? Maybe not. Her eyes struggled to focus through cracked eyelids. They smiled. She smiled back.

"Daddy asked us to check on you," said the girl.

Sam's mind reached for the name, the one on the card.

Izzy.

That was it. She wondered if it was short for something.

"Feeling better, Mamma?" The boy stepped towards the bed, one hand behind his back.

Izzy giggled. The boy, *Will*, shot her an annoyed look. He brought his hand around revealing a bouquet of wildflowers.

"We picked new flowers, Mamma," said Izzy.

Again, Will glared at her. "We were supposed to say that together."

He pointed to a new vase that now graced the nightstand.

"May I put them in?"

"Thank you," said Sam, startled by her raspy voice. "Yes. Thank you."

Will arranged the flowers and Izzy bounced to the foot of the bed to pet Socks. The cat stood, stretched, and walked close enough for Sam to reach out and scratch behind its ears.

"He likes guarding you," said Izzy, hopping alongside him as he walked. "You're his favorite. Mine, too."

"What's he guarding me from? Maybe ... myself?" Sam grinned.

"Mamma needs rest," said Will, a harsh glare aimed at his sister. Izzy looked down at her feet.

"It's ok," said Sam, trying to soften the mood. "I'm feeling better, Isabella."

Yes, *Isabella.* Izzy was short for Isabella. An image of Will calling the girl *Dizzy Izzy* and being gently reprimanded appeared in her mind's eye. A memory? She tried to focus, to see the moments surrounding the event, but the image was an island in her mind. Moving in any direction from it, she encountered frothy, uninviting waters. If she squinted, she could see there was something out there, something important. She was supposed to be doing something, preparing something. Throbbing welled inside her skull.

Isabella. The girl's name was Isabella, and when he was feeling impish, Will called her Dizzy Izzy.

Both children grinned, as if spectators to the inner workings of her mind.

"Daddy asked if you want to come to the table or have breakfast in bed," said Will.

Despite her confusion, a trip out of the room sounded inviting. Her mind narrowed in on one word.

"Breakfast? What time is it?"

"It's 9 o'clock in the morning, Mamma!" Izzy said, bouncing, her pigtails taking on a life of their own. "Daddy said to let you sleep in."

Sam turned her head and saw an indent in the pillow next to hers. Her hand slid over, under the covers. The sheets were cool, but a memory of when they were warm, then hot, crept in. Blood rushed to her cheeks.

"Do you want breakfast in bed, Mamma?" Will tapped on her shoulder, startling her.

"No. No, I want to leave the room. Tell him I'm coming."

Will nodded. Izzy beamed. They both ran out the door to relay the message. Socks sat and watched Sam push herself up.

My guard.

She slid her legs out from under the sheets and set her feet on the floor.

Nice and slow. Remember what happened last time.

Sam stood, but kept her hands and the backs of her legs pressed against the mattress. She took a few deep breaths. The bedroom door opened and a middle-aged woman entered, shutting the door behind her. She wore jeans and a white t-shirt. An apron circled her waist. When she saw Sam, she rushed over.

"Ma'am, let me help you. You shouldn't get up by yourself. It takes time."

"What takes time?"

The woman brought her robe and offered her arm.

"Time for what?"

Their eyes met. The woman looked away.

"You had an episode. It always takes time after an episode, ma'am."

Sam leaned on the woman's arm and the two made their way to the door.

"My name is Marta, in case you don't ... remember."

How can I remember something I never knew? I probably won't remember any of this when I wake up ... if I wake up. And, if I have this dream again, you'll have to introduce yourself all over again. The thought tickled inside her. She sealed her lips to contain a chuckle, which escaped in the form of an audible puff through her nose.

"Everything ok, ma'am?" Sam nodded.

When they reached the door, Marta extended a fist and knocked a few times, which was odd, since they were leaving a room, not entering one.

"In case someone is walking by the door. I don't want to knock anyone over," said Marta, though Sam had not asked for an explanation.

Could Marta, a housekeeper of some kind, read her mind? It seemed like everyone else could. Also, didn't bedroom doors usually open *into* the room? She remembered reading something in a magazine about flow, pulling positive energy into the room.

The door swung open revealing Izzy in a pale yellow jumper with a large sunflower on the front. She was carrying a glass of water. The moment she saw Sam, she darted over to give her a hug. Sam rested a hand on the girl's head. She sure was an affectionate little thing.

Those curly chestnut pigtails bounced about, almost hypnotizing. Sam closed her eyes and an image (*a memory?*) ran through her mind like the promo for a Hallmark special. It was the woman, Marta, pushing Izzy on a swing. The girl's pigtails bounced and swayed in the breeze.

"Come on, Izzy. Your papà is waiting," said Marta, her voice chasing off the image. Sam opened her eyes. "Izzy, let your poor mama go so she can have breakfast, please."

Izzy relaxed her grip and stepped back. She looked at Sam, then at her own hand, as if suddenly remembering the glass of water.

"Mamma. I brought water. Are you thirsty?"

Actually, yes, she was very thirsty. She reached out to take the glass, miscalculating and knocking it from the girl's hand. Water spread out across the floor in front of them.

"Oh Isabella," she said. "I am so sorry."

Izzy cast her eyes down, her smile contorting into a trembling grimace. Tears streaked down her cheeks. "I'm sorry, Mamma. I'm so stupid."

The last statement stung as much as any slap ever had. Sam looked at the little girl, whose commanding presence had melted into insignificance ... and saw herself.

"No, honey. No. It was an accident. Accidents happen."

Marta pulled a yellow dust cloth from her apron and knelt to mop up the puddles. The cloth swirled about, stirring a memory. But, when Sam stretched her mind to reach for it, it dissipated like mist in a breeze. When the mess was tidied, the trio continued toward the kitchen.

The little Cape Cod was immaculate, each room warm and welcoming. Each piece of furniture positioned where Sam would have placed it if she'd designed the home herself. Photos adorned the walls, arranged in little themed groups. A closer look revealed images from a life she hadn't lived. Yet, there she was with the kids on a beach, celebrating a birthday with the Jimmy she'd just met, locked in an embrace with him.

This has to be a dream.

But, it felt so real. She reached out and took a picture from the wall, felt the weight of it, the texture of the wooden frame. Her index finger traced the smooth surface of the glass, leaving a smudge.

"Sorry," she said, using the sleeve of her robe to wipe it away.

"It's ok, ma'am. I understand," said Marta, taking the photo and hanging it back in its place. "I'll clean it later. Let's get you to the table."

When they walked past a window in the living room, Sam's muscles tightened and her brow furrowed. It was a gorgeous day. The sun was shining and fluffy clouds speckled the sky like sheep ripe for shearing. Off in the distance, mountains where there should have been factories and warehouses. Mountains. Beautiful, snow-tipped mountains. A dull ache throbbed behind her eyes.

In the kitchen, Jimmy and Will sat waiting at the table. They stood when she approached. Jimmy pulled out her chair, guiding it back once she was situated. Izzy bounced over to her place, and everyone sat but Marta.

The table was set with an array of goodies, from pancakes and waffles to bacon and bagels. There was a bowl of fresh fruit at each place, and a vase filled with roses sat at the table's center.

"Coffee, ma'am?" asked Marta.

Sam nodded and raised her cup. She closed her eyes and drew in a breath, letting the very real, very fragrant blend of aromas enchant her. All at once, she didn't care if it was a dream or even if she was dead. It felt like home. The thought spread through her, entering her bloodstream, warming her, and bringing a smile to her lips.

She opened her eyes, looked around, and she saw the family, her family, smiling back. They looked relieved. Will grabbed a piece of bacon and popped it in his mouth, chewing through a grin. Izzy blew Sam a giggly kiss. And, Jimmy gazed, sending her secret romantic messages over his coffee cup with his deep green eyes. Even Socks the cat looked satisfied. He slithered around her legs under the table on the way to a bowl of milk set out on the floor.

Music drifted in, as if carried on a breeze. A song she knew and liked floated around in her head. She heard the music not with her ears, but through melodic vibrations that entered her pores.

A burning sensation refocused Sam's attention. On her wrist, several red spots blossomed. Below it on the table, droplets of freshly spilt coffee steamed.

"So sorry, ma'am," said Marta, pulling a yellow cloth from her apron. "Are you ok, ma'am?"

Sam nodded. *I'm fine. I'm happy.*

She observed Marta. The housekeeper's eyebrows furrowed ever so slightly, her lips pursed, then smoothed into a tight neutral smile. Could she hear the music? Sam leaned closer. Marta's pupils were dilated, two shiny obsidian disks. And, underneath her not-a-care-in-the- world smile, Sam saw panic. Her pulse quickened.

"I'll get ice for your arm, ma'am," Marta said, anxiety peeking out around the edges of her smile.

Her eyes flicked to and fro, assessing the family, then back to Sam. The others continued to chat and enjoy their breakfast, seemingly unaware. *Those eyes.* Those eyes said, "run."

"I need to use the bathroom anyway, I'll run some cold water on it," said Sam, thinking that a splash of cold water on her face might help her focus.

Will pushed his chair back. "I can help you, Mamma."

"That's ok, sweetie. You enjoy your bacon. Marta can make sure I get there ok."

Marta looked surprised, but nodded. "Of course, ma'am."

"Just holler if you need anything," said Jimmy, adding more pancakes to the stack on his plate.

Izzy stared. Sam felt like the girl was scanning her for signs of trouble.

"I'll be right back, Izzy." She winked playfully and blew a kiss, which seemed to reassure the girl.

Marta helped her up and offered an arm to lean on. They made their way to the powder room.

"Hurry back, pumpkin!" Jimmy called.

When they were out of earshot, Sam whispered, "do you hear the music, Marta?"

"No, ma'am. What music?" She was hesitant. It sounded like a lie.

"Marta. What is going on?"

Marta's body tensed and her brows drew together. She tightened the corners of her mouth as if trying to make a decision. "Ma'am, you are happy here, right?"

Sam nodded. She was, very. Marta's expression smoothed.

"Then, relax. Go soothe your burns. Everything will be fine."

She opened the door to the powder room and helped Sam inside, opening the faucet before backing out.

"You'll be fine." Her eyes still said the opposite. Sam was going to say as much when she noticed Socks had followed them. She nodded.

"I've got it from here. Thank you," said Sam, closing the

door before the cat could slip in.

She lowered her arm under the stream of cold water, feeling instant relief. Then, cupped her other hand to wet her face. She could still feel the music coursing through her. She closed her eyes, its volume intensified.

"My radio," she whispered. "Where's my radio?"

After David Bowie's "Major Tom," a familiar voice echoed in her head. Where had she heard it? The voice joked about *another day of rain*, something about *cats and dogs* and *canoeing to work*. Snippets of discourse pelted her like sleet, jarring her consciousness.

Then, the voice grew serious. She focused on the signal in her mind, imagined herself inching a knob forward, then back ... until the static cleared.

A local elderly woman has been hospitalized after being severely beaten by her neighbor, a Mr. James Anthony. When officers took Mr. Anthony into custody, he claimed that the elderly woman was hiding his wife somewhere. The man's wife, Mrs. Samantha Anthony, has been missing for almost a week now. A missing persons report was filed after she failed to show up to work at an open house. Mrs. Anthony's empty car was found in front of the abandoned home she was scheduled to show. Police are asking for anyone with information on her whereabouts to please contact them. The elderly woman, Mrs. Claudia Turner, is in critical condition.

The voice continued, but Sam lost focus.

Mrs. Turner. Claudia needs me. My friend needs me. The thought spun circles in her brain, strengthening like a funnel cloud until it fully consumed her. The perfect little powder room seemed to shift, to slant.

Where am I? What is this? The only thing she knew for sure was that she wanted to leave. She needed to get back to the closet, to find her way out.

I need to get to Mrs. Turner.

When she opened the door, Marta was waiting for her. Urgency blazed in Sam's eyes and Marta, whoever she was, understood. She rested a hand on Sam's shoulder, and Sam felt she had an ally. Somehow the cat, too, understood. It hissed and ran toward the kitchen.

"Run," said Marta, this time not just with her eyes. She pointed to the corridor leading to the main bedroom. "I'll buy you time."

"Marta..."

"Run. If you want to go back, you can't hesitate. Run."

Sam sprinted down the hall. The floor now rolling under her feet, its wooden planks bending and bowing with each wave. Furniture bumped against her. She reached out to catch herself, but when she touched the walls they sank in like putty, oozing around her wrists. She yanked them out and continued forward, timing her steps to the rhythmic movements of the floorboards.

"Mamma!" a voice cried out behind her. Sam turned to see Izzy burst from the kitchen. "Mamma! Don't you leave me!"

Marta stood between Sam and the girl, holding out her hands to create a barrier.

"Run!"

Sam shook her head at the little girl. "I'm sorry. I don't belong here," she said and turned back to focus on her destination.

"You *do* belong here." This was Jimmy's voice, but there was something of the old, possessive Jimmy now. "You're happy here. Everything's the way you want it here."

"Mrs. Turner needs me," said Sam looking back at him.

"*We* need you, Mamma," said Will, stepping up next to his father. "We need you more."

They started toward her. Marta spread her arms to block

them, but they brushed her aside, a mere inconvenience.

"Hurry ma'am ... Sam," said Marta. "If you don't go now, it'll be too late. If you don't go now, you can never change your mind."

Marta sobbed, and Sam understood she spoke from experience. She turned toward the bedroom again and pushed through the confusion until she reached the door. Frantic footsteps clapped then scraped the boards behind her. Each sound screaming that if she turned to look, it would not be the lovely little family behind her. Marta shrieked, prompting a burst of adrenaline in Sam. She lunged for the doorknob.

Once inside the room, she slammed the door and reached down to secure it, but the lock was not on the inside.

"Shit!" She kicked at the knob bending it toward the door frame.

In her panic, Sam hadn't noticed the cat slip into the room with her. It darted past her to the closet, turned, and arched its back. The animal seemed much bigger now, almost the size of a small wolf. The bedroom door clicked behind her, but jammed against the knob when someone ... or *something* tried to pull it open.

Sam threw her hands toward the cat, in a desperate effort to shoo it away.

"Move! Go away! I want to leave!'

The cat flattened its back and sat.

"Do you, really?" it asked.

Sam's eyes widened and her mouth gaped. The cat lifted a paw and licked it a few times.

"Do you, really? Think about your life there. The moment you stepped foot in this house we knew you needed us, that we need you. When was the last time you heard that nasty voice in your head?"

The room had steadied and the house was silent. Sam tried

to swallow past what felt like her heart in her throat.

"You have a family here, a family that adores you. You can be happy here, we don't ask for much."

Somewhere in the distance, the music. The music from her radio. The radio that Mrs. Turner had given her. Mrs. Turner, her friend. Her friend who was in the hospital. Her friend who *Jimmy* put in the hospital ... because of *her*. A thought occurred to her, reoccurred from somewhere deep in her mind.

It seems a thing can look absolutely precious, and still be seeping poison.

And, she realized that she needed to get out. She steeled herself and rushed the cat.

"This is not real. You are not real. And, no matter how hard it is, real is better than a lie!"

The cat leaped forward and swiped at her arm. Sam side-stepped, but felt claws stripe her shoulder. She snatched the vase from the nightstand and threw it as hard as she could at the beast, which was looking less and less like a cat. It dodged, leaving a clear path to the closet door. Sam ran to it and yanked it open.

"Wait!" screamed the cat.

But it wasn't just the cat. The voice that called out, that reached *inside* and twisted her organs like twine, was an amalgamation of the cat's voice and that of the children and the man they called Daddy. And, though they spoke as a chorus, each voice echoed separately, begging her to stay and flooding her mind with pictures of an imaginary life with them. Until, one word broke the spell.

"Mamma, please." It was Izzy, sweet Izzy. Yet, it wasn't.

"Mamma."

Sam's free hand slid down to her lower abdomen. She ducked into the closet and slammed the door.

Smothering darkness pressed against her, around her. She

sat shaking, her fingernails biting into the floor.

Fake it till you take it.

The thought conjured an image of Mrs. Turner smiling and wagging her finger. Sam slowed her breaths, and the beating of her heart quieted to a steady *thump thump,* no longer assaulting her ears. And through the darkness, the sound of music, mixed with just a hint of static. She crawled toward it, an impossible distance for a bedroom closet. Bits of fabric brushed the top of her head. She crawled through an acrid smell of stored must and across items scattered on the floor, feeling shoes, wallets, and purses under her hands.

Then, something long and hard. A stick? She grasped it, shuddered, and tossed it aside. It clattered against other, similar sounding items. A thought flooded her mind, an image of bones stacked in a pile. She lurched to the side, bile and panic racing up her throat.

The music. Focus on the music. Music makes the brain happy.

She crawled forward until her forehead bumped up against something. The wooden panels of a door, a knob. She half-expected to find it locked, sealed shut, but it offered no resistance.

* * *

Sam stumbled out and slammed the door behind her. The room was lit by pale moon beams through a window on the far wall. When her eyes adjusted, she could make out the shape of a bed frame and mattress. A concentrated beam illuminated a small dark spot on the floor, the dead roach from what seemed like an eternity ago.

Her mind was thick and doughy, but the dizziness had

subsided. She made her way through the dim, musty house to the kitchen. There, she reached out and flipped the light switch. The room remained dark. She remembered the light exploding in the closet.

Did I trip the breaker?

Did I fall?

Bump my head?

Sam put a hand to her head and felt for lumps. Instead, a throbbing pain called from her shoulder. It burned like hot coals when her fingers brushed the long deep gash left by the cat, or beast, or whatever it was.

Loud knocking and scratching sounded from the direction of the bedroom, the closet. Sam knew what she had to do.

She fumbled through the cabinets and drawers until she felt a matchbook. On the floor in front of her lay a dirty yellow dust rag. She scooped it up and brought it to her nose, inhaling the pungent smell of cleaning chemicals. Sam set it on the counter and pulled a match from the book. She struck it and a flame jumped up, throwing shadows to dance on the walls. The rag caught quickly, as if eager to be a part of the light. She carried the growing flame to the closet where she had seen the cleaning supplies and tossed it in. It flared up in unnatural colors, waltzing around the chemicals and licking the walls, spreading faster than she'd thought possible, threatening to overtake her. She stepped back, but the heat beckoned. The house called to her one last time, its words pulling at her like strands from a web.

Stay here. You'll be happy here. We need you here.

Sam turned and made her way to the front door. She stepped out into the cool, crisp, night air, untainted by the rising smoke. Leaving the door open just a crack to feed the flames, she proceeded down the front walk and turned in the direction of Memorial Hospital.

THE KIPLING LAMP

ERIC D. LEHMAN

U pon finishing my Masters of Fine Arts in Fiction, I moved to Brattleboro, Vermont. I was a big believer in the importance of place for a writer, both to the act of writing itself and to the later memory of renown. Since I grew up in Concord, Massachusetts, you might understand how this idea took root in me. A year rarely went by when I wasn't dragged by a teacher or parent to the house of a writer: Emerson, Alcott, Hawthorne. We swam in Walden Pond as children. I learned how place could inspire and then hold the memory of your work long afterwards, keep your words on the lips of the locals, and give future admirers a shrine for pilgrimage.

I had passed through Brattleboro a number of times when I was a child on trips to northern Vermont. We would take Route 2 west and I-91 north, and by Brattleboro we needed to pee. It had the usual strip malls and fast food outside of town, and seemed a very ordinary, even mundane town. Then in grad school my friends and I rented canoes there for a paddle down the Connecticut, and I discovered a charming downtown with food co-op, coffee shops, and old brick buildings. So when I graduated with no job prospects but a nice inheritance from my recently passed grandmother, I decided to take time off to write, and chose this town, telling my friends it was a "random" choice. But in reality, I chose it because it had not been chosen before. No Hemingway or Melville had staked out Brattleboro, no famous college filled its streets with the exploits of genera- tions of memoirists, no artist colony had painted it for all time. Or so I was made to believe after years of American Literature classes and a quick search on the internet. The internet was barely functional back then, anyway, but I trusted it, and trusted my own instincts.

Not everyone was on board. My girlfriend of two years, Anya, wanted to stay in Boston, and had a job as an editor lined up even before graduation. "No way I am moving to some hick town in Vermont," she said. "It's bad enough living in Boston and not New York."

I planned a bed and breakfast stay that would dramatically change her heart, but she cheated on me before I got the chance. I had to cancel at the last minute, and lost a deposit. When I told my parents my post-graduation plans, they chuckled at my ambitions, as they always did. "I bet he lasts six months and leaves as soon as he finishes a rough draft," my mother said. "I bet he lasts six months and leaves before he finishes anything," my father countered.

I rented a studio apartment in one of the repurposed facto- ries, and settled into my novel writing routine, shopping at the co-op, sitting at the coffee shop with my Moleskine notebook and fountain pen, exploring the nearby hills on my mountain bike. It was lonely and romantic to be in this small town that time had passed by, to know that I would be the one to capture the feeling of its faded glory. No one else had appreciated it like I would. I met a few people: a muscled, dreadlocked worker at the co-op, a sexy bun-haired lady at the library, and a gray ponytailed local antiques dealer named Bill, who seemed to spend all his time in the coffee shops rather than his store. "How's the novel?" he would ask when we passed each other, which was often. It was a small town.

I think I was getting a croissant at one of the competing bakeries when a woman in line began to talk about Rudyard Kipling. I didn't think much of it, maybe she had a kid in elementary school or a husband from England. Then a week later a couple in a coffee shop mentioned the name.

"I'm sorry," I said in my confident, gregarious way, probably starved for conversation. "This is the second time I've heard someone mention Kipling this week. Is there a convention or something?"

"Oh, we're staying at his house," the woman said, waving a hand to indicate a vague direction.

"His house? In England?"

"No, it's just up the hill, only like a mile or two?" She looked at her husband.

"That's right," he said. "It's an amazing place. We're sharing it with another couple and our children." He also waved a hand vaguely. "Getting some alone time this morning."

I took the hint and turned back to my coffee, but unsaid questions bounced around in my skull. I walked to the small library and made a casual inquiry of the sexy bun-haired lady at the desk.

"Oh, yes, he lived here, or rather over the line in Dummerston."

"How long?"

"I don't know, a few years I think."

Only a few years–that was a comfort, and he didn't really live in Brattleboro either. I sighed with relief. Then, the bun-haired lady walked with me to some shelves and gave me a book about Kipling's life in Vermont. My heart sank again. If a whole book had been written about it, then it wasn't just a vacation, was it? I checked it out and read through it, affecting a superior sort of incredulousness at what a hash he had made of his life here, battling against the American press, against the locals, against his drunken brother-in-law. He never really became part of the place, did he? And he didn't write much about it, except in letters and maybe a poem or two. However, I had to admit that he wrote *The Jungle Books* and *Captains Courageous* while living here, but they weren't connected to the place, nothing that anchored him here. And a few people mentioning his name didn't mean that he owned the town, did it? He hated Brattleboro, as far as I could tell, and his experiences with his wife's brother put him off Americans forever. No, Kipling's places were the dusty streets of India and maybe Pook's Hill in England. Not here.

So, I ignored this minor crack in my literary plan for a month or so, crafting my own chapters, bringing the town, or my version of it, into life on the pages of my journals and then shaping them later. One day in November, though, I biked out of town on Black Mountain Road, thinking of heading to the mountain itself for a hike, when I saw the turn-off to Kipling Road. It was irresistible. I pedaled up a steep hill, past some sort of international school, and as the road paled into gravel, I saw the house pictured in the book. Like some great ship it floated on the side of a hill above a meadow, long and tall, unlike any house I have seen before or since. A man stood on the porch at the south end, gazing out at the mountains of New Hampshire, sipping from a mug. For a moment I thought it was Kipling himself, and a surge of annoyance pulsed through me. That was ridiculous; he hadn't lived in the house for over a hundred years. But the feeling persisted, and I continued along the road past one of those majestic Vermont farms, past maple-sap tubing, to another paved road, which I took back to town, my desire to a hike Black Mountain gone.

My irritation toward the ghost of Kipling soon bled into irritation at myself for having yielded to temptation and biking up that road. I couldn't unsee the house now, perched on the hillside like a huge slate green sentinel, watching my pathetic attempts to write a novel, smug and impregnable. When I visited the library to look up a detail for my own work, and to flirt with the librarian, I saw the huge Kipling section, including an imposing row of collected works. My anger focused like a laser on my stupidity for not having done the proper research before moving here. If I wasn't so lazy and romantic, I could have found the Kipling connection with just a little more effort.

All that winter I tried to dismiss him as snow piled up outside the old factory buildings. Just a children's author, I scoffed. Racist, imperialist, colonialist. Claptrap written for the masses. But that didn't work. My novel sputtered to a halt, weighed down by that huge house. Would my apartment in this old factory ever be bought and rented out by the Landmark Trust? Not likely! I was a pretender, a dabbler, a monkey with a diploma.

In the midst of this funk I ran into ponytail Bill at the coffee shop, as he slouched in the corner with an old wool army coat and two-day old stubble, looking like a transient rather than a successful antiques dealer. "How's the novel?" he asked.

Not sure whether he was being ironic or genuinely interested, I answered in a brusque negative. Nevertheless, we began to talk–he was bemoaning the fate of his son, who had graduated from an art school in New York, a degree that Bill alternately respected and thought "suicidal." This brought my own situation back into the conversation. All at once I blurted out "I'd never have come here if I'd known Kipling was here first."

He laughed at this, and when I explained, he laughed even harder. But when he saw how seriously I took the situation, he frowned. "Don't you understand that it is the past that gives our lives meaning?"

"What a surprise for an antiques dealer to have that perspective."

His laugh downgraded to a chuckle. "But surely you see that the history makes the place richer, gives it more resonance?"

No, I did not see, or rather I did, but wanted that history to start with me. I couldn't articulate that to Bill, so I nodded and changed the subject. As he stood up to leave he looked carefully at me.

"Come by the shop sometime, not today, I've got an appointment, but tomorrow or Friday. I have something I want to show you."

Having nothing else to do, on Friday I went through his door, weaving my way through sideboards and roll-top desks, ducking to avoid canoe oars and tavern signs. Bill stood at the cash register in the back ringing up a customer. I browsed the pewterware and ceramics.

"So, do you want to see it?" He waved me over.

"See what? You haven't told me what *it* is."

"That's true!" he said. "First you have to promise not to tell anyone else, or write about this in one of your stories."

"Okay." My interest perked up.

He opened one of the barrister bookcases with a key and pushed a few *objects d'arte* aside. With a dramatic flourish he pulled out a double wicked brass oil lamp. "Behold! Rudyard Kipling's lamp."

I laughed. Bill often made preposterous claims, and this one was no different.

"No, it really is his lamp. You know about his house, of

course, well they needed money a few years back and sold me a couple of pieces. This is one of them."

"Right."

Shaking his head, he dug around in the closed bookcase again, producing a small framed sketch with Kipling's signature. "Does this look fake to you?"

"I have no idea. I'm not an expert in these things," I scoffed.

"Well listen, I know you have this thing against Kipling and I thought I would do something to help reconcile the two of you. I know you can't afford something like this, but if you sign an I.O.U. I will let you borrow it. You can write by its light, or whatever, and be inspired."

I laughed again, but peered at it more closely. He handed it to me, and I turned it over and over. "Naulakha" was stamped on the bottom–the name of Kipling's house. Maybe it was real, or maybe Bill was just trying to be nice.

"If it makes you happy I will try it out for a bit."

"How does a week sound? You're not going anywhere, right?" A suspicious note crept into his voice.

"No, of course not."

"All right, let me draw something up." He turned to a small obsolete computer and typed for a while. He printed something out on an old dot matrix printer, and I examined it, filling in my driver's license information and credit card number as "guarantee" for the $5000 item. Now I was suspicious and hesitant, but he was a business owner, a fixture of the community, so I gave him the paper and took the lamp. He dug around and found some lamp oil and gave that to me. "A dollar?"

I handed it to him with a wry grin.

Back at my studio I set it on the cheap Swedish desk, feeling foolish. I didn't believe for a second it was Kipling's lamp, but it was an antique of some sort, and since I had it for a week, I thought I might as well try it. I poured the oil into the reservoir, adjusted the two wicks, and lit it. A scribble of black smoke headed to the ceiling and I sat down to write. After an hour a few things came, and soon I had to refill the lamp. The next day I scoured the town for more oil and, having discovered a small can in a local, family-run hardware store, I continued. By the end of the week the novel had advanced over 10,000 words, a personal best. I reread what I had written. It was good, better than anything I had done in the previous six months in Brattleboro. The lamp may not have been Kipling's, but it was certainly good luck.

The day I had to return it came too quickly, and I found myself reluctant.

"Well?" Bill asked when I slouched into the shop. "Are you friends with Kipling again?"

"Ha, ha," I said. "But it's nice. Can I keep it for another week?"

"What does this look like to you? A library? No." He took it and placed it back on the shelf. "I have a potential buyer coming in from England this week."

"Uh-huh," I said skeptically. "Maybe I could rent it?"

"You've really become attached, huh? Nope, five thousand dollars, my friend."

"One thousand," I blurted out.

Bill's eyebrows shot up and he adjusted his ponytail. "I was just kidding, man, you can't afford this. Besides, I couldn't go less than four."

"I have a little money saved up," I said, thinking of grandma's inheritance, recalculating rents and electric bills, gaming out a shortened lease. "Two thousand, no more."

"Now you're just teasing me. You don't have that kind of cash, and if you did I wouldn't take it from you. Besides, it's on an internet auction with a starting price of $3000."

"Then why'd you say five?"

"I'm a businessman, kid," he growled.

"I thought we were friends?" I whined. "I only have two thousand five hundred in my savings account. And that means I won't eat for the next couple months."

Bill looked me up and down. "All right, for a friend two five."

I wrote a check and he gave me a scrap of paper supposed to be "provenance." I took the lamp back with me to the apartment, and over the next two months used it regularly, polishing off and polishing up my novel. The Kipling house now seemed a benevolent mentor rather than a dark sentinel, just as Bill prophesied. As spring cleared the roads, I took my bike out again and waved a thankful hand to the house. In May I happily walked to the post office with my novel, an insightful family chronicle about the nature of time and fiction. I began to plan out my next one, maybe a period piece, late 19th century. But before I could do more than jot down a few notes, I had a pair of unwelcome visitors at my apartment. The knock came just as I put down my groceries.

"Yes?" I opened the door to find two policemen smiling grimly, one in a uniform and one in plainclothes with a badge in hand. They asked my name, asked to come in, and, mystified, I acquiesced.

"Do you know this man?" The uniformed man asked, showing a mugshot of Bill.

I gaped. "Yes."

"How?"

"Well, I met him downtown—"

"Did you have any dealings with him?" The plainclothes man cut in.

"Uhm..." I looked across to my desk and for a second thought about lying, but did not. "I bought that lamp from him a few months ago."

The uniformed officer walked over and picked it up. "This is it," he said to the other man.

"Do you have a receipt for it?"

"I guess, I mean maybe I kept it," I said weakly. "Let me look." I opened a kitchen drawer while the two men watched me, the uniform fingering his revolver. I broke into a sweat. Did they think I might have a gun in the drawer? What was going on?

Luckily, I had the receipt stapled to the "provenance" paper. I gave it to the plainclothes man, who held up a matching receipt and checked them. "You have a bank statement? You paid for this with a check?"

"No, those are online. Or we can go to the bank."

"Open it up on the computer."

I did, finger trembling over the keys, and found the online statement that had been emailed to me, showing the $2500 taken out of the account. The cops nodded to each other, satisfied.

"So," plainclothes said. "You knew this was Rudyard Kipling's lamp?"

"What? I mean, that's what Bill said, but it's not really." As I said that, I realized that it must be the lamp, and surmised that it was stolen. I stupidly began blabbering. "So it is real? Did Bill steal it? Is that why you're here? I mean, I didn't really think it was his lamp..."

"Then why'd you pay $2500 for it?" uniform asked sharply.

I told them what had happened and it sounded ridiculous, even to me. The cops looked confused and bothered by the story, and it was clear they didn't believe a word.

"Well," uniform interrupted my tale, "we're going to have to talk about this at the station. Receiving stolen goods is a crime."

"But I didn't know!" I sputtered.

"Ignorance of the law..." the other trailed off. "Let's go down to the station. We'll need you to sign a statement."

A statement? Did he mean a confession? For what? I stared at the shining lamp in the officer's hand and it seemed an agent of evil, transformed utterly in those few minutes. I followed the man to the station on foot and wrote down my story. They looked at it and made me cut parts out, which I did unquestioningly, though later realized how dangerous that had been. However, no changes were filed, no rights were read to me, and I didn't even spend that night in jail. They were simply building evidence for the trial against Bill, and getting the lamp back to its owners. I found out later that it was one of a group of household items stolen in the dead of night in a daring raid. Bill eventually went to jail for the theft, or maybe just for selling the goods, I never found that out, because by that time I had left town.

During the interrogation one of the officers had asked me what my job was, and when I told him I didn't have a job, that I was a writer, the two men started whispering. I knew that they were marking me for future reference or surveillance, and I began to think about leaving. More likely they were just laughing behind their hands, and in fact an older man might even have found the entire experience funny, but I was much too serious. Things were not going well with the librarian, either, and my apartment had an ant problem. So, I applied for editing jobs around New England and with mixed feelings, I accepted one in Hartford, Connecticut. Authors like Mark Twain, Harriet Beecher Stowe, and Wallace Stevens had lived here, and I wasn't in any danger of becoming the dominant literary figure.

My Brattleboro novel was picked up by an eager editor at a small press, who loved the way I wove themes of creativity, longevity, and locality into the story of a family's slow disintegration. It came out to good reviews, received a spit of fanfare, and promptly sank into oblivion. My parents bought it, and the sexy bun-haired librarian, but that's about it. The $500 advance was never exceeded by the royalties, and the rights reverted to me with a brief note.

"It's a shame," the editor wrote, "that we can't compel readers to claim your novel as their own."

COPPER

BRITTANY BELL

When my parents realized their dream of homeownership after years of chasing jobs up and down the east coast, they wanted to set down roots that would take hold and grow deep. They found a small group of homes circling a central green in College Point, Queens. Cut off by an expressway and an abandoned airport, College Point is one of the most isolated neighborhoods in New York City.

We moved over the Memorial Day weekend. Our modest attached brick home did not belong on the street, which was lined with expansive houses built just after the turn of the century, the kind with wrap-around porches made for sipping lemonade on hot summer days. My first memory is of my father showing me the boundaries of the cul-de-sac, telling me I was allowed to play anywhere from "here to there," his tan index finger gesturing to the borders of my new life.

Our house sat adjacent to a yellow colonial whose landscaping my mother was always redoing in her head (and often out loud to my father). The owners of the house were hosting a barbecue and invited us to join them.

Will and Beata Nowack had a daughter, Anna, who was also three years old like me. We became fast friends. The distance between our front doors was a few dozen feet, so Will Nowack's decision to cut a hole between the fence that divided our backyards was born out of symbolism more than convenience. It facilitated so many comings and goings between our two families that it never occurred to any of us that he should be compelled to seal it back up. But indeed that is exactly what he did one sunny morning in early July, eight years later.

The incident was unexpected. To this day I am still not sure precisely what precipitated so much resentment. It occurred during a barbecue at Anna's house after the children had been sent to bed. The adults had continued sitting around the table drinking and playing cards. I slept over and woke up early the next morning and saw Anna's mother sitting at the kitchen counter with bloodshot eyes and last night's clothes.

"I think you'd better go home," Anna's mother said.

What little I could ascertain about the situation had to be meticulously gathered, like someone lost in the forest following a breadcrumb trail already half-eaten by birds. The only information my mother would offer when I got home was that the adults were having problems.

"Try not to worry. It will all blow over eventually." She wouldn't look me in the eyes.

The rest I learned from listening to conversations held in hushed, angry voices through the forced air vents in our house. I kept hearing something about a closed door and too much to drink. It seemed even my parents were not certain of what had transpired.

I saw Anna at the park a few days after the barbecue and walked up to her at the sprinkler. I kicked off my sandals and extended my right leg into the stream of water like an olive branch.

"My parents said I can't talk to you," Anna said.

"That just means you can't come to my house right now," I explained.

"They really mean it. I should go."

Watching Anna walk away without looking back left me feeling like a stunned bird that had just flown into a sliding glass door. We had never bothered to make other close friends, although, as it turned out, I did not have to go far in order to make another.

Mrs. Walsh lived in the second to largest house on our cul-de-sac, and used just two of its generously sized eleven rooms. In my mind, she had been born old. Neither Anna nor I paid much attention to adults in our distracted, self-absorbed cloak of childhood. That's why it took several attempts for Mrs. Walsh to get my attention one evening as I caught fireflies. She was standing on her front porch, waving at me.

"Your name is Jenny, am I right?" she asked as I approached.

I nodded. "And your name is Mrs. Walsh?"

"That's right." She was holding a mason jar covered with a piece of cheesecloth.

It had a damp paper towel at the bottom. "This is much better than your old milk jug," she said.

"What's the paper towel for?" I asked.

"Fireflies like it to be humid," Mrs. Walsh explained.

"Did you know fireflies produce a chemical reaction inside their bodies?" I asked.

"Did they actually teach you that?" she scoffed. "Fireflies are summer magic. Forget what they told you in school, and go catch some lightning bugs. No sense standing here talking to an old lady."

"Would you mind if I asked how old you are?"

"Don't worry. I stopped being embarrassed by that question two decades ago. I'm ninety-four."

"Almost one hundred," I noted, immediately wanting to kick myself for being rude.

"I like you," Mrs. Walsh laughed. "Come over tomorrow. We can make muffins."

Her invitation served as a map to that summer. I was delighted by Mrs. Walsh's tales of life before cars and computers. She told me about horse drawn carriages on our street, which was probably not accurate given the timeline of her life, but she had likely seen them during her childhood in Brooklyn. In this way Mrs. Walsh rearranged details to convey the essential truth in her stories.

Every day we ate cucumber sandwiches without crust and used Mrs. Walsh's china tea set. I always called her Mrs. Walsh. She wasn't like other adults who are often so eager to get children to like them.

With most adults it was: *"Mrs. Russo is my mother's name, not mine! Call me Maria."* That is until something would spill or until we wanted to ride bicycles across town, and then the parent would pull the adult card that had been so desperately concealed at the bottom of the deck. Mrs. Walsh never insisted that I call her anything else, and it made me feel important. She was my *important* friend.

She knew how to bear witness to the little secrets and truths of life without interjecting judgment. I confessed my strong suspicion that Anna and I were the only girls in sixth grade that still played with dolls. I disclosed the time a horrible man in a white van exposed himself to me while I was waiting to cross the street. In turn, she told me things that she also couldn't discuss with anyone else, such as how her daughter was trying to convince her to move.

Mrs. Walsh said it was an absurd idea. "I have my own

home, thank you very much. I would never move to *Long Island*."

She told me about how her other daughter wanted her to move her bedroom to the first floor of the house. "Like it's some kind of compromise. My husband and I slept there for over sixty years before he passed. Two of our children were *born* in that bedroom." Mrs. Walsh confided that one of those babies had been stillborn, his slippery little body born limp and purple.

"Aren't you afraid to sleep in there?" I asked.

"Only young people are afraid of ghosts," she said.

Mrs. Walsh and I spent a lot of time amongst the outdated pine cabinets and floral wallpaper in her sunny kitchen. The table could seat six, although that many people had not sat there in some time. Mrs. Walsh said if she closed her eyes she could see her husband and hear the pitter patter of children's feet (she would have described them as thunderous at the time, but memory has a way of softening the edges of one's life). A white cabinet with a butcher block top sat to the left of the table, and above that was a long shelf that housed boxes of index cards, so yellowed and stained, her daughters feared they'd never be able to interpret the family recipes.

"Of course this is a ridiculous fear," Mrs. Walsh explained, "both of them are well into their sixties and will soon be turning holiday dinners over to their own daughters. I think my granddaughters get all their recipes on the Internet."

Three copper pots hung from hooks underneath the shelf. The pots had been passed down by Mrs. Walsh's grandmother, the full collection having been divided evenly among the girls in the family at the time. "The only problem is I have more granddaughters than pots," Mrs. Walsh explained. "But they'll have to figure all that out when I'm gone. For now I'm just going to keep enjoying the way the morning sun hits them. Lovely, isn't it?"

Mrs. Walsh waited until our friendship was well-established to ask about Anna.

"Whatever happened between you and the Nowack girl? I always used to see you together."

I shifted my weight, sending the porch swing back rather abruptly. "Our parents had a fight, and now we're not allowed to talk to each other," I explained.

"What was it about?"

"No one will tell us."

"That must be frustrating," Mrs. Walsh acknowledged. "My children only listened to half of what I had to say, which was a good thing because that's about how much of it I actually meant. Anna will come around, even if her parents don't."

The next morning I sat in my kitchen eating a bowl of soggy cereal. "Are you going to Mrs. Walsh's today?" my mother asked.

"Why?" I responded, knowing that my mother detested answering a question with another question.

"I don't think you should spend so much time there. Maybe you should talk to people your own age."

"Thanks to you and Dad I'm no longer friends with Anna." I slammed my spoon down so hard it sent the milk into ripples and splashed over the sides of the bowl. I pushed past my mother.

Mrs. Walsh would usually be sitting on the porch already, but I knew she sometimes lingered over a second cup of coffee. I didn't bother knocking because she wouldn't be able to hear it from the kitchen. I was able to let myself in because she didn't believe in locks. I made it through the foyer and could see that she was not sitting at the table, but I assumed she was in the bathroom. I put a kettle on the stove to boil. After a few minutes I decided to check on Mrs. Walsh. The bathroom door was wide open.

That's when I knew. I wished Anna was with me. She was the brave one. For a moment I thought about going back to my house and telling my mother what I suspected, but I found the resolve to walk towards the staircase. I had only been in Mrs. Walsh's bedroom once or twice to fetch some old photographs. The door was open.

I could see Mrs. Walsh in the bed. Her skin was purplish-gray, and, as I approached, I saw her eyelids looked tighter, her jaw stiffer.

"Mrs. Walsh?" I asked and slowly reached out.

She felt cool to the touch. I wanted to say goodbye, but the word got lost in my throat, strangled by a single sob. The tea kettle whistled downstairs.

I moved through that afternoon and the next day in the haze of grief, forcing myself to take small bites of crackers and sips of water that my mother offered. I hoped that Anna's family would be at the funeral, but I knew they'd been little more than distant neighbors. At most her mother would send a mass card with the illustration of some forgotten saint.

The mourners gathered at Mrs. Walsh's house after the burial, dozens of strangers hovering over cold cut platters and casseroles. I noticed that someone had removed the copper pots, leaving three discolored circles imprinted in the wallpaper. My mother was busy talking to someone she knew from church, so I made my way over to the sofa and sat down, balancing a plate of cheese and watery potato salad on my lap.

As we were getting ready to leave, one of Mrs. Walsh's daughters approached us. "Thank you for coming," she said. "I know how much you meant to her."

"She was like a grandmother to me," I managed to respond. In actuality, Mrs. Walsh was the only grandmother I'd ever really known since my father's mother lived in Cape Cod, and my maternal grandmother had passed away when I was a baby.

"She wanted you to have something. My sister isn't happy about parting with something that has been in the family for generations, but it's important to honor my mother's wishes. I'll be right back." She returned holding the copper pots. "Ma said one for you and one for your best friend. She seemed to think you'd be able to figure out what to do with the third."

"Thank you. I'm sorry for your loss," I said, accepting the pots.

"That was unusual," my mother commented as soon as we got to the safety of the curb.

"Not to me," I said, wondering if I'd ever have the chance to give Anna her copper pot. "I have something I need to do in the yard." Somehow I knew exactly what to do.

I waited until my mother went inside. I knelt down and began digging a hole underneath the patched up fence that had once so easily connected us to our neighbors, using my hands to move clumps of dirt and rocks aside. After a few minutes I heard the front gate that led from our driveway to the yard swing open. It was Anna. She knelt down next to me and began cupping her hands in the soil, pushing it into piles. We dug for a minute or so. "What are we burying?" she asked.

"Mrs. Walsh gave me three copper pots: one for you, one for me, and one for good luck."

Anna picked up one of the pots, admiring the way the afternoon light cast a muted glow on its surface. "I heard you're the one who found her. What did she look like?"

I thought about Mrs. Walsh's ashen skin and the dozens of lines around her mouth and eyes that had tightened in death. "She looked like someone who had lived a very long time," I answered.

"Do you think she was ready to die?"

"I think she would have liked one more cup of tea. She enjoyed little things like that."

"Were you scared?"

"Not really." *Only young people are afraid of ghosts.*

We kept digging. Once the hole was deep enough we placed a pot inside and covered it with soil. Anna reached out for my hand and gave it a squeeze. I watched her walk home, and she looked over her shoulder two times. I drew my hands up to my face.

They smelled of copper and earth.

ALL FOR YOU, SARA SUE

KEN GOLDMAN

The moment a child is born,
the mother is also born.
She never existed before.
The woman existed, but the mother, never.
A mother is something absolutely new.

- **Bhagwan Shree Rajneesh (1931-1990)**

Would it mean anything now if I told you that I loved my husband? I know that's hard for you to swallow considering what's happened, but I do mean it. No woman could ask for a finer man than my Elliot, least of all a woman like myself. Just look at the sacrifices he made for us. How could anyone with a beating heart not love a man who would suffer for his loved ones like that?

And we both loved our Sara Sue so much, you know, so very much.

Ever notice how in those Hollywood movies these beautiful couples always manage to meet real cute? Some Jennifer Aniston type breaks her heel on the streets of New York and then—*Wham!* This prince of a guy shows up to help her, he just materializes out of thin air for lovely Jennifer, and he's usually some beef cake, or maybe he has this really charming accent every woman in the audience immediately goes wet for. And of course, despite the inevitable complications, love happens in the space of the next ninety minutes, during which time, for the women in the theater, there's not a dry seat in the house. Everything wraps so perfectly, just in time to cue the syrupy love song they run with the end credits. Yeah, those movies, they're always the same. Some boy wins some girl, but then loses said girl or she loses him, and then—well, I've already told you the rest. My point is, everyone goes home happy.

I'd like to say that's how it happened with Elliot and me. Yes, I'd like to, but I can't. Oh, we started happy enough during one rainy afternoon when he sat alongside me at the Charlestown Avenue Starbucks and didn't speak a word for ten minutes. See, it was crowded, and that seat was the only one available. And when he finally did speak, he asked me for the time. I gave it to him, he thanked me, and—well, end of story. Almost. Because when I ran into him on the bus later that day, again only one seat was available. So, I sat next to him expecting at most a smile of recognition. But no, that man spoke right up.

"Well, this must be kismet," that's what he said, and only then did I realize how attractive he was. Not movie star attractive, of course, but easy enough on the eyes. I'll admit I was startled the man said anything considering I sat there soaking wet and looked awful. I mean, look at me. Do I have the kind of face men would remember?

"What's that?" I asked.

"*Kismet?* From this old late show '50s musical of the same name. It means fate, destiny. And I'd say there must be some kind of fate working here, sitting next to each other again like this, wouldn't you?" He smiled, offered his hand. "My name is Elliot. And who might your soaking wet self be?"

I smiled, but didn't answer his question. The man seemed to be coming on to me, and that didn't happen often—or ever. So instead I said the first thing that came to mind, which was unfortunately something stupid.

"Elliot. That was my father's name. He's dead now."

Dumb, I know. But my hesitation didn't put that man off for one second. "It's not a name you can do much with. Too humdrum to shorten into anything. Not much wiggle room to do that. I mean, come on—El? Ellie? Try surviving the school yard when kids call you that."

I smiled politely again, although I could feel my heart beginning to race. We seemed pretty awkward talking such nonsense, so I went for the save, leaning closer as if sharing a secret. It was a daring move for me.

"My real name is Darcella Etheridge, but everyone calls me Darcy. I'm not sure how that started, but I'm glad it did. Anyway, you can call me anything you like." I had no idea what that meant, but Elliot seemed to think I had said something very clever. He grinned, leaned close too.

"So, you're suggesting I call you?"

It wasn't the stuff great romance stories are made of, I know. But that's how we began, and by the end of our bus ride, I felt I had been talking with an old friend. No Reese or Julia or Jennifer meeting Hugh Jackman or Clive what's-his-name while Celine Dion warbles on the soundtrack. Attractive as Elliot appeared, I doubt anyone would mistake him for Mr. Jackman, or me for—well, I can name about a hundred movie stars to whom I bear no resemblance whatsoever. But to Mr. Elliot Hanover, that didn't matter in the least. And when he spoke my name, my heart pretty much supplied its own soundtrack. I suppose I'm getting much too talky about that first day, so I'll go easy on all the love stuff that followed. Oh yes, there was quite a bit of that, in case you were wondering, but I'll skip to the serious parts you ought to know about, okay?

We married. It didn't take long. A woman knows when it feels right. Hell, I practically jumped into that man's arms when he asked me to be his. Somehow he managed to present me with a beautiful ring too, although to this day I couldn't tell you how he could afford such a thing working in the city mail room at the time. But we were both so young, and with youth comes foolishness. I've no doubt Elliot probably spent most of his life savings on what he placed on my finger.

Our wedding ceremony wasn't anything to make those English Royals envious and the small apartment we moved into fell considerably short of palatial, but none of that mattered. I knew this was as perfect a life as I'd ever hoped for, and only one thing could make it more perfect. Elliot felt the same, so we got to working on beginning our family right away. We were young. We didn't know—we just didn't know.

See, it wasn't really anyone's fault, my not being able to conceive, but it didn't seem in the stars for us. So after many months trying, we decided to find out if maybe we had been doing something wrong. Turns out it wasn't Elliot or me who got it wrong. No, nature herself had made that decision for us; it was what Elliot had called kismet. Well, fate can kismet my ass. Dr. Byron over at the County Medical Hospital, he informed us that my eggs weren't doing what a woman's eggs are supposed to. But that wasn't all. Because see, Dr. Byron also tested Elliot, and—well, let's just say that Mother Nature decided to hit us with a double barrel. I must have cried myself to sleep for weeks.

"We can adopt," Elliot tried reassuring me. "I swear, we would love that child like it was our own, Darcy, I'm sure we would." But I knew it wouldn't be the same, not for me, and besides, we could never have afforded what those agencies were asking. Talk about a hard pill to swallow, and I really did try. But knowing I could never be a mother, that I could never hold my own infant in my arms, it was just too much for me to stand.

That's how Sara Sue came to be. She was Elliot's idea, and maybe at first I thought it seemed crazy. After I'd spent so many nights bathing my face in tears, one morning Elliot sat on the bed alongside me. He wore this huge grin, something I hadn't seen for weeks. Taking my face into his hands, he kissed me.

"I think maybe we're going to have that child after all. See, I've been doing some thinking, Darcy, and I believe you're going to give birth to our child any day now."

I had no idea what he meant. Unless my new husband intended to kidnap some infant from its crib, I didn't see any child in our future. But doing something so wrong wasn't Elliot Hanover's style. I sat up, managed a few words.

"You want to tell me how that's going to happen, considering the doctor explained that a newborn coming out of me is as likely as one coming out of that old bowling ball of yours?"

Elliot's grin grew wider. He rubbed my stomach, then put his ear to it. "Why, I believe I've just felt that baby of ours kick. She's going to be a healthy one, our Sara Sue, I just know it. I'm so proud of you, Darcy. You'll be such a wonderful mother." He turned serious. "Are you following me on this?"

"Not at all." I'll tell you right now that at that moment I felt certain my Elliot had completely lost his mind. Either that, or he had something up his sleeve I couldn't begin to guess. As it turned out, he did.

"Okay, then, I'll explain this only once, and after today I'll never say another word about it. You can either agree to it or not. Whatever you decide will be all right, but I'm hoping you'll see this situation the way I do."

I might have felt frightened had those words come from a man less rational than my husband, but I knew he was dead serious and that his feelings for me never had proved less than solid gold genuine.

Elliot took my hand, held it tight. His words sounded as if he had rehearsed them for hours. Likely, he had. But he spoke with such assuredness, such certainty ...

"Our Sara Sue will be born in a few days. We'll need time to fix up the place, of course, maybe purchase an old crib at the thrift store, some baby clothes too. You'll deliver a little prematurely at home, and it may seem somewhat touch and go for a while, but I'll be there to deliver our child and it will be a perfect birth. And from that day forward you and I, together we'll watch our daughter grow every day, and we'll ask her how her time at school went, soothe her when she skins her knee, laugh and cry with her when circumstances call for it. Most important, we'll love that little girl every bit as much as if—"

He seemed to almost choke on the rest of that sentence. I finished it for him.

"As if she were real?"

Those words did not come easy. I looked hard into my husband's eyes to determine if maybe something had gone seriously wrong with his thinking to cause him to suggest something so preposterous. But I saw a clarity there that I knew meant he had earnestly weighed the pros and cons of his proposition.

"She *will* be real, Darcy. To us she'll be more real than anything else in the world." Elliot squeezed my hand, then kissed it. "Our Sara Sue will be the most perfect child a parent could want, and you—*you* will be the perfect mother."

I didn't know whether to laugh or cry. I did neither. What Elliot had suggested was possibly the most insane idea a man could propose, or maybe it was the most incredible demonstration of love of which any husband was capable. Knowing my man the way I did, I didn't have to question his reasoning for very long.

"Why 'Sara Sue?'" I asked.

His smile reappeared. "You wanted a girl, right?"

I nodded.

"Well, then, why *not* Sara Sue?"

Thinking over what he suggested, I felt so much love for my husband I knew no other response would do. Elliot had found a way to give us our child, and I threw my arms around him, held him as close as I could. "I know our Sara Sue will be perfect," I whispered. "I know she will."

It was an amazing moment, all right. I was laughing while tears clouded my eyes. And Elliot and I held each other so tight for the next hour as if we were each afraid to let go.

And maybe we were.

* * *

Elliot proved true to his word. Never once did he imply that Sara Sue would be anything less than our flesh and blood daughter. So I played along, even down to his providing all the skills necessary to make our imaginary child's imaginary birth anything but imaginary. I'll spare you the details of that day, but I will admit that I screamed and pushed just as accurately as any woman going through the wonderful agony of childbirth, and Elliott stood by me the whole time wiping my forehead with a moist towel while coaxing my breathing. When it was over I felt exhausted, and I really was bathed in sweat. Moments later, there stood Elliot holding the most beautiful imaginary infant a new mother could ever hope to see. Yes, I knew that wrapped inside the pink blanket was probably a bag of flour, but I swear, for a moment I really did see our new daughter in her father's arms. And I'm telling no lie when I say my heart nearly burst with happiness when he handed Sara Sue to me.

In the days that followed when Elliott returned from work his first words always were "Where's my little angel? What wonderful thing did our daughter do today?" And I would answer, I'd say, "Oh, you should have seen her! She was so good, Elliot, the way she ate all her carrots, and without so much as a whimper the entire afternoon. She's fast asleep now. Come, look." But sometimes Sara Sue could be difficult too, and I'd complain, "Oh, God! I think I want to scream. That child just refused to eat anything today, and I must have changed her diaper ten times!"

During the night, Elliot would often climb from our bed, tell me, "I hear Sara Sue crying. You go back to sleep, Darcy. I'll take care of it." Other times I would sit for an hour rocking her to sleep and singing gently to her "Hush little baby, don't say a word ..."

And so it went ...

* * *

"Oh, Elliot! Sara Sue spoke her first word today! Mama—she said Mama!!"

"Look, Darcy! I think—Yes! I think she's trying to take her first step right now!"

"Hush little baby ..."

"Who's Daddy's perfect little angel? Who? Who?"

"First day of school! Let's get going, munchkin!"

"Elliot, come see what our daughter drew in class today!"

"Love you ... Love you ..."

* * *

No there was nothing there to see, I knew that. But another part of me disregarded that empty space, and instead I saw the most precious girl child on this planet. And like a madly spinning carousel the years seemed to pass too quickly...

* * *

"Sara Sue got picked for head cheerleader today, Elliot. Head cheerleader!"

"Doesn't our daughter look beautiful all dressed up for the dance?"

"Tell her, Elliot. Tell her how boys sometimes can seem cruel like that ..."

* * *

Sara Sue came laughing to us when she saw the first robin of spring, told how she caught lightning bugs inside a jar on the first day of summer, rolled in the autumn leaves or made snow angels in the park. They were such wonderful years. Sara Sue was our life.

No, that's not correct. She was more.

Sara Sue kept us alive!

But then during the darkest days of winter our old friend Kismet reared her ugly head.

Elliot came from our daughter's room. "Darcy, do Sara Sue's eyes look a bit swollen to you? She's been complaining about stomach pains and she can't seem to move. I think there's something seriously wrong."

Of course, I realized a child's illness was a problem all parents face. Our daughter was an adolescent now, but never had she been sick, so some kind of illness seemed inevitable. I entered Sara Sue's room, looked into the empty bed and waited a respectable few minute. Returning to my husband I told him, "You may be right, she doesn't look so good. There's some fever too." Then I added the only thing a concerned parent would say. "I think maybe we should see the doctor."

I had barely got that sentence out before Elliot grabbed his coat, so I went for mine. But he told me, "No, Darcy, you stay home," always wanting to protect me from anything disturbing. Although my maternal instincts disagreed, I chose not to argue, certain that within the hour Elliot would return, explain to me that our daughter had just caught a bad virus, or something like that. I heard him tell Sara Sue to put on some clothes, watched through the window as our old Camry drove off.

For hours I waited but Elliot didn't return, and when I called his cellular he didn't answer. I prayed our Sara Sue would be all right, all the while realizing the foolishness of that prayer. I suppose when you believe in something hard enough, you make it so. That night, I realized how authentic Sara Sue had become to both of us, understood the fear any mother would feel for her ailing child. Near dawn, Elliot appeared at the door. I could tell he hadn't slept, and the look on his face was one I had never seen.

"Sara Sue isn't with you?" I asked.

Without removing his coat he sat on the couch, just looking at me. "Darcy, I think you had better sit too." Taking his hand I could feel his trembling. "It was her heart, Darcy. The doctors, they tried and tried, but Sara Sue just wasn't strong enough. She didn't make it."

The world stopped in that instant, and I couldn't form even the simplest rational thought. "That's—That's not possible, Elliot. She's just a young girl, hardly into her teenage years. A child's heart—*our* child's, it just doesn't quit like that. It *can't!*"

"Sara Sue's heart did. It just stopped, Darcy, like some busted watch. Just like that."

She isn't real, Elliot. She never was. You know it. I know it. How can she die?

But Elliot insisted our child lay in the morgue at County Medical. I heard growing anger in his voice and I reached for him, but he pulled himself from me, told me he needed to be alone for a while. I understood, or at least a part of me thought I did. I'm certain we never felt so lonely in our lives as we mourned the tragic death of our child, arranged for her burial, spoke of her funeral—all without leaving our apartment. We opened imaginary cards of sympathy from imaginary friends, shared them, answered imaginary calls. I guess after all those years I just got caught up in the pretending, and I almost believed our daughter's death to be so. I knew Sara Sue seemed real—*but she wasn't!* Still, the grief felt as real as anything I'd experienced, although what followed after weeks of mourning our loss—well, I couldn't have seen it coming in a million years.

Searching for answers, at first I believed maybe Elliot decided Sara Sue had to die because he hoped we might grow closer in our grief. But that didn't happen. We stopped talking, ate little, slept less. Sometimes Elliot disappeared for the entire night. I knew better than to ask where he had been because the alcohol on his breath told me. But that wasn't the worst of it. Often at night Elliot would leave our bed and scream like a man gone mad. I could no longer suggest that our Sara Sue existed only in our imaginations. He would glare at me as if I had uttered something reprehensible, my words deserving no response beyond his complete contempt that I had suggested such a terrible thing. His misery grew so terrible that now it seemed I mourned more for my lost husband than for Sara Sue.

I should have seen it coming—I should have seen it!

He had managed to do it so quietly while I slept, I never heard a sound from the bathroom. I found Elliot in the morning slumped in a spreading puddle of his own blood, the razor's blade still in his wrist, a smeared note at his side.

I'm so sorry, Darcy. I just can't take the pain any more.
I love you.

I won't go into the details of the awful scene I found. I really can't do that without bringing myself back to it. Seeing my beloved husband there on the floor, and the blood, so much blood—well, just talking about it, I'm sorry, but I don't want to say any more about that. I can't tell you how I felt either. I couldn't get my mind to comprehend what Elliot had done or why he had done it. I still can't. No matter how I look at it, it makes no sense at all. Well, maybe that's not entirely true. See, I always knew my Elliot was more man than a woman like me ever deserved, and I love him still despite the terrible thing he did. So there's one thing I do understand. It's been almost a year now since my husband and our Sara Sue have been gone, and that one thing rings pretty clear.

Loneliness, it does terrible things to a person's head—terrible things.

Yes, I know it wasn't right, my taking that infant from its carriage. But when I saw her at the Charlestown Mall left unattended for that moment—well, I just did what I did without putting much thought into it. That little darling looked so much like our Sara Sue, it seemed my hands developed a mind of their own when they snatched her. After I'd done that, all I could think to do was just run. So there I was, standing in the middle of that parking lot holding some strange woman's infant, having not the slightest idea what to do next. I found this large plastic trash bag in a bin, emptied it to put the infant inside. I wanted to hide her, that was all. I wasn't thinking clearly, you have to know that. I just wasn't thinking clearly.

Would it mean anything now if I told you how sorry I feel for all I've done? Because I do feel sorry, you know—so very sorry for whatever sorrow I've caused. It's just that I miss my family so much, even knowing our Sara Sue never really—she never—

... not really ...

Damn! Oh damn!

Do you think you could turn off that recorder device now, please, Sergeant? I've told you all there is to tell, and I'm feeling so tired.

* * *

5th POLICE PRECINCT: CITY OF CHARLESTOWN
12: 47 a.m.

After a third replay of the recorded confession of the woman who called herself Mrs. Darcella Hanover, Sergeant Harry Servitto felt damned tired himself. Arresting officer Will McCormack poured two cups of coffee and spoke Harry's thoughts.

"She's wrong about that last part, Sergeant. There's more to tell, all right. A dozen witnesses saw her take that child, a dozen more claim there always seemed something not right about her. I saw that close up when we busted that woman's door and found her singing some 'Hush Little Baby' song to that stolen infant's corpse. Never looked up, just kept singing her damned lullaby like we weren't there, as if that dead baby was gurgling happily in her own mother's arms."

Servitto raised a pair of bloodshot eyes. "To that woman you *weren't* there, William. People see what they want to see. Maybe doing that, they goose up fate into being whatever they want it to be. She wanted a real Sara Sue. I guess she found one. But fate has her way of biting you in the ass. Kismet, like the lady said." He stubbed out his cigarette, stared at the ashes. "Christ, it's too late to be getting philosophical."

Looking as tired as his superior, McCormack sipped his coffee. "Go figure what crazy shit goes on inside a lonely woman's head to make her self-destruct like that, eh? Guess we'll have to let the court shrink decide that."

Servitto nodded agreement. "You find anything about this Hanover guy?"

The officer shook his head. "Not a damned thing, Sergeant. Elliot's her late father's name, Hanover's the family name of some local garage mechanic says he took this Darcella to a movie once when she was about fifteen, and he hasn't seen her since. But there's no record of any Elliot Hanover in this woman's life, not a signature on any document or canceled check, not one person in that apartment building who's ever seen a trace of the man. No one's never seen her sporting any fancy ring like she spoke about, neither. She's never been anything but Darcella Etheridge. Court shrink's going to have a field day with this one."

Servitto forced a tired smile, quickly gave it up, and reached for his coffee.

"Loneliness is one mean mind fucker, all right. A woman wants a family, she figures a way to have one. Imaginary dead children and husbands don't mean a whole lot, legally speaking. But now we've got a dead infant for real here. Write it up by tomorrow morning, will you? Go home and kiss your wife and kids." He glared into his cup. "Anything else, William?"

The young officer took a moment to consider the question. He shrugged.

"Coffee's gone cold," he said.

BASEMENT BOB

BRITTANY BELL

"**M**an, if you gotta ask, you'll never know." This sentence ignited something in us the way a single match can send a forest into flames. Perhaps it was because Erica and I were already curious about Basement Bob when we asked Joshua Parker what he knew about the recluse who lived on his street. The fact that we were eleven and Josh was already in high school likely contributed. Perhaps it was simply because we didn't like being told we would never know. Whatever the reason, everything was set into motion when Josh uttered these words.

Basement Bob was our town's version of Boo Radley. As far as we knew, he never left the basement of his parents' two-story, beige stucco house. All of the neighborhood children knew about Bob. Some of our more callous peers tapped on the basement windows with sticks as they strolled by.

Erica and I were convinced that Basement Bob had to leave the house eventually and made it our mission to ensure that we would be present when he did. The house across the street was owned by an elderly couple who went to Florida for half the year, so their stoop became our post. Sometimes we took shifts, but we usually kept watch together, sharing a pair of binoculars that my grandfather used to bring to baseball games.

We had seen Bob peer through the cheap, vinyl blinds that covered one of the basement hopper windows exactly four times. We knew he was there because we saw movement when he used his thumb and index finger to separate the slats and then quickly let them drop after his glimpse at the world. One time we were feeling brave and crossed the street. We got close enough to see the whites of his eyes before shrieking and darting back to our post.

Erica began growing impatient after a few days. I kept catching her picking at the scab on her knee or piling pebbles instead of looking out for Bob. "Do you think Josh will ever like one of us?" she asked during one of our stakeouts.

"I think he likes us," I said. "He always says hi to us when he sees us around."

"Not *that* kind of like."

"You mean as a girlfriend?"

Erica rolled her eyes. "A guy like Josh Parker doesn't have just one girlfriend."

"Fine, whatever." I was annoyed. We were supposed to be on the lookout for Bob.

"This is getting boring." Erica started picking at her scab again. The skin on her knee was pink and looked angry.

"Look, it's fine if you want to give up. But he has to come out sooner or later."

"Josh said he never leaves."

"Okay, so go find your precious Josh, and leave me alone." I knew this statement would get to Erica because we'd recently made a pact never to let a boy get in the middle of our friendship, a promise based on books and movies in the absence of real life experience.

She plopped back down and gestured for the binoculars. "Give me those."

"Do you see anything?" I asked.

"Just the same thing you see."

"We need a better plan," I admitted.

"Do you have one?" Erica dropped the binoculars and let them hang from the string around her neck.

I thought for a while, and my mind wandered. My mother would have a fit if she knew we were spying on Basement Bob. She had told me to "leave the poor man alone" and warned us that he wasn't right. As soon as I got home, she would probably nag me about selling Girl Scout cookies and wag the empty order form in the air for dramatic effect.

That's when it came to me. "I have a plan," I announced.

"Finally!" Relief flooded Erica's face.

"Let's ring the doorbell and try to sell his parents Girl Scout cookies."

"That's your plan?" Erica wrinkled her nose, which made her look like a pug. I would have to tell her not to do that around Josh.

"Everyone loves Girl Scout cookies," I pointed out.

"How does that help us?"

"Maybe he'll come upstairs when the bell rings. We've never seen anyone ring the bell before. It would be a big event. Even if we don't see him, we'll get to meet one of his parents. The only hobby parents have is talking about their kids. They'll probably tell us all about him while they're ordering cookies."

"*If* they order cookies."

"They'll order cookies."

"What makes you so sure?"

"Come on, you've eaten Thin Mints before." I had once seen Erica eat an entire sleeve of them at a sleepover.

"I guess it could work. Let's get the order form."

We went to my house and returned to Bob's block wearing our Girl Scout uniforms and sashes. We walked up the four brick steps to Basement Bob's house. Erica placed her index finger on the doorbell. I could see its orange glow through her translucent nail. She looked at me, and I nodded. She rang the bell.

A woman in late middle age answered the door, presumably Basement Bob's mother. She wore a magenta tracksuit, despite the fact that we'd never seen her go for a run before. Her only other distinguishing feature was an exceptionally bad perm. I could hear a Louis Armstrong song playing in the background, the kind of music my grandparents played. I was surprised to think of Basement Bob's parents sitting around listening to jazz while their son stayed down in the basement. I didn't know how to feel about it.

"Girl Scouts!" she exclaimed. "I was a Girl Scout, too, but that was ages ago, of course. Are you selling cookies?"

"Uh huh," I stammered, realizing that talking was my role. Erica rang doorbells, and I did the talking. "Would you like some? We have a new flavor this year, along with some traditional favorites—"

A male voice, presumably belonging to Basement Bob's father, called out from the living room. "Are those Girl Scouts, hon? Make sure you get some Samoas!"

The woman smiled. "I'll take one box of Samoas and one box of Thin Mints."

I unfolded the order form and made a tally mark in the appropriate columns. "Thank you! Now, I'll just need your name and phone number," I said, conducting the transaction the way our troop leader had taught us.

Just then, a bellowing, guttural voice was heard ascending into the main floor of the house. We saw him. Basement Bob had long, stringy black hair that waved in front of his eyes. His skin was ghostly white. His fists were clenched, but gesticulated wildly in the air. "I TOLD YOU! I told you they were watching me!"

"Honey, these are Girl Scouts selling cookies," the woman said, her hand shaking as she scribbled her name in the appropriate box on the order form. Her voice was as slow and syrupy as a kindergarten teacher's.

Basement Bob lunged across the living room, but was intercepted by his father who tackled him to the floor. Erica gasped, and Basement Bob's mother dropped the pen. "I'm sorry, you'll have to excuse me. My son isn't well." She shoved the form back in my hand and closed the door abruptly.

Erica looked at me. "Well, we saw him."

"We saw him," I repeated.

We walked in silence for a few minutes before she asked, "What are we going to do when the cookies come in?"

"What?" I asked, unsure of what she was alluding to.

"Are we actually going to bring her the cookies?"

"Of course not," I snapped.

"Because she didn't pay?"

"No, not because she didn't pay."

"Because we did a bad thing?" Erica asked.

Man, if you gotta ask, you'll never know, I thought.

THE WEEPING SCIMITAR

VINCENT CZYZ

"The least tinge of the Tartar taint is as difficult to efface as that of Africa: the elongated eye, the spreading nostril, the unhealthy, jaundiced hue, are sure to be revealed ..." —an anonymous western traveler [as quoted in Thomas De Quincey's *The Revolt of a Tartar Tribe*]

The sky was shrouded, the river's voice damp, the air clammy as the sides of an old well. It was the kind of morning that muffled the ring of steel and doused sparks before they could disappear with a bright flourish. Nearly the whole of the village, men and women alike, had converged on the river. Leather boots as stiff as wood slipped on dead leaves, on rocks, and on fallen logs coated with moss and settled mist. The villagers planted themselves like battle standards along the river's banks, arms crossed over chests, while they waited to see whether Dargo Peshren would survive judgment.

There'd been a quarrel, an exchange of insults, a drawing of knives, and Dargo had killed his best friend, Mesun Kalmuk. Now, on a day that smelled of moldering leaves and wet wood, he was to be thrown into the river, which would carry him over the falls. Plummeting more than a hundred feet, he would disappear into the seething white where the waters collided, and a permanent cloud hovered. Either his body would be shattered on the rocks or, if the river spirit watched over him, he would be cupped by a pocket of water and heaved back to the surface.

Nothing is in the world but Sila is also in it.

"There's no hope for him." Dargo's aunt shook her head. "Look at this weather ... so gray that if a wolf were watching, we'd see only his eyes."

Her neighbor, a man with a great drooping mustache, nodded gravely. "Last night I heard the call of an owl. Three times."

She clucked her tongue unhappily. "The bird that perches on Death's shoulder." She shook her head again. "No hope."

They cocked their heads as though they could hear the tumble-washed bones of the drowned stirring fitfully in their beds of swaying weeds.

Dargo stood on the bank of the river, too young to have more than a wisp of a mustache, his dusky face impassive. His eyes had changed since his friend's death. Something had gone out of them, the way certain stones, brilliantly colored when first picked out of the water, become pale and dull when they dry.

Two men held him by either arm while others lined the banks to make sure, once he was in the river, he didn't try to swim ashore.

The tradition was clear: it fell to Mesun's father, Husgan, and to Mesun's younger brother, Chahtay, to avenge his death. Knowing he was now *kanli*, Dargo should have fled to the mountains and joined an Azak tribe or lost himself in the crowds of Samirska. Instead, he had admitted his crime.

Husgan had behaved in similarly uncharacteristic fashion. "Why should another father lose his son? How will a mother's grief be recompense for mine?" He was known to have a weakness for the truth.

Nonetheless, there were murmurs of disapproval from elders with hardly a tooth left with which to menace their meals, men who insisted that tradition must be unchanging, like the sky and the return of birds in spring. But there were also grandfathers who brushed away this objection with withered hands. While they agreed that something had to be done, they reminded their neighbors that the sky changed its aspect every day, that blizzards had been known to bury spring's upstart green in startling white, that balmy winds sometimes fretted glassy snowdrifts to tepid puddles even during the Moon of Creaking Ice. A youth need not always pay for his foolishness with blood. In the end it was decided that Sila, acting through the falls, would be the arbiter who would either take Dargo's life or spare it.

A burly farmer held Dargo by his wrists while a second lifted him by his ankles. Sagging between them like a rolled carpet, Dargo was swung into the water.

Frigid no matter the season, the river startled his heart and turned the breath in his throat into a stone. When he could manage a gasp, he sputtered and flailed as the current swept him toward the falls. Villagers who watched his head bob past also saw it disappear as though something unseen had grasped him by an ankle and jerked him under. He fell like a fallen tree or the remnants of a smashed boat, without a shout or a cry.

A handful of men waited at the bottom of the falls, peering into the mist and white foam. Husgan was among them, his peasant hands leaden at his sides, his youngest son a step behind him. Although Chahtay's face was dispassionate, he prayed silently that Dargo had been killed, that he and his family wouldn't have to bear the shame of allowing his brother's murderer to live.

"There!" One of the men pointed while others went splashing into the river.

Dargo churned the water like a panicked dog.

Hands grabbed hold of his shirt and hauled him ashore.

Blood made a tiny red country with spreading borders on his forehead. Dripping with river water, slightly bow-legged, he stood facing Husgan. His long hair bedraggled and his clothes sagging like skin falling away from the bone, he seemed even more a boy than he had before they'd thrown him into the river.

Husgan embraced him, his outsized hands with their blunt fingers splayed on Dargo's back. He turned to Chahtay. "He's your elder brother now."

Chahtay found it almost intolerable to open his arms to a man he wanted to see dead, but he obeyed his father. A wet cheek pressed against his own numbed his face.

"I know you wanted me to drown," Dargo said in his ear, "I know I can't replace Mesun, but no *kabrek* will be more loyal."

Chahtay's nostrils flared as he turned away from Dargo.

Seizing Chahtay's hand, twisting it palm-up, Husgan drew his knife across it.

Chahtay would much rather spit in Dargo's face, but he placed his bleeding palm on Dargo's forehead and held it there. "Now," he muttered, "we're of the same blood."

Amid nods and shouts of approval, the two kissed each other's cheeks.

* * *

As the Moon rose over the hut his great-grandfather had built, Chahtay glanced at the cushion on which his brother used to sleep and listened to the wind whine through chinks and ill-fitting seams. On the other side of a rug hung to divide the hut in two, his parents slept. He stared at the ceiling until it dissolved into haze, and he was taken by a dark undertow.

Mesun, not unlike the wind perhaps, found a crack or a fault through which he was able to return home. The hairs on the back of Chahtay's neck raised themselves up as though predicting a brush with lightning. He was sure it was Mesun standing beside him, but when he lifted a candle, the light died on shadowy features as if his brother's face were still shrouded in the murk of the World Behind the World.

"Dargo killed me in a moment of anger." Mesun's voice had not changed. "Let it pass."

"I can't."

"No one is better to take my place."

"No one should have to."

"Better a *kabrek* at your side than another body to bury."

His brother said nothing else, the candle guttered out, and in the morning, the first thing Chahtay did was look at Mesun's cushion. It hadn't been slept on. But the tightness that had squeezed his chest since his brother's death had loosened. Unfastening a flap of oiled cloth that covered a window, he lifted it to find that a thick mist had replaced the fields. The vague white hung like overlapping veils between the world and him, and at that distance he found the world easier to bear.

He heard his mother, Ruya, preparing breakfast on the other side of the rug partitioning the hut.

Broad and thick-thewed, Chahtay tended to dominate conversations among other boys with a voice that tumbled out of him like a barrel shoved down a staircase. This morning he sat down in silence to the bread and cheese his mother had set out.

Not until the meal was finished and Husgan had stood up

was the silence broken. "Without Mesun, we'll have to work harder."

That was always his father's solution, no matter the problem—work harder. Putting on a sheepskin jerkin, Chahtay followed him outside.

Dargo, a rag wrapped around his head, was waiting for them.

Chahtay thought about waiting for the right moment and splitting open Dargo's head beyond bandaging with a shovel, but he remembered his dream and pushed his anger aside.

Husgan put a hand on Dargo's shoulder. "We're glad you came."

Chahtay and Husgan got used to seeing him on the doorstep in the morning, the way you get used to anything that gives the impression it will perpetually repeat—winter, full moons, bad weather—and after a month or so, Chahtay told Dargo about his dream.

Dargo smiled. "Even in death your brother's a friend to me. Trust him. I'll be the same to you."

"I'll do my best, but don't be surprised if one day I reach for my knife instead of my rake." Already Chahtay had a reputation for being—even for a Tazta—skillful with a blade.

Unlike his son, Husgan was in love with the land. "Even the dead hover before a favorite view or lengthen like a shadow on the grass before they head off to the World Behind the World." Husgan was content returning from the fields to a wife who waited for him every evening and lit his pipe for him after dinner. He sat and smoked, looking out on the twilight as though contemplating the day when he himself would be a shade gazing his last.

Chahtay envied his father's peaceful nature, just as he admired the hands that could scoop up as much loose soil as the blade of a shovel. He envied the way the land seemed to need him as much as sun or rain.

Nonetheless the harvest didn't go well that year, and Husgan wasn't able to pay his taxes. Yes, King Hugo had made reforms, had awarded lands to the peasants who worked them, but the more land they owned, the more taxes they owed. It didn't matter to the government whether frost killed a harvest or drought ruined a crop; the taxes had to be paid.

Peasants who had rejoiced at being property owners began to despair when they fell behind in their payments. If the land reverted to the crown, the peasant families once again became serfs in all but name or worse, were dispossessed entirely, and the land was sold off.

Husgan refused to give up so much as a clod of tillable earth. Instead, he worked more, tending not only to his own groves and fields, but also cutting wood to sell or hiring himself out, sometimes earning less than a single *kroshten* for a day's labor. He slept little, swilling tea to keep his eyes open and his muscles alert. In spite of heartier meals, his bones began to shadow his skin.

Chahtay despised toiling in the fields, swatted at the biting flies that circled his head, resented the acrid musk of the manure he shoveled. But whenever he stopped to ask himself what he was doing with a farm tool in his hand, he had only to look over at Dargo, who silently kept pace with Husgan, or to remember how his father's ribs had begun to look like a potter's stack of clay coils.

* * *

Winter swept in from the nearby mountains to the west and from the distant steppes in the east. Anything left outside froze into a block. Beards turned white with frost and mustaches drooped with icicles. If the wood used to repair a house was too green, it split open, sometimes startling a family out of sleep.

Turuk's one tavern, its whitewashed walls stained with soot, had as many idlers as drinkers. Chahtay and Dargo were playing cards with Suluga and Artem. The losers would buy the winner a bowl of hot plum brandy, which the tavernkeep, always on the lookout for a bargain, had bought from a passing Gypsy clan.

Noses curved like blades, wispy mustaches and triangular faces—severe cheekbones and sharp chins forming the apexes —Artem and Dargo could have been brothers. Artem, however, had arms conspicuously too long for his body. The two of them liked to insinuate that Chahtay, with his heavier frame and squared-off jaw, his blunt chin and straighter nose, had inherited his looks from a Slav ancestor. After tacking an insult onto his denial, Chahtay reminded his friends he was darker than any of them. Suluga, who was the tallest ("You make the biggest target," Chahtay liked to say), had the least ability on horseback, with bow and knife. He was always the last to break into song, having fallen into the trap of studying long-dead philosophers and their weighty arguments against optimism.

Chahtay played a card that made Suluga groan and fold his hand.

Holding a fan of cards with one hand, Artem kept the other hand shoved into his felt pants, which was the only way he could warm it without standing in front of the smoky fireplace. He would happily cheat given the chance, but his friends were well aware of his tendencies and frequently cast suspicious glances in his direction.

Suluga would be leaving Turuk in the spring to attend the university in Samirska. His father had had to sell off a good deal of his land to make the first payments.

"We'll petition the king for a tax based on the harvest rather than a fixed tax on acres of land ..."

Chahtay shook his head and played another card. "You'll change nothing." Dirt that had seeped into the cracks in his skin gave his fingers the crazing of an old vase.

Artem threw his cards on the table with a slap and an oath. Straightening up in his chair, he shoved both of his hands into his pants.

"Aim at nothing, Chahtay Kalmuk, and you're sure to hit it."

Chahtay sipped his brandy and then squirted it through his teeth.

"Bastard son of a goat!" Suluga wiped his face.

"My aim's not so bad, eh?" He looked down at his bowl, a little regretful that it had been plum brandy he'd wasted. "One of these days, Hugo the Fat is going to lose patience with the student protests and send you all to the mines."

Suluga and Chahtay had been taught to read in a farmhouse rented by an idealistic Slav who was usually paid in blemished potatoes or battered fruit, a scrawny chicken or a pig's haunch. He'd been the one who'd loaned his philosophy books to Suluga, who'd enticed him with descriptions of Samirska's broad avenues and gas-lit streets, its great baroque buildings and Gothic cathedrals, its immense libraries and marble corridors echoing with the footsteps of men in black gowns who'd dedicated their lives to scholarly pursuits.

While Chahtay had given up lessons to help Husgan work the muddy fields, Suluga sat in the schoolmaster's farmhouse whenever his father gave him leave and read from textbooks stained by spilled tea or smudged by dirty hands.

"Are you going to be a farmer all your life?"

Chahtay shrugged. "I can't abandon my father."

"I can stay and do your work," Dargo said. Nothing in his

face changed as he threw down a card that furrowed Chahtay's brow.

"University's not for me. Even if it were, there's no money. You're father's a brave man to sell off his livelihood."

"You can find work in Samirska until you can pay for your studies."

"I told you, books don't suit me. Nor does a job in a Slav city." He snorted and spread his cards on the table. "Show!"

The seam of his lips wouldn't have admitted a chisel, and his eyes were as blank as erased chalkboards.

"Show!"

Dargo put his cards down.

"Hah! That's eleven brandies you dung-collectors owe me."

"Another hand!"

Artem reached across the table without leaning forward; it was his turn to deal. "Why don't we go to Samirska?"

"Eh?"

Artem held up a finger. "If we rob one rich Slav while he's tottering home from a tavern, we'll have money enough to last a year."

"Only we'd have to steal a horse to get to a town west of the Kaldovians."

"Unless we find a merchant passing through."

Suluga poked Chahtay's chest. "*That's* how you end up in the mines."

Chatay knew that Suluga was right, but breaking the law appealed to him more than university. Since he couldn't steal from Taztas (it would be like robbing his own family), the only solution was to leave Turuk. There was something like a whirlwind inside him, and even when he was still, it kept his thoughts going in circles.

Long before his brother's nocturnal visit, Chahtay's dreams had been disturbed by ghosts. Even awake, he could dowse an unmarked grave. Suluga, who'd been reading the philosophy of the Sceptics at the time, had once dug where Chahtay had pointed—and had been astonished to turn up a moldering skull and ribs as gray as driftwood. Maybe the windstorm was his own spirit spinning with tales told by the departed while he slept. Maybe the riot in his blood would quiet if he traveled as far as Samirska or even Tatavnia.

He looked at the dingy tavern wall and nodded as if to the Kaldovians beyond it. "It's settled then."

* * *

Bows in hand and quivers on their backs, Chahtay and Dargo left on foot in winter, which was the only time when Husgan could afford to do without them. Experienced hunters, they rarely misplaced an arrow when their aim was unhurried.

They returned three weeks later on horseback, their grins like curved knives.

"Where did you get that animal?" Husgan asked.

"A Slav who insulted me." Chahtay patted the horse's shoulder. "I gave him a choice: draw his knife or give me his horse. He chose wisely."

"The gendarmes will consider that brigandage."

"And if I had killed him, they would consider that murder."

Husgan shrugged. "If they come for you, you'll go to the mines."

"We were west of the Kaldovians, they'll never track us this far, I promise you."

Husgan, his wife, his son, and his adopted son worked the fields as they had the previous year, and the harvest was better but not much. Meals were meager throughout the winter. Husgan, worn down by lack of sleep and the long days of the growing season, began to wheeze and cough. He spent more and more of his day in bed, his breath rattling in his chest. Ruya brought him bowl after bowl of cabbage soup red with pepper. Chahtay squeezed one of his father's outsized hands. When he was a child, he'd thought there was nothing his father couldn't do with such hands—hold back a horse, splinter a door, crush a stone.

"Dargo and I will go into the hills. Fresh meat will restore your strength."

"Yes, a little meat and I'll be fine."

With fresh snowfalls hampering their progress and obliterating the tracks of their quarry, Dargo and Chahtay were gone three days before they were able to bring down a deer that had escaped the wolf packs. Dargo returned on foot while the deer, relieved of its entrails, shared the saddle with Chahtay.

Ruya, who had seen her son approaching like a shadow advancing across a white waste, waited for him at the door, a wool shawl draped over her shoulders.

"I couldn't bury him." She glanced at the frozen ground. "He's in the barn.

Husgan had grown even thinner before he'd died. His pale skin was stretched over the bone, the flesh sunken as though it had reached the end of a long retreat.

Chahtay's tears seemed as indifferent as water seeping out of a cliff face. He bent down and kissed each of his father's eyes to sweeten what he saw in the afterlife.

"Hugo the Fat," he said as though the wind would carry his words to the winter palace in Samirska, "his death is on your hands. And so are the deaths of the Slavs I kill to pay our debts."

After the spring thaw allowed his father's body to be properly laid to rest, Chahtay claimed the scimitar that had been in the family for generations and should have been passed on to Mesun. Its name was Gusyaslakash—archaic Tazta that translated roughly to Weeping Woman. Holding the curved blade aloft, he admired it from various angles. It was uniquely patterned by the two different steels from which it had been forged.

"Not even the king can tax this."

Although he couldn't read the motto, which was inscribed in the Arabic alphabet, he knew what it said: *The finest steel is nothing compared to the hand that wields it.*

After the day's work was done, Husgan sometimes practiced with Chahtay the repertoire of strikes and parries he'd learned from his own father. Ruya had disapproved of these lessons. "Only brigands and soldiers carry swords. Since he'll never fight for the king, you'll wind up making a brigand out of him."

No rake or shovel fit Chahtay's hand so perfectly, no ax handled so naturally. While Suluga apprenticed himself to the schoolmaster, Chahtay spent his spare time with Urfan Darkosov, who sometimes demonstrated his swordsmanship by cutting pairs of thrown apples in two or slicing buttons from vests. Last year, when Chahtay was 16, he'd competed with a wooden sword in the Festival of the Fourteen Clans. He'd defeated six men before losing to an Azak named Mustafa.

Tearful Woman at his side, Chahtay kissed his mother good-bye before mounting his horse. "I'm taking Dargo with me, but we'll be back with enough money for you to hire someone to help in the fields."

"A bullet or the mines, you're going to leave me without any sons."

"Would you rather I died like my father?"

"I would rather you live with respect for the law."

"If the law had the least respect for us, I would."

Chahtay left his mother standing in front of the hut his grandfather had built, which wasn't quite square and tilted a little to one side. She didn't wave but neither did she go inside, remaining motionless, like the stones marking the graves where her first son and her husband lay buried.

* * *

Chahtay woke up on the ground, shivering in his cloak. His hands trembling as he put wood on the embers of the fire, he knew, no matter how warm the stove at home was this morning, he'd never pick up a farm tool again. He owed nothing to anyone, owned only what he carried, and the whirlwind inside him had diminished to an intermittent gust.

He was not yet 18.

He kicked Dargo awake. "Don't call me Chahtay anymore. I don't want my name to get back to the gendarmes."

Dargo bent closer to the awakening fire. "How about Husband-To-A-Goat?"

"Ulash is shorter."

"Ulash?"

"How about you?"

Dargo shrugged. "Bury my last name."

"Since you wake up chirping like a bird, how about Dargo the Cheerful?"

Dargo shrugged again.

"That's why you're the only one who ever beats me at cards —that face, it's like trying to read stone."

Ulash cropped his hair short so there'd be less chance of a snag at close quarters, but Dargo left his long as a taunt to his enemies. Guards hired by wary merchants should've killed them or the gendarmes should have caught up with them, but they learned to glide past as silently as clouds, to recognize silhouettes by moonlight. On their first foray they made off with three horses without letting fly a single arrow because a drunken Slav had fallen asleep on his watch.

Inspired, they traded one of the horses for a crate of *ambruca* and posed as itinerant merchants near Tatavnia, where they sold half a dozen bottles to a pair of carpet dealers and their retinue. Doubling back to follow their customers, they waited until the last badly sung song had faded into the dark to rob them not only of their horses but also their weapons, their money, and their last bottle of *ambruca*.

Chahtay and Dargo drank until one joke was funnier than the next, until nothing seemed more natural than pissing with one leg in the stirrup. They shivered in blue dawns and built roaring fires to compensate for frozen sunsets. They inhaled the musk of their horses and sometimes hugged the muscular necks for warmth. Returning to Turuk to pay off Ruya's taxes, they spread the rumor they'd won their money gambling in Samirska.

Returning to their new occupation, they misjudged their first daylight raid—there were one or two men too many—and the back of Ulash's head was gashed by a Kurg arrow. Fortunately, the horses they'd stolen were good ones, and they disappeared into the forest. The blood clumping his hair, sticky on the back of his neck, made him giddy. Wheezing, coughing on what remained of his laughter, he put a sticky handprint on Dargo's forehead for good measure. His smile wilted as he realized that he was closer to Dargo than to the shirt he hadn't changed in weeks.

One day Ulash reined his horse to a stop at the edge of a forest. He watched steam plume rhythmically from his horse's flared nostrils, felt the ribs between his legs rise and fall.

"I think it is time to admit it, Dargo." He reached down to pat the horse's shoulder. "Sila cast me in the shape of a brigand. It's the only one I have."

"Maybe. Maybe we're just lazy thieves who don't mind killing to fill our pockets."

"We haven't killed anyone, yet."

"It's bound to happen."

Ulash shrugged. "The fields ripen, the grain is ground into flour, and the bread feeds a village—this is Sila. An earthquake shakes a city to pieces and whole families are crushed to death in their sleep—this is also Sila. How are we different?"

"We're not Sila."

They'd been robbing travelers for more than three years when Artem told them Suluga had been sent to the mines.

* * *

Sparks flew as Suluga's pick struck a cavern wall, but he didn't see them. Chips of stone sleeted his face, his hands, his body.

"There's a trick," a blue-gummed old Slav had told him. His nickname was Methuselah. "You close your eyes as you swing."

Stretched out, you could have used Methuselah to tie up a bale of hay. When the patched-up rag he called a cap came off his head, his white hair stuck up in every direction and he looked like a dandelion gone to seed.

Methuselah's advice had come too late. Suluga already had a patch over an eye in which he was now blind. His hands and feet were wrapped in torn strips (his boots had worn out weeks ago). Swinging his pick again, he tried to conserve strength without drawing the attention of a guard. His breath came out of him like a steam leak. Harder than ice, the chunks of wall he dislodged were nearly as frigid. After 12 hours, his hands were numbed and his bones as dead as the handle of the pick. Cold sent the exhaustion deeper, made it almost impossible at the end of a shift even to lift the heavy-headed tool.

On his first day in the camp, a huge guard with a ragged

beard framing his smile had said, "There are only two certainties in Yedrensk—one day will be your last, and the day after that you'll be forgotten."

He didn't tell the gloating Slav—Shelenka, the captain of the guards—that he'd been sentenced not to life but to only 10 years. Shelenka would have laughed. *You won't last 10 years.*

"Tatar bastard! Why are you slowing down?"

A guard shoved him with the butt of his rifle, and Suluga swung his pick again with the vigor borrowed from anger. Nothing was worse than hearing, somewhere behind you, the cock of a rifle. If you didn't turn around, seconds lengthened while you waited to be shot. If you did turn around, you were presumed guilty, and if you weren't shot, you were beaten. If you were beaten, you still had to work the next day with one or two fewer teeth to chew the crust of bread they gave you.

If only there were meat in the miserable mush they got twice a day! If only there were more than a single slice of bread to go with it. No matter how hungry they were, they ate slowly, savoring the few moments out of the day when there was something in their mouths that could be swallowed, when there was a taste—bland as it was—to press against their pasty tongues. Convicts who despised each other could share the same table as quietly as nuns, justifying a camp adage: *Even a snake doesn't bite a prisoner during his meal.*

At night, stinking of old sweat and dried urine, of rotting gums and the dark ferment between folds of skin, they sank into their bunks. There was never enough wood for the stove so the convicts slept bundled in what clothes they had. Because it was slightly warmer—or thought to be—closer to the rough-hewn rafters, there were sometimes brawls over who would get the top bunk. In summer the lower bunks caused fights. But by then at least half a dozen men would have died in their sleep or fallen face-forward, pick in hand, calling for new sleeping arrangements.

Who knew how, when a guard barged in blowing his whistle, they reassembled themselves in the morning, their faces unshaven, their stares vacant, their bodies held together by rancid-smelling bindings, and mustered the will to move. Suluga's only dreams were of roasted meat, roaring fires, and a soft bed. When he woke, it was always to the same crude barrack full of reeking men in various stages of decomposition.

Visitors weren't allowed. Letters sometimes came, thrown at the prisoners in crumpled balls. They were forbidden to speak while they worked; the chunk and clink of the pick were all the guards wanted to hear. If the toes poking through their wrappings turned black with frostbite, the convict was taken screaming to the infirmary, where he didn't need a doctor to inform him there was nothing for it but amputation. The older men didn't scream; some even grinned. Three weeks, maybe more, they wouldn't have to get up at dawn, have their legs clasped in irons, shuffle and clank to the mines where they gave up even the meager pleasure of watching the sun fire the sky.

While they worked, an icon of the Virgin Mary glowed above a feeble lantern. To Suluga it was nothing but a painted face darkened with soot. Only a painted face could do nothing while students and the few men brave enough to speak out against Hugo the Fat were chained together and forced to burrow in dank caverns like moles. Only a painted face could stare day after day at men so broken they could be reduced to tears if someone on the outside sent so much as a pair of wool socks.

It had been six months for Suluga. A boot or a rifle butt, sometimes the lash. Whistles to get out of bed, to end the day, to call attention to another man dead in his chains or in his bunk. The monotony of steel biting into stone. Sometimes cramped into a space so small he was able to swing his pick only a few inches while lice made him itch under his shirt. The curses of the guards who liked none of the convicts but liked Tatars still less.

"Doesn't it bother you that God made you the same color as shit?" The other guards laughed no matter how many times they'd heard it.

The prisoners had their own jokes. *What's the difference between a criminal and the king? No one can send the king to the mines.*

From time to time Suluga thought of the idealistic schoolmaster in Turuk who'd introduced him to the Stoic assertion that a spinning cosmos was also a living cosmos, to the geometry of Euclid, to political equations in which monarchies were replaced by parliaments, who had unintentionally landed him in this underworld with nothing to light his way but the sullen glow of a painted face.

Aleksander, a Slav with green eyes and curly brown hair sprouting from beneath his hat, reminded Suluga of his old teacher. He was the only guard who wasn't above giving out cigarettes to the prisoners—not the kind rolled with newspaper and shag tobacco but clean white ones that came like a row of soldiers bedded in a fancy box.

"One day," Shelenka bawled, "one of these Tatars, who shouldn't've been more than a stain on a whore's sheet, is going to repay you with a piece of steel in your back."

Aleksander would answer with a shrug. He was still youthful, was, in fact, the same age as Prince Lev when he had turned back the Taztas at the Battle of Tatavnia: 20.

As another shift was ending, Methuselah crumpled to his knees while trying to heave a rock into a cart. His poorly wrapped hands turned white holding the side of the cart, but he couldn't pull himself up. Suluga rushed to his side, but a guard began lashing them both. Suluga gave up, and Methuselah lost his ragged grip and fell. The guard's attack grew more frenzied.

Aleksander stopped the guard's arm in mid-arc. For a guard without rank, it was unthinkable. "He's older than my grandfather, and he works harder than both of us." Without raising his voice, he'd stated a fact as blunt as any pick handle.

The guard, who struggled for a second or two, let his arm sink as though the lash had suddenly become too heavy to hold up.

Aleksander lifted Methuselah. The convict's head lolled on his scrawny neck, his arms dangled uselessly, and the strings that pulled his legs had been cut. Aleksander laid him across a saddle and led the horse to the infirmary.

Shelenka spit out the shreds of a smoked cigar and lifted his chin toward Aleksander. "He won't last."

Neither did Methuselah; he was dead before morning.

The true criminals—the thieves and murderers who ran the barracks—were even worse than the guards. They didn't like the political dissenters, who were educated and could rarely show tattoos or worthwhile scars. Soft as fat bookworms, the Politicals couldn't forge a nail or carpenter a table, couldn't handle a blade.

A Criminal who'd lost his name in the mines and was known simply as the Kindjal, could get most any convict to do what he wanted with a word or a look. Blond, hairy, his muscles knotty (extra rations always found their way into his bowl), he might have been nicknamed Socrates in honor of his broad nose except that his only notable bit of philosophy had been to remark that a life sentence wasn't always as generous as it sounded. Had he been born in another place, another time, he might have served the Russian tsar whose elite guard was composed entirely of pug-nosed recruits—all chosen for the simple fact that they shared his own distinguishing feature.

A few days after Suluga had arrived in Yedrensk, the Kindjal had singled out one of the students for an unprovoked slap. Ivan, a Slav from Tatavnia, spun in half a pirouette and fell to his knees.

"You're lucky I didn't make a fist." The Kindjal bent closer to Ivan. "While you were in a university, I was in a prison. Let's see who learned more."

Straightening up and leaping onto his bunk, the Kindjal ordered Ivan to pull off his boots (the Kindjal's feet were never in rags).

Willowy and pale, his cheekbones exposed by his habit of buying books instead of food, Ivan wiped the blood from his mouth and complied.

"Now, press your thumbs into my feet and if I don't like the way it feels, you'll get my fist after all."

The bones in his pale hands standing out, Ivan kneaded the Kindjal's feet as if they were an exceptionally unyielding dough. The Kindjal's head rocked back on his neck and his lips curled back like a contented dog. A tooth glimmered with bronze. Since the last inmate whom the Kindjal had assigned to his feet had died less a few weeks ago, Ivan was summoned almost nightly to the Kindjal's bunk.

Ivan, who'd been studying law at Samirska University, learned to take off the Kindjal's boots without being asked, to pick lice out of the blond carpeting on his back, to fetch the Kindjal's towel at a nod, to scratch behind the Kindjal's ears if his chin dropped to his chest. Gradually, no one called him Student or Lawyer or Ivan; he was Toe-Picker.

Shelenka had been right on that first day—Suluga was too tired to do anything but avoid the guards' whips, their rifle butts, to keep the Kindjal from making an example of him. It wasn't worth the salt in a tear to torture himself with memories of the father who'd sold his land to send him to school, the mother who'd feared for him in a city of Slavs, or the friends who couldn't help him. It was best not only to be forgotten, but to also forget.

If he hadn't cast the past adrift, he would have sung out on the way to the mines one morning when he spotted two convicts who looked exactly like Chahtay and Dargo. He would have been incredulous, stricken when they passed him as though they'd never seen him before.

The story about the pair of Tatars—the Wolf and Stone Face— that came to the Kindjal went like this: they'd been involved in a brawl in the Yedrensk, and hadn't been able to keep their mouths shut when the judge sentenced them to a few days in the local jail. They earned two months in the mines.

Gaspar the Gem-Cutter, who'd been relieved of one eye by the mines and whose name had been reduced to Gem by the other convicts, shared a barrack with the new arrivals. One evening he commanded the Wolf to fetch wood for the stove. The Wolf didn't bother to answer him. When Gem informed him that the Kindjal and the Criminals ran the place, he said, "You and the Kindjal can go to hell on the same horse." Gem pulled out something like a long nail affixed to a handle, but the Wolf deftly blocked his thrust and stabbed him three or four times before Gem had a chance to attempt another. Holding a blade of skillfully worked flint, the Wolf stood over the body, which sporadically juddered like the last efforts of a minnow hooked for bait.

No one approached the Wolf after that.

"Bring the slant-eyed pile of donkey droppings," the

Kindjal whispered to Shelenka. Over the years, he and the guard had established a rapport. "He needs to learn there's a hierarchy, and if a Criminal wants a cushion for his ass, his Tatar head will do."

Shelenka, ever one for throwing another snake into the pit, had both of the Tatars transferred to the Kindjal's barrack, and the guards, who approved of the fact that a Slav had established himself as the most feared convict, that the underworld of Yedrensk reflected the legitimacy of the monarchy, placed very long odds on the Tatar to survive the next month.

After soup and bread in the mess hall, the Wolf and Stone Face were shoved through the door of the Kindjal's barrack. In spite of the emotion Suluga felt swelling under his ribs (but to which he could no longer put a name), his face didn't so much as twitch.

The Kindjal, too, acted as though the guards had dumped trash on the floor—one more chore for Toe-Picker.

Suluga, the Wolf, and Stone Face didn't exchange a word all night although the new arrivals had an argument with a pair of Slavs over where they were going to sleep.

With a look, the Kindjal settled the matter in favor of the Tatars.

The contest had begun.

* * *

In the mess hall, seated at a long table before bowls of porridge, the three Taztas clumped together like crystals.

The Wolf shook his head at Suluga. "We thought farm work was bad—there's hardly anything left of you!"

Suluga jerked his chin at him. "I knew you'd end up here."

"I'm a fool who breaks laws, you're a fool who believes in

them." The Wolf shrugged. "How else were we going to get you out?"

"You mean you came here on purpose? You *are* a fool."

"After I swore never to swing a pick again, never to bow to a shovel ... yes, I must be."

They came up with the most archaic words they knew, used as much village slang as possible, exaggerated their accents, spoke rapidly, and swallowed syllables so that only a native speaker of Tazta could follow their conversation.

"Now what will you do?"

"Pick lice from our eyebrows," snapped Stone Face.

"We were sentenced to 60 days. That's how long we have to get you out. Artem says he's going to lose three friends instead of one."

"He's right."

When they'd used their fingers and tongues to get the last of the film clinging to their bowls, Stone Face and the Wolf stood up. The Wolf slapped Suluga's bowl off the table and both of them spat on him. Suluga jumped up, toppling his chair, but a threatening look from a guard made him sit back down.

The Kindjal, at a nearby table, was convinced of his initial appraisal of the Wolf: he was a Criminal, not merely a drunken brawler, and his swift killing of the Gem-Cutter wasn't a fluke.

During the next weeks there was a kind of flirtation, a courting that the Kindjal had initiated by settling the bunk dispute. Better to have a new lieutenant than a new rival. Because the Wolf was no more interested the Kindjal's over-tures than he was in the slag carted daily out of the mines, Ice was appended to his nickname.

With the truce refused, an unspoken duel ensued. The other convicts watched as though the names of the pardoned were being called out. This was not the usual contest—

VINCENT CZYZ

although it would end in the usual way, with blood and a corpse to be buried—this one would involve the whole barrack and would have repercussions throughout the camp: the Kindjal's rule was being challenged.

* * *

Desperate to break the dreariness of the mines, prisoners would bet on anything, even a lice-infested head. A crust of bread might be put up against a handful of tobacco; whoever could pick more lice out of his hair in a counted-off minute was the winner. Correctly predicting the day on which the first flake of snow would fall might garner a pair of ragged underwear.

The deck the Kindjal was shuffling had been made from glued-together sheets of newspaper. Tucked in the corner of his mouth was a cigarette that also relied on a torn-up gazette. As the Kindjal inhaled, the ragged edge of orange crept along an article about a new ballroom added to Hugo the Fat's winter palace on one side while on the other an advertisement for a French perfume was slowly consumed.

The Ice Wolf sent up a stinking cloud from an unraveling cigar. He had reached the age at which a very distant relative of his, Mehmet the Conqueror, had smashed the last of Byzantine resistance and sacked the long-coveted city of Constantinople: 20.

The smoke made the rafters look like the ribs of a skeletal ship sunk in fog. A burning taper set in a cut-down tin can yellowed the haze. The two men sat cross-legged on the Kindjal's bunk. The Slav wore a lead cross that flattened out chest hairs as though it were a grave marker that had fallen on sunburnt grass. His snub nose seemed to scent possibilities as he played.

The Ice Wolf's skin was the color of bronze that had

tarnished without the usual green rime. His eyes, in their twin caverns, were mostly shadow.

"The better part of your father ran down your mother's leg when you were conceived." The Kindjal slapped down a card.

"It will be interesting to hear what you have to say when I mount you in the shade of the tree I planted between your mother's legs." The Ice Wolf drew a card.

"I'd pay a ducat to see you do that when I have your Tatar peas between my teeth."

"What will you pay when you hear my oranges slapping against your shaggy Slav rump?"

So it went, the night through, a game that called for a thousand points according to a complicated system that penalized a player for holding too many cards, for throwing down the wrong card, for picking up at the wrong time, for misjudging the cards he couldn't see. One of the Kindjal's lieutenants, who held a stubby pencil between his thick fingers, kept score. So did the onlookers gathered around the tin-can lamp like a circle of hyenas waiting for the leavings of larger predators. They kept silent, careful not to so much as shift their buttocks and squeak a spring until a hand was over. Then they cleared their throats, whispered the score and maybe another bet.

The rest of the barrack was as dark as the mines.

After hours of play neither convict had pulled much ahead of the other: a sweeping win would be followed by a resounding loss, a small loss by a minor triumph. There were pyrrhic victories in which the energy expended, the concentration involved, the clever moves engineered amounted to a gain of only a few points. There were foolhardy risks taken, gambits that cost heavily, straight-faced bluffs that went undetected.

The candle stuttered, and shadows on their cragged faces wavered.

By the time most of the prisoners had crawled into their

bunks, leaving only a determined handful of onlookers, drinking tea from a rusty can passed from hand to hand, the Ice Wolf was falling behind.

The Kindjal's face, with the perennial look of belligerence that his nose engendered, showed nothing. His lieutenant sneered.

The Kindjal won another hand. "Praise the Tatar whore who bore you!"

"Curse the dog and the donkey whom all Slavs can point to as their first ancestors."

The Wolf lost another hand and the game. His cards landed on the bed with a slap.

The Kindjal took the Wolf's head in his rough hands. "You're mine now." A smile spread across his face like a swift-moving shadow, and his bronzed tooth glinted in the lamplight.

"You need a new toe-picker?" The Ice Wolf snorted. "Any boy can tickle your feet." He shoved his scarred forehead against the Kindjal's. "Why don't you let me kill someone for you?"

The Kindjal let go of the Wolf's head. "Who do you have in mind?"

"You won't be grinning when you find out."

* * *

Shelenka despised everything about the dreary town, the isolation, the shabby quarters allotted to the guards, the glacial winters, the mines that bred ice and damp. But he had a weakness for gambling and to escape his debts in Samirska he'd given up his place in the army to become a guard in Yedrensk.

Even if he put every *drima* he made toward his debts, he'd gambled away his earnings for the next 10 years. There was no going back for him. There was only *ambruca*, small card games here at which he cheated and usually won, and the Tatar whore who propped him up when he was too drunk to find his way to his bed.

He hated Aleksander.

If Aleksander weren't a Slav, if he weren't as big as Shelenka himself, Shelenka would have found an excuse to kick out his teeth. Although Aleksander's dumb adherence to the camp rules was a source of irritation to the other guards, who grumbled about his softness, Aleksander himself they found likable—all the more because he was always good for a cigarette, a drink in town, a loan of a *kroshten* or two.

The most despicable thing about Aleksander was his absurd belief that he was somehow doing good. Prisoners, he said, could still be turned into good citizens. Idiot! He did his duty in Yedrensk cheerfully because he believed he was protecting society, and he was on his way to wearing the yellow-topped boots of an elite division of gendarmes.

"Let him waste his youth in this anteroom to hell!"

The last guard out of his miserable shack this morning, Shelenka held his hands to the stove one more time before putting on his gloves.

"Good Christ! What a frozen dawn!"

He straightened up like a jackknife when he heard the first shot. There was another, followed by a third and a fourth.

He yanked open the door and a gust of icy air scraped his face. It was still dark, but he could hear shouting and more shots fired. His anger turned to fear when he saw the Kindjal standing in front of him—with a *rifle* in his hands! His feet weren't shackled, and other convicts stood behind him.

The Ice Wolf pushed the Kindjal aside and stepped into the cabin with steel knife in his hand.

Shelenka didn't even have time to overcome his shock.

The knife thumped into him just below his ribcage, and he lost both his breath and his ability to draw another.

"Sorry, old friend." The Kindjal's lips peeled back in a glittery smile. "That's the way it goes sometimes."

The knife came up again swiftly, brutally, and Shelenka thudded to the floor like a slaughtered cow.

The Ice Wolf wiped the blade on Shelenka's uniform. "My debt is paid."

The Kindjal snickered. "Be a good Tatar and kill some of these guards on your way out."

When the Ice Wolf had first offered to kill Shelenka, the Kindjal had shaken his head. "He gets me what I want in here."

"But can he get you out of here?"

"Escape?"

"Why not? One fine morning upon which we all agree, the Criminals attack the guards who come in to blow their whistles. We take the keys, get our hands on a few muskets, and disappear in different directions. Most of us will be caught. A lot of us will be killed." He shrugged. "You and I will get away."

"We get the whole camp to rise up against the guards just so you can kill Shelenka?"

"With him dead and the camp in disarray, with a few guns, we'll get a few hours start on the gendarmes garrisoned in town."

The Kindjal threw back his head and roared with laughter. "Agreed!"

While the Kindjal and his lieutenants ransacked Shelenka's quarters, Suluga, Stone Face, Ivan, and the Ice Wolf headed south with two good knives, two rifles, some shot and powder.

"We'll never make it without horses," Suluga said between breaths. "They'll set the dogs on us in a few hours. We'll be outnumbered. They'll ride us down like wild pigs." Even with his tortured feet in Shelenka's stolen boots, Saluga, body depleted by six months in the mines, was the slowest.

"Forget about your mouth and move your feet."

The terrain, cut with rough trails, was no different than the wooded hills near Turuk.

When the sun rose above the treetops, they welcomed it like a brother returning from the front. But by the time the day had warmed up, they could hear the dogs baying in the distance.

"We won't make it!" Suluga moaned.

"Better a dead lion than a caged rat!" Ulash snapped.

He, Dargo, and Ivan stopped to deal with the dogs, while Suluga, who'd been slowing them down, kept running.

Ulash shot the first of the dogs to reach them at almost point-blank range (he'd been afraid he would miss).

Dargo killed the second.

They handed their rifles to Ivan. "Reload them!"

Before Ivan had readied a musket, a snarling hound was on them. Dargo and Ulash—one wielding an empty rifle, the other a knife—kept him at bay until Ivan put a lead ball into him.

They hurried up a slope and caught up with Suluga who was wheezing at the top.

"Do you hear that? Horses!"

"Let's give them a Tazta welcome!"

The first rider to appear was leading three horses with empty saddles. It was Artem.

"Where've you been? Prying some whore's legs off your waist?"

Artem shrugged. "You aren't the only convicts who came south."

There were only four horses; Ulash had not planned on Ivan.

"He rides with me," Suluga said. "He weighs almost nothing, and he knows better than any of us how to load those muskets."

"All right!"

* * *

During the first day of the chase, when the Taztas had gained a hilltop, they glimpsed the gendarmes in the distance. There were only 10 or 11 men tracking them; they'd expected twice that number. When, after the second day, they saw the gendarmes again, they counted three or four men fewer.

On the morning of the third day, Ulash brought his horse to a stop in a narrow pass. "Enough running!" He glanced over at Ivan. "Can you aim as well as load?"

Ivan nodded.

"Five men surprising seven or eight ... we have our bows with a full quiver each. They'll have three shots each: two pistols, one musket. We have to get half of them in the ambush."

They rode on, leaving no tracks breaking away from the trail until they were out of the defile. Dismounting, they walked their horses up its steep slopes and doubled back. Suluga and Artem made their way along an easterly ridge, while Dargo, Ulash, and Ivan took one on the western side.

Not an hour later they spotted the gendarmes in their yellow-topped boots, all but one.

Artem drew his bow and let go the first arrow. Then Suluga's bow twanged and feathers streaked the air with dark colors.

Two gendarmes and a horse lay in the defile before they realized where the attack was coming from. Fleeing the eastern side of the pass, they retreated north and west—where Ulash, Ivan, and Dargo opened fire on them.

Only two gendarmes and Aleksander survived.

The Taztas, leading their mounts along the ridges, regrouped at the mouth of the defile.

"They're done!" Suluga shouted. "They've gone back to Yedrensk!"

Dargo, always the most cautious card-player among them, had posted himself on a slope. He sang out a warning just as shots were fired.

Ivan's opened-mouth smile collapsed as a spray of red burst from his chest. He muttered a final prayer. One of the horses fell beside him.

Dargo let fly an arrow.

A scream went up as it skewered an arm.

The Taztas leapt for the nearest cover. Dargo ran tree to tree hoping to flank the three gendarmes who, doubling back, had circumvented the pass and had the high ground.

Realizing they couldn't afford to have Dargo behind them, the gendarmes concentrated their fire on him. Ulash moved in closer, saw an exposed face and buried an arrow in an eye.

Dargo hit the man he had wounded a second time, the arrow lodging mid-shaft in the throat. The gendarme fell clutching the shaft.

Only Aleksander was left. He fired at Dargo; tree bark exploded. Out of ammunition he threw down his gun and drew his saber.

Ulash pulled his sword out of its scabbard. "Aleksander! You treated us well at the mines, and we are men of honor. Go back to Yedrensk."

"God was on my side when I lifted up fallen prisoners, He's on my side now."

Dargo held his bow drawn, unsure of whether he should kill Aleksander or obey his *kabrek*'s wishes.

"You are one and we are four."

"There's a way to live in this world, and sometimes it means dying."

"But it's not merely a possibility," Ulash countered, "it's a certainty. Why should you throw your life away?"

"Then, as men of honor, come at me one at a time!" Without waiting for a reply, he rushed down the slope at Ulash. The smaller man was also quicker. After a brief series of strokes, he slashed open Aleksander's forearm.

"You shot a student!"

"The students tried to incite an insurrection. They're enemies of the state!"

"We wanted nothing but tax reform!" Suluga shouted.

Moving his bulk with surprising speed, Aleksander hacked at Ulash, and the brigand stumbled back. Spinning away from the next slash, Ulash countered. Sparks flecked the air as saber and scimitar rang on each other in rapid succession. Aleksander was strong, had skill with a sword, and the slope didn't favor a man who had to maneuver. Ulash had hoped to tire the guard, to disarm him or force him to surrender, but when his cheek was slashed open, his dark eyes glimmered with rage. Finding an opening, he thrust his damascened blade into Aleksander nearly to the hilt. Ulash pulled the scimitar out with a jerk and the huge Slav fell to his knees.

Wiping blood from his cheek, Ulash looked down at Aleksander.

The guard seemed startled more than anything else, as though he were meeting the king or had just learned that a wealthy uncle had willed his estate to him. Ulash watched the handsome face blanch, saw the trembling lips turn white, and resented the sword that had been given a woman's name.

"Why didn't you turn back!" Ulash shook his sword in the ashen face. "You'll take a whole day to die with that wound!"

"If you're a man of honor, you'll give me a clean death." He coughed and blood gushed out of his mouth. He fell forward on his hands. "You'll take a letter ... from my jacket pocket." He began to breathe rapidly as though he had to support the staccato heartbeat of a hummingbird. "You'll tell my father." He gurgled and choked again. "How I died. The address. On the envelope." He shook his head violently as if to dispel the pain or deny his fate.

Ulash, unable to watch anymore, leapt forward. Aleksander's head conveniently bowed, he sheared through bone. Aleksander fell face-forward in an abrupt shush of leaves and pine needles, his head at a ridiculous angle that made him look like a huge puppet.

The Taztas gathered around the fallen guard. They sang to Aleksander's spirit and would have gone on singing even had a full company of gendarmes been bearing down on them.

You will not be ashamed
  To stand before your ancestors.
  May we die as well when our time comes!
  May we meet again, honored enemy,
  In the World Behind the World,
  Where no man raises a sword to another.
  You should have been born a Tazta!

While they stood with their faces uplifted and gusts of wind scattered their words, a tear as dark as a ruby swelled at the point of Ulash's scimitar.

THE GEISHA IN THE ATTIC

DALTON MIRE

I slowly lifted the lid of the old leather steamer trunk and tugged out a black silk purse jammed in the side. When the wooden handles were pulled apart, sunbeams shining through floating dust motes danced off gleaming coins. My eager hand dove inside to retrieve a fistful and could not believe my luck—there was gold in Grandma's attic.

My grandmother passed away, and her granddaughter, that's me, was chosen to clean out the junk from under her hot tin roof. I wheezed and sneezed my way into her musty smelling third floor attic on a steamy Virginia summer day and pulled the top box off a tower of cardboard. The stack toppled over and buried me under an avalanche of grime. Sputtering, choking, and coughing, I scattered the boxes to each side and wiped dirt from my eyes with the bottom of my once white t-shirt. After shaking years of filth out of my blonde pixie cut and off my red shorts and long legs, my treasure chest was waiting.

I returned the shining riches to their dark hideaway and searched the trunk for more. I held up a gorgeous bright orange silk dressing gown emblazoned with elaborate floral designs that glistened in the attic's muted light. It was an, ah, oh, what do you call it? A kimono, that's it! Beneath it, there were other clothes, and then I spotted a stack of letters tied tight by a red silk ribbon. Using a dirty box for a seat with the purse in my lap, my fingers slowly pulled open the long-tied bow. The letters were old—no envelopes or stamps. Just folded paper with an address and postage scratched in ink turned brown from age. Many included the name of the ship that delivered them from Japan. *Japan?* Curiosity made me unfold the top one.

Dearest Catherine:

In this summer of 1862, I have finally made it to the ship that will take me to the Japans. After riding trains from Richmond to St. Joseph, Missouri, I had to endure nineteen days on the Butterfield stagecoach before we reached Los Angeles. Traveling by stage was torture for the mind and body. Every day, you are tightly packed between odiferous bodies. The ripe smell reminded me of the pigsty at home. If you open the Isinglass windows for a breath of fresh air, you are showered with dust. Stops are infrequent and the water is only for drinking. Every bump has a bounce, and every rut tosses you from side to side. After the first day, hoop skirts and starched crinolines were abandoned. There was no room for them, and the ride made them unbearable to wear. I am reduced to the status of a pauper with underpants, a chemise, and only two petticoats under my dreary black missionary garb.

I miss you terribly. My Baptist traveling companions do not believe in idle conversation and frown whenever I cough or share a thought. Please write of home. Beyond sisters, we are best friends. This is the last letter before my voyage to a new land.

Holding My Nose,
Rebecca

* * *

After that introduction, I had to read at least one more.

Dearest Catherine:
A young Lieutenant caught my eye and showered me with atten-
tion on the wave-wracked voyage to this foreign land. When our
feet touched land, romance introduced me to love that ended in
lust. Mother and Father would be shocked to learn their
daughter was one with a sailor, but in many ways, it was their
fault. Their domineering attitudes and strict Baptist upbringing
created a life without joy. They kept us home when girls in beau-
tiful gowns and handsome boys in their gray uniforms danced at
grand balls. Father insisted I become a missionary when Yankees
invaded our home. You must remember how I leapt at the
chance—anything to get away from him. I will never forgive
Father for selling Nat to the slave traders from Mississippi. His
only sin was teaching me to play the banjo. Father did it to
spite me.
Mother packed my bags, and Father exiled me without a wave
goodbye.
In the cramped quarters of the mission, my lieutenant seduced
me, or possibly, I seduced him, but my lack of experience
exposed our tryst. I forgot to lock the door and we were caught in
the frenzy of coupling. Puritan hypocrites called me a harlot and
drove me from the foreign quarter of Yokohama. Torn from my
past, I was alone and abandoned. My lover's Captain rescued
me by convincing the proprietress of a House of Geisha, a Lady
Mitsuko, to provide refuge. It was horrifying to be thrown into a
"House of Ill Repute," but there was no other choice.

Fate's Prisoner
Rebecca

Excited fingers opened the next installment of this century old gossip.

Dear Catherine:
After a night of tears, slumber was tossed aside when Lady
Mitsuko poked me with a stick and motioned for me to get up.
My new bedroom houses ten girls from eight to eighteen who
were all staring at me. Mitsuko glared and tapped her stick on
the other futons that were neatly rolled up against the wall. Not
wanting to offend, I did the same with mine. She motioned
toward the door, and I followed her on a tour of this house of
fallen women. Still shaken by the repudiation of Christian
missionaries, I followed like a whipped puppy. The second-floor
hallway revealed Geishas, still sleeping, in their own rooms that
they share with their senior attendant, or maiko. A dormitory
room at the other end held more attendants. Downstairs, we
traversed hallways with dark polished wooden floors past two
interior rooms that led to two that overlooked a beautiful garden
with a pond and trees behind the house. My tour revealed that
servants, cooks, and caretakers were hidden from sight in hovels
behind fences on each end of the garden. My introduction ended
in front of the house as we stood before double doors with round
filigreed windows on each side that have paper covering the
inside. At night, candles are placed behind these patterned
windows to attract guests with their cheerful light. Brass
figurines hold burning incense that permeates the house with a
mystic smell. Large timbers support a balcony stretching across
the second floor. Carved filigree windows welcome light during
the day and strings of brightly colored ribbed paper lanterns are
strung across the railing to draw attention to the house at night.

My New World
Rebecca

To delay my dive into the mess around me, I kept reading.

Dearest Catherine:
After listening to the preachers at the mission condemn all
geishas to hell, I dismissed Lady Mitsuko as a sinful "Lady of the
Evening," but quickly learned the words from the pulpit were
blasphemy. This demure lady is a multi-talented entertainer.
She plays the Japanese harp, guitar, and banjo and has a voice
that would shame a mockingbird. She dances with grace and
performs short plays for her patrons.
At first, I dismissed these Japanese sinners as silly gossips who
spent their days dressing like dolls and sharing trivial secrets,
but it did not take long to learn how wrong I was. Drawn to their
music after playing the church organ and strumming the banjo
at home, I admired their talent.
My language lessons on the long journey across the less-than-
united United States and the sail across the less-than-tranquil
Pacific have served me well. They let me participate in the gaiety
and zest for life in this house of women. Something I never expe-
rienced in the mission or at home. Luck has challenged me, but
has not deserted me.
My letters will continue to be sent through Anna so that you can
hide them from Father's prying eyes. Guard them well.

Respecting Others,
Rebecca

I paused and sighed. I can understand why she was upset.
A guy stole my heart during my senior year in college. He
proposed on one knee in front of a glowing tree and my parents

on Christmas morning. My dream of forever ended on spring break. He went home and sent a sterile email asking for his ring back—he had reconciled with his high school sweetheart. Graduation rescued me from the sympathy of friends, but could not end the humiliation of returning home with a broken heart. I still miss that ring.

A call echoed through the dust and dirt, "Nora, Nora, where are you?" Mom arrived in her jeans and soon-to-be filthy, bright yellow short-sleeved blouse with her red hair tied back in its customary ponytail. She stood above me and stared down, "What are you doing? You've hardly started."

I held up the letters and told her, "I've been reading these."

"What are they?"

"Letters from Japan that I found in that trunk. Did someone in our family go to Japan back in the 1860's?"

Mother thought for a moment, itched her temple with her forefinger, and pointed it at me, "Your great, great Aunt did." She nodded her head to confirm the thought. "Yes, she went there with missionaries during the *War Between the States* and did something over there that upset her parents. I'm not sure just what. Who are they from?"

"A Rebecca is writing to a Catherine."

"That makes sense. Rebecca is your great-great-aunt and she is writing to her sister, Catherine, your great-great-grand-mother. Now put them up and help me clean this place."

"Wait, there's more." I fished out a handful of glittering coins and Mom just stared. Stunned, she took one from my palm, looked at it closely, and mumbled, "Gold?"

"Yep, they were in this trunk with the letters."

"Amazing. Your dad will be able to tell us about them." Mom dropped the coin in my hand, and I slipped them into the purse, put it in the trunk and flipped down the top. An old paper label was addressed to: Miss Catherine Andrews,

Queens Creek Road, Williamsburg, Virginia. Surprised, I exclaimed, "That's his house. Gram's house, but the date says 1897."

Mother broke out of her golden trance, "For some reason, your great-great-grandmother left the plantation and built this house for her family. Look at the Japanese writing. My bet is that this trunk was sent home after Rebecca died. You should study our family history. It could make a good story."

* * *

Back in my room, the black purse and stack of letters landed next to the laptop on my desk before sweaty clothes hit the bathroom floor. The sweet breeze from the window air-conditioner cooled my body as I slipped out of the shower and mounted the bathroom scale. A long day of hauling dirty boxes down two flights of stairs melted three pounds off my 5' 8" athletic frame.

When my cheeks got chubby as a kid, my father introduced me to running. Now, I run every day, and we still hit the pavement on weekends. Running has always provided a Zen moment to clear my mind and organize my world. A clean black tee and white tennis shorts made me feel like a new woman.

I sat on my double bed and pulled on low-cut socks and running shoes. This is my inner sanctum. This room has evolved from the pink of a little girl to the subtle lime green walls of an adult. My double bed is in the middle and the door on the left of the bed leads to a bathroom with a large walk-in closet. My desk sits in front of a picture window that looks out on a forest of pines and oaks whose branches inspire a myriad of thoughts. Next to the desk, on the left, is a folding table littered with books, projects, and a printer. A recliner in the corner provides a comfortable place to edit and read. On the other side of the room, a yellow yoga mat and a set of weights wait for a chance to keep my twenty-two-year-old body flexible and strong. Two bulletin boards on that wall hold mementoes of high school and college. Tall bookcases stand as sentinels on each side of the door and hold volumes by authors who have inspired me.

Finding gold was incredible, but discovering a *geisha* in the attic was my real surprise. I am a Language Arts graduate living at home, searching for ideas. As a writer of unpublished short stories and one unwanted novel, literary agencies and publishers send rejection letters or emails that encourage me to keep writing, but add that my submission doesn't meet their current needs. I live for the day when my first acceptance letter arrives.

Devoid of inspiration after an exhausting day, I sat in my recliner and returned to Rebecca's letters.

Dearest Catherine:

Lady Mitsuko teaches song and dance each morning, and today I applauded after she finished a beautiful ballad. She appreciated my response and asked me to sing. My fingers strummed one of her instruments, and I sang a medley of spirituals from the ol' South. These women clapped to my simple tunes and were surprised by the notes I managed to extract from their strange guitar. After this debut, Mitsuko invited me to take part in her morning vocal and instrumental lessons. The tunes of Japanese music seemed discordant at first, but I have learned they have a haunting beauty.

Lady Mitsuko has become a true friend. We share tales upstairs in our living quarters when she isn't entertaining downstairs. She teaches me about the life of a geisha and, whenever possible, drains me dry with questions about the world I left behind. I have abandoned western clothes and wear the brown and gray robes of an everyday Japanese woman. Hoop skirts and corsets no longer appeal to me.

Today, I achieved my first success in the Chrysanthemum House. Mitsuko is pleased with my ability to copy her notes. Her standard is to play a tune three times without a mistake—a true challenge without printed music. Old Nat taught me to play by ear and this skill and practiced repetition let me complete one song on what I know now is a Japanese pear-shaped guitar with four strings called a Biwa. It is my favorite because it reminds me of a banjo.

Fresh from my triumph, I asked Mitsuko if I might play for her patrons. She evaluated me with a practiced eye, and her estimate of my looks was so critical I almost cried. Considered slim and attractive in our southern home, her estimation of my looks did not seem fair. She was not impressed by what she called "your enormous breasts and huge waist." My hope of joining her troupe of performers seemed to end before it began.

But my hair, my beautiful golden hair, saved me. Mitsuko felt it was a redeeming quality and told me, "Your sunny hair may distract men from your deficits. No one has that color in Japan." She traced her fingers across my lips and nose and held up my chin, "With makeup, I could make your mouth and nose appear smaller. You are taller than my patrons. You must learn to use grace to fold your long legs under you."

Then she turned to my eyes and was worried her patrons have never seen such things, but added, "The sky blue may be a delightful novelty. You have possibilities."

Your gigantic sister,
Rebecca

* * *

My great, great Aunt was blond with blue eyes, traits I may have inherited from her.

Mother called up the stairs, "Dad's home. Bring down your gold."

Downstairs, I took out a handful and his eyes widened, "Oh, my God. Let's spread them out on the coffee table in the living room." When the coins filled the table, my father said, "These are Japanese gold from the Tokugawa Period and here are some American gold pieces. Over here are British sovereigns from the early Victorian period." He pointed at the top of the table, "I think these are Spanish doubloons. Look at that date, 1788. All these coins were used for trade in Asia during the 19th century. This is more than gold. It is rare gold that is worth a fortune. How did they get in that trunk?"

"Mom thinks they belonged to Great-Great-Grandma, Catherine."

I left him to search the internet and went upstairs to sit in front of a dark, daunting screen, hoping to arrange words that could change the world, or at least, make one person think a new thought. My fingers lingered over the keys as I searched for ideas and wondered if Pearl Buck ever had moments when ideas were scarce. I've wanted to continue her tradition, but haven't had much luck.

Before surrendering to Morpheus with his dreams, the stack of letters called to me.

Dearest Sister:
Write to Robby. Soldiers are lonely and long for words from home. He is a beautiful boy. I always liked him. You are lucky to have him as a friend and lover. Funnel the letters to him through Anna. She will keep your secret from Father.
I am excited. Mitsuko has agreed to let me perform. However, she told me, "There is still a problem. Your teeth are offensive.

They are bright and white like the fangs of a wolf. You must blacken your teeth if you want to entertain."

This custom has always offended me. The Christian community called this practice the work of the devil, fit only for fallen women. After broaching my concern to Mitsuko in the garden, she simply replied, "Black teeth are considered a mark of beauty in our society. This practice is often used by powerful Samurai and members of the Imperial family. Will painting your teeth black be a problem?"

I swallowed my pride and forced a smile, "Of course not."

The next day, I sat on a small stool, a bit scared. A senior apprentice knelt on the tatami next to me and mixed a foul-smelling witch's brew to put on my teeth. She ground Sumac nuts into a fine powder, mixed in iron fillings, and poured in vinegar to make the solution bubble. Other attendants shoved their fingers in my mouth to pull back my cheeks so this woman could paint my beautiful white teeth a dreadful black.

The guck did not taste bad and once the foul-smelling bowl was removed, my nose was no longer offended. After waiting for the solution to work, a mirror appeared in front of my face. Much to the glee of my attendants, my hand covered my face, and eyes peeked out from between my fingers: ugh, ugh, ugly. My horror was not ameliorated by the cheers of my maikos, who thought I was, now, most beautiful.

I licked my teeth. They felt different, but not unpleasant. The only redeeming feature of this beauty aid was that I could not see it without a mirror. Lady Mitsuko appeared, and my lips revealed my first black-toothed smile. She clapped her hands and declared my transformation complete. Being declared beautiful by this woman is a standard I accept and value.

Open to new experiences,
Rebecca

* * *

Rebecca's description of life in Japan reminded me of Pearl's pages. Exhausted, I fell into bed, but images of a "Southern Belle" trapped in Japan haunted my dreams. I pulled my tired body up from the soft hug of my foam mattress and unfolded another letter.

My Dear Catherine:
I am devastated to learn Robert was killed at Gettysburg. That bloody war has claimed the lives of far too many fine young men. If I was there, my arms would surround you and my bosom would catch your tears as I stroked your hair. Being so far away when you need me creates a hole in my heart. I meet each ship from home, hoping for words from you. I know you are grieving but keep writing. I treasure your letters and devour every word of the newspapers you send.
Lady Mitsuko reveres her society's rituals, and I have learned to respect them. I poked fun while learning the intricacies of a tea ceremony and questioned why a hand must twist just so when the masher thing is set down after pulverizing the green tea. My behavior forced her to take me aside for a harsh lecture.
She told me, "You must respect Japanese ways or leave."
Her threat was frightening. I have no place to go.
Being graceful is impossible for me. The idea of grace in this society is to make precise, often awkward, movements seem effortless and natural. This includes sitting, kneeling, reaching— the list never ends. This concept seemed beyond my grasp until a senior apprentice, Emiko, was assigned to help. She focused on the larger movements and taught me to relax. Her sense of humor won the day, and I have improved.
One afternoon, Mitsuko and I strolled under the blooming cherry trees next to the pond in the garden behind her house.

Huge gold and orange fish splashed hoping to find a bug on a glorious sunny day with the scent of spring in the air. We sat on a stone bench under a branch burdened with pink blossoms with our feet just above the water. Fish rushed to us hoping for a handful of rice. After a silent moment, she clasped my hands, "I am honored to make you a part of my house. With your hair, you will be known as the 'Golden Geisha.' Yosuke, my benefactor, has scheduled a visit and you will perform for him. He is a good man and has tolerated apprentices in the past."

Learning to Survive,
Rebecca

* * *

Rebecca's letters were the real treasure in Grandma's attic. These echoes from the past could be my ticket into Pearl Buck's world. Research into geisha life could be combined with vignettes of family history to create a very interesting story. Her words called to me—she became my muse—my pages were no longer blank.

* * *

Little Sister:
I remember squeezing berries and smearing the remains on our lips and cheeks to make them red. Today, attendants painted my face white with pink cheeks and rekindled memories of our fun. My hair was fixed in a style called Icho Gaeshi. Mitsuko chose this style because it does not require a hairpiece. They don't have any that match my sunset gold. Thoughts of black teeth vanished when a mirror revealed what they had created. My hair, piled high on my head, was beautiful.

Oh, I forgot to tell you that we bathe each day. First, you wash off with a cloth and then you soak in warm water. My body has never smelled so sweet, and my clean hair has never shined as bright.

Next, I donned white satin undergarments, followed by a kimono of black silk crepe embroidered with crescent moons. Standing in front of the garden pool to see my reflection, I grabbed the edges of this gown and wrapped them around my figure to the sheer horror of my attendants. I had pulled the right side of the kimono over the left. This, I learned, was not proper. Only the kimono of a corpse was tied that way. I quickly pulled the left side over the right to correct this grievous error.

A silk Obi Shigaraki sash embroidered with silver chrysanthemums on a gold background was pulled tight around my waist. It was hard to breathe but the results were stunning. My little girl's dream of becoming a princess had come true.

Living a fairy-tale
Rebecca

*   *   *

The slap, slap, slap of muffled footfalls created a hypnotic rhythm that let my mind soar. Today, lost love dominated my thoughts. Why did I accept Ralph as a lover and potential spouse? He was not particularly good-looking and a bit ordinary. We met in a park as we walked to catch our breath after long runs. I guess that gave us something in common, but why him? Probably because we were both shy and naïve. That's it. Our demons made us reluctant to make bold moves and confront the world of the more accomplished. Together, our arms protected us from their derision. And . . . and then this scrawny no-account left me. *Son-of-a-bitch!*

I returned to our white colonial breathless from a run in the park and spotted an envelope with my ex's name on the return address. I snatched it off the small table near the front door and ripped it open. He has reconsidered and wants me back. *Eat your heart out, you bastard. You had your chance.* I crumpled it into a ball and hesitated, *that was a nice ring.* A ring rang out when my well-aimed toss deposited his memories into a tin wastebasket.

* * *

My Dearest Catherine:
Yesterday, Mitsuko entered the dressing room and announced,
"You will be performing for my retainer and a Prince Mito."
Emiko straightened my kimono when I stood up, and I walked
calmly down the hall with as much grace as I could muster.
Nervous didn't begin to describe my state—panic was closer to
the truth. Lady Mitsuko's reputation would be tarnished if I
failed. I entered and bowed to Yosuke and the Prince. Yosuke
was a short man with dark penetrating eyes, but the gaze of this
gorgeous prince captured my attention. His face was chiseled
into the most handsome one I have ever encountered. His stare
warmed my body.
I quickly folded my legs under me with practiced grace to
conceal my height and sat down. The prince turned to Lady
Mitsuko and asked permission to touch my golden hair. She
agreed and nodded for me to bow. He stroked my silk locks and
asked if it was real. I tugged a tuff to show it was mine.
Emiko handed me my biwa, *and after a nod from Lady Mitsuko,*
I used a bachi, *a wedge-shaped pick, to pluck each note as my*
voice trilled the beautiful words of a Japanese lullaby. Mitsuko
complimented my performance with a wink while the last note
still floated in the air—not one mistake. She has taught us to

never look directly into a patron's eyes, but the coal-black orbs of
this prince searched for my heart. He exuded a gentle power I
had never experienced.

When the prince asked for another song, I wasn't sure what to do
—I had exhausted my repertoire. Lady Mitsuko, torn between
disappointing her benefactor and embarrassing me, was not sure
how to save me. I dropped the pick and used my fingers to strum
this Japanese guitar like a banjo. Notes flew from my nimble
digits and happy tunes in English that I learned from slaves
filled the room. I was not sure if Lady Mitsuko could blush
under her make-up, but her cheeks seemed to flash a brighter
shade of pink. She and our attendants held their breath while
songs from the Old Dominion echoed through the room.

I finished with a little jig I used to dance with the Negro children and made my first mistake of the evening—a big one. My
voice was soaring, but my silk slippered feet slipped on the
tatami. My biwa went flying in the air, and I fell, but opening
night luck was with me. My guitar descended into the waiting
hands of Emiko, who caught it and bowed. Everyone thought my
toss was part of the act. Me, I landed in the prince's lap. He was
surprised but not upset. He gently kissed my cheek and kindled
a fire that burned deep in my soul. Not to be distracted by a
patron's touch, I jumped up and bowed.

Silence descended on the room. Was I to be damned or praised?
Finally, Mito and Yosuke broke into raucous applause, and an
astonished Lady Mitsuko and our attendants joined in
demanding another bow. After my performance, the talk in our
quarters was of the prince. He was beautiful and had kissed my
cheek. Lady Mitsuko entered our quarters after ushering Yosuke
and the prince from the house and announced, "Prince Mito
would like to become your retainer and has offered three times
the price I would set as fair. He told me that if his proposal does
not please you, you should set a number that will."

My first thought was, I would pay to be with him, but that is not how things are done here. This is business, not foolish love. I asked Mitsuko, "What should I do?"

She told me, "His offer is fair, but a geisha always negotiates for twice the offer. Prince Mito knows the rules and is expecting you to insist on more. You must counter with a number that includes a monthly allowance for food, clothing, and board for you and your attendants. You must insist that all payments be made in gold."

I immediately accepted, and everyone celebrated my good fortune. My dream of being alone with my prince turned to disappointment when Mitsuko explained it would take days, even weeks, to complete the contract, but the prospect of, one day, holding this man close excited every inch of my body. The final celebration of my first evening performance was held late that night upstairs in our private quarters. My companions mimicked my voice and folk songs as the sake flowed. Emiko threw my biwa in the air for me to catch and then landed in Mitsuko's lap. This bonding topped off a triumphant evening, but thoughts of home crossed my mind before I nodded off. My dreams as a young woman never imagined a life so free. I am free to entertain thanks to the gift of music taught to me by slaves. I now understand the meaning of freedom and no longer cheer for the Confederate gray. Lincoln's emancipation is a cause worth fighting for, and yes, worth dying for. Freedom is for everyone. Uncle Amos and my friends in the cabins taught me to sing and dance—the skills I needed to become a free woman. They, too, deserve to be free.

Free at last,
Rebecca

* * *

My aunt was talented, but for me, the jury was still out. She dared to perform. My past has made it easy for me to hide in the background and watch. Must an author be brave, or is that trait only reserved for your characters? My characters have never disappointed me, but I have learned that betrayal is part of the real world.

After the high school cross-country coach saw me run in a freshman gym class, he recruited me for his team. Dad encouraged me to give it a try, so I joined the team. My career ended when the coach's hugs became too familiar after we won a meet, and his hand touched my thigh after I accepted a ride home. I wanted to tell Dad, but did not want to stake my word against a popular coach. That incident still haunts me and has made me wary of men.

Inspired by Rebecca's letters, my passion for writing turned into an exhilarating experience. The Zen of tapping fingers has created a new fount of creative thoughts.

* * *

Catherine:

In your last letter, you asked about intimacy. There is no shame in sex here. A geisha entertains by exhibiting her talents, not her body. A retainer will try to establish a contract if he desires her. If she accepts, only then will they join. There are no relations with the ordinary patron. If those patrons are excited, they go to a brothel after the performance.

I was nervous when the arrangements with Prince Mito were complete. My attention has cost him a "King's Ransom." My mind cried out, what if I do not, please him? I shared my concerns with Mitsuko, and she showed me a "Pillow Book" to calm my fears. The pages shocked my Baptist soul, but my eyes could not turn from the graphic woodblock prints of geishas and men performing. Mitsuko read the Hiragana script as I perused illustrations that left nothing to the imagination. I was surprised to discover there were so many ways for a man and woman to couple, but the possibilities piqued my interest.

That night, the paper-covered screen door slid open, and Mito stood before me—his stare captivating—his rippled body enticing as he shed his robe. The world disappeared with joy and delight at each touch. Passion consumed us as we joined in a variety of ways. Our performance ended at the same curtain call—he was pleased with me and I with him.

Dearest sister, I have learned that love without marriage is still love.

> Find yourself a man,
> Rebecca

* * *

My aunt's introduction to triumphant sex made my temperature rise. Images of naked bodies made me sigh, but memories of my only lover left me feeling empty. *Is there a prince out there to ravage me?*

I opened Rebecca's last letter. The others were dated 1862 or 1863, but this one was dated April 2, 1873.

Dearest Catherine:

I am excited and overwhelmed at the prospect of seeing you. We sail first to San Francisco and then down the coast to Panama. A train will take us across the isthmus to a ship waiting in the Caribbean. Then wind-filled sails will bring me home to you and my Virginia.

> Longing to See You,

Rebecca

* * *

A good story needs a great ending, but her narrative just ended. What happened to my aunt during the lost years between letters? What happened when she set foot on Virginia's sacred soil? Who was the "we" she mentioned? I thought of writing new letters to fill the gap, but doubted my imagination could create a narrative true to her life.

My mother noticed my grim demeanor when I went into the kitchen and asked, "Why the long face?"

I filled a mug to the brim with a bitter dark brew and sat on a stool as I waited for it to cool. "I have a book without an ending. Rebecca returned home. That's all I know."

Then mom saved my project. "Catherine's diary is somewhere in the attic. I read it once as a teen. I think she mentioned her sister. Maybe that will help."

We headed upstairs and searched trunks, boxes, and drawers in old furniture, but could not find it. Puzzled by our failure, my mother thought a moment and pointed downstairs, "Your father's book collection."

Mom went to a high shelf in Dad's den and pulled down an old brown leather volume with DIARY, in faded gold letters, stamped on the front. She handed it to me, and I plopped down on dad's black leather couch and opened this weathered memoir. I was deciphering Catherine's tiny script when my mother returned and put a steaming mug on the coffee table. My caffeine-aided exploration provided an ending—not a happy one, but a dramatic one.

* * *

Thursday-June 12, 1873

I fretted at the gate with Mother and Father in the noon high sun while we waited for Rebecca to arrive in the carriage Father had sent to the train. He does not approve of public displays of affection and would not allow us to meet her at the station. I had a foreboding that Rebecca's return would be fraught with angst when she once again stepped foot under Father's roof.

Excitement filled my breast when I spotted the matched pair of speckled gray Tennessee Walkers pulling Rebecca's black carriage home, but her visit started with a shock. Rebecca's husband was Japanese—we did not know. Introduced as a Prince, he was still foreign. Father refused to shake his hand and called him an epithet I shall not repeat. Father stormed away and Mother and I chased him down the path until he mounted the steps and stood between the fluted white columns of our plantation home and shouted, "That heathen and his sinful consort will not darken my door."

Incredulous, Mother frantically stepped to the porch to calm him, but he wouldn't listen. He shoved her away and stomped into the house issuing the string of vulgarities common to his rages. Mother trailed behind hoping to alleviate his concerns, while I returned to my sister and her husband to mediate the tension. We could hear our parents argue as my father continued to be his typically inflexible self.

Mother was despondent when she returned to the porch and announced, "My dearest Rebecca, please forgive him. This residence is not a welcoming abode for you and your husband. You will find no tranquility here. You must leave."

I was horrified by the mean nature of Father's false virtue and begged Rebecca to damn only him. I assured her that his anger was not mine.

Wiping away a tear with her lace-gloved finger, Rebecca

told me, "We will spend the night at the King Arms Tavern and sup there. You and Mother are welcome to join us if you wish. Tomorrow, we travel to Washington. My husband has an appointment with President Grant."

Father insisted that mother and I stay in this evening and forgo Rebecca's invitation, but for the first time, I defied him. His epithets colored the air as I walked out. Mother, frightened to the core, did not dare accompany me. I spent a pleasant evening with Rebecca and her husband, Mito, and begged for an opportunity to catch up with my sister. I explained that I have missed her ear and needed her counsel after enduring long years under Father's roof. My plea ended when I pointed out, "Rebecca has seen the world. I have not."

Mito, a true diplomat, understood and politely agreed to stay another day. He bowed to me before I left.

Father was waiting at the door with a buggy whip in hand when I returned home, but stepped back when my stare and clenched jaw challenged him. The coward uttered oaths that burned my ears, but he did not have the stomach to raise his hand to me as he has done so many times in the past. I refused to stop and went to my room. I do not know what I would have done if he had tried to whip me, but I'm sure he would not have been pleased with the outcome. I was ready to defend my sister and, finally, stand up for myself.

Friday-June 13, 1873

On a sunny afternoon, my sister and I strolled the dusty streets of Williamsburg under frilly parasols. Rebecca wore a fashionable dress she purchased in San Francisco, and I was dressed in my Sunday best. She complained about having to return to starched crinolines and leave the comfortable Japanese dress behind. Tales of her life filled me with wonder and disbelief. She is an actress in a House of Geisha and lives a life free from mundane chores. Mito is not her husband, but her benefactor.

I looked over my shoulder to make sure no one was eavesdropping before listening carefully to learn the difference. I was both shocked and excited by her daring. Mito represents Japan as a diplomat, and Rebecca travels as his wife to conform to our society's standards. Her skill with both languages will help him navigate the challenges of Washington society. He will be the first Japanese representative to meet a President.

Rebecca noticed a boy waving to us and asked who he was and mentioned that he was good-looking. I told her that was Tom Andrews. He was a nice boy, but Father had rejected him as a suitor.

My sister ended the day by giving me a beautiful orange silk kimono adorned with silver flowers that I will always treasure.

Saturday-June 14, 1873

The black train with its bell shaped smokestack bellowed clouds of steam and was about to chug away when I hugged my sister and bowed to her husband. Rebecca shouted above the rumble, "Leave that house. You'll never be happy under his roof." She slipped a heavy black silk purse with wooden handles into my hands and boarded the train.

I waved goodbye as the black snake slithered away with a mustache of gray trailing behind. Thoughts of life clouded my mind. Father has rejected every suitor. That should be my prerogative, not his. Why have I let him steal my chance for love? I must learn from Rebecca and become my own woman.

After the train disappeared, I pulled open the wooden handles of the purse and peeked inside. A golden treasure *greeted my eyes. More than enough for a life independent of Father. My sister had granted me the gift of freedom.*

* * *

I had an ending—one I had not anticipated. This project was ready for Mom and Dad. My father knocked on my bedroom door the next evening and entered with my manuscript in hand. I turned from my computer as he sat on the end of my bed and told me, "This is a good read. It shows how much you have grown as an author. Your mom and I are proud of you, but your great-great-aunt and great-great-grandmother have taught me something. You must leave this house."

"What?" I exclaimed.

"Reading Catherine's diary made me realize it's time to kick you out of the nest. Make you live on your own. Your mother and I love having you up here in your room, but you're no longer a child. You need to become an independent woman. I had a friend appraise your gold. You are now a rich woman. Use that check and your inheritance from Gram to build a new life."

"I don't want to leave. I like it here."

"Of course, you do. It's safe. You need to explore the world. Take chances. Make mistakes. See what you have missed. Rebecca made me realize that you need to experience life to write about it. Follow the footsteps of Buck. Go to Asia and beyond. There are ideas out there waiting for you to capture."

"I . . . I don't know what to say."

"Don't say a word. Just be out of this house by the end of the month."

I stared out at the trees after he left. Their tangled branches etched a thought as the setting sun turned the sky to a golden hue.

Dad is kicking me out? Well, it can't be just him. Mom must be a part of this. This is my home for God's sake.

Days later when the shock wore off, I realized they were right. I had been hiding at home to heal a broken heart and hide from men. Bedroom walls and childhood relics do not inspire. I traded adventure for security and needed to strike out on my own. My prince is out there. My heart knows only a parent's love, and I want more.

* * *

The angry Hong Kong Riot Police attacked, swinging their batons at the heads of students marching for democracy. The crowd stampeded, and a girl tripped. I pulled her up as batons rained down on my back and shoulders. We stumbled away and escaped down an alley. My fast feet made it easy to outdistance men with clubs and shields.

Fingers flew over the keys as I tapped out a story of what I had just witnessed. After mail was stuffed under the door of my small flat, I stopped to brew green tea and stood next to the stove. Waiting for the kettle to whistle, I admired the two-karat star ruby ring set in platinum on my finger. Hong Kong has rings galore, and I have learned I don't need a man to get one. I sorted through the letters and tore open a business-sized envelope from the University Press. They want to publish my book —Rebecca's book—our book. After a quiet moment of reflection, I realized my fortunes have changed and thought, *this will be the first of many.*

A breathless Li Yuan burst through my door. High on adrenaline from the chase, his frantic words described how he had just managed to elude the police. He is a reporter for an underground newspaper, and I'll guarantee his sculpted features rival those of my great-great-aunt's Prince Mito. His arms surrounded me as our lips touched. We were tempted to compare notes on the demonstration, but we were hungry—hungry for each other. Swept up in his arms, we landed, laughing, in the soft embrace of my bed. After relentless sexual gymnastics, we collapsed in a tangle of arms and legs, gasping for air, completely spent. Safe in the arms of my lover, tears of joy streamed down my cheeks until the Chinese police blasted down my door.

STATUTE OF LIMITATIONS

GARY ZENKER

"**D**ebt?" I asked.

"Four to ten years, depending on the state," she replied.

"Taxes?"

"Federal—three years following filing of the return. Six if they determine fraud."

"Sexual misconduct?"

"Look at the news recently with Cosby and Weinstein. Apparently, none."

"Murder?"

"No limit. They can come for you at any time." She interrupted her own rambling. "So who?"

"It's just a theoretical."

She stared me directly in the eyes. "I know you. You don't know *how* to do theoretical."

I bit at the cuticle of my right thumb, then spit a small piece of skin onto the floor.

"As your attorney ..." she began.

"As my attorney, you are bound by lawyer-client privilege," I finished for her.

"*Only* if you come for my representation *afterwards*. *Not* if I know about the crime ahead of time. And certainly *not* if it's a capital offense." She cited some legal brouhaha I didn't care about. "You can't rely on spousal protection, you know." Spouses can't be forced to testify against each other. But we aren't married any more.

We had an amicable divorce five years prior, at MY instigation. That is, if you can consider being forced to give your ex seven-eighths of everything you own with the exception of a classic Gibson Guitar collection, to be amicable. I am sure that her having to win at everything is a terrible burden for her ... almost as much as it was for me. I'm not sure which she hated worse: my filing for divorce, or her not inability to clean me out entirely. But I did win my freedom. Well, if you can believe living in a one-bedroom efficiency and struggling to pay my rent each month to be a win.

It improved our relationship. We could now sit in the same room together without arguing about virtually everything. And now, once every two weeks or so, we grab cocktails and dinner, then hump like animals no matter who either of us may be dating at the time. It's strange how a divorce and a forced colonoscopy can make someone more attractive. She still makes me pay for the dinner, of course.

"What's your motivation ... money? Revenge? Lo-ove?" She emphasized that last word like one teenager goading another. I didn't respond. "Ah, it's love, then." She nodded, and her lips curled to what appeared to be a tight smile. "So let's see. She's otherwise involved. Maybe married ... probably married. You need a clean path. The husband has money. You aren't doing it for that, but it would be a nice bonus. You could use it, and she would lose it in the divorce."

This is why she is the lawyer and I am living where I am.

"So you need a plan. An alibi. And maybe a defense in case the alibi isn't enough. Of course, I'm not really having this discussion with you, so..."

There's nothing like a lawyer to help you plan out your next illegal act—they are the masters of loopholes. Suddenly, our dinner has become a business meeting, and I expect a bill much larger than the dinner check is coming my way. Lawyers don't offer anyone a *friends and family discount*, especially to ex's.

Two hours later, I have a plan better than I ever could have thought up myself, with all the angles covered. I have a plan, an alibi, and a smart lawyer in my corner.

A week later, I'm with Betty and her soon-to-be-deceased husband in an expensive hotel suite in a city hours from where they live together. A business trip for him slash romantic surprise from her slash murder opportunity for me. It's cliché, but I watch from the closet. One more sip and two more minutes, and he'll collapse to the floor. Five more minutes and his breathing will stop completely. The trick that the ex taught me wasn't to hide the cause of death, but rather point the blame in a different direction. It works in the courtroom all the time, she assured me.

As I emerge from the closet, she kisses my cheek. I flip open the top of a medicine bottle and jiggle two pills onto the floor and kick them under the dresser, to give the detectives a reward for their detailed examination of the room. He'll be discovered by housekeeping tomorrow, dead and wallet-less. Toxicology will show high levels of drugs in his system, matching the pills they found. The obvious suspect will be a mystery woman from a discreet out-of-town encounter while on business. Another cheating husband on a business trip. Not original, but entirely believable.

Before we leave, his beautiful widow will go home to play the confused spouse when the police visit to inform her of the murder. But it's a shame to waste the untainted champagne, so she and I take a moment to celebrate with clean glasses. We'll take them with us and dump them in a can at a convenience store between here and home. It's all so perfectly planned. We toast and drink.

Suddenly, I can't keep my balance. The room starts spinning, and speeds up quickly. I drop the bottle and glass, then fall to my knees. My love falls beside me. I'm paralyzed, but still conscious. My ex exits from the bathroom and appears over me, smiling. She was hiding here before me? Too many damn hiding places in this luxury suite. My head spins.

Our perfect plan.

Her perfect plan.

I poison the hubby, and then his wife (my new woman) and I "accidentally" poison each other. All wrapped neatly in a bow for the police.

"I hate when there's anything still left on the table," she says from above. I can't be sure if she's referring to the champagne or my guitar collection. As my executer, I'm sure she'll figure a way to get the guitars after all.

Statutes of limitations. I forgot the most important one. A woman scorned. Apparently, there's no time limit on that one, either.

PEOPLE ON THE ROADS AND IN THE GARDENS

MYKYTA RYZHYKH

People on the roads and in the gardens.

Sunny bunnies' eyes, hands, sounds of whispers of people, plants, wind. Sheaves. State institutions. And in every way so rich. Fresh buns, honey, clean water, hot morning coffee, cold morning dew, evening clean air, morning bells of hemingways, evening prayers and excitement—suddenly someone will hear, suddenly someone is still in heaven.

The abundance of grass, the variety of fire, the rain, the light, the mud of the roads, the nonsense of the neighbors, the flights of birds, the scent of flowers, the black circles under the eyes, and the minibusses are not adapted to happiness.

"I don't know what to do now ..." the woman despaired.

- Everything will change tomorrow! - her husband's hope.

- When I grow up, I will not become an adult?— whether it is hope or despair of the child.

Hotel room for one person.

The address of the former. Lover's phone. Despair. Tears of silence.

Little boy with a toy in his hand and hope in his heart.

Kindergarten with painted wallpaper. Kindergarten is a garden. Eyes, like beetles, and want to fly, like Exupery. The mother finally comes to the nursery after a long working day and takes the child home. The guard nods disapprovingly. The mother pretends not to notice. The country pretends not to notice. The guard finally falls asleep quietly on the post. The robbers finally wake up calmly and take up their criminal post.

Taxi again ... Apology of good and mythology of evil. Three dots. Question mark. Two for punctuation. Four for content. Three points for the failing, unsatisfactory essay. The teacher puts his hand over the journal with grades and for a moment ...

A woman sings an aria of a virgin at the opera house, as if she were in fact a virgin. And the night club, which is not so far from here, is about to close due to someone's vandalism and— law enforcement officers, and above them—someone else and— someone else, according to the hierarchy.

A cup of tears, drunk with a trembling grandfather's eye.

Firecrackers under the window.

The final stop—the cottage.

Curves. Hands, their intersection. Plexus of bodies.

Animal bodies. Kitten, bunny, piglet, puppy, duckling, baby. Well, just grace! And still— forcemeat in the city market.

Umbrella instead of blue sky, grayness instead of self.

Abyuz underfoot, comet tails, space rockets.

Movies after ten in the evening, when the younger sister finally went to bed. Sometimes she's really mad.

The afterlife of my grandmother's village.

Chocolate Santa Claus, who remained in the refrigerator through the New Year holidays and miraculously survived.

The face of untruth. The face of the grass.

Walt Whitman, Charlie Chaplain, Uncle Misha from a kiosk on the next street.

Bookshelf of the spirit.

Perfume associations.

A birthday present, and a huge cake (and cousin's complaints about low wages).

Burning. Giants. Giant mountains. Giant people. Mountain people. And somewhere nearby—stone ceilings of misunderstandings, Easter eggs of complaints, easels of cries, dwarfs of humiliation—as soon as it is tolerated.

"New songs are always reminiscent of..." Key: "Delete message."

Stars above your head, a dream of space, grass, roadsides, a smile on your face—and we are on the way to a fairy tale, but it's time to grow up.

In short, it is impossible to convey this feeling of a home that no longer exists.

THE FISHERMAN

KIM RANSLEY

A long time ago, a great storm barreled across the Pacific, stirring sky and sea into a violent rage and bringing ruin to anything it found in its path. It pummeled many islands, wrenching limbs from trees and drowning lowlands in hurtling floodwaters. Some of the wreckage made its way out to sea and would wash up on beaches the next day alongside hefty mounds of seaweed that had been brought in by the turgid water. There was all manner of floating debris—branches, giant shells, palm fronds, cuttlefish—and among the vast collection of things that had been wrested from their place in the world and deposited on the sand was an old, weather-worn fisherman, who lay in the shallows, spurting seawater and desperately clutching a small splintered plank.

After the fisherman had expelled the ocean from his body, he lay still for a time, his mind rolling in and out of lucidity. He could not remember how he had gotten onto the beach, but he remembered the moment when the clouds had appeared out of nowhere, and the realization that his threadbare sails would not see him clear of the storm. He also remembered the deafening sound as the ocean had heaved its contents upward, and the sudden eerie darkness towered over his boat, hiding him momentarily in an ill-fated cave. The rest, he supposed, was as it seemed.

Eventually, he willed himself up off the sand so he could go in search of water. He found a stick to support his weary body and ambled inland, resting often, and reminding himself to pay attention to his surroundings. He saw that the island contained many useful things—papaya hanging from trees, jagged-edged rocks that could be used for cutting, and broad-leafed trees that would do for shelter at a pinch. Soon enough, he came across a little stream and guzzled the trickling water through his blistered lips. A small crab scuttled along the riverbank, and he picked it up, thinking it would do for his lunch.

Over the next few weeks, he spent his time exploring the island, and building tools and comforts from the natural resources he had available. He found a shallow cave, and furnished it with logs and soft leaves so that he would have somewhere to sleep, and somewhere to sit as he whittled and carved. Because he lived in an age where day-to-day things were still done by hand, he managed to make a fire with much less trouble than it would have taken you or me, and crafted an ax out of rock that he could use to cut lumber. Now that he had an ax, he had means to make a spear, and then, with a bit more effort, a small, but functional raft. These he could use to catch fish in the waters around the island. With further improvement, the raft might manage bigger seas, and so be able to carry him to other nearby islands. With a little more still, it could be made suitable for the open ocean, and might one day carry him back to the place from whence he had come.

Perhaps through boredom, or perhaps through some innate need to tell his tale, he spent the last few hours of each day etching pictures on the wall of his cave with a sharpened rock. He drew the sea, wild and black, for it was always on his mind, and filled that sea with creatures that cavorted in its depths. At first, the creatures were the many types of fish he had encountered in his years working the seas. But as the days passed, and his hands flowed more freely across the rock, he began to adorn the figures he drew with strange appendages, and his etchings grew wilder and more savage. Sometimes, he drew serpents that thrashed violently against the waves, or hideous sea-monsters with bulbous eyes and oversized teeth. At other times, he drew mysterious dark forms that lurked in trenches on the sea floor, coveting dead things. The more he drew, the more violent the images became until eventually the cave was transformed into a macabre undersea battleground, with each hideous creation frozen in a different heinous act.

Every evening, the fisherman would fall asleep watching the strange creatures be taken by darkness, and every night he would dream strange dreams. In these dreams he would play out the battles he had drawn, watching as the victors doled out their savage deathblows and the losers sank listlessly through the cold black depths. Sometimes, his dreams would fill him with terror and he would wake suddenly, heart pounding, and drenched in sweat. But more often, he found himself oddly captivated by his gruesome undersea world, and felt the same morbid exhilaration that the old nobles must have felt watching gladiators plunge their swords into the soft flesh of their conquests.

The fisherman's fascination with his creatures crept into his waking hours, where he began to hear the hiss of serpents under the dull roar of the waves and see the shadows of undersea monsters flicker on the surface of the water. Every time one of his strange creatures crept across his mind he felt more familiar with its peculiar quirks, and better acquainted with its barbarous ways. And the more he knew each of them, the more obsessed he became, and the more he yearned to be part of their murderous world.

One day, when he was out on his raft trying to spear marlin from the shallows, he noticed a tiny dot on the horizon that he could not recall having seen before. He thought at first it might be one of his creatures, but its movements were too subtle, and it didn't match any of their boisterous styles. He thought then that perhaps it was the carcass of a great beast that had floated up to the surface—or perhaps an artifact that a creature had dredged from the bottom of the sea to give him as a gift.

Intrigued, he dug his oar into the sea and paddled for what felt like hours, stopping now and then to peer towards the rogue object. Eventually, it became clear that the object was neither gift nor carcass, but rather a small boat that had been propelled there by a man much like himself. Many thoughts raced through his mind. He had the wherewithal to know a boat might mean rescue, and to know this was something he had once coveted. But as he sat on his raft looking out at the boat, he struggled to remember anything of the life to which he had once hoped to return. He could bring to mind snippets—the house he had lived in, the jetty where he unloaded his haul each night, the portly old woman who sold him his bait—but the people and things he remembered didn't feel connected to him in any way. He felt neither love nor grief for these remnants of his past life, but only a vague familiarity, as if they existed purely as an abstract collection of things he could have been looking at in a museum.

He tried to settle himself, thinking that perhaps his reticence was just a fear of change, and that with time he would slot back into the comforts of his old life. But his reasoning felt forced and hollow, and the more he looked at the boat, the more he felt it to be an alien scourge on a pure and cherished territory. He looked down at the sea, angry now, and tried to calm himself with its steady rhythm. As he did this, he noticed a shadow slide across the surface of the water, and began to hear a hiss building against the sound of the waves. He let his mind settle on these familiar sights and sounds, and immediately his body began to pulse with the fear and exhilaration that came to him whenever he dreamed of his creatures. As the pulse thrummed through his body, he felt it cleanse his mind of wayward notions, and all of the tension that had built since he had first seen the boat melted away.

In a moment of perfect clarity he grabbed his spear and used its sharpened tip to etch a long set of gills into either side of his neck. Then, with one decisive movement, he thrust his body off the raft and plunged into the sea.

RICOCHET

MARK WILLIAMS

"Ricochet" first appeared in *Scarlet Leaf Review*.

PHWACKK

Weaving through Shawnee National Forest, then hugging the Ohio River's meandering banks a hundred miles before circumventing horse farms and tobacco barns southeast through Kentucky, the road from southern Illinois to Bardstown in 1970 had been as circuitous as Harlan Dillbeck's subsequent journey: from teenage, five-string banjo prodigy, to three-time Master Bourbon Taster Champion of the Kentucky Bourbon Trail. If seventeen-year-old Harlan had waited a few more years to begin his drive, Interstate 64 would have been completed. That road would have been far straighter. As for his life, who knows?

Tonight, sixty-three-year-old Harlan—failed *four*-time Master Bourbon Taster Champion, as of moments ago—is in the Louis Philippe room at Bardstown's Talbott Inn waving his Glock in the air. "Rigged, is what it was!" he shouts.

Is Harlan aware that Louis Philippe I, exiled King of France, stayed at Talbott Inn in 1797 while traveling to Nashville? Does Harlan know that King Louis, or one of his attendants, painted the mural of a French garden that the gun is aimed at now? Does Harlan realize that Jesse James, after spending a debaucherous evening downstairs in Talbott Tavern —site of tonight's Master Taster Taste-Off—plugged the French birds and butterflies with shots from his six-shooter? Yes, yes, yes. And like Jesse, Harlan takes aim at the mural, though standing to the side for fear the bullets might ricochet off the protective Plexiglas at him. But in the instant before Harlan fires, tonight's Taste-Off judge, the Reverend Sam Boone, enters the room.

PHWACKK-PHWACKK-PHWACKK-PHWACKK

From the souls of his loafers to the top of his head, Sam is little more than five feet tall—each shot zinging off the Plexiglass above his white comb-over.

"Goddamn, Harlan!" shouts the Reverend Sam as he drops to the floor.

PHWACKK

"Didn't see you coming, Sam," says Harlan.

"How about that last shot, you fool?"

"Fool, you say," says Harlan, waving the Glock's nose in Sam's direction as footfalls strike the stairway leading to the upstairs hall. "Not fool enough to know I've been cheated."

"You've been hit," says Sam, raising his arm from the floor and pointing at Harlan's feet, where blood is puddling on the hardwood. "Serves your ass right."

As it so happened, two of the ricocheted bullets had entered the plaster above Sam. A third had bounced off that wall and entered another. And two bounced off the third wall as well, completing their trip around the room, one plinking off the Plexiglas, another grazing Harlan's right buttock, from which a trickle of blood ran off his shoe. Harlan's ass had been served.

"I'll be damned," says Harlan, exploring his bloodied right cheek through the hole in his trousers before six Taste-Off contestants bound into the room and subdue him. Three contestants to each of Harlan's arms. "Easy boys, I was just letting off some steam," he says, just before Reba Fenway, master taster at Heaven Knows Distillery, runs into the room— her long black hair in pursuit.

Legs as long as a thoroughbred's. Eyes as green as blue grass. Two years ago, Reba would have feared for Harlan's safety. "You all right, sweetie?" asks Reba, rushing to Sam, whose comb-over has flopped over in the fracas.

When Harlan was seeing Reba, their fifteen-year age difference never struck him as unusual. But *Sam* and Reba? Good God.

"The Lord laughs at the wicked, for he knows their day is coming," says Sam, standing with Reba's help and pointing at Harlan. "I'd say it's come for you today."

"Not now, Sam," says Reba. "You okay, Harlan?"

"Been better. This isn't over, Sam," says Harlan: butt-shot, blood-stained, angry.

Dolly Time
1967

"There must be something fishy going on."

From the kitchen, where fourteen-year-old Harlan was helping his mother with the dishes, the soprano voice sounded like nothing he had heard before. "Get a load of that!" Harlan's dad shouted from the living room couch, where he was watching *The Porter Wagoner Show* on the family's 21-inch, Zenith color console. Across the room, Harlan's little brother, Duncan, was lying on the carpet shooting marbles at a row of plastic green soldiers, standing in dense green shag.

"*I guess some largemouth bass left that lipstick on your shirt.*"

"You're old enough to be her father, Franklin," said Harlan's mother, June, stepping from the kitchen for a look. "Oh, my. She's about to bust out of that dress. I liked Norma Jean's voice better."

"Bust is right. Who cares about her voice?"

"Now, Franklin," said June.

"*I think there's something fishy going on.*"

Curious, Harlan stepped into the living room behind his mom, a dripping washcloth in his hand. "Whoa," said Harlan, eyeing Norma Jean's replacement. Harlan thought this girl looked as good as she sounded.

"Let's all give Miss Dolly here a hand," Porter said as the studio audience broke into applause. Were it not for the washcloth, Harlan would have clapped too.

"Got him!" said Duncan as a marble rolled a soldier to the loom.

Little did Harlan know, the seed of his life had been sewn. After that night, Harlan and his dad never missed *The Porter Wagoner Show*. "Dolly time!" they'd call to one another. And though his interest in Dolly did not wane, Harlan also enjoyed listening to Porter's band, The Wagonmasters, and specifically to Buck Trent the banjo player. While listening to Buck, Harlan's right thumb and first two fingers would pick against his shirtfront as his left hand fretted up and down an imaginary banjo. It was as if, before this life, he had been a picker in another. But another seed had also been sewn.

Almost fifty years later, Harlan will call his brother,

Duncan, from the Nelson County jail, asking him to drive from Illinois to Bardstown and pay five thousand dollars in bail. "For shooting my ass and threatening another," Harlan will explain. "A preacher, so-called."

In the course of the conversation, Duncan will inform Harlan that, as boys, they had consumed life-altering amounts of perchloroethylene from their well water. For Duncan will have recently discovered that their childhood home had been built atop a dry-cleaning dumpsite. "We drank that stuff for years, Harlan. The doc says that's why I hear things—you know, my voices. Could be why you get so angry."

"That and about a million other reasons. You still hear the Irish kid, Dunc? Why didn't you tell me this sooner?"

"Yeah, I still hear Kevin. And others. But I just found out about the water a few months ago. I would have told you sooner, but there's nothing we can do about it. I thought knowing this might make you even more pissed off. Besides, everybody's got to live with something or other."

"Percho what?"

"Perchloroethylene. PERC, they call it. For me, it took forty years to kick in. For you, I'm guessing sooner."

"Who knows? Hey, Dunc, they want me back in my cell. Coming, Dharma."

"Dharma?" says Duncan.

"Deputy Dharma. See you tomorrow, Dunc."

"You'll see Darlene too. She won't let me drive anymore. She's afraid Kevin might tell me to go off a bridge or something. Slow as Darlene drives, probably be more like tomorrow night before we get there."

"Take I-64 through Louisville."

But that December, 1967, after badgering his dad for a banjo the past three months, Harlan's dad relented, driving to Evansville, Indiana, where Harlan found a Kay five-string for fifty dollars—his dad's fifty dollars—before picking up a copy of *Banjo Made Easy* by Buck Trent himself.

"Merry Christmas, Son," said Franklin.

The Final Dram

Earlier tonight, seated at the Talbott Tavern bar with nine other Taste-Off contestants, Harlan suspected there was something fishy going on when he caught more than a hint of vanilla in the final round.

Harlan thought that he'd done well, though the third round had given him some trouble. Swishing that dram between his cheeks, he couldn't decide whether it had aged five years or six. "Six," he'd guessed, after sensing a bit more smoke from the barrel and spitting the bourbon into a Talbott Tavern glass.

The contestants, master tasters all, had now sampled nine drams from his or her distillery and guessed the number of years the tastes had aged in charred, white oak barrels. Each dram, a full three scruples, had been poured by the Reverend Sam Boone, pastor of Sudden Glory Fellowship and director of Forever Yours Funeral Chapel in nearby Shepherdsville. With Sam standing barely taller than the bar, it was hard for Harlan to imagine Sam Boone's blood coursing with even a scruple of his distant relative Daniel's courage.

"You have one more minute to guess," Sam said to Harlan, leading off round ten. Sitting next to Reba Fenway, at first Harlan thought her perfume was throwing him off. Euphoria, Harlan recalled from the two years they had dated. But no, it was something more than that.

Harlan had worked at Rowan Brothers since he was seventeen, working his way up to master taster. At sixty percent corn,

Rowan Brothers tended toward the sweet side. But this . . . you could use it on a pancake, Harlan thought before spitting into the glass, now ten drams full of a Rowan Brothers blend.

"That's wheated bourbon. Didn't come from any of *our* barrels," said Harlan.

"Thirty seconds to name a year," said Sam.

"You've made a mistake. Or someone has. I'm telling you, that wasn't Rowan Brothers."

"Twenty."

"Come on. What's this all about?"

"Ten," said Sam, smiling at Reba.

"Alright, *ten*. Ten goddamn years!"

Minutes later, Sam announced, "From Rowan Brothers, with nine correct tastes, this year's runner-up is Harlan Dillbeck. And our Master Bourbon Taster champion, from Heaven Knows Distillery, Reba Fenway! A perfect ten. Congratulations, Reba. Harlan, *wait*."

But by the time Sam had finished his announcement, Harlan was off his barstool, pulling his Glock from its holster and heading for the Talbott Inn stairs. Stairs that Jesse James himself once trod.

Maryann by the Hand, Martin by the Neck
1968 — 1969

By summer, Harlan was picking "You are My Sunshine." By fall, he'd mastered "Will the Circle be Unbroken." Soon after that, "I'll Fly Away," which he was ready to do. If Harlan had had his way, he would have turned sixteen, dropped out of school, bought a car, and headed for Nashville.

Harlan's break came while playing "Blue Moon of

Kentucky" at his high school's spring talent show. Jerry Lawson, lead guitarist for The Illinois Ramblers, was there that night to accompany his daughter Maryann on his Martin twelve-string. Maryann had just knocked "Crazy" out of the Shawnee High gym when Harlan took the stage. Six bars in, he was surprised to hear a twelve-string rhythm to his five-string melody. Looking behind him, there stood Maryann and her dad. *"Blue moon of Kentucky, keep on shining,"* crooned Maryann, soon to be announced, along with Harlan, that night's co-winner. *"Shine on the one that's gone and left me blue."*

That summer, 1969, Harlan and Maryann traveled throughout southern Illinois, southern Indiana, and western Kentucky with The Ramblers, playing county fairs, church socials, and VFW's. Onstage, Jerry introduced Harlan by saying, "I could tell a natural when I heard one, folks. Before I knew it, I grabbed my Maryann by the hand, my Martin by the neck, and took the stage with—Harlan Dillbeck, everybody!" Then Harlan would play a few riffs of "Clinch Mountain Back-step," his favorite.

Those were heady days for Harlan. Taking up the lead from Jerry on "Cripple Creek" or "The Ballad of Jed Clam-pett," Harlan noticed teenage girls drifting toward the stage, clapping and dancing as he picked. Out of the corner of his eye, he could tell that Maryann, onstage to his right, noticed too.

For the first time, he saw Carbondale, Vincennes, Paducah. For the first time he saw real money. At thirty dollars a show, by August, sixteen-year-old Harlan had earned enough to buy a 1960 Plymouth Belvedere with one hundred forty thousand miles and two white-walls. It was in this car that Harlan saw much more.

Harlan had always admired Maryann. She'd played Laurey in the school musical, *Oklahoma!* With legs as high as an elephant's eye, Maryann high-jumped on the boys' track team. She jumped as high as she was tall. District champion.

One night that August, The Ramblers played the Saint Ambrose Bierstube in Jasper, Indiana. They had finished their final set, and while Jerry and the band imbibed beer inside a tent, Harlan and Maryann imbibed each other inside The Ramblers' van. They made love a second time inside an empty goat pen at the Vanderburgh County Fair. The remaining times, in the Belvedere's back seat, became a blur in Harlan's mind. He guessed he'd wait awhile to go to Nashville.

In October, with Harlan cheering her on, Maryann ran a consistent fourth *man* on the boys' cross-country team. By November, five pounds heavier, she was running seventh. There would be no high-jumping for Maryann next spring.

Deputy Dharma

Harlan and Maryann's son, Lawson, had been thirty-two when Harlan last saw him—fourteen years ago at Harlan's father's funeral. Franklin had had a heart attack while watching The Rock defeat Hulk Hogan on Pay-Per-View.

As Deputy Dharma escorts Harlan to the lobby, at first Harlan thinks his sister-in-law, Darlene, is standing next to an overweight guard and a prisoner. Duncan, wearing khaki slacks, has gained weight. Lawson has that look.

"Hey, Lawson. Hello, Darlene. Put on a little weight there, Dunc," says Harlan before awkwardly hugging all three.

"It's the psycho drugs they've got me on," says Duncan. "They make me hungry. I'm up fifty pounds. Why are you limping?"

Pointing to the hole in his pants, Harlan says, "I told you, I shot myself in the ass."

"Oh, yeah. Well, good to see you."

"Good to see you, Dunc. Pretty as ever, Darlene."

"Right. They let you drink in there, Harlan?" asks Darlene, blowing salt-and-pepper bangs from her eyes.

"Sober as a judge. Didn't expect to see you, Lawson. How's your mother?"

"Fine, I guess."

"The boy could use some help," says Duncan—the *boy* only nine years younger than he. "What kind of help?"

"Could you take this somewhere else, Harlan?" asks Deputy Dharma, looking up from her desk, her skin several shades darker than her khaki uniform.

In the past eighteen years, Deputy Dharma had booked Harlan into jail five times. But with only the faintest of laugh lines beside her large brown eyes, her age was hard to tell. "Shift change," says Dharma. "We try to clear the lobby. You'll be getting notice of your court date in the next few days."

"Thanks," says Harlan, "I know the drill. Dharma, this is my sister-in-law, Darlene, my brother, Duncan, and Lawson, my son. How about some dinner, everybody? On me. There's a diner not far from here. You, too, Dharma. We'll wait."

"Maybe next time you're here, Harlan," says Dharma, smiling as she stands. "Nice to meet you all."

Harlan had heard that Dharma teaches Jazzercise week nights at the high school. Looking at her now, as she walks ahead to open the door, he believes it. "Next time—good one. I'll take you up on that."

My Old Kentucky Motor-In Inn

1970

In March, Harlan was called into his music teacher's homeroom. Facing Mrs. Kleinschmidt at her desk, he took a seat on the piano bench and eased back against the keyboard. "I think this might be an opportunity for you, Harlan," Mrs. Kleinschmidt said, opening a colorful brochure. "Have you ever heard of Stephen Foster?"

"I think he lives in Kentucky."

"No, but I can see why you might think so. He died a long time ago. They put on a play about him every summer at the amphitheater in Bardstown. With the way you play that banjo..."

Mrs. Kleinschmidt went on to say that she thought it might be a good way for Harlan to earn money the summer before his senior year. "You'll need it," she said. "What's your baby's name?"

Everyone knew about Harlan, Maryann, and their baby. And word had gotten around that Jerry Lawson had no intention of letting Harlan play with The Ramblers. Mrs. Kleinschmidt was right. Harlan could use the money. Maryann kept telling him that her dad would come around, but in the meantime, Harlan couldn't even come to Maryann's house to see his son. "Lawson," answered Harlan.

"I made a call to Bardstown," said Mrs. Kleinschmidt. "The auditions are in two weeks. They said that you should be prepared to play the three songs I've written down on this brochure. They'll ask you to play two songs in the key that's written down beside each song."

"Thanks, Mrs. K," said Harlan, leaning forward for the brochure. "Why not?" he asked, striking a discord on the piano keys as he leaned back.

After learning "Ring, Ring the Banjo" in F, "Oh! Susanna" in D, and "Camptown Races" in G, after telling Maryann he would see her in a few days, and giving Lawson's foot a squeeze (at Harlan's house), Harlan jumped into his Belvedere, weaved through Shawnee Forest, hugged the Ohio River, and wound around Kentucky horse farms and tobacco barns on his way to Bardstown. With his banjo on his knee.

Slipping ten of thirty dollars from his banjo case, Harlan paid for a room at My Old Kentucky Motor-In Inn, across Stephen Foster Avenue from My Old Kentucky Home. "The place that's in the song?" Harlan asked the desk clerk.

"That's the one."

The auditions were to be held at Bardstown High the following day. After a cheeseburger, fries, and a vanilla shake at a nearby diner, Harlan returned to his room and ran through the three songs again. He was fidgeting with the rabbit ears on a black and white TV when he heard a banjo playing "Camptown Races" in a nearby room.

Was Harlan impressed by what he heard? Did he think that this rendition compared to his own? Did he fear for tomorrow? Yes, possibly, no. For why would anyone auditioning tomorrow, no matter their skill, be playing "Camptown Races" in D? After checking the brochure one last time (*Camptown Races: G*), Harlan turned off *The Wild Wild West* and fell asleep, never dreaming years would pass before he'd see Maryann, Lawson, or home.

Kevin's Plean

"Ate here the first night I came to Bardstown," says Harlan, after arriving at the diner from the jail. "April, 1970. Seventeen years old."

Sitting in the booth beside Darlene, across the table from Harlan and Lawson, Duncan asks, "Was it called Camptown Diner then?"

"Same name. Same booth," says Harlan, squirming on the well-worn red vinyl. "The doc said my cheek could be sore for months."

"How'd you shoot yourself again?" Duncan asks.

"Again? Pass the ketchup, Aunt Darlene," says Lawson.

"No, just the once. And it's a long story," Harlan says. "Ketchup on a hot brown?"

"Don't worry, he won't," says Duncan.

"What do you mean, he won't?"

"No, I was telling Kevin not to worry. You won't be telling any long stories, will you, Harlan? Kevin hates long stories."

"No, guess I won't," says Harlan, frowning at Darlene.

"His doctor says it's best for him to *engage* his voices," says Darlene. "I'm not so sure."

"Anyway, what kind of help do you need, Lawson?" asks Harlan.

Twenty minutes later—after listening to Lawson explain how he might have helped his friend Timmy steal what some people call drugs from Duke, a bad dude who might have killed them if Timmy hadn't cut off Duke's little finger, and how Duke, never mind his drug raps, called the cops and fingered Lawson and Timmy, but the cops said that since Lawson had been in no trouble compared to Timmy, he could skate with one hundred hours community service if he rolled on Timmy, which, since the whole idea had been Timmy's, Lawson did, but after working off his CS hours cleaning kennels at the pound, he heard that Timmy was so pissed ("sorry, Aunt

Darlene"), *mad* at him for rolling, Timmy put out a thousand dollar contract on him—Harlan sides with Kevin. He hates long stories too.

"Some friend," says Harlan.

"We thought he should skip town," says Duncan. "And here we are. This is some serious coffee."

"What's your mother say, Lawson?" asks Harlan.

"It was her idea for me to come here. Mom says if anyone would know what to do, what with all the trouble you've been in—"

"Not now, Lawson," says Darlene.

"No, your mother's right. I've had my share of run-ins," says Harlan. "Now I almost killed a mortician. The water made me do it, right Dunc? You all about finished? It's almost nine o'clock. They'll be closing soon."

With the moon over Kentucky barely shining through the clouds, they get into Duncan and Darlene's Dodge Ram—Darlene driving, Duncan beside her, Harlan and Lawson in the back seat—and head for Harlan's house near the high school.

"I heard what he said. I'll ask him," Duncan says to—Kevin? "Thought you said the guy you shot at was a preacher, Harlan."

"Claims to be. Has his own church and funeral parlor. Gets them coming and going."

"What's with you and him?" asks Darlene. "Turn here?"

"Next light. Sam and me, we go way back. Another long story. Don't worry, Kevin," says Harlan, staring at the back of Duncan's head.

"Maybe don't get him started. It's getting late. He has trouble sleeping as it is," says Darlene, stopping at the light.

"A church *and* funeral home?" asks Duncan.

"Bingo," says Harlan.

"Way *bleedin'* back, you say?"

"Bleedin'?"

"Sometimes he talks like Kevin," says Darlene. "County Sligo."

Unfastening his seat belt, Duncan turns toward the back seat. Smiling in the red glow of the streetlight, he says, "We might just have us a *plean.*"

"Plean?" asks Lawson.

"Irish for plan," explains Duncan as his smile turns green.

Driving through the intersection, Darlene says, "Oh, no," as though she's been down this road with Duncan and Kevin before.

"You missed the turn," says Harlan.

Doo-dah in D

1970

After a breakfast of eggs and grits at Camptown Diner, Harlan drove to Bardstown High. Eager for his audition to begin, he had to sit in the auditorium for two hours as, one-by-one, college-age girls sang, "Why No One to Love?," "Wilt Thou Be Gone, Love?," and "If Only You Had a Mustache"—each girl performing two requested songs. By the time the girls finished, Harlan thought he could have grown a mustache. But then it was the boys' turn to sing, "Open Thy Lattice, Love," "Jeannie With the Light Brown Hair," and "Beautiful Dreamer," unendingly, it seemed. Though several girls had caught Harlan's eye, his ears had had enough.

"We'll break an hour for lunch," announced a large man in baggy madras shorts and leather sandals. "Then we'll hear the banjos."

With only three dollars in his wallet and twenty hidden in

his banjo case—figuring two for supper, ten for that night's room, a buck-fifty for breakfast, and eight for gas money home —Harlan found a corner market, where he bought an apple and a Snickers bar for lunch.

Back at the school, he was bending down to the water fountain outside the auditorium when someone said, "You pick a mean banjo, *brotha*."

Lifting from the fountain, Harlan turned and, across the hall, saw a painting of a grim old man with a coonskin cap on his head, a rifle on his shoulder, and a hound by his side. Only then did Harlan realize he was looking over the top of someone's blond buzz-cut.

"That's my great-great granduncle Daniel. I'm Sam Boone," said the little guy, extending his right hand toward Harlan while holding a Gibson banjo in his left. A Mastertone, Harlan noticed. "What you got there?" Sam asked, nodding at Harlan's case.

"A Kay," said Harlan, shaking the smallest hand he guessed he'd ever shook. About the size of baby Lawson's foot. Couldn't reach three frets, Harlan thought. "Name's Harlan Dillbeck. Where'd you hear me play?"

"In your room last night. Never would have guessed that was nothing but a Kay. I'm two doors down from you."

This was who he'd heard playing? Harlan had heard that Earl Scruggs has small hands, but Sam Boone's hands are no bigger than a cat's paws. "Where you from, Sam?"

"Paris," Sam said. "Kentucky. Good luck, Ferlin."

"It's Harlan. Good luck yourself."

Ten minutes later, baggy shorts led the six banjo hopefuls backstage. Taking their seats in a row of folding chairs, four of the boys looked to be in their early twenties. As for Sam, it was as if a teenage voice was coming from a ten-year-old's body.

"How long you been playing?" Sam asked, sitting beside Harlan.

"Couple years."

"Couple years? When I started, my banjo was bigger than me."

"Still is, looks like," said Harlan, eyeing the Mastertone standing in Sam's lap, its tuning pegs two feet higher than Sam's shit-eating grin. The little guy was getting on Harlan's nerves.

"Okay, boys, we'll go in alphabetical order," baggy shorts said before disappearing through the stage curtains. "First up, Rusty Baker," the same voice, amplified, said as a red-haired boy two seats down from Harlan stood and parted the curtains with the neck of his Vega Sunburst. "'Ring, Ring the Banjo,' Rusty," the voice said, followed by a banjo's ring.

Harlan was thinking Rusty wasn't half bad when Sam said, "Sounds like his finger rolls are missing a thumb." Slipping a silver pick onto his own right thumb and a blue plastic pick onto each of his first two fingers, Sam asked, "What do you say, Ferlin?"

"I'd say give the guy a chance," Harlan said as Rusty wrapped up "Ring, Ring the Banjo" and, as instructed, kicked off "Oh! Susanna."

"Lighten up," said Sam, popping each knuckle, shaking both hands, and swiveling his head from shoulder to shoulder. By now Sam was no longer getting on Harlan's nerves. He had reached the summit and planted a flag.

"Next up, Sam Boone. 'Oh! Susanna,' Sam," the voice said.

Earlier that year, Harlan had heard James Taylor sing "Oh! Susanna" on the radio. He sang it like a love song. But here was Sam playing like he was off to "Camptown Races." Harlan's version of "Oh! Susanna" took three minutes. Sam had wrapped it up in two.

"Little quick there, aren't you, Sam?" the voice said to Harlan's satisfaction.

"Anyone can play her slow, sir," Sam answered.

"Well, let's see what you can do with "Camptown Races.""

Sam had not made it to the first *doo-dah* when Harlan realized he was playing in D, just as he'd played last night. Why weren't they stopping him? Meanwhile, aside from Rusty, the other contestants were squirming in their seats. "D?" one boy said. Here again, Sam was managing to turn twelve furlongs into no more than eight. He'd already reached the finish line.

"Now that's more like it," the voice said, pleased with the speed, it seemed. "Thank you, Sam. Now let's hear what Harlan Dillbeck can do. Same two songs, Harlan."

With his mind on "Camptown Races," Harlan parted the curtains, took the stage, and played "Oh! Susanna."

"Played like the love song it is," said baggy shorts, seated in the auditorium's front row.

"Thanks, sir. Uh," said Harlan, fingerpicks twiddling, "I think we're supposed to play 'Camptown Races' in G."

"Let's see," the man said, fumbling through some papers. "That's right. G it is."

"But he played in D," Harlan said, pointing to the curtains with his Kay.

"He did? Well, I guess you'd better play in D too. Don't you boys tune in G?"

"Yeah, but—"

"Blind man could play in G. Give us what you got in D, Harlan. Only fair."

"Yes!" a voice shouted from behind the curtains. Sam's "yes," no doubt.

Normally, Harlan could have played this song, any song, in D. But he'd been practicing in G. And he was angry. The little fucker planned this all along, Harlan thought as he ripped into the strings.

If they had stopped Sam from playing in D, he probably could have played in G. He'd no doubt practiced in both. Sam must have hoped they'd play in alphabetical order, that he'd be asked to play "Camptown," and baggy shorts would require the others to play in D—a key in which they had not practiced. Sam had nothing to lose and principal banjoist to gain, Harlan thought. *ALL THE DOO-DAMN DAY!* Harlan's banjo wailed.

"Good God, Harlan, it's a song, not Chickamauga," baggy shorts said. "But thanks, I guess. Roy Jones, you're next. Any relation to Grandpa?"

Upset with Sam, baggy ass, and himself, Harlan's banjo nearly took out Roy Jones as they passed each other through the curtains. "Gets a little tricky in D, don't it . . ." Sam began with a wink as Harlan walked toward his seat.

Had it occurred to Harlan to grab his case, jump into his car, and head home? Yes, yes, yes. And he more than likely would have had Sam not added "*brotha?*" to his question, at which point Harlan grabbed Sam's Mastertone and shouted, "Brother my ass!" Then, with one hand on its neck and the other on its tailpiece, Harlan snapped the banjo on his knee.

Counting Jail Cells to Sleep

An hour ago, Harlan, Duncan, Darlene, and Lawson, after springing Harlan from jail and eating dinner at Camptown Diner, arrived at Harlan's house. Now, lying in his bed, staring at a water-stained ceiling, it occurs to Harlan that this is the first night he has ever slept under the same roof with his son. How is that possible?

It had all started the day he turned Sam's Mastertone into a mandolin and his own life into one of confinement in Bardstown—at first involuntarily, but then, aside from a few weekend getaways, he just stayed.

One Saturday, years after quitting the banjo, he'd finally driven to Nashville. That night, across the alley from the Ryman at Tootsie's Orchid Lounge, after hearing a man call Tennessee whiskey, "bourbon," Harlan broke the man's jaw and spent four nights in jail. On a trip to Graceland, he'd threatened a tour guide (Harlan said Elvis copped out to Hollywood, the tour guide disagreed) and spent three nights in the Memphis can. If not for his undisputed skill for tasting, Rowan Brothers would have lost its taste for Harlan years ago.

Counting jail cells—the time he'd booed Pete Rose in Cincinnati, the time he put a nine ball through a mirror in Knoxville... —Harlan falls asleep.

The next morning, Harlan ties on his Rowan Brothers, *Bottoms Up in the Bluegrass* apron and fries some bacon and eggs. At the sound of footsteps, he turns from the stove to see Duncan and Darlene entering the kitchen from the guest room. "Some apron," says Duncan. Looking down, spatula in hand, Harlan sees two bare butts—a man's and a woman's, unmistakably—poking up through blades of grass.

"Bacon and eggs all right?" asks Harlan. "Coffee?"

"Sounds good," says Duncan, pulling a chair out from under the table and scooting in beside Darleen. "So, Harlan, what kind of terms you on with that mortician preacher?"

Arriving at Harlan's house the previous night, everyone went straight to bed—in Lawson's case, a foldout couch in the basement. They'd planned to discuss Kevin's *plean* in the morning.

Turning to the stove, with his back to Duncan and Darlene, Harlan says, "Terms? I told you, I fired five rounds at Sam."

"Thought you said you guys go way back."

"Back to hell, I'd say."

"Well, Kevin thinks that Sam, being a mortician, could say Lawson's already dead. Then we run an obituary here and in the *Southern Illinois Times*. That way Lawson's friend won't send anyone to kill him. He'd already be dead."

"You don't get it," says Harlan, bringing bacon to the table. "Sam and I don't talk."

"And being a preacher, he could say a few words at the funeral," says Duncan. "Charlotte says it's okay for fathers to cover up for their sons. She says Confucius said so. Tell the preacher that. Pass the bacon, Darlene."

"Confucius? And who's Charlotte?" asks Harlan.

"His Unitarian minister in Vermont voice," says Darlene. "Just be glad he doesn't start singing with her."

"Singing?" Harlan says when, with the look of a dead man, Lawson walks into the kitchen.

"Morning, Lawson," says Duncan, "What do you want on your tombstone?"

Rubbing his eyes with his thumbs, Lawson bumps into Darleen's chair and says, "I never gave it much thought."

"Not bad," says Harlan. "More coffee, Dunc?"

Three cups later, Duncan still hasn't let go of the plan, explaining how a funeral would be necessary to convince "*eegit* Timmy" that Lawson's dead.

"Irish for idiot," Darlene explains.

But by Duncan's fifth cup, Harlan has to admit that Kevin's *plean*, despite Harlan and Sam's history and the annoying Irish expressions, makes sense. "Suppose I could talk to Reba."

"Reba? The woman you used to see?" asks Duncan, helping himself to more bacon.

"She's with Sam now. She might get Sam to listen."

"You know, Harlan, maybe you should get a cat," says Duncan.

"Why would I want a cat?"

"Keep you company. We wouldn't take a million dollars for Robinson Crusoe. We found him stranded at an interstate rest stop on our way home from a Cards game. Didn't we, Darlene?"

"That we did," says Darlene. "And his litter box needs to be changed."

"In that case, we'd better get going," says Harlan. "Let's write us an obit."

"Now we're suckin' diesel," says Duncan.

A Career is Born

1970

Before shortening Sam's Mastertone, there were three things that Harlan had failed to consider: first, the agility of a large man in madras shorts and sandals; second, the malicious damage laws in Nelson County, Kentucky; and third, the noon checkout time at My Old Kentucky Motor-In Inn. At the crack of a banjo and Sam's "*Sumamabitch*," baggy shorts had leapt onto the stage, run through the curtains, and grabbed Harlan in a bear hug. "Someone, call the police," the man said. Meanwhile, the motel clock kept ticking.

Following an explanatory phone call home in which Harlan's father said, "Night in jail might do you good," Harlan spent not one but five incarcerated nights, each one accruing an additional ten dollars in motel fees. That fifty dollars, plus court costs, two hundred thirty-five dollars for a new Mastertone, and one hundred in punitive damages, meant Harlan would not be leaving Bardstown anytime soon. After learning that Harlan was almost five hundred dollars short, Judge Rowan said, "You can catch up on your schoolwork this *summa*. Can you lift an empty bourbon barrel, son?"

Unbeknownst to Harlan, Judge Rowan and his brother were co-owners of Rowan Brothers Distillery. Harlan had just had his first job interview. "I suppose," Harlan said.

"*Yes!*" shouted Sam, rising from his seat in the courtroom.

Sam in the Purse

As Duncan, Darlene, and Lawson finish breakfast, Harlan calls in to Rowan Brothers for a personal day. Then, over another pot of coffee and occasional objections from Lawson, the four of them compose his obituary.

Satisfied with their efforts, Harlan suggests that his guests take a tour of My Old Kentucky Home while he contacts Reba about Kevin's plan. "The place that's in the song?" asks Lawson.

"That's the one."

Intending to catch Reba at work, Harlan gets into his van, a black pearl Honda Odyssey. Driving northwest out of town, he passes warehouse after warehouse filled with aging Rowan Brothers bourbon before veering northwest onto State Highway 245, bound for Heaven Knows Distillery in Bullitt County. Seems impossible, Harlan thinks. Forty-six years since he rolled the other way, thinking he would win the audition, make some money, and earn Jerry Lawson's respect.

All these years Harlan had assumed it was Sam Boone that had gotten under his skin at Bardstown High. But maybe— what had Dunc called it, percho-something?—maybe that had too. It would explain some things. That first summer, he'd lobbed a cherry bomb onto *The Stephen Foster Story* stage during Sam's performance. Shortly after that, he'd inscribed *PAID IN FULL* with his thumb pick on the motel owner's car hood, costing four more nights in jail, three hundred dollars in damages, and another six months in Rowan Brothers servitude. One night in February, 1971, after learning Maryann had married The Ramblers' drummer, Carl Baumgart, Harlan heaved his banjo into the Beech Fork River. On a summer day in 1979, after batting fifth for the Rowan Brothers Softball Hotshots, he took out Sudden Glory Fellowship shortstop Sam Boone's left knee with a cleats-up slide. Then there was the broken jaw at Tootsie's, the argument at Graceland, and so on.

Time was, about 5:00, Friday afternoons, Harlan would walk into the office at Heaven Knows and say, "Working hard, Connie?" to receptionist, Connie Arbeit—a woman about his age with big blonde hair—before walking into Reba's office, unannounced. There, he'd wait as Reba finished entering notes from that day's tastes into her desktop. Then he'd follow Reba to her house in Shepherdsville, where he kept a weekend's worth of clothes.

They had met at Reba's first Taste-Off, held annually at Talbott Tavern. Harlan finished third that year, but first in another respect, for that night Reba had agreed to a drink that led to two that led to dinner three nights later.

"Working hard, Connie?" Harlan asks now as Connie looks up from her desk.

"Harlan Dillbeck!"

"Never could fool you, girl. Reba busy?"

"Let me check," says Connie, tapping the phone on her desk. "How you been, Harlan? Other than shooting yourself."

"Heard about that, did you?"

"Reba, there's a Harlan Dillbeck here to see you. Good looking fella. With a limp, looks like . . . Uh, huh . . . Go on in, Harlan."

Harlan knew, as everyone did, that Reba got the job as Heaven Knows master taster thanks to her father, Forest Fenway. Before Forest retired, he'd master-tasted for Heaven Knows for half a century. The night Harlan met Reba at her rookie Taste-Off, she'd said, "Thanks to Daddy, I could tell wheat bourbon from a rye time I was ten."

Though it had only been two years since Harlan dated Reba, walking into her office feels like stepping back fifty. Gilt-framed photographs of Whirlaway, Citation, Adolph Rupp, and Joe B. Hall line the mahogany paneling. Irving Stone biographies, the complete works of James Michener, and Forest Fenway's many First-Place silver Taste-Off snifters fill the converted, cherry gun case shelves.

"See you haven't changed a thing. Other than your trophy," says Harlan, nodding at the shining snifter on Reba's walnut desk."

"About that, Harlan."

"No need."

"Well then, have a seat."

There was a time when Reba shared Harlan's opinion of Sam. "An arrogant little man," she'd once said. But then one June Sunday morning at Reba's house, all that changed.

Harlan had awakened to find himself alone in Reba's bed.

He was about to get up, when she walked into her bedroom, dressed. "Where you off to?" he'd asked.

"The Lord's house. Be back in a few hours. Sleep in, sweetie."

Lying on his back, staring at the revolving fan above the bed, Harlan guessed it had been forty-some years since he'd been to church—other than his parents' funerals. And though he'd never known Reba to attend, he figured which church she was heading to was none of his business—as long as it wasn't Sam's church. But good God, the Lord couldn't live there. Plus, he'd heard her car door slam. It was summer; the sun was shining through the blinds; and Sudden Glory was just two blocks up Plum Street. If she was going there, she would have walked. Besides, Reba knew how he felt about Sam, the little bastard. Harlan went to sleep, awakening a few hours later to the sight of Sam, hanging from the bedroom doorknob, grinning from the corner of a Sudden Glory bulletin inside Reba's purse. Grinning like he'd won another contest.

"It doesn't mean a thing," Reba had said, kicking off her shoes inside her closet. "We ran into each other at Walmart. In light bulbs. He said he was preaching on forgiveness, and that we should come. You in particular."

Flinging the sheet from his body, Harlan said, "Got a better chance of seeing me in one of his caskets than his church."

"That's what I told Sam, pretty much. I know how you feel about him. Truth told, it's a shame you didn't hear his message," said Reba, stepping from her dress. "And *my*, can he play that banjo."

"Played you for a fool is what," said Harlan before he jumped from bed, pulled on a Rowan Brothers T-shirt, stepped into his jeans, and left.

The following week, Harlan didn't go to either Heaven Knows or Shepherdsville. But after not hearing from Reba in almost two weeks, he'd driven to her house on a Saturday, hoping to talk, when the Forever Yours hearse parked at her curb had left him speechless. After slamming his Odyssey into the hearse's rear bumper, Harlan found his voice and more. For within seconds of contact, the hearse's rear door opened and Sam, wrapped in a sheet, jumped out, giving Harlan a clear view of a stretcher. There, wrapped in nothing, lay Reba.

"Thing is," says Harlan, lifting the snifter from Reba's desk and buffing it with his shirtsleeve, "I got a favor to ask."

52 19 G
April 6, 1980

After unloading empty barrels for years, Harlan now oversaw the placement of them, bourbon-filled, in Rowan Brothers' twenty-five warehouses. Twenty thousand, fifty-three-gallon barrels per house. One morning in September, he was in Warehouse 19, walking down a barrel-lined aisle streaked by east-facing sunlight. He was looking for a barrel that had been in place for ten years. As long as he.

Like him, the bourbon had aged. Like him—aside from his few solitary trips to Rupp Arena, Churchill Downs, and Nashville—it had not moved.

He'd bought a little house not far from Bardstown High. Summers, he played left field for the Hotshots. Dated a few girls. Even came close to marrying Betty Moffett, a Bardstown vet tech. One night after dinner, Harlan picked up Moses, a big, orange tabby, and sat beside Betty on her couch.

"I asked you over tonight to say I'm sorry," said Betty, "but

I've prayed on it, and as long as you make spirits for the Devil, I can't marry you."

In Harlan's way of thinking, the closest thing to the Devil was the anger that was prone to surface in himself. He would look back with pride to turning his back on Satan that night. For without one word, Harlan smiled at Betty, lowered Moses into Betty's lap, and walked out.

Day after day, walking down rows of barrels, Harlan had begun to think of them as friends, quiet friends who never judged him. Looking up at stacks of barrels, he imagined the bourbon inside, soaking up tannins as it aged.

Many years later, Harlan would look back and wonder how his life had passed so quickly. Aside from occasional romances and obligatory Rowan Brothers parties and picnics, he'd spent his life alone. If not for his three First-Place snifters and inter-mittent jail time, he'd hardly lived at all.

But that day in Warehouse 19, as Harlan walked down the aisle with instructions to pull barrel 52 19 G, *Fill Date 04 06 70*, it occurred to him that this could have been the day he'd snapped Sam's banjo. One *crack*. Everything had resounded from there.

Searching for Mushrooms at NASCAR

As Harlan returns the shirt-shined snifter to Reba's desk, she says, "Let me get this straight. You want Sam, who you tried to shoot, to put your son's obituary in our paper and the *Illinois Times*. Never mind he's alive. Then Sam performs a funeral service—closed coffin, I hope—followed by some graveside words. Surprised you don't want a meal at the church after-wards. Anything else?"

"*Southern Illinois Times*. And a meal might be nice," says Harlan, smiling.

"Who writes the obituary?"

"Got it right here," says Harlan, pulling a sealed envelope from his back pocket.

Reaching for the envelope, Reba says, "I'll talk to Sam tonight. I owe you that much. But I doubt you'd do this for him."

"No, don't guess I would, seeing as how he steals a man's woman, fixes contests, and I don't run a church or funeral home."

"I beat you fair and square, Harlan. Sam said so."

"Take Sam's word plus a dollar, and you've got fifty cents."

"And as far as him stealing me, Sam was there for me when you weren't."

"In the back of a hearse, you mean."

"No, that's not what I mean. With that temper of yours, you'll never get close to anyone. At least not me. Everyone's out to get you, according to you. It gets old, Harlan. Sam, he sees the best in people."

"That's because to him everyone is some fool to best. Company included. And when did I ever lose my temper with you?"

"Look, Harlan. I said I'd talk to Sam. I'll give him this envelope and let you know what he says. I think you'd better go now."

Overtaking Citation, Harlan turns and says, "Tell Sam this needs to happen yesterday. Could mean life or death for Lawson, and Duncan needs to get home."

"Your brother still hearing things?"

"You might say."

* * *

Southern Illinois resident, Lawson F. Dillbeck, 46, died tragically Wednesday, April 18 after falling off his father's roof in Bardstown, Kentucky. A graduate of Shawnee High in Jefferson County, Illinois, and owner operator of Lawson's Lawns and Such, he enjoyed hunting mushrooms in Shawnee National Forest and NASCAR. He is survived by his mother, Maryann Baumgart (stepfather, Carl); father, Harlan; uncle, Duncan (aunt, Darlene; cousins, Ron and Don); and ball python, Carl. The Light shines on the enlightened, and Lawson was well lit. Memorial service to be held Saturday, April 21, 3:00 at Forever Yours Funeral Chapel in Shepherdsville with burial at Rose Hill Cemetery to follow. The Reverend Sam Boone officiating. He will be missed.

"You write this, Harlan?" asks Reba, lowering *The Kentucky Standard* to her desk as Harlan, Duncan, and Darlene enter her office. "No wonder the envelope was sealed."

Reba had convinced Sam to help. He'd taken the obituary to *The Standard* yesterday.

"Reba, this is my brother, Duncan, and my sister-in-law, Darlene," says Harlan as Reba walks around her desk to greet them. "We thought Lawson should lay low."

"Good thinking," says Reba.

"We've heard a lot about you," says Duncan, accepting Reba's hand. "Sorry things didn't work out for you and Harlan. Nice office."

"Pleased to meet you," says Darlene, giving Reba a hug. "Your perfume . . . Euphoria?"

"Yes, it is. Harlan, pull up some chairs to my desk," says Reba, touching his shoulder and catching his eye.

There was a time, looking into Reba's green eyes, Harlan

saw his reflection as if cast from a bountiful sea. Looking into Reba's eyes now, knowing they were more apt to reflect Sam, Harlan felt like he was drowning. "We all pitched in a word or two," he says, nodding at *The Standard.*

Returning to the chair behind her desk, Reba asks, "Why a fall from your roof?"

"That's the kind of thing he does, cleans gutters—and such," says Harlan.

"Reads like he searches for mushrooms at NASCAR. Did he find his snake there too?"

"Jesus, Reba. It's an obit, not a book."

"What's this about being enlightened?"

"Charlotte's idea," says Duncan. "She's a minister."

"According to this, *Sam* will be missed," says Reba, folding *The Standard* and tossing it aside.

"Not likely," says Harlan.

"Listen, Harlan. I didn't call you over here to insult Sam. We have some planning to do."

"We want the cheapest damn coffin he's got."

Seems like a lifetime ago, Harlan thinks before realizing it *was* a lifetime ago—when he stood behind red velvet curtains as Maryann walked through them and sang "Crazy." Only this time there is an organ droning in the background as Harlan parts green tweed for her to exit. Looking as though she could still high-jump her height, Maryann leaves the anteroom at Forever Yours Funeral Chapel, places her hands on the casket (closed), and starts weeping. "I saw your mother act like this in *Oklahoma!*" says Harlan.

"What were you doing there?" asks Lawson from a corner

of the anteroom. "Who do you see by my casket, besides family?"

Family—a word Harlan had not considered until now. Lawson, Duncan, Darlene, Maryann, and even her husband, Carl. Took a funeral to bring them together. "Sam, glad-handing a few friends of mine from work," says Harlan, "Connie Arbeit, Reba. There's Deputy Dharma."

"But do you see anyone who doesn't belong here?"

Turning toward Lawson, Harlan says, "You mean other than a man at his own funeral with a snake around his neck."

"I told you, the name is Carl," says Lawson, stroking the snake between the eyes. "Just like my dad."

Since Duncan informed him of the water they once drank, Harlan imagined it rising through Illinois soil much like the voices that rise in Duncan and the anger in himself. But this time, it's not anger, it's disappointment that surfaces at the sound of "my dad."

"Did you ever think of me as your dad?"

"Not at first. I was only a year old when Mom married Carl. He *was* my dad, far as I knew. But by the time I turned sixteen, I couldn't stand the guy—always telling me what to do, don't smoke this or why'd you do that and shit. I named my snake Carl to get even. Started telling friends my real dad lived in Kentucky."

"Don't see why you can't have two."

"Cool," says Lawson, stroking Carl's skin.

"Sam's about to start. Just stay where you are and enjoy your funeral. And hold onto Carl," says Harlan, parting the curtains, giving Lawson a glimpse of the chapel.

"Some coffin. What is that, plywood?" asks Lawson.

"Pine," says Harlan before slipping out the anteroom and into the chapel.

Around ten o'clock the previous night, Maryann and her

husband arrived at Harlan's house with Lawson's snake, which had been in Maryann's care since Lawson fled Illinois. Harlan learned that when Maryann's Carl wasn't drumming, he ran a paint store. "I could give you some suggestions," Carl said as he looked at Harlan's drab walls.

They had gathered in Harlan's living room, and all but Duncan capped off the day with shots of Rowan Brothers' best. "None for him. He hears enough voices as it is," Darlene had said.

"Suppose my walls could use some color," said Harlan before turning toward the couch, where the snake lay extended across Duncan's and Lawson's shoulders.

When the python's head swiveled, Harlan noticed an unusual marking between its brown eyes. In the center of a coppery splotch, a smaller brown splotch looked like another eye. A three-eyed snake with a flickering forked tongue. "You have somewhere you can put that thing tonight?"

"Carl sleeps with me," said Lawson.

"Not tonight. You and I'll be sharing the foldout in the basement. The day I sleep with a snake . . ."

"We'll sleep in your van."

After finishing their bourbon, they turned in: Duncan and Darlene to the guestroom; Lawson and Carl to the van; and Harlan to his basement, just below his bedroom, where Maryann and her Carl slept.

But now at Forever Yours Funeral Chapel, seated in the front row between Harlan and Carl Baumgart, Maryann stands, steps to the casket, and sings, "Tears in Heaven," tearfully.

Sounds as good as ever, thinks Harlan. And with Lawson alive as ever, Harlan is impressed by her tears. But surprisingly, by the third stanza, Harlan feels tears welling too. Exactly who he's crying for—who knows? Lawson? Eric Clapton? *"'Cause I know I don't belong here in heaven,"* sings Maryann.

"Oh, but we do!" Sam shouts from behind a shortened pulpit. Wearing a black suit with a black string bow tie, white hair plastered in place, he continues, "Thank you, Sister Maryann. Folks, in Psalms 6:6, King David said, *I am worn out from sobbing. All night I flood my bed with weeping, drenching it with my tears.* Like King David, we have wept. We have flooded our beds with tears for Brother Lawson."

Could sell tears to a baby, thinks Harlan.

"But in Acts 21:13, Paul asks, *Why are you weeping and breaking my heart?* And that's what I ask you today. Why are you weeping, folks? This should be a day of celebration!"

He'll be pulling out his banjo next, Harlan is thinking when he hears a door creak from the rear of the chapel.

"Can I get an *amen!*" shouts Sam.

The Five Susanna Chorus

1998

To this day, twenty-eight years after arriving in Bardstown, Harlan had not seen *The Stephen Foster Story* (aside from the time it took to heave a cherry bomb at Sam onstage). But Harlan's parents were visiting, and his mother insisted they see it. The problem was that Harlan's father had insisted on a pre-play tour of Rowan Brothers, where, beginning with a taste of the 160-proof *white dog*, straight from the pot still, and ending with a sampling of eight aged, bottled bourbons, Franklin got sloshed. "They all same the taste to me," he'd said after sipping a sweet blend.

Running late for the show, Harlan took his parents to

Camptown Diner. But after downing the roast beef special and drinking four cups of coffee, Franklin was no less sloshed. Thirty minutes later, ten rows in front of Harlan, Franklin, and June, a young Stephen Foster was singing "Oh! Susanna" (too fast, thought Harlan, but at least Sam's not on banjo), when all five Susannas lifted twirling skirts to their faces and grabbed bright-colored garters from their thighs.

"Get a load a that!" said Franklin.

Taking his eyes off the stage, Harlan saw his father reaching for a garter as it sailed into the audience, reaching . . . reaching . . . before tumbling onto a woman in row nine, sending both Franklin and the woman into row eight on top of a young girl. "*Oh Susanna, don't you cry for me,*" faux Stephen Foster sang as a large man—the girl's father, presumably—heaved Franklin into row seven.

One day, Harlan would attribute the rage he felt to the dry-cleaned water he'd consumed as a boy. But that day, with the help of his twenty-five-years-of-service Rowan Brothers ring on his finger, he broke the large man's nose with no thought at all.

That night, Franklin, who had come to his son's defense in the ensuing ruckus, slept soundly in a cell he shared with Harlan. Awake on his bunk, Harlan wasn't thinking of the nose he had crushed, the play he had stopped, or the jail time he faced. Instead, he thought of the young deputy, Deputy Dharma, who had found an extra pillow for Franklin before removing the weapon from Harlan's right hand—the ring that had splintered a nose. "Procedure, Mr. Dillbeck. We'll take good care," she said with a voice as smooth as twenty-year bourbon.

In Cold Blood

"*Amen!*" replies everyone to Sam but Harlan. Instead, turning toward the door-creak, Harlan sees an orange *Fighting Illini* hoodie and camouflage pants walking up the aisle—the face inside the hood, a man of forty, maybe fifty years, sporting a braided red goatee.

But it's not the goatee, it's the man's bandaged right hand that grabs Harlan's attention. Hadn't Lawson's friend Timmy lopped off a man's finger? With his good hand, the man lowers his hoodie and grabs a seat beside Reba, three rows back. Harlan turns toward Lawson in the anteroom. Between its green curtains, a blue eye grows large.

As for the celebration Sam called for, it isn't much of one. Duncan says, "No one sharpens mower blades like Lawson." Maryann tells how Lawson once stayed up all night kneading Carl. "His snake," she explains. "It swallowed a squirrel."

Following Sam's benediction, as the mourners pay final respects, Harlan positions himself beside Maryann and Carl-the-husband in front of Lawson's casket. With one hand on the lid, Harlan is prepared if anyone, namely the red-bearded stranger, tries to look in. But when the man approaches, he barely glances at the coffin. "Sorry, dude," he says, offering his left hand to Harlan.

"You a friend of Lawson's?" asks Harlan, scanning the ink on the man's left knuckles—*D U K E*—before giving them a shake.

"You might say. We both know a guy who asked me to see old Lawson off," says Duke, whose amber eyes quiver like bourbon in a shot glass.

"Thanks for coming, Duke," says Harlan.

"How'd you know my name?" asks Duke. Harlan taps his own left knuckles. "Oh, yeah. See you at the cemetery," Duke says.

Next in line, wearing a flattering black silk dress and white pearls, Deputy Dharma takes Harlan's hand in hers. "I'm so sorry, Harlan."

"Thank you, Dharma. Nice of you to come."

"I don't want to alarm you," Dharma says in a near whisper, "but we received word from the Jefferson County, Illinois, jail. They overheard a threatening conversation between a prisoner and a visitor named Howard Earl, who goes by Duke. The man you just shook hands with. I overheard. That's why I'm here today, partly." Continuing in a normal voice, she says, "I'm sorry for your loss, Mr. and Mrs.—"

"Baumgart," says Maryann. "Thank you for coming."

"Dharma, Maryann. Maryann, Dharma," says Harlan. "I owe a lot to Maryann and Carl, Lawson's other dad."

"Hear that, Lawson?" says Carl, performing a two-fingered drumroll on the coffin."

Judging by the thumps, Harlan can tell that Sam forgot to fill the coffin—with newspapers, bricks, whatever—to give it heft. Duncan had suggested kitty litter. Kevin, empty bourbon bottles.

"Lawson's *only* father, more like," says Maryann, as though anger had been surfacing in her too.

"Nice to meet you all," says Dharma. "See you at the cemetery, Harlan."

"No, wait. I'll walk you to your car." Then, looking at Maryann, Harlan says, "I appreciate you and Carl being there for Lawson when I wasn't."

"You mean for the first forty-six years?"

"You have a right to be upset. It's just that one thing led to another. Your marriage for one. Then it seemed too late. Maybe now things can be different—for us all," says Harlan, glancing at the anteroom.

"We'll see. At least you got off to a start this week. I'll give you that." Turning to Dharma, Maryann says, "It would have meant a lot to Lawson, rest his sweet soul."

* * *

A short time later, Duncan, Darlene, Maryann, and Carl Baumgart join Harlan near the hearse, parked outside Forever Yours. "Pretend it's got a body in it," Harlan tells them before Sam's nephew Danny, the hearse driver, steps from the car. With Danny pinch-hitting as sixth pallbearer, they lift the coffin above a dented bumper into the hearse. A dent for which Harlan had paid to be fixed. "Must have been a little guy," Danny says as the pallbearers get into the car. Judging by Danny's smirk, Harlan suspects Sam has filled him in. But all has gone well so far. Why take any chances? Aside from Duncan singing the chorus to "This Little Light of Mine"—and Darlene whispering to Harlan, "He's singing with Charlotte"— they drive to Rose Hill Cemetery in silence.

Winding through the cemetery, Harlan spots a fluttering white tent above an open grave. Soon the hearse comes to a stop. Behind it, Dharma, Connie Arbeit, and Duke step from their cars—a beat-up Dodge van in Duke's case. Orange. After the pallbearers feign Lawson's dead weight to the gravesite (even Danny affects a grimace), a black Lincoln Town Car drives up; Reba and Sam step out; and Sam begins.

"Four days ago, it pleased God to lead Lawson to his daddy's rooftop. But brothers and sisters, Lawson did not die that day," Sam says with a grin aimed at Harlan. "And though we commit his earthly vessel to the ground, Lawson is with his heavenly Father now, standing on the *rooftop* of heaven. Hallelujah!

"Lawson's family invites you to share a lunch that the good ladies at Sudden Glory Fellowship have prepared. Now, may the grace of our Lord Jesus, the love of God Almighty, and the spirit of the Holy Ghost be with you today and evermore. Amen."

* * *

An hour later, Harlan is standing in the desert line at Sudden Glory Fellowship with Deputy Dharma. He's scooping cherry cobbler into a bowl when he feels a tap on his shoulder. "Got a question about Lawson's snake," says Duke.

"Duke, Dharma. Dharma, Duke," says Harlan.

Up to now, standing in line at Sudden Glory, Harlan had managed to avoid Sam. What was there to say? *Thanks*, to a guy about to make five thousand dollars? ("He'd normally charge six," Reba had said. "But since there's no body . . .") But here Sam is, cutting in line, envelope in hand. "That a bill you got there," says Harlan, squirting whipped cream onto his cobbler.

"Now, Brother Harlan, we'll get to that soon enough," Sam says, stuffing the envelope into his suit pocket. "Nice to see you again, Deputy. We met when my nephew Danny got into a little trouble," Sam explains to Harlan. "That where you two met? Who's your friend?" Sam asks, looking up at Duke.

Tomorrow morning, Duncan and Darlene will depart for Illinois. Tomorrow afternoon, Maryann and Carl Baumgart will leave too. The next day, Sam, Dharma, and Harlan will meet with Judge Rowan, old Judge Rowan's son, to discuss Harlan's Talbott Inn charges. In the judge's chamber, Dharma will offer to create a Jazzercise for Anger Management Class, JAM; and Sam will consent with the judge's decision to sentence Harlan to one year of JAM attendance (Wednesday nights at Bardstown High). Given the importance of Harlan's master taster status and the fact that this Judge Rowan, as did the preceding one, has much at stake in the distillery, Harlan will not be surprised at his honor's leniency. But Harlan will be grateful to the judge, to Dharma, and to some extent, Sam. But today...

"Duke, Sam. Sam—" Harlan says in the dessert line. But faster than Harlan can say *Duke*, Duke yells, "Snake!" at the sight of Carl slithering from the kitchen, serpentining beneath the desert table, and coiling behind Sam. Faster than Lawson, running from the kitchen, can reach Carl, Duke pulls out a Smith and Wesson from underneath his *Fighting Illini* sweatshirt and takes aim—the snake a clear shot if not for Sam in the way. Giving no thought to more than forty years of grievances, Harlan lowers his shoulder and drives Sam into a double-frosted chocolate sheet cake.

PHWACKK-PHWACKK

"Drop the weapon," says Deputy Dharma, squeezing Duke's bandaged hand and yanking down.

"Shitsake!" yells Duke, dropping his gun and himself to the yellow linoleum.

Rising from the sheet cake, wiping chocolate from his eyes, Sam looks to his right and says, "He's been hit!" (Standing beside Sam, Harlan runs his hand across his butt and thinks, not again.)

"Hands behind your head," says Dharma.

"I was aiming for the snake!" yells Duke.

Securing Duke's hands with her pearls, Dharma says, "Harlan Dillbeck, you have some explaining to do. I thought your son was dead—before now."

Before now? thinks Harlan, turning from Dharma. And there, beneath the dessert table, motionless atop his snake, lies Lawson—a red rivulet running across the floor.

Two months from now, leaving Wednesday night JAM with Dharma, Harlan will say, "I could never bring Carl to class. The vibrations from the music would scare her. She curled into a ball this morning when a fire truck went by. It's what ball pythons do when they feel threatened. Like that day at Lawson's funeral."

"Wait, Carl is a she?"

"Yeah. Lawson didn't know that when he named her. He didn't think much of his other dad back then."

"You know, Harlan, if you called her Carla it would clear things up."

But for now, at Sudden Glory Fellowship, it's still Carl. And the only visible part of Carl is the tip of her tail, sticking out from beneath Lawson, whom Harlan falls upon to embrace.

Meanwhile, Duncan, Darlene, and Carl Baumgart rush to Lawson's side. "Lawson!" Maryann shouts, squeezing into the space beneath the table atop Harlan. Despite the shock of the moment, Harlan imagines the picture this would make: a stack of Carl-the-snake, Lawson, and Harlan himself, topped by Maryann beneath a table filled with cobblers and pies.

"Mom, Dad, you're getting heavy. Carl's been hit," mumbles Lawson from below.

"Praise God!" shouts Sam. "He's alive!"

Maryann is first to stand, followed by Harlan, then Lawson. In a bleeding mottled ball, curls Carl. "It's just a flesh wound, looks like. Someone, get a towel," says Carl Baumgart, the cue for Sudden Glory Parishioner, Connie Arbeit, to run into the kitchen and hustle a dishtowel back. With two wraps around the python's body, Carl staunches Carl's cold blood.

Still on his knees, Duke says, "You gotta believe me," his red goatee braid swinging from Harlan to Dharma and back as he pleads. "I didn't come here to shoot nobody. I seen the obit, and I figured Timmy being in jail hadn't, and since he was willing to pay a stack to kill Lawson, why not cash in? So, I visited Timmy and told him I thought Lawson might be in

Kentucky with his daddy. I said I'd come over here and kill him and bring back the proof. That snake took me by surprise, is all."

"What kind of proof?" asks Lawson, lifting Carl to his shoulders.

"That three-eyed snake. Everybody knows you wouldn't go nowhere without it. Timmy said, 'Bring me back Carl, alive, and I'll know the snitch is dead.' Timmy always liked that snake. Me, I thought whoever wound up with it would be happy to give it up. I'd tell Timmy I pushed you off your daddy's roof, show him the obit, and give him the snake. Anyways, I was about to ask where the damn snake was, when there he was. Who's in the damn casket?"

"So, you tried to kill your proof, dumbfuck?" says Lawson.

"Sorry, Reverend."

"Probably would have if I hadn't shot left-handed," says Duke.

By this time, Reba has cleaned the chocolate from Sam's face. She's dabbing his lapel with a napkin, when Sam asks Lawson, "Love that serpent, do you?"

"Yes, sir," Lawson says, stroking Carl's third eye.

"Couldn't see your way to give it up?"

"No, sir."

With Duke on his knees, Sam, short as he is, looks Duke in the eyes and says, "Look here, you go back and tell this Timmy fella you got here too late. Lawson was already dead. You seen his body at the funeral. Make sure Timmy sees the obit, and tell him Harlan wanted the snake. How much for you to do that, Duke?"

"A thousand?"

"How about two hundred?"

"Deal."

"Harlan, give the man his money," says Sam.

"And trust him to do what you say?"

Leaning into Duke's left ear, Sam says, "Well, the Lord works in mysterious ways. Don't He, Duke? First your finger, then God knows what. I have me some friends in Paris. They might just like to take a motorcycle ride to Illinois."

"Bang on *boyo!*" says Duncan.

"I catch your drift, Reverend," says Duke. "Paris?"

Ladling a drink from the punch bowl, Sam says, "Now then, Harlan, let's have us a word. And thank you, Dharma. Those pearls make a nice pair of cuffs."

Following Sam upstairs into his office, Harlan sees two five-string banjos, a Deering standing in a chair and a Gibson lying in an open case across Sam's desk. "Have a seat," says Sam.

Harlan has not held a banjo since he tossed his Kay into the Beech Fork, but picking up the Deering, he can't resist playing the riff he used to play when Jerry Lawson introduced him in the Ramblers.

"'Clinch Mountain Backstep.' Not bad," Sam says, before lowering his fruit punch to the desk, picking up his Gibson, and playing the first nine notes of "Dueling Banjos." Pausing, Sam looks at Harlan while grinning that shit-same grin from decades ago.

If it were up to Harlan's mind, he would not accept the duel. More than forty years since he'd last played. He'd have to be a fool to accept Sam's challenge. *Da-da da da da da da da daa*, Harlan's fingers reply.

Da da da da da da da daa, plays Sam before Harlan's mind wins out. Lowering the Deering, Harlan sits and pulls out his checkbook. "What do I owe you? Let's get this over with."

After putting the Gibson in its case, Sam reaches into his suit pocket, opens the envelope, and says, "According to this, five thousand three hundred eighty dollars and thirty-seven cents—for the Norwich Pine, taxes, and my services. But seeing as how you might have saved my life, let's call it an even five thousand three hundred. Fair enough?"

"How about five thousand four hundred and you put in a word for me with the judge."

"About you almost shooting me at the Talbott?"

"What else would I mean?"

"Fifty-four hundred it is. But just so you know, I did this all for Reba's sake. I could lose my license over this."

"Your license to steal, you mean," says Harlan as he rips out a check.

Picking up the Gibson, Sam launches into "Camptown Races," in D, to no surprise. Glaring down at Sam, Harlan picks up the Deering and, in G, joins in—discord the likes of which raises Reba up the stairs and, for all Harlan knows, Stephen Foster from the dead.

* * *

Two months later, leaving Wednesday night JAM, Harlan says, "Good point, Dharma. But Lawson's called her Carl for nearly thirty years. Be hard to call her Carla now."

"Thirty years? Pythons live that long?" asks Dharma, walking hand-in-hand with Harlan down the steps from Bardstown High, a full moon shining in the east.

"Out in the wild, they don't. Kind of like us in a way. You and me could live a long time, now," says Harlan, giving Dharma's hand a squeeze.

"Listen to you," says Dharma, squeezing back.

Looking down at their clasped hands, in the mix of moon and streetlight, Dharma's slender brown fingers complete the back of Harlan's white hand. "Lawson's working graveyard tonight. A shipment of barrels came in late," says Harlan. "How about you stay at my house?"

Up to now, Harlan and Dharma's relationship had consisted of meals at Camptown Diner and Jazzercise at Bardstown High. But last Wednesday night had ended with a hug on Dharma's doorstep. Harlan had hopes for tonight.

"I have to be at work by seven in the morning. You'll have to drop me off at my house by six."

"Yes, officer."

Walking down the sidewalk toward Harlan's Honda van, Dharma says, "I've been meaning to ask, that day at the church, when you and Sam went into his office, what did you talk about —before you started playing?"

"Nothing much. Sam wanted his money."

"That's it?"

"That and he wanted me to know that he did Lawson's funeral for Reba's sake."

"Well, he did talk to Judge Rowan for you," says Dharma.

"Between you and me, I paid him to speak to the judge."

"I didn't hear that," says Dharma as Harlan aims a key at his van and punches the opener. "What is it between you two, anyway?"

"It's a long story. But just because two men can't stand the other, it doesn't mean they can't help each other out when—Oh hell, I don't know. Let's go home," says Harlan, opening the door for Dharma to his Odyssey.

THE MEMORY BENCH

BECK ERIXSON

White steam off two raspberry hot cocoas braids into the frost-kissed night air, tickling at my face as the man in the midnight blue peacoat offers his usual late-night nod. His skin is pale, licked from years of whipping wind, and his eyes permanently heavy from life. We're both out here among the other souls wandering late, avoiding what sleep brings, lost in ourselves.

The darkness of the sky cuts the bright glow of the shops through grand glass panes and glittering holiday lights twisted amongst the branches of each leafless tree, illuminating the path to my waterfront haven. Petrified branches on either side hold their forced dress like a corpse at a funeral, only these will reanimate in the spring and the binds of the wire between each twinkle of festive white will be cut away, freeing the confines to stretch until they are bound again. If only life were simple enough to cut binds and grow before they come again.

A shudder slides from the base of my skull down the hairs on my neck with the sharp wind tickling the backs of my ears. The misty cloud of my breath draws up the brick street towards the glow from a fading streetlight hovering over an iron bench overlooking the muted river. Wandering up the path to the bench, I can sense the man is cautiously close, following, but allowing enough space for us both to exist in respective bubbles of comfort.

The warmth of the streetlight works to pink my cheeks as I steady the hot chocolate and take a seat on the far right of the bench. Placing one drink at my side, I cup the other in my palms, letting the heat burn the tips of my fingers as they poke through my gloves, reminding me I'm here. The river is so calm it appears more like planting soil than water.

The man in the coat clears his throat, helping to send a gentle sign he's present, close. I don't have the heart to tell him I already knew. Instead, I offer a nod at the river, imagining a parade of one-man sailboats each the tone inside of a sunset moving through a field of rust-colored sunflowers and a creamsicle sky ahead. Ridiculous, yes, but at my core I'll always look for beauty to fight the waves of numbness, of darkness, that intertwine with my past.

He clears his throat again, appearing on the far left of the bench in my peripheral view, clutching a tweed flat cap. His soft white hair draws my focus. The darkness of the sky and the blackness of the quiet water return. The still air allows us to breathe, calmly existing near one another. Willing my gaze back out at the water, I take a sip of the hot chocolate, letting the raspberry coat my tongue while giving him the time he needs with the river.

His sigh catches my own exhale, leaving only one breath to sit in the air before dissipating.

"It's late..." His voice wanders, almost searching for the thought.

"Late is the best time to go out and think," I say, keeping my tone gentle.

I turn to him, acknowledging his presence, and controlling the rise and fall of my chest with soft, calm breaths. Unlike my green version of his coat—which comes to the back of my knees with flair rather than ending below my waist and is marred with minor snags here and there with scattered stains from water droplets—time suspends the fabric of his. There's limited wear despite the age of his threads, however, his hands are another story. Scars on his thin skin cling to his bones without elasticity, and his knuckles are so thick his fingers cannot fully touch.

"This bench is new," he says. Short, tight, sweet. Not needing to finish or find the initial statement he was going to make, nor releasing anything personal.

With a nod, I gesture to the empty seat next to me. "I've wandered through most of this town and each time, I've found this spot to be my favorite."

"This is where I stand. There's a bench where I stand to look out at night." His words twist as if he's unsure who would have the audacity to place a bench in his standing space.

I peek over and catch his eyes studying the bench's placard, his brow creasing while he stares, lips moving without sound.

"This isn't your bench," he says. His brow softens and the side of his mouth lifts, showing off straight white teeth. He chuckles, but the laughs come out unsure.

"Do you think the owner would mind us sitting here?"

"I suppose it's late enough they'll not care, or even know." His eyes shift to look at me, searching back and forth.

A dog bark echoes across the openness of the small park. In concert, we turn and check over our shoulders. There's no being visible, offering one another a shrug as we rejoin our positions to resume conversation. A sailboat in the distance flicks on a light and the water glitters around the hull. More restless souls.

"I've never understood the idea of buying one of these things. They're all over town, a graveyard of memories socially acceptable to toot on." His eyebrows lift, and I swear a sparkle hit his eyes, then as fast as it came it fades, and he shakes his head. "Supposed someone would rather be remembered as a tree so they can provide fruit or shade, or as a beehive to help sustain the earth."

"Is that what you'd want? To be a beehive or a tree?" I watch as a figure moves about the sailboat in the distance.

"Seems a bench may last longer than a tree or a hive. If you're going for longevity, I'd go with the bench." He nods and clears his throat.

"What changed your mind?" I ask.

He heaves a deep sigh. "A tree has more risks. The tree may not take, it could get disease, and then you die again, the second time might even be more painful. People may break parts of you, or you could get cut down. All depends on where the tree is, but I don't think a tree would get this view either."

"Makes sense. The danger with the hive feels similar, though I do love the idea of the beehive. Protecting the earth and being a force to help new life grow. Such a tiny gesture with a massive impact."

"A hive wouldn't be bad. Much better than a gravestone. Gravestones are where sadness grows and laughter dies. I'd want people to not feel like they have to visit a fading stone and cry. On a bench you can laugh, cry, or simply be." He looks down at the bench and tilts his head, eyebrows twitching at one another. "Maybe both a bench and a hive. Only what if one of the bees stings someone at the park? The hive can't be in the park. You have to keep people safe."

"This means we're back down to a bench." My chest presses down and breathing is harder. The sadness that comes with discussing death shouldn't bother me. I've been around a lot of death in my life.

"Is that for anyone?" He gestures to the extra cup at my side.

The pressure leaves, releasing my lungs to reclaim a hesitant rhythm of breath, and my mouth draws to a smile. "It's hot chocolate—for you." I stare out at the grand houses across the water, wondering if anyone's noticed I come here each night.

"I'm not too thirsty, but I'd love company." His posture is strong, almost youthful despite the years worn on his face and a bit of the blankness in his dull eyes. "This is my favorite spot in town."

I nod and clasp the cup between my hands, bracing for a dip in the worn wood slats of the bench that never comes. He happily stretches his legs in front of him and leans forward, his hands clasping the front of the bench seat.

"When I was younger, I rode sculls on this river." His breath, unlike mine, fails to leave a single stream of fog in the air as he speaks.

"Do you remember a lot about when you were younger?" The stillness of the air settles around us and the quiet of the river hushes the wind from interfering in our conversation.

"Not too much." He shifts his jaw and keeps his gaze out to the river. "What about you? Do you remember a lot from when you were younger?"

I shake my head and swallow back the sludge of emotion pulling at my face and throat. "I never learned a lot. Other things I've accepted—been forced to pretend to accept that I'll never know."

"I'm not sure which is worse. Not remembering, or not knowing."

"Neither are better nor worse. They simply are."

He nods and nods. Seeming to forget where he was in the

conversation. "I don't want to burden a stranger, especially one who brought me hot chocolate. But when I saw you sitting here, I was worried because it's late and you're alone."

"I'm alone a lot."

"What about your family?"

Speaking slowly to myself, and then to him while I process how to answer what I'm tired of—people pitying me or having to come up with another off-handed response when they don't understand the pain of not knowing. "Mainly dead."

"Oh. That's a shame. Grief is hard."

I shift and keep my focus on the river, like answers or some magic potion will rise from it and soothe me. The river does center me. When I concentrate hard, it enchants my focus, and the rest of the world blurs awhile. Even when I'm walking up the main streets, I can sense it peeking through the alleyways at me like a good friend wondering when I'm going to come for a long visit.

"I lost my son when he was thirty." His vivid tone pulls to light. "He'd skip school to take out art books from the library, and they'd call me to let me know he was right here, where we're sitting. There was no bench then. I'd check on him from across the street and the back of his little head would move back and forth while he studied the pictures. He didn't know I knew, but he was happy and safe. Who was I to say no?" He removes his cap and resets it so it covers his pale eyes a little more. "My wife died a few months before him. He was suffering, and she couldn't watch him die before her. She stopped eating...and then was gone. And then he was gone." His voice fades and a gentle wind blows out where I'd imagine his breath to be.

"I lost my dad when he was thirty. My grandmother left us a few months before him—so I'm told. So the death certificates say."

"You don't remember?"

"I can't. I was too little." My heart beats so hard it feels bruised.

He stops, I can feel him thinking. Processing. I need him to find it or he'll disappear. I've rushed this moment before, and it's spooked him.

"You were a baby then?" His tongue clicks against the roof of his mouth and his eyes widen.

"Nearly a toddler." The bench creaks while I lean back, letting the rigid boards hug me.

When I look over at him, his mouth is moving through what looks like names. "Alice." His favorite aunt. "Lily." His late wife. He removes his hat, presses his fingers tight against the bridge of his nose and rocks forward, then back. His hand drops and he studies my face. Forward, then back. "Maya." One of his two granddaughters. He shakes his head, and the pain spanning his face is evident. "Baby Freya..."

Tears well, and the wait to open the conversation is over.

"Hi, Pop-pop." I'm nearly forty, but having him call me baby is what I need right now and my eyes sting of salt.

"Baby Freya. I'm sorry. I don't remember—"

"It's okay, I remember you."

With that, we both stare out at the river in silence again. Taking in the moment the way we do each night, taking in the bond we have, and letting the light above continue to warm our skin despite the patches of snow on frost-laden grass.

"Baby Freya." He taps his fingers on the bench as he mouths my name a second time, stitching it across his lips and reinforcing it in his forgetful mind. Perhaps it's not forgetful, but full of the long ago. Before my existence, the loss of our family, himself. I understand his desire to connect back, and wish I could peek at where he goes when he fades out.

We both pause, detaching from emotional soreness in our

own way. Him, likely to the past. Me, to my imagination, filling in what's unknown to me but trapped in his head. I'd have liked to picnic here, with him and them. In this very spot overlooking the undulating waves of the river on a cool summer day with juicy watermelon, sprawled out together on the quilt my grandmother made that I instead wrap myself in each night. I pretend to know their laughs, their humor and quirks. Their preference for a little salt on the watermelon and a special dusting of ground fresh mint from his overgrown herb garden. Pretending to know and creating my own history only pushes out the hollowness for so long. Then part of me feels lost again. Here, he and I are lost together with the mediocre comfort a cold bench offers.

"Do you—you haven't touched your hot cocoa." I slide my tongue across the back of my teeth, swallowing the questions I want to ask.

"Yeah, I'm okay." He blankly stares out towards the boat.

Sadness drips from his slumped posture.

A long breath fills my chest and the wind tickles at my neck.

"Your face is...eyes are hers and his, but you were a child..." The wheels in his head are spinning, big gaps of time pass between words and his eyes twitch while he concentrates on mine. "If it weren't for the eyes..."

"I like my eyes." My tiny genetic tie to the people I don't know. He can't answer my questions, I know this. I like to believe his head protects him from more pain, blocking out the hurt. He'll forever know me as a child, but at least I know in the depths of his mind he knows me and I know him. That if nothing else, we're bonded by memories. We're distant, existing in our fullest capacity at very different places in time.

"Eyes are good, their eyes were bad." He leans back, his fingers tugging the edge of the bench, stretching his arms. "Bad

isn't the right word. They weren't evil or ugly. Their eyes are...
were...beautiful... they couldn't see a lick without their glasses,
though." He chuckles under his breath. "I'd move their glasses,
not too far, but far enough to tease them. Enough to hear them
say my name with a harmonious loving groan at a morsel of
family humor...I miss the whine, the jokes...the house is so
quiet...everything is so hushed..." His fingers release from the
front of the bench and he slumps back, rubbing his ring. "You
don't want to hear about this, Baby Freya."

"I'm here for the company, and to listen." My heart
squeezes, hoping he'll share more, but remaining steadfast on
the outside so as not to scare him off or confuse him. "Your hot
cocoa is getting cold."

"Maybe tomorrow. Do you want to meet again tomorrow? I
know we haven't seen each other in so long, and I don't want to
be greedy about your time. But this was so nice, sitting on this
bench. Being here with you."

I suck in the air, letting it coat my dry mouth. "I'll come
tomorrow."

"Oh." His gaze falls to the ground.

"What's wrong?"

"I'm worried. What if you come, and I...I miss you? Or..."

"You'll remember," I say. "I'll bring you a hot cocoa."

His gaze changes to my face with bright sparkles in his
eyes. "The diner has the best hot cocoa." His tone drops to a
cheerful whisper. "If you ask nicely, they'll even add raspberry,
makes it delicious."

"Sounds delicious. I'll be sure to ask them tomorrow." I sip
the last bit of my cold drink, letting the raspberry linger on my
tongue before swallowing.

He checks over his shoulder and looks at my face. "You
shouldn't walk home alone."

"I can drop you off at your house on my way, this way we

can spend a little more time together." I stand and lift the extra cup from the bench.

He points out the trash can to the side of someone else's memorial tree, done up with a small plaque and a mishmash of purple and green graffiti crochet up the trunk. "I'm adding bad outfits to the reasons for not wanting a memorial tree."

Silent chuckles burst from my chest. I don't want to wake or startle anyone else who is wandering tonight. I nod over to the can, and he follows me while I throw out our cups.

His footsteps are silent, but I can feel him drifting from me as I walk. When I turn, he's standing, hand on the front of his cap, looking back at the bench.

"You bought the bench." His voice trembles.

"The best spot in town needed somewhere to sit." I swallow down at the dry thickening in my throat. "We should get you home."

Three blocks later, we take a sharp right onto his street. On the last block, both of our steps grow slow, savoring the company, knowing our time together is winding out.

"Hot cocoa tomorrow on our bench." He's repeating, reinforcing, but I know what's to come.

"I'll be ready." My fingers fidget with the cold keys in my pocket on one side, and the smooth surface of my phone on the other. It's one way to stop myself from trying to hug him, to keep myself from breaking down and crying in the street late at night. Fighting the raw emotional soreness growing in me while I work on lifting my gentle smile is a standard play in my battle of eternal mourning.

He waves at me before disappearing through the amber colored door. Not a single light goes on, nor as much as a flicker of a curtain. The numbness infiltrating my body isn't from the cold or sadness. Rather, it's the way I've learned to parse processing through my unknown. The streets here offer comfort. They've memorized his steps. My energy lives here now like theirs and every other person who's walked through like Alice, Lilly, and Dad. I take comfort in knowing one day in the future someone may gain the same comfort that I too walked these streets.

The air pauses as if cradling me in a held breath on the three blocks it takes to get home. I could've bought the house he lived in, or the one three doors down his parents lived in. But even for me, that'd be a little too much. That house is his space. My house is mine. The bench is ours.

The lights are on in the living room when I get home and I walk through the house as quiet as I can to the bedroom to find my husband hugging my pillow while he waits for me. The house is toasty and a simple glance at his sweet face washes away my numbness with loving warmth. I kiss his forehead and curl up with him, tugging up on the well-loved quilt.

"Was he there?" my husband whispers.

"On time, like always." I know he doesn't understand or believe what happens each night. But for me, he lets me have the moments. He doesn't make comments about the interactions not being real, or my family being gone, or the answers I'll never have.

The bench was, in large part, his idea. Less cold or intense than gravestones long overdue for purchase, and a place I've connected to through other people's memories.

He pulls me between him and the pillow, kissing my shoulder and wrapping his arm tightly around my waist. He waits for me here each night, never questioning why I need the late night walk to clear my head. Nor my insistence on buying two hot chocolates and sitting by myself on the memorial bench night after night for the past three years.

We have ice cream and laughter with our girls on that bench in the summer. Picnics with bubbles in the spring.

Together we work to fill the air with life and love to leave our own positive imprint in the ground while remembering the energy of my family that once sparkled there. We sit there sometimes watching the rowers or reading quietly. Picking dandelions to make tiny bracelets—but Pop-pop only wanders at night. I like to imagine I'll turn around one bright day sitting on the bench, and he'll be watching me the way he watched my dad. He'll be there again tomorrow night, and so will I, with two drinks.

He'll remember me.

BEGIN AGAIN

IBTISAM SHAHBAZ

Her: Age had weathered his face. Where sunkissed spots once lay, now rested wrinkles of time. Worn leather boots had traveled cities it seemed, marred by scraped and soil. As the distance enclosed between them, his footsteps became in tune with hers; a metronome to her fastening pulse.

Him: She flowed with an ease of an old soul. Luscious black hair had faded to gray, the luster of a novel spirit adding its own shine. A maroon scarf framed her face, entwining her with poise. Crow lines had replaced her once kohl-lined eyes. But she had never needed the kajal. Her thick lashes knew the darkness surrounding the moon. A contrast hinting at an ethereal presence, one high in the sky and deep in her bones. I had never met eyes like that; a doorway to a sunken well, a prison, or an escape. Sometimes, that darkness, sent something back.

The slightest sliver of curiosity, shrouded by a bashful tilt. Her lashes lowered again as she fiddled aimlessly with the threads of her scarf. I guess some things never change.

Her: Age had made him finer. A pressed blazer, woven with navy hues. Was it a woman's touch? He was pieced

233

together from head to toe. Weary with the time that had passed, but all the wiser. His shoulders were dipped forward, strained from a weight that had compiled since we had last met. Or perhaps it was hidden underneath, a river held together by a mental dam. Yet, when I lifted my eyes to meet his, I saw it there. The magma burning inside. The never-ending flame fueling him, melting my surroundings as we spoke. And I was totally, utterly mesmerized. I could only see that flame.

Him: Meeting the fullness of her gaze was to become the ink that spilled onto parchment. Realizing the utter permanence of the stain you have found yourself in. The weary had fallen. The tether broke. The only thing keeping me rooted to reality was her name, repeated in silence under my breath.

Her: I saw life writhing inside him.

I had been so, spent. So, exhausted. For years, repeating the one day. Everything would fade to grey by noon. But now in front of me, I saw the very spirit of life exemplified. Glowing, burning, and writhing. We were feet apart, but the heat from his body I could feel on the crevices of my fingerprint. With that blaze, my pain was burning from the edges - the pages of my past set alight by a touch.

His smile caressed something broken inside me.

It shone on the emptiness and resentments, the past and the would-have-beens.

The aversion disappeared—healed—and suddenly emotion was pooling out of me, laced with molten gold. How empty I had been and how quickly, born anew. His love was not just enough, it was infinite. It baptized me with a single embrace. I could not register how dissociated I had been; emotion itself felt so foreign. To feel anything at all. I had forgotten what is was like to miss. Feelings held together under a placated facade. Yet here I was now, passion unfurling faster than Monstera leaves. And it was all channeling from my sun.

Him: That half smile was my undoing. How could someone be so soft in a sharp second? That one almost grin would be enough. With that memory, I could dream another decade. But she was here. We were here. This was real. My hand reached for hers, brushing supple skin as fear devoured my receding confidence. Fear warned me of loss, but I could sense the power of faith above. How could one ever look away?

Her: I inched closer. This battled heart. How many days to waste? How many lovers to bite the dust? Regret, remorse and yet, here we were still. Hope. Monsieur Hope.

My beloved had returned.

Him: I let my apprehension escape as she stepped into the safety of my arms. Her threaded scarf tangled with silvering hair, both flickering in the breeze. For her, for this, I would wait a thousand times over.

Lovers: So, there they stood, time of no relevance or relative. For mornings that had never began, and evenings spent in a lonesome trance. Fate could be cruel, but self-inflicted misery had been worse.

But still, there in the chambers of his heart, had stood an eternal flame. One he tended at dusk, her name is his morning prayers. On her moonless nights, he was a novel laid open at her desk. Reading in-between the intervals of conversations, transporting to her favorite story; theirs.

But here they were. In life and in flesh. Standing as one. Chapters of a shared past leaking into each other, held together by a love stronger than a bookbinder's glue. In silence, a vow made to never let it be lost again.

RESPITE

JENNIFER CINGUINA

The cherry red nail polish on my toes popped against the cedar floor of the outdoor shower. My wet, sandy hair plastered my cheeks and chin, water dripping from the tips and polka-dotting the wood floor. Though dusk approached, the sun was still overhead, and I lifted my face to it, squinting, feeling safe in this solitary small space.

I was protected on all sides from everyone who needed me to be a wife, mother, daughter, sister, friend. From schedules, carpools, class projects, art lessons and dance classes. From grocery shopping, the orthodontist, overdue library books. From worrying about my aging parents, about saving for my daughters' college. From wondering about mistakes, about regrets.

Throughout the day, rhythmic waves of the Atlantic struck the seashore, seagulls squawked. Small plastic shovels scraped the densely packed sand. Little feet pounded the seashore as kids ran in and out of the water's edge. Now, stillness settled over the block, interrupted only by an occasional backyard gate squeaking open or a neighbor snapping a towel before hanging it on the line to dry.

In this tiny fortress, there was only room for me, water, sun, and air. And in the absence of everything else, there was bandwidth for my own musings. What surfaced, like a riptide or strong undertow, was unexpected.

Fragrant cedar filled my lungs, engulfed me like a freshly pressed white cotton blouse.

I opened the tap fully, hoping the water would warm up faster that way, and hung my towel on a silver hook. On the small corner shelf, I placed a bar of soap, shampoo, and a bottle of Bud Light Lime.

I tested the water with my left hand. "Ouch, waaaaaay too hot," I said aloud. I adjusted the tap. While I waited for the water temperature to cool, I stood aside and reached for my beer.

I'm not a drinker. Full-bodied sauvignon, supple pinot noir, rich chardonnay, Russian vodka, Tennessee whiskey, Southern bourbon—all of it—wasted on me. I never understood the allure. Red wine made my tongue feel hairy. Scotch burned the back of my throat. But a cold beer in an outdoor shower in the summer at dusk after a day at the beach? Perfection. The smooth swallows eased the sting of sunburn beneath the grimy residue of sweat and suntan lotion.

According to my husband, I liked bad beer. "Ew," he said, grimacing after a sip of my Bud Light Lime once. "Reminds me of apple juice." Precisely why I liked it. It tasted like childhood.

I tilted my head back and took a long drink. The light amber liquid blended seamlessly with the sinking sun.

I stuck my left foot into the water's path to test the temperature and when I realized it was just right, I returned my beer to the shelf, and stepped directly into the shower's stream. Warmth surrounded me.

I grabbed the hem of my tankini top and hoisted it over my head then lowered the bottom of my suit, caught it on my big toe and tossed it into the air, catching it with my hand, the way my five-year-old used to change her princess underwear in the morning. At an earlier point in my life, I would have ensured there was no sightline to my naked body outside in the shower. But heck, as a 43-year-old mother of three I'd be flattered if someone considered my naked body worthy of gawking. I rinsed my suit and swung it over the shower door.

Water flowed from my scalp to the sandy spaces between my toes. It was impossible to trace one rivulet of water the full pathway down my body, but I tried. Some fell off my chin. Others escaped between my breasts or were trapped in my belly button. Many made a sharp turn at my hips, where I could feel them cascading down the small of my back.

Sand was everywhere. Across my ribs. Between the creases of my elbow. In my ear. I turned my back to the sun, faced the shower, let the water rinse it all away, broken bits of shells and the lone piece of seaweed, gone. I watched the water's own force remove what was left of my day at the beach.

Slowly, the water's warmth spread from my face to my chest, around my torso and down my thighs, as if the sun were acknowledging me—all of me—establishing my place on Earth. Validation from the universe. Relief inundated me. I was a woman, and I embraced her. In this moment, I belonged to myself.

As I took another sip of beer, I held it in my mouth, not allowing myself to swallow, my eyes zeroed in on the single water droplet suspended in the silken symmetry of a spiderweb in the corner of my cedar retreat. I stooped closer and water pounded my back. The droplet quivered, as if holding on for dear life. It mesmerized me. Two molecules of hydrogen and one molecule of carbon hanging in the balance of the geometrical patterns built instinctively by a spider. Both nature's creations, but somehow out of sync. Among the web's silken threads, the droplet continued to quiver—perhaps a silent request for support? Then, without warning, the droplet fell from the web's perch. Gone. Immediately undecipherable from the rest of the water in my Atlantic hideaway, and no sign that it had ever existed on the spiderweb—no matter how momentarily—in its simple beauty. Two molecules of hydrogen and one molecule of oxygen. Now it mixed with millions of droplets, finding its way out of the shower. I stood, my captivation with the web's beauty suddenly broken. I swallowed my beer and, with the bottle, swiped at the web, destroying it.

As I lathered my hair with shampoo, grains of sand trapped in my scalp accumulated beneath my fingernails. Soap slid down my back and flowed out the side of the shower and down the walkway. Suds pooled around my feet, like they didn't want to leave.

Me neither.

Being alone didn't conjure loneliness for me. It was invigorating, because, in these moments, I emptied my mind of everything the world constantly tried to stuff inside it, like a tangled ball of yarn. And I'm constantly pawing at it, toiling over it, trying to find the loose end so I can unwind it, untangle it, look at it linearly and make sense of it. But this ball of yarn only exists on the other side of the shower door. Here, I am knot-free. Unwound.

I lathered my hands with soap and wondered how long I'd been in the shower. Fifteen minutes? This seashore house was filled with my husband and daughters, my parents and siblings and nieces and nephews, and thankfully, no one had discovered me missing yet. It was only a matter of time. If I'd been at home, someone would have knocked on the door by now looking for a ride or a snack.

I wrung my hands together. On the ring finger of my left hand, beneath my fingernail on the right side was the sizable bump Mrs. Grant had promised me in second grade would appear if I didn't change my pencil grip. When I've been writing a lot, it swells. I smiled. Proof of a commitment I'd made to myself to start writing again. I'd only ever been encouraged to get married, then, have babies, and while those dreams fulfilled me, something nagged at me, something I couldn't define. Outside, it was unfocused and intangible, but, in here, dreams were crystal clear. The bump on my finger would never be ugly to me.

I rubbed the bar of soap across my ribs and down to my belly button, which, like me, never returned to its old self after giving birth. The stretched skin around my new navel created wrinkles that still encircle it, much the way a child draws a circle for the sun and yellow lines all around to signify rays of sunlight.

As I stand back up, I can see the line from my bathing suit where I'd gotten too much sun today. "That's going to hurt later," I say aloud.

I closed the tap, grabbed the towel, and dried off. As I took the last swallows of my beer, in the distance, I heard the *smack, smack* of little flip flops growing closer. Time was up. I wrapped the towel around me and picked up my soap, shampoo, and empty beer bottle. I unlocked the door, and the smell of warming charcoals hit me.

"Mom?" Amy was calling me.

"Here I am, Amy," I said.

Amy rounded the corner of the house, donned in her kitty pajamas. Her hair was still damp from her shower.

"Mommy, where were you?" she asked. She sounded panicked. "I couldn't find you."

Smiling, I walked up and kissed the top of her head. Mmmmm, baby shampoo.

"Right here, Amy," I replied. I inhaled deeply, filling my lungs completely. "I've been right here the whole time."

THE AUDITION

BRITTANY BELL

My sister's death was an accident, but I killed her just the same. I remember finding her facedown in the creek that ran behind our house. We lived in farm country, and one local newspaper served the entire county. "It's a fucking tragedy," the police officer who was asked for a comment by the sole reporter covering the incident said.

Everyone asked me what had happened, but all I could remember were her blonde head and slender limbs forming the five points of a fallen star and the panic that rose in my throat. I was told that I had retched at the scene and left a trail of vomit as I ran through the field separating the creek from our house.

My stoic father became even more withdrawn after the accident, although he dutifully attended every science fair and band performance, standing in the back without speaking or smiling. The only reason I knew what his voice sounded like was from him saying, "Pass the salt" at our silent family dinners, where I purposefully placed the saltshaker out of his reach when I set the table, looking forward to this meager exchange each night.

My mother spent entire days after the accident sleeping in my sister's bed, burying her face in the pillow where my sister used to lay her head, furiously wrapping the comforter around herself as if to wrap herself in my sister. One day I came home from school and found my mother crying in a heap at the bottom of the stairs. I raced up and found the contents of my sister's room neatly packed into cardboard moving boxes. My father was standing on a stool and painting over the daisy wallpaper with long brushstrokes. At the time, I tucked this episode away as evidence of his cruelty, but now I understand that he thought it would help.

My parents were too sad to bicker. Grief bound them together. They did not speak during the day, but at night they clung to one another, their bedroom bordered by their dead daughter's room on one side and her murderer's room (*mine*) on the other.

Amy's death went everywhere we did. People in Walmart would turn away when they saw us, pushing their carts in the other direction as if tragedy were contagious. They spoke about us in whispers. I imagined they were saying, *That's him. That's the boy who killed his sister.*

I never tried to take my own life because I was already responsible for one death and did not want three more bodies on my hands. Losing another child would have killed my mother. I knew that my father was the kind of person who would not hesitate to swallow the barrel of a gun. A considerate man who hated to inconvenience anyone, he would carry it out next to the creek when it was raining so that some of the mess would wash away.

As time passed, we all found ways to cope. My father started making and selling furniture to summer tourists who frequented the Catskills. My mother began knitting caps for premature babies and took them to the hospital in Oneonta.

She volunteered in the special care nursery twice per month, cuddling the babies so their mothers could go home and shower or rest. She was someone who understood the fragility of life.

My parents couldn't afford a child psychologist so they took me to a local Baptist preacher for counseling. Pastor Ricky neither helped me remember the circumstances of Amy's death nor did he bring me a sense of peace, but he did have an old mahogany upright piano sitting in the foyer outside of his office. The second or third time my mother and I went me to see Pastor Rick, he asked us to wait until he finished a phone call with a parishioner. My mother sat in one of two folding chairs that flanked either side of his office, but I sat on the piano bench.

After a few minutes I grew restless and spun around to face the piano, spreading my fingers out onto the cold, white keys and curving them slightly. I extended my index finger to tap one of the black keys without emitting any sound. I looked down at the three pedals and pressed one with my foot, feeling a slight vibration. Next I pressed down on a white key, which made a pleasant sound and reminded me of a sunny day. I moved to the right and pressed a key, finding it was high pitched like someone crying out in pain. A key all the way down on the left was deep and low like my sadness.

"Benny, please stop," my mother said. "The Pastor is on the phone."

Pastor Rick's door opened. He smiled. "That's quite all right. Do you know how to play?"

I shook my head no.

"I'm afraid music isn't my department, but Sally, my wife, plays beautifully. I'm sure she wouldn't mind giving you some lessons."

Pastor Rick's wife smelled like mothballs and had holes in her sweaters, but I liked her. Sometimes it hurt when Sally corrected my posture by poking me with a pencil or stomped her foot on mine to help me find the tempo, but she was patient and encouraging. She was the kind of teacher who could not hide her excitement when I finally mastered something new. She talked too much, but I found comfort in the sounds of her words and the piano notes swirling around the room, filling the silent spaces of my life. I learned that lightly tapping my fingers over the keys in legato play resulted in smooth, connected notes that sounded like springtime, while winter could be brought on simply by moving an octave lower and pressing the keys harder.

After a few months my father surprised me by purchasing a secondhand piano at an estate sale. He left the house one morning without telling me where he was going and returned with a small upright piano sitting in the bed of his pickup truck. Pastor Rick and another man I didn't know helped him move it into the house using a four-wheel dolly. My mother made lemonade, and everyone sang along as I played a song. It was the only truly happy day we had as a family after Amy's death.

I practiced every day, learning to let the weight of my arms push the keys down, allowing the notes to be loud and even. I began to relax my wrists and play with my entire upper body. I learned how to play the piano like a child learns to read, the initial striking of notes like individual letter sounds. Over time, I began to play groups of notes like words that finally evolved into phrases that formed musical sentences.

I continued weekly lessons with Sally. I began having difficulty with signatures outside what is often called common time once we moved on to more complex pieces. She brought a metronome to practice one day. It was a small, black piece of wood with a pendulum to keep time. "At first, we'll slow down this piece to help you learn it, and then we can use the metronome to help you speed it up." She turned the winding key clockwise slowly and moved the sliding weight, pulling the beat selector and finally unhooking the pendulum.

The metronome began clicking. Tick. Tick. Tick. "Please begin," Sally said, gesturing to the sheet music in front of me.

Tick. Tick. Tick.

It sounded like a clock or a heartbeat getting louder. My fingers stiffened up on the keys.

Tick. Tick. Tick.

A familiar panic rose up in my throat. My lungs filled with air that could not escape. *Amy.* I attempted to stand, but my gelatin legs would not allow it. I crumpled to the floor, my back sliding down the rigid piano bench. I vomited on the tan linoleum, tears streaming down my face. Sally turned off the metronome by rehooking the pendulum. She kneeled down beside me and took me in her arms, rocking me back and forth. "Shh, it's okay. It's all right."

"I loved Amy, but we fought sometimes," I said between sobs. "How do I know we weren't having an argument?" I paused for a moment, trying to catch my breath. "How do I know I didn't push her?"

After my breathing slowed down and the tears stopped flowing, Sally put her hand under my chin and lifted it up. "Listen to me," she said. "Music will set you free."

I nodded, not fully grasping what she was trying to tell me, yet fully understanding that I had to escape the whispers in Walmart and the rushing of the creek that scolded me every time I stepped outside. I practiced harder and longer.

Then, ten years later, I found myself sitting at a piano in New York City on an unseasonably warm day in early March about to audition for Juilliard.

As I waited for the signal to begin, I squeezed my eyes shut and saw my eight-year-old self stepping out of bed. I could see my toes touching the worn throw rug on the floor, then my legs, and finally all of me came into focus.

A voice said, "Please begin." My fingers were frozen on the keys. I fluttered my eyes open and shut, this time watching eight-year-old me descend the staircase that led into the kitchen. Intuitively, I knew I was seeing myself on the morning that Amy died. If I just let the memories come, I would know what happened.

The voice repeated, "Please begin."

"I'm sorry," I said, clearing my throat. I got up from the bench as if I had not just spent the previous ten years working to earn this opportunity. I fled the room, the door slamming behind me. I ran out onto the New York City Street and headed south.

I made two rights and a left. Another right took me to Broadway. It was only my second time in Manhattan. The other time had been a family trip to see the tree at Rockefeller Center when Amy and I were small. I could still picture the immense tree with its twinkling crystal star on top. Amy hadn't been able to take her eyes off the sunken rink, a stream of skaters moving in concentric circles.

I felt for my phone and took it out of my pocket, comforted for a fleeting moment by its familiar glow and feeling in my cupped hand. I brought up the map and decided to make a left on West 50th Street. A quick right brought me to Rockefeller Center. I remained on the street level, looking down at the lower plaza. The scene looked different than it had that day over ten years before. The tree had been taken down for the season, and there were just a few skaters circling the rink. The crowd of tourists posing for pictures had been replaced by people in suits ferrying laptop bags and trays of styrofoam coffee cups across the plaza. I focused on the statue of Prometheus sitting in a fountain in the background, an image that felt familiar from watching the televised Christmas tree lighting with my mother every year.

As I watched the jets of pristine water spurt into the air surrounding the statue, I couldn't help but think how different this water was from the creek. The creek was murky and brown. Its bed was rocky and marked with pebbles. A series of flat stone fragments in one section of the creek made a decent footpath that Amy and I used to attempt to traverse without falling. The creek was surrounded by overhanging trees, which offered us shade on hot summer days and kept the water brisk and cool.

I tried to conjure the feeling I'd experienced sitting down on the piano bench during the audition. I closed my eyes and tried to visualize what Amy must have looked like when I sat down to eat breakfast with her that morning, as we did every morning, but I just couldn't do it. I still couldn't remember anything that happened after waking up that morning to the time I found her, except the new images of my feet touching the threadbare throw rug on the floor next to my bed and going down the staircase. Why had the memories come so easily and stopped so suddenly?

That's when I realized I never should have left the audition and that the answers weren't located in a gilded cast bronze sculpture or being inscribed by skates on an icy rink. I ran back to Juilliard, dodging past street vendors and sprinting through crosswalks. The audition room was empty. I sat down at the piano and began to play. As I played, the memories came flooding back.

I recalled asking our mother to go play at the creek, which we did often that summer. She said yes and gave us the usual warning to stay on our property and stay together. We went off. At first we gathered flat, round stones to skip. Amy still didn't know how to get them to bounce off the water. Her stones sunk right to the bottom so she'd quickly lost interest. Amy had brought a red rubber ball with her, one of those quarter machine prizes. She made a game of tossing the ball in the creek, letting it bob along the surface for a second or two before scooping it back up. At some point I made her put it back in her pocket, and we continued walking. We approached the neighbor's property line, so we turned back towards our house. That's when Amy realized that she didn't have her ball.

I squeezed my eyes shut because I knew I was close to remembering everything I ever would about that day. I was about to experience the last memory I'd ever have of Amy. I hoped that it wasn't entirely my fault.

"Stay right here," I told Amy, "I'll go look for it." I had told her to stay, knowing we were too far from home and that I'd be able to find it faster by myself. I retraced our steps, scanning the surface of the creek for a red ball bobbing up and down. I also looked along the sides of the creek in case she'd dropped it in the dirt. I couldn't find it. Fearing I'd been away too long, I hurried back to where I'd left her. That's when I saw her face-down in the water, her arms and legs suspended.

My fingers played the final note of my piece, and I was startled by the sound of clapping. I looked up and saw one member of the audition panel standing there. "Oh, I didn't even know you were there," I said. "I'm sorry about leaving before."

"Cold feet?" he asked, peeling off his tweed jacket and sitting down.

"No, I never get nervous when I play, but sometimes I can't stop thinking," I said. "Anyway, I'm sorry for wasting your time."

"Where are you going?" he asked. "Sit down and play."

"But I walked out in the middle of a Juilliard audition," I said.

"I'm well aware. You certainly won't be the last." He paused and half-smiled. "But you are the first to come back."

As I placed my fingers on the cold piano keys, the memories continued flowing. Amy, facedown in the creek. My sister, the fallen star. The sound of my mother's knitting needles clicking together. My father saying, "Pass the salt." The way he communicated he was proud of me after I executed a difficult piano solo by cupping his hand on my shoulder, refusing to look me in the eye. The ticking of Sally's metronome. All of these things had led me to that moment at Juilliard.

I began to play.

NEVER ENOUGH

CAROLINE SHANNON DAVENPORT

F unny, the things I never noticed about this man—thought I, sitting across from him, staring at him—things that were starting to penetrate my consciousness. We were in my uncle's delicious aroma-smelling kitchen—my Uncle Harald, the fine art gallery owner, college renowned literary professor and gourmet chef—as we waited for Uncle's cooking extravaganza of a dinner to be ready. A gastronomist's treat to come to be certain. After a busy day, the three of us are in for a quiet supper. Me, visiting Uncle in this college and artistic-centered town.

Glancing over to Uncle's friend, I decided it was a fair oversight of what I hadn't noticed. Considering the dazzle of his friend's usual surroundings, it was but a small wonder. He had appeared bland in comparison. A big man, yet shallow of complexion, and although red of hair, it was the color that resembled desert sand—dusty looking, a tone that blended with the skin so readily as to barely leave a distinction. Next to all those golds and all that brilliance in that house of finery of his, he had been a fade-out.

In my mind, the only things that stood out had been those horn-rimmed glasses he wore and that well-modulated voice. That voice that had me now listening with an attentive ear and realizing how much I liked its sound. Even more, how much I liked its content. He had a way of speaking so as to place each word in a sequence of tone and meaning to lead one up to a point as if by way of a horse-drawn carriage down a keenly manicured lane. The trip was such a delight that one was in no hurry to get to the destination.

A real storyteller. Better yet, a fascinating person, to be sure. Not that I hadn't an inkling, but as I said, my attention had been diverted elsewhere. Just earlier in the day, over some strong and hearty Bloody Marys with cold shrimp nibbles for chasers, we were at his house to view the unpacking of a shipment of priceless antique china from China. And now and then, ripping my eyes off the prize as he and his mother unwrapped each piece, I had watched him with more than a little inquisitiveness as he relished in his acquisition of rarity, thinking, "I'll get to you later."

This one was not one of those types you gave a quick once over. Of that, I was sure. A plum to save for a more appropriate time. Fifty-something was my guess. But Roth Jennings was not one you would think to classify by age. I couldn't imagine him being old. But then, I couldn't imagine him being young, either. It seemed to me that he had probably been old the day he was born. Wise, this one. A cross between a hawk and an owl. At least, when it pertained to others ... By profession an antique shop owner and dealer, *par excellence*, and also occasionally, a professor of art history. But a private collector first. A true connoisseur. A scholar. A world traveler. Brilliant. Charming. Elegant. And most sophisticated.

Then, there were other assorted facts of interest. Just enough to whet the palate. Never been married. Lived with his mother. Who, I might digress to tell you, struck me as some interesting specimen herself. Although, at least in her eighties, she had the appearance of one mighty strong lady: long gray hair, tall and large-boned with a mind like a whip. And a tongue that could likely crack just as fast if given the altercation. One got the impression that, like her son, she had eyes that ran a computer scan on you the first time they set sight. He and she—no difference there. Shrewd. These people were masters. And one as gracious as the other. Which, perhaps, had to do with why these robust, strong-bodied, and minded people didn't appear at all out of place among all these extremely delicate oriental and French furnishings. Furnishings so exquisite as to rival anything anywhere. Museum pieces, of which they were worldwide procurers.. The sort of quality one feels inclined to view with a reverence akin to saintliness.

And in, no less, an equally magnificent setting. A home with rooms and ceilings fit for a king's palace adorned with decorative moldings of scallops and cherubs and shells. Walls and tapestries of lords and ladies in their storybook depiction of riches and finery and flora and fauna of gardens of color ablaze. Floors of gleaming wood and polished marble left to peek from beneath the cushiony lushness of rugs of velvet beauty aflame with efflorescent wonder. Brocade and silk on window seats and pillows and chairs. Figurines of china and porcelain and bisque. Pillboxes and snuff boxes and ornaments encrusted with diamonds and jewels. And the glint of gold and silver everywhere. If that wasn't enough, crystal dripping from chandeliers and compotes and chalices to catch and shatter the eye to the point of vertigo. It was overwhelming. Standing in the middle of a room, I had felt faint with the glory of it. Treasures! And one object as beautiful as the next. It was almost too much gathered under one roof for the mind to comprehend.

Lord, I thought, *why would there be any reason to go on collecting? What more*
could anyone possibly want? It would seem almost redundant. Piggish! Almost childish!

But things are not usually as they seem, are they? Or are they?

So, as you can tell, the seeds had been planted earlier in the day. Now, with no distractions after finishing a scrumptious meal, mellow and thoughtful from a glass of wine, intrigue was on the rise as I listened to my Uncle and Roth discussing the shipment of china Roth had managed to capture—snag—with all its exclusiveness. Uncle was heaping his admiration on Roth for his expertise in pulling off such an endeavor.

What was Roth about? I wanted to know. How had all this acquisition started? The collecting? Not as I imagined, as it turned out. So much for my supposition of inherited wealth and aristocratic background.

"Actually," he said, "I grew up with a few antiques, but my father's friend had a shop. He was an older man and had no kids. He knew the good stuff. I was curious and fascinated by his stories of how and where things were made. He taught me. I was about eight. He took me to some estate sales at old farmhouses in the area. I watched the dealers haggle. They would grab everything, trying to be first at getting the best. And the best deal. Haggle over the price.

"Anyway, I learned what they liked. What they collected and sold. What maybe I could sell to them? One guy bought up all the antique bottles. So I started knocking on doors asking housewives if they had old bottles, anything old. I suppose, a small kid ... I started carting all sorts of things home with my bike and a wagon, sticking them out in an old barn we never used or up under the attic eaves where my family didn't go. It was fun knowing I could get things that even the dealers would have coveted but couldn't get. I could get it all!"

"What did your parents think," I asked.

"Oh, my parents never paid much mind, he laughed. "Daddy was always involved in some new venture. Most didn't pan out. He lost more than he ever amassed. Including money. Mother was the college librarian, and even though—and while —she was worrying about Daddy and his shenanigans and his bad heart, he died young. She was into her books. Which is where I learned to look things up—antiques, vintage. Some of what I got was covered with years of grime, brought from the old countries and stored away in garages and sheds, that the housewives let me paw through. Often, just let me have whatever I found. My parents just thought it was junk—old junk. Some was. It wasn't until later they paid attention.

"While I was away at college, I got a call from my younger sister. Mother was dying and Daddy was broke. What had happened was Daddy had invested everything in raising quail, and they all died from one of those dreaded diseases sweeping the country. Mother needed an operation to save her life. Daddy didn't have the money. Never held on to anything. But I had," Roth said with a wry smile, then continued.

"So I came home and started dragging things out of the barn and attic, polishing, cleaning. Ran a big ad in the papers. We sold for the entire weekend, got my sister and friends to help. From sunup to sundown. Then, the following week, I ran around the countryside and picked up everything I could lay my hands on. I knew where all the good caches were. I had been to every house in the county since a kid. Had another sale. Mother got her operation, and I paid off the debts."

"That was the start so many years ago. Now, I don't know. I like to get there first. Can't let anything slip away. I just have to have whatever I see ..."

SCHMEARED REPUTATION

GARY ZENKER

I'm sitting in my parked car with my camera lens pointed at the second floor window on the east side. From where I sit, there's a pretty good visual whenever he walks near the window.

I'm waiting for the money shot, one of him in the place he shouldn't be, doing the thing he shouldn't be doing, on the day he said he was someplace else. It's like the triple lutz of detecting. If you're the kind of schmuck that mixes metaphors. I'm not.

The target, one Sidney Goldfarb, has a wife who believes he's cheating. All indications say she's probably right. But at $250 a day plus expenses, I don't have a horse in this race. I get paid either way.

Penny Jill Goldfarb picked me specifically for this gig. I remember her visit to my office.

"So you're the big detective? The one who helped out Selma last year?" I put down my chopsticks. I always eat my Chinese with chopsticks. Otherwise you may as well eat a pastrami with mayo. They're both a crime against nature ... and God's law on being kosher.

"So what can I do for you Ms...."

"Mrs. Mrs. Penny Goldfarb."

"I think he's cheating on me," she explained and went into details. I pretended to listen while I mentally calculated whether my account would be overdrawn after the office rent check cleared.

"New suits," she said as I focused back on her words. "Nice ones. Like he doesn't have a closet full already." I looked at her Louis Vuitton designer purse on my desk, then down at her Jimmy Chu flats. Then up again at her Dr. Ira Finestein double D chest. First class work.

"He's a big man at the synagogue. President of the Brotherhood. We have seats up front with our name on the plaques. But we don't use them much. Anymore. Together." She had money and position. I was thinking about a very specific position when she spoke up again.

"I need someone I can trust to follow him and find the truth. I'll pay you well. If I can trust you."

And that's why I'm here in a car, two hours before sundown, exactly one week after Rosh Hashanah when Sidney prayed to atone for his past year's sins. Now, I guess, he's planning new ones for the new year.

Finally, he approaches the window and the picture I've been waiting for presents itself. I take it. And another. And another.

He's cheating, but the details are a surprise. He's got something on the side, all right. It looks like three sides from here. I'm not a guy easily surprised. I think about the implications and realize that if I were another man, these photos would be my retirement fund. An annuity of cash.

But no. I was hired for a job—I do the job. Folks are more likely to seek a Jew lawyer or Yid doctor than a sha-bbat shamus, but here I am. There's no doctor's payday, but it's an all cash business. Kind seeks kind, even if I am a more sinning than Synagogue kind of a Jew.

I carefully stow my gear and drive back to the office. It's just past sundown, but my Shiksa assistant, Sharon, is still there. I drop the photo card on her desk and ask her to print out 8 x 10s to show the detail. "Don't forget the date and time stamp," I tell her.

"Another old guy trying desperately to stay young by burrowing between some girl's legs?" she questioned in her southern drawl, which makes it sound all the dirtier.

"He's more cheesy than cheater," I tell her and leave it at that. I call the Mrs. and leave a message on her voice mail. No doubt that today, by now, she's at a friend's home feasting.

Two days later, she walks in my office. I'm working on my between-job dart throwing skills. Different handbag, different shoes, same chest. I should have gone to med school. I pull an envelope from my desk drawer and hand it to her.

"He's not cheating on you," I say as she opens the envelope. "He's cheating on his diet. Sneaking away for knishes and bagel schmears and corned beef sandwiches. I think you'll find that if you check the suits, they are a size or two larger than what he was wearing before."

"Oh," she smiles as though the weight of the world has been lifted from her. So I know the next part will rock her world.

"There's one more thing. It's bad."

"There's no other woman. How bad could it be?"

"Take a look at the time and date stamp on the photos."

So she does. First puzzlement, then she connects with the date. She goes from anger to tears almost instantly. "No. We'll be ruined. How could he?"

I have no answers. After seeing all of the horrific sides of humanity, I still cannot explain why people do what they do.

She pulled open her designer purse and fumbled in it until she withdrew a lighter.

"Are these the originals?"

"Yes," I replied.

She burnt the photos and melted the flash card, then turned to me with pleading eyes. She didn't need to say anything.

"Privacy between a PI and his client is sacred. I never break that trust. Especially when I'm paid promptly." She reached into her handbag and pulled out a handful of crisp new bills. She counted them out and kept counting beyond our agreement. Then she turned and walked out the door.

I watched her rear as she walked away. The tennis lessons had been a good investment. Maybe ... and that's when my secretary interrupted my thoughts.

"I don't get it, boss," my blonde, blue-eyed receptionist said. "What is the big deal about cheating on his diet?"

"It wasn't the diet," I explained. "It was the timing."

She was still puzzled. I pointed to a date on the calendar hanging on the wall. She read the bold words printed under the day. "Yum kipper..."

"Yom Kippor. The Jewish New Year." I explained. "The big one. The holiest of holiest. Christmas without Christ for the Jews. You're supposed to fast."

She nodded, but I think that Christ comment confused her.

I took the cash and placed it into the bank deposit envelope.

Looks like it was going to be a happy new year. For me at least.

L'shana Tova.

THE RESULTS

JOSEPH A. SCHILLER

E than stepped up to one of several elevators of a high-rise of medical offices and clinics and promptly indicated he wanted to go up with the corresponding button. He only had to wait a few moments before the elevator made the expected dinging sound indicating its arrival before the door to the elevator opened before him, welcoming its latest guest with open arms. After stepping in and selecting the button for the fifth floor, the door of the elevator quickly closed and subsequently began to climb quickly upward as directed. The building did not seem to have a soul within, Ethan noted, except the security officer sitting behind the reception desk on the first floor. After getting off the elevator, he moved down the empty hallway toward his destination—his footsteps creating an echo as the leather heels of his shoes clicked on the hard linoleum.

When Ethan finally reached the designated place at which he had an appointment, he paused. It was only a momentary hesitation, but enough to make Ethan feel embarrassed by the cautionary impulse. *You're being silly.* Almost to overcompensate, he stepped into the clinic waiting room as if his arrival were somehow greatly anticipated, only to find two other guests looking up uninterestedly at him from their seats. Ethan took a few awkward steps up to an electronic interface screen on the other side of the small room.

Approaching the display in the wall triggered a series of electronic noises from the device before a surprisingly life-like female voice sounded. "Welcome. Please place your right wrist face down over the biometric scanner. This process may take several seconds. Do not lift your wrist from the screen until directed to do so. If you have any questions or require assistance, press the 'Help' button."

Ethan pulled the sleeve of his shirt covering his right arm a bit to his forearm and promptly placed his wrist down upon the small glass screen as instructed. A bluish-green light moved quickly back and forth under the glass, flashing as it did, indicating the device was reading the identification chip just under the surface of his skin.

After a couple of seconds, the woman's voice returned. "Welcome, Mr. Malvic. You are now checked in for your appointment. Please take a seat, and your name will be called shortly."

Pulling his sleeve back over his wrist, Ethan turned and took a seat along the side of the wall a few chairs away from one of the other two patients, exchanging a compulsory smile and nod as he did. He remembered from his initial visit just how thoroughly clean and sterilized the clinic was maintained, with a hint of disinfectant lingering in the air.

Or, perhaps they pump something in through the ventilation system.

Either way, all he knew for sure was this was a level of cleanliness impossible for a person to achieve.

They are clearly using a humanoid service.

There would only be a few minutes at the most to wait. One of the benefits of the advent of automated medical services over the past century was the addition of increased efficiencies, one of which was that appointments started and ended with remarkable precision while physicians, nurses, and reception staff had been replaced by AI. There was also the added anonymity and sensitivity as well. Patients entered through one automatic door and were ushered out another when finished. What Ethan could not reason was, however, with all of the tremendous advancements that had been made, why there was still a lingering necessity to ever physically visit a clinic just to receive the results of a set of lab tests. Ethan's profession, that of a school teacher, he reasoned, had long since migrated online for virtual or asynchronous lessons. In his short six years as a teacher, he never had, and would never meet any of his pupils face-to-face.

If I can collect assignments from home, I can certainly get these lab results sent to me digitally.

Eventually finding himself alone after the other two patients were called in for their appointments, Ethan had a quick moment to himself in silence before the automated voice came over a speaker to announce his turn. "Mr. Malvic, please step forward and enter. Room 5 has been prepared for you."

Stepping forward as requested, Ethan walked up to a door that led into a back hallway which then led into a series of small spaces. When he was standing directly under the door, a sensor was triggered, and the door slid open, allowing him to enter. Ethan walked halfway down the hallway until he found the entrance to the room labeled "5", and the door to the cubicle opened immediately revealing a small capsule with a single chair facing a computer interface.

Ethan took one step forward to the chair, but stopped, and just stared down, the door closing behind him. He slowly, gingerly, moved toward the chair, reaching out to grab the back of it to pull it away and sit, before pausing again.

You wanted this. Remember that you wanted this.

Sitting down, Ethan faced the screen and, almost squirming, adjusted himself in the seat. Electronic beeps sounded from the interface before the AI-generated voice spoke to him. "Mr. Malvic, please place your right wrist face down over the biometric scanner. This process may take several seconds. Do not lift your wrist from the screen until directed to do so. If you have any questions or require assistance, press the 'Help' button."

Much more reluctant this time, Ethan reached forward to rest his right wrist upon the glass biometric scanning screen, sensing his anxiety rising. After quickly having his identity verified, Ethan waited for the interface to respond. "Mr. Malvic, thank you. The results of the examination you requested are now available. A printout of your results is forthcoming. There are eight minutes and twenty-eight seconds remaining for your appointment. Feel free to use the remaining time to review your exam results. We know you have alternative service provider options, so thank you for trusting us with your business. Should you have additional needs in the future we hope that you will consider our services again."

When the AI-generated voice had concluded its message, a brief whirring sound came from within the interface before a small piece of paper was released from a slip in the device. Ethan did not immediately reach for the exam results, but rather, sat back in the chair, leaning and stretching backward, then slouching a bit. He turned his face to look up at the tiles of the ceiling and closed his eyes, taking slow, deep breaths. Ethan felt his heart pounding in his chest. Several more long breaths passed in and out before Ethan sat forward again to face the wall monitor. He sighed, then extended his hand to take the slip of paper sticking out of the module.

Just take it.

Forcing himself to look at what was printed on the paper, Ethan read,

5 years, 3 months, 2 days, 6 hours, and 24 minutes

AS MY FATHER WAS DYING

CAROLINE SHANNON DAVENPORT

"Father is dying."

What the hell was my sister talking about? I had just talked to him a few days ago. My healthy, robust father. Dying?

I was sitting with a glass of iced tea in hand at four in the afternoon, on my computer researching a possible well-earned Caribbean vacation, lost in a world of warm water and sand between my toes, when the phone rudely rang. Answering, a familiar voice nearly fifteen hundred miles away pushed me from the feel of a comfortable, caressing beach towel onto a hard, cold floor, dropping me with a thud.

Living in a big southern city, in my complex, overextended, overcommitted lifestyle, I was almost always prepared with a plan of action. I am a business executive, a writer, a wife, and a mom with numerous friends and responsibilities.

I have a propensity for order that allows me to juggle all the moving parts no matter how chaotic. I also have the advantage of keeping anything outside my sphere of control at bay, like the relentless drone of jarring daily newspaper headlines and media horror, all the political hate and nastiness, yellers and screamers, bad players, sad tales of human suffering, and all the awfulness happening somewhere else in the city, somewhere else in the county, somewhere else on the planet, and to someone else. Simply put, I look for and find ways to navigate around distraction. Lest it come too close.

Always being prepared and getting ahead of the game. I was convinced those were the keys keeping calamities, pain, and sadness from befalling onto life—mine and everyone else's. I do not react well to the unexpected—more like a tortoise who comes up against a solid two-foot wall than a scintillating agile hare who hesitates only a split second to assess the situation and bound for the other side. So, when something happens without an inkling of prior warning, I am momentarily at loose ends with my otherwise well-thought-out routine disturbed and derailed.

I am, by nature, a long-range and meticulous manager of people and events. It is a position that I hold in the booming commercial real estate firm my husband and I own and run. I am the slow mover that plots, plans, and pulls everything and everyone together, concentrating on individual personalities and details for optimum outcomes in business and social envi-ronments. So, when something unusual, confounding, or in this case, terrifying happens, I flounder, frantically grasping to orient my protesting brain.

My father dying?

My sister said he had an emergency operation the night before. He had been with one of his old racetrack buddies, watching the ponies, but he had to leave before the races were over. My surprised mother met him at the door.

"It must be another kidney stone, Mom," he told her. "I've got that low back pain and pressure in my groin again."

Taking an aspirin, his panacea for all ailments, he went to bed. Understand, in his almost 65 years, the worst and only illness had been kidney stones, which he had refuted would never happen again, the careful eater he had become.

Sunday morning, he got up and did the grocery shopping for my mother, *his Margaret;* he called her. Always called her his Margaret, apple of his eye. But he said the pain was not going away when Mother asked, worried. By Sunday night, he was unable to urinate. So, said my sister, my 25-year old baby sister, little Marie, the surprise package when I was almost eleven, who had taken him to the hospital on doctor's orders to be catheterized, had waited while they tried, had left when they said he would have to be admitted, and who had later returned with my mother to sit huddled in fear in stiff plastic chairs in the waiting room after they said it was serious, that his bladder would burst if they didn't operate immediately. . She did not hold up well under stress, especially when dawn broke on a new day, and they said my father was in critical condition.

Why hadn't she called me sooner? I wanted to know. *And how was Mother holding up? And who were* they? *What doctors? Which hospital?* I needed to ask all the right questions. I could see that. Put on my best authoritative voice. Someone needed to take charge here. That much I knew, even in my dim-witted floundering state of mind.

Go for the facts.

In any emergency.

It was my personal fear buffer, the finger in the dike, my private arsenal of artillery. Just keep firing those questions! Never mind that I am not fast at assimilating the answers into any coherent depth of understanding while the battle is raging, the adrenalin pouring. Never mind that the answers are just bouncing around in my head, filling space—molecules in a state of supersonic excitation.

Let's face it. It makes for a good appearance! But it is not until later, after the weakness in the knees, the sickness in the stomach, and the clanging in the head stops, that those molecules find their way along the right channels and replay themselves to form precise meaning.

Now, only the bare rudiments of understanding were being gleaned from Marie's shaky words. Most of all, I wanted to know what she meant by *critical*. Either critical didn't sound critical coming from Marie—might she be over-fearful? Or else, I did not want it to be as bad as the word implied. I was holding out for that one final hope of reassurance that I would hear, get, and feel. I wanted my father's calm voice. His steady arm around my shoulder. A fathomless dive into the depth of his deep blue eyes.

I called his doctor. A man I had never met and about whom I knew nothing other than the name Marie gave me, along with his phone number. And in my efficient-sounding direct way, I asked for the truth, and in his efficient-sounding direct way, Dr. Ronald M. Dasher gave it to me. He said kidney failure. Complete kidney failure. The kidneys were not functioning. I wanted to know why. He said he didn't know why and that they hadn't been able to find out why.

What did you mean?

He explained that when they performed emergency surgery, they found an obstruction of tissue, but before they could explore further, they ran into complications of profuse bleeding and had to close after removing only the tissue blockage. And there were other problems. More complications. My father was a very large man, and in such cases, the doctor said, kidney failure often means heart failure.

Fool that I am, I asked the jugular question, "How much of a chance will he survive? How much of a percentage?"

Hesitation on his part as my legs went numb, forcing me to sit holding the phone, waiting.

"Oh, I would hate to say, but not good, less than fifty percent."

Less than fifty percent.

Less than fifty percent.

Less than fifty percent.

It never stopped droning through my brain as I ended the call and started a new one to Marie.

Listening to the rings—*Get a grip.*

I told Marie I would be there as soon as I could get a flight. I then called my husband, who was on a business trip for our company. He didn't pick up. I left a message. Then called our assistant and told her briefly what was happening, tried to keep my voice steady as I gave her instructions for the week, and then I called and got plane reservations and a rental car.

I forced myself to focus, and from the moment I secured the way forward, I was meticulously thorough. Organized. I planned. I took care of business! I raced around like a top on a spin. I cleaned and straightened everything on my desk. Preceded to leave notes around the house and for my teenage son, so nothing would be left to chance in my absence. That was the only way to go—never, never leave anything to chance.

While I was hauling a suitcase out from the hall closet, my husband called with deep anxiousness in his voice. And like a star pupil asked to recite in class with the feverish glow of an overachiever, I gave him all the information and filled him in on everything. *No need to worry.* I had it under control.

I did some laundry and packed, mindful of what all I might need. Already deciding to take only a carry-on with essentials to get off the plane fast, I would ship the rest UPS—no waiting for luggage. I ran through the checklist in my head of clothes I would need. It was Autumn in the North, and I needed warmer clothes, jogging clothes to keep exercising—shoes, dress, casual, nightgowns, slippers, make-up, and on and on, checking my mental list. I packed, intending to be ready for every eventuality. Even packed that *little black dress* along with extraneous other "just in case" sensibilities, but pushed away the thought of *less than fifty percent* as quickly as it came. I barreled through the house to get out the door and to the airport.

A friend was picking me up, and we talked non-stop all the way there. She was a close business and personal friend, and I knew I could trust her to hold down the fort until I returned. We went over every detail of all I had scheduled in the coming week or so. Once at the airport, I quickly checked in, thankful the weather was good, and that it wasn't a busy time. I grabbed a sandwich and some bottled water. Luckily, I sat down next to a lovely woman my age, and we had a lively conversation about the city she was headed to for a business meeting. I knew it well and told her where all the great restaurants were, a museum there I loved, and all the best places not to miss. Then, it was time to board.

And once settled in my assigned spot, as my whisper jet began its vibratory whisper, there was a cold, clammy, oscillating hum in my head that kept time with the jet engines on their rev. All morning my motor had been running full throttle, but lo, it had been feeding off the fuel of frivolous practicalities.

But once buckled into this narrow, suffocating seat enclosure sandwiched between two tired, no-nonsense, can't-wait-to-get-home male business types elbowing on both sides—the only fuel for thought was the final, unavoidable enormity of where I was going and why.

As the last vestiges of the skyline of my home base receded from my mournful view, I looked around, fully realizing the terrible predicament I was in—trapped in this plane, this seat, with nothing to do but think for almost three hours.

Panic!

Now, for those who cared to notice, aboard this wide-bodied gleaming Tri Star 8B was a reasonably attractive, slender woman dressed in a navy-blue suit, matching shoes, and a crisp white blouse, wearing a warm, quick, confident smile with a bright-eyed look.

Mary Poppins with hands folded neatly in her lap.

Calm.

Self-assured.

Deceit! That calm, *nice lady* exterior was nothing but a fraud. Already a strange sort of metamorphosis began to take place inside her mind—a metamorphosis that was to come and go with hardly a speck of prior warning as future events unfolded. She was growing smaller, like Alice in the fairytale stepping through the looking glass. Only, unlike Alice, it was not size she was losing. No, there were no outward changes in that friendly, adult appearance. But alas, years were falling away with the blink of an eye. She was growing younger inwardly. Approaching childhood. She was in a time tunnel going back to *Daddy*. Woe be to the unsuspecting.

Somebody was saying something! Somebody was talking to her. Mr. Businessman on her right was making airplane conversation. *How nice.* In response, she felt her grown-up facade crinkle in the proper politeness of smile.

As shrinking, terrified little Alice was down there silently screaming in fear and rage, "leave me alone, leave me alone, can't you see I don't want to talk to your dull, stupid, little accountant's face? My FATHER is dying. My FATHER, you idiot!"

All the while, she heard a *grown-up* voice with all the nuances of an educated robot-like reply, "No, I'm afraid this isn't a business or pleasure trip. My father's taken ill."

And it was little Alice that looked out of her eyes at Mr.

Businessman as he gave a perfunctory response, thinking to her childish self, *You jerk, is that all you can say!* Little Alice wanted to talk now. Needed to talk now. Oh boy, did she ever. Keep those little girl fears from exploding into absolute bogeyman hysteria. What she could use was a nice, grandfatherly type: gray hair, rumpled suit, big ol' soothin' Southern gentleman sayin', "Now, don't you worry none, honey, that Pappy of yours gonna be alright."

But little Mr. Businessman, soon to be discovered as little Mr. Tight Ass unwilling to give up a smidgen of sympathy, little Mr. Short Conservative Haircut, wire-rimmed glasses working his way up the corporate ladder, mother sickly since he was a boy and still hangin' on, no care for dying parents, *bet I could show you a good time* glint in his eye, *jerk*, insensitive clod —didn't like little girls.

Sure, as tootin', little Alice had had the good luck to sit next to an in-need-of-a-strong- woman type, a son lookin' for the mother he never had, a poor baby boy, with, no less, lust on his mind. But little Mr. Tight Ass was the best that fate had offered up. Mr. Businessman on the left was hunched next to the window staring into nothingness and conspicuously not inter-ested in conversation. So, what was to be done? Dumb, scared little Alice was willing to play any game now as long as it kept those words coming and kept the silence of disengagement from fueling her tender child fears.

But if that didn't beat all, here she was, looking for some reassurance, and before she knew it, she was giving it out instead of getting it. Little Mr. Tight Ass, ten-year-old whiny, bragger kid, was telling her all about his job and a significant monthly report, the first-ever he was getting ready to give. And her running off at the mouth about knowing too well the diffi-culty, having just given a big one at a conference, all supportive of his plight. Assuring him, it would get easier. She did them all the time. Second nature.

In that case, *really, wow,* he wondered if she could take a peek at his speech, and give him some pointers on his opening, wanted it to come off with a pow!

Little Alice was in for it now. And it never let up. All the way across the cold night sky and even into the taxi up to the gate. *Gee! Gee! Gee! Was she really married?* If she looked out the window to the right, she might even see the lights on top of the enormous hangar and the lounge his company owned for their private planes.

With the cabin lights still low and the runway lights blinking by, her new best friend leaned in to talk low in her ear, gesturing with his hands. As his pointing finger came too close to her face in one instant of madness, she was tempted to bite down. But the idea snapped back to reality in the nick of time by a grown-up voice in her head. As other planes on the runway flashed past, she had the thought that this felt like the longest taxi on record. Then, trying not to laugh, the idea hit her of the absurdity of the teenage-boy-girl-show-you-my-trophy situation.

And her role in this little charade. Adult Alice knew why little Alice had appeared and played. Not to say it couldn't have been better. But for all her bitter complaining about little Mr. Tight Ass, little Mr. Ship Passing In The Night, Little Big Bad Wolf hadn't been that *bad.*

He had kept the real wolves from gnawing at her mind and pawing at her shaky terrified emotions. Cabin lights on.

Now what...

LAST KISS

GARY ZENKER

I f the secret is known by the person it is meant to be kept
from, is it still a secret? That's what I am wondering as I
look at this girl I used to date, who I cared about, who was my
deepest love.

"Good to see you," she greets me, but we both know the
words aren't entirely true. Breakups are never easy, especially
when one of you is still in love. There's usually guilt involved
on the part of the other person. Usually.

"Good to see you, too," I offer back. At least I know the
feeling behind the words when *I* say them. If it wasn't for the
scowl on her face, I might even believe she meant hers.

We sit, she with her coffee and me with my soda. The high-
top table literally and figuratively separates us, although the
secret would have effectively done that by itself. One person
would refer to it as straying and justify it with a variety of
reasons. The other would call it cheating, with no reasonable
explanation possible. The same act, viewed so differently by
the two people closest to it. Both right. Both wrong.

We look at each other. Two people who talked about everything ... well, almost everything, who can't find the words to open a conversation. The air is heavy. We sip at our drinks.

"I'm sorry," I offer and outline a list of regrets in my actions and behaviors. She listens and nods every so often in a rhythm unrelated to the words. It seems less about agreement and more in reaction to thoughts in her head.

"I'm sorry, too," and she takes the opportunity to list a few of hers. We are both being honest as far as they go, but it doesn't represent the true problem that existed.

But the secret remains unspoken, hidden behind the words we speak ... and those we don't. There is silence ... again.

That silence makes it clear that the end of our conversation has arrived. There won't be others, despite any words left unspoken.

I take a deep breath. "Would you like a kiss?" It's an honest question for which I honestly don't know her answer.

"Okay." There's no change in her facial expression to indicate what "okay" really means. She stands stiffly, and I move around the high-top table to her. She visibly shifts her weight from one leg to the other.

This kiss has nothing in common with the kisses we shared before. No hands behind the head or on the small of the back. There's no actual body connection as we both lean forward as if specifically to avoid that very thing.

She doesn't close her eyes ... which I realize when I open mine, mid-kiss. Her lips are unmoving. Soft pillows that provide no comfort or warmth, and hide any emotion ... if any still exists.

I pull my face back and look into hers. Although physically here, she is someplace else. Maybe it's with her new someone, or she's in the past. It's anywhere but here. A definitive end and answer to the question "is there any residual spark left?" The closure I had hoped for, one way or another.

I gather the folder and hold the door for her. As she walks through it, she thanks me, but for what, I'm not certain. Being a gentleman and holding the door? The kiss? Meeting her in the first place? Not making a scene?

I'm in the car and just settling in as her car already drives past. I wave, but I can see that she's not looking in my direction. She's looking straight ahead, beyond me. And I'm already in her rear view mirror.

I buckle the seat belt and then look over at the passenger seat. Lilies, her favorites. Two bunches. They sit there. So smart not to have brought them in with me. I reach over to grab them by the stems and swing my arm across my chest to drop them out of my driver's side window. The growing wet spots on my shirt aren't from the dry stems.

It's ten minutes before I can see clearly enough to put the car into gear and drive home.

ART PROJECT

JOHN TAVARES

On a lark, Taglia bought a lottery ticket, after joking with his favorite convenience store clerk over the size of the jackpot, twenty-four million dollars. Meanwhile, he bought his nightly takeout coffee and a pint of chocolate peanut butter ice cream, which usually constituted his last meal of the day.

Then, against all odds and expectations, Taglia, an aspiring visual artist, won twenty-four million dollars in the provincial lottery. He was utterly astonished and partially silenced of his critique of society and capitalism and social inequity and racism and all societal ill. The money allowed him to pursue his aspirations as an artist, so he felt gratified. Perhaps now he would have the opportunity to focus his energies on attaining critical respect and attracting media attention to his artwork.

If he didn't succeed as an artist, Taglia consoled himself with the reassurance that finally he would have no money worries. He even hired an accountant and a financial advisor. These business professionals prudently and wisely invested his money. Having gotten the opportunity to know him, they invested the jackpot to provide him a sufficient income to, in their words, pursue his wild and crazy and whacky art, his art projects, his conceptual art, his installations.

Meanwhile, he was fascinated by the widespread adoption of smartphones. Having been born and raised in a rural area with landlines, he felt comfortable and most at home and at ease with a simple basic rotary telephone (although he used a cordless telephone, which his real estate agent gave him when he bought the condo from her). So, he deeply immersed himself in computer technology and digital art projects.

Perhaps his refusal to adopt a smartphone was related to the fact he didn't expect to receive or make many calls, at least until after he had won the lottery, when calls from the financially distressed and opportunists cascaded. Anyway, after he thought long and hard about what would be his next art project, he decided he would surreptitiously gift up to thirteen smartphones, under the numbered corporate name his accountant and financial advisor set up. He decided to abandon the smartphones at various public venues across the city, at beaches, squares, parks, libraries, subway trains. He figured that random people would pick up one of these smartphones. As long as he paid for the calling and data plans, these unwitting art project collaborators could continue to use the smartphones.

Taglia set up and configured the smartphones so that he would have access to the accounts, data, and storage. He would harvest the phone recordings, images, videos, texts, e-mails, and social media as raw material for his art project, Thirteen Smartphones. He would edit the material, and present clips and excerpts in an art installation. Eagerly, he set about his artistic journey and endeavor.

Taglia left a smartphone at Hanlan's Point Beach, where he sometimes sketched landscapes and nudes. He thought this location was perfect: the vibe was cutting edge, anti-establishment, and progressive at the beach. He expected whoever picked up the smartphone could soon provide a rich source of artistic material. Instead, when he downloaded the media from this smartphone, he found countless nude photos, surreptitiously recorded at the clothing optional beach. While he believed some of the material might be useful in his art installation, he righteously and hypocritically considered the majority of these images exceedingly sleazy, prurient, and voyeuristic. The video of gay men having sex along the cruising trail wending its way along the shoreline he found a complete disappointment.

This new artistic material almost caused him to abort the project, but then he saw the user had taken some stunning and beautiful sunsets along the western shoreline of the Toronto Islands facing towards Etobicoke, and these vistas and landscapes looked simply stunning. Once again, he believed he might be on the right and righteous artistic path.

The second smartphone he left in Nathan Phillips Square. This smartphone he soon discovered was picked up by a transgender sex trade worker. He found her fascinating, but as she exchanged intelligent and thoughtful texts with fellow graduate students and tutorial assistants, he realized he may have been in over his head. The academic jargon and terminology he didn't understand; however, some of the phraseology he found eminently quotable. The texts from the sex worker's adventures with clients were the stuff of scripted commercial movies: scary, creepy johns; stolen wallets and handbags; arguments over condoms and protection and risky unprotected sex; daring sexual encounters in public spaces, shopping mall washrooms, parks, corporate C-suites. Astonished at the wealth of raw artistic material and the social and philosophic questions it raised, he carefully curated and archived this material, as was his usual practice, burning digital files to DVDs and recording the data to external hard drives and USB flash drives and data cards. Then Taglia left a smartphone in Dundas Square. A teenage skateboarder found the smartphone. Following connection, synchronization, and data transmission, Taglia found the image folder filled with images of pizza slices the skateboarder took at various pizza restaurants across the city. The skateboarder gave him the impression he was homeless, as he crashed on the couches and sofas of countless friends, uncles and aunts, and cousins, and even park benches, and underneath bridges, alongside his skateboard, but, as Taglia surmised, Mason the skateboarder was instead a free-spirited youth with an entrepreneurial family. Indeed, there were countless unanswered voicemails and texts from his parents complaining about his skipped classes and high school absences. His parents also complained about the emails and calls they received from his high school teachers, guidance counselors, and the school administration. If Mason dropped out of high school, during his last senior year, which he was forced to repeat, when he was only a few credits shy of graduation, they would have to charge him rent. He would be forced to work as a hamburger flipper at a fast-food restaurant or a box boy at a supermarket, or as a clerk at his father's convenience store and gas bar. Still, Mason continued to explore the concrete jungle on his skateboard, eating large pizza slices at his favorite pizza parlors along the route of skateboarding nirvana. The video he shot of skateboarders in mid-flight, leaping, spinning, jumping, crashing, were spectacular and amazing. Taglia thought that he would project the images and overlay these motion pictures and stop motion still captures with quotes of the youth's text messages arguing with his parents.

Next, Tanglia left a smartphone in the section of heavy

texts and formidable scientific journals in the huge reference branch of the Toronto public library, just north of Bloor on Yonge Street. However, he didn't realize he had left the books in the medical reference section. Soon he discovered texts in German, a foreign language for him, which he translated online, using his favorite internet browser and search engine with enhanced privacy features and automatic English-to-German translation, once he selected the appropriate features.

The texts were between a graduate student and her parents. A striking person, Helga liked to take selfies. She was a large woman, but he also thought she was attractive and possessed a certain Rubenesque beauty. Helga messaged her parents that she needed money, Euros, after she suffered a stroke. Meanwhile, Helga was unable to resume her PhD studies in neuroscience because of her brain hemorrhage, which left her confused, dizzy, with vertigo, memory deficits, and brain fog.

Helga confessed to her parents in her mother tongue that she suffered the stroke after she overdosed: She snorted cocaine of unexpected purity, and her blood pressure skyrocketed. After succumbing to peer pressure, Helga wished she followed the advice of her circumspect and geeky fellow neuroscience student who worried about contamination with fentanyl, synthetic opioids, designer drugs, or other potentially toxic impurities. Still, Helga insisted that it was the first time she had snorted cocaine, and all the other graduate students were using the illicit stimulant that festive night, which became even more celebratory when they were forced to stay overnight because of the snow blizzard. In fact, the stormy winter weather also delayed the arrival of paramedics and an ambulance when her medical emergency occurred, thereby exacerbating her condition.

Despite whatever brain fog Helga said she still suffered,

Taglia admired the precision of her prose, the technical language, and her methodical thinking. So, he couldn't help wondering how someone so intelligent could be so rash and naïve—to snort black market cocaine, which she said she obtained from another graduate student in neurology at the Christmas party.

That would be the tabloid-like headline Taglia would project over her German texts and selfies superimposed over screenshots of the academic articles she had published as a graduate student in neuroscience journals. Now he could observe from her own selfies that Helga suffered mobility issues, as she struggled with her cane, walker, and wheelchair. He thought the short video clips and selfies Helga produced might also make, in a disparate section of his art installation, an excellent chronicle of a young woman's recovery from nature's retribution.

The smartphone that Taglia left on the subway train as he departed at Yonge Station was found by a teenage runaway girl. Stacy had apparently told her parents that she was moving to Toronto to attend community college, study culinary arts, and become a pastry chef. But Taglia noted from the official e-mail Stacy received from George Brown College's school of hospitality that her application was rejected because she didn't have sufficient high school credits. Moreover, Stacy wasn't old enough to apply as a mature student.

Now, judging from the journal entries Stacy made on the smartphone, she spent her days reading paperback books on the subway. She spent what little money she had on coffee, lattes, espresso, and cappuccinos in cafes and biscotti, sherbets, gelatos, and gourmet ice cream in tiny cafes in Greektown on the Danforth, where she resumed her reading. Then, after she did her straphanging act to the opposite side of the city on Bloor Street West, Stacy ate parsimoniously at the fancier restaurants and cafes on the patios and boulevards, where she continued reading her favorite books and magazines she picked up from recycle bins. Stacy admitted she felt guilty because her exacting and fickle taste wouldn't permit her to eat considerably more inexpensive snacks and cheap meals from fast food restaurants.

Stacy was couch surfing, too, sleeping in a spare bedroom of an uncle one week, the sofa of an aunt the next, and a high school friend's upper bunk bed the following week. Her friend even got her pregnant and, after a violent argument, during which his parents called the police, she was subsequently forced to live in a shelter. Stacy realized she wasn't ready for pregnancy—which she kept secret—or parenthood[1] . After she overdosed on antidepressants, she talked to a counselor and decided to obtain an abortion.

Taglia felt so badly for the young woman, especially when he read she was shoplifting from grocery stores and supermarkets to eat. He entertained the idea of offering her one of the spare bedrooms he used as a studio, but he feared that would compromise the integrity of his art project.

Then Taglia had a smartphone he originally intended to leave in the lounge of the bus terminal or ferry terminal, at the foot of Bay Street, near the financial district, on the shore of Lake Ontario in the Harbourfront. But he forgot this smartphone—at his favorite bar and café, where he read newspapers and drank coffee, a place he first discovered when he was a student in art college, where artists, and pseudo artists and pseudo intellectuals, Taglia joked, with some cynicism, loved to hang out. He left the mobile device when he was distracted by a woman in a short leather skirt with a crisscross cut-out crop top and a barking Pitbull.

Soon Taglia found he was looking at cryptic texts for what he could only conclude were illicit drugs and drug shipments.

He began to receive the impression that the smartphone had been hijacked by a high-level drug dealer. There were photographs of various types of pills, tablets, capsules, and powders in sandwich baggies, and then large shipments, packaged in rolls of duct tape, shaped like bricks, of what appeared to be illicit drugs. The material and images he observed and studied were like photos police released to the media showing smuggled and concealed drug shipments. Why would a drug dealer be so imprudent to use a phone he found castaway in a bohemian café, where the avant-garde thrived. Taglia could only surmise the drug dealer knew more about smartphone technology and apps than he did.

The texts between the drug dealer and his associates were written in slang and argot Taglia barely comprehended. He deciphered and unencrypted the jargon through liberal use of an online urban dictionary. Alongside the images, these messages became extremely graphic and the violence disturbing. When Taglia saw the images of an amputated finger from a drug mule and addict who owed tens of thousands of dollars, he thought he needed to find a way to disconnect this smartphone from the network or even retrieve the device surreptitiously. When he saw a graphic image of a decapitated head, Taglia thought he hit artistic gold, but, at the same time he found the image so graphic and disturbing he considered ending his artistic project.

Then, the global positioning system on the city map of his desktop computer screen showed the smartphone getting closer and closer to his own condo. The bleeps sounded loud warnings through the high-fidelity speakers of his digital studio, with its desktop workstations with dual monitors, purchased with lottery money, in the east end of the downtown core.

The end came with a simple rapping, accompanied by a polite, firm, and loud voice, at the door. The bleeping from the honing device software for the smartphone combined with the loud knocking abruptly alarmed Taglia, interrupting him in his evening labors, when he was processing, editing, and manipulating mixed media, text, images, and videos at his workstation. He clenched the receiver, his tense fingers primed to hit the numbers on the cordless telephone. When the pounding resumed and he didn't recognize the voice, he hit the preprogrammed emergency number button for 911 for fire, ambulance, or police. Taglia answered the door and a man in a fedora and a tasteful blazer over what looked like a very expensive T-shirt told Taglia that IT technicians and cartel hackers tracked the smartphone to this address. Taglia hoped for the arrival of the police as he clung to the ceremonial dagger a Sikh, whom he had befriended as a teenager, had given him as a parting gift. Meanwhile, Glasgow weaseled his way inside Taglia's condominium and showed him his handgun.

When the police officer arrived, Glasgow stood near the open door, which she closed. Glasgow apologetically explained that he was attempting to return a lost smartphone when Taglia suffered a panic attack. This jived with what the police officer assumed and presupposed, Glasgow's forthright assertion confirming her suspicions. Besides, when she saw who the caller was, she took an instant dislike to Taglia. Her body language showed she was uncomfortable with the summons, as she shifted on her shapely hips and legs, shrouded in neatly pressed striped trousers. The officer pursed and twisted her lips in some odd contorted facial expression, as if she was dealing with a perp who hadn't washed in months. She didn't want to deal with Taglia.

In that instant Taglia thought he understood. He remembered her as the gorgeous constable who had come to his door during a past encounter. He had attempted to shoo this constable away, like she was some pesky pest, despite the fact he thought she was most attractive.

That evening, before she arrived at his condominium, she conducted a quick database search and traced the telephone number to records of a wellness check she herself had coincidentally done on him in a neighboring house. She was the police officer who responded after a neighbor called and expressed concern over his frantic pacing, frenetic activity, restlessness, and pressured speech, which she could hear through the walls and in the hallways. In a manic painting spree, fueled by energy drinks, protein bars, and methamphetamine, Taglia didn't leave his boarding house room for two weeks. Meanwhile, he worked on his art and painted and stroked and daubed, brushing his way through several oversized murals, for a crucial project for art college. The massive murals ultimately ended up getting hung up around several high-rise construction sites, surrounding massive holes in the construction grounds for condo tower developments.

When a moment of mutual recognition occurred, Taglia felt ashamed at the sight of this officer, embarrassed by how disrespectful and verbally abusive he had behaved towards her when she attempted to question him. He remembered how several years ago, as he splashed and slopped gobs of brightly colored paint with exotic pigments on his canvas, he attempted to shoo her away. He hurtled spiteful sarcastic retorts, when she told him she was merely there after she had been summoned to his room by a concerned neighbor. He could see she didn't wish to respond to a call for police service at his apartment. Now, believing that the situation was safe and under control, she found reassurance in the words and manner of the slender man, dressed in a light-colored suit, pastel shirt, boat shoes, and a fedora. This suddenly ingratiating figure, who had invaded Taglia's home, the constable found encouraging, and Taglia found frightening and dangerous.

When the constable was ready to leave, Taglia made several gestures in pantomime, including that of a handgun, concealed in a coat pocket. Meanwhile, Glasgow caught wind of his performance and body language. Taglia realized his message wasn't registering with the constable and became desperate. Taglia showed her the ceremonial dagger and said he was ready to use the weapon to defend himself from the intruder if she didn't call backup. Glasgow pulled out his revolver. When the constable reached for her weapon, Glasgow shot her. Then, he aimed at Taglia at point blank range, but, virtually instantaneously, Taglia stabbed Glasgow in the middle of the chest. Still, Glasgow managed to fire a bullet into his torso. As Taglia stood bleeding, clutching his stomach, he was giddy with the knowledge he was the last person standing. Still, he reached for his drafting chair for support and soon collapsed.

Glasgow and the police officer were not stirring or moving after they apparently lost consciousness due to their injuries. Taglia struggled to use his misplaced art project smartphone, which had fallen beside him on his floor, but Glasgow had— sometime after Taglia had downloaded the pictures and texts— applied a passcode, which barred access to the cell phone and cyberspace. This ending he found too abrupt, too melodramatic, for his art project; his hubris ended too soon his hopes for his artwork project and his innovative subjective reconfiguration of the lifestyle changes induced by mobile telephone technology.

Succumbing to his wound, Taglia fell to the floor and [2] attempted to crawl across the room to his cordless telephone. He managed to inch his way across the floor to the end table, where the telephone was mounted, but, weak, nauseous, and in extreme pain, he collapsed in exhaustion.

The base of the telephone beeped a muted warning because the battery was low on power and close to dying. He needed to move the cordless handset to its mount to charge its battery, but he could hardly move. He couldn't even shout or scream for help, where he lay helpless on the hardwood floor, alongside the two other victims.

Taglia faced the uniformed police officer and gazed into her motionless eyes. Entangled in her long dark blonde hair, he lay directly beside her in the pathos. He found her beautiful and considered the romance of suffering and perishing beside this woman in a uniform as he felt his arms go cool and lost the sensation in his hands. To die beside such a woman was beyond his wildest dreams. If he could chronicle and document the moment, he thought, his artistic ambitions, his mixed media project, would be complete.

As his thinking grew incoherent and cloudy, he felt excruciating pain and fulfillment, laying in this puddle of blood beside this woman, alongside her for an infinity, he imagined, drifting through an abyss of confusion. At that moment his field of vision became a grainy scintillating screen.

He blacked out and completely lost consciousness, a casualty of harsh reality.

MONSTER

JERRY PURDON

Jim Rader delivered the message. It was brief, concise, and as non-emotional as possible. Exactly, how the man across from him had taught. Funny how a few promotions later, the messenger changed though the words might as well have been carbon copied. Without question, every drop of information was understood.

"Sam," Rader said, "look man, I don't have all day. You know the deal. I've seen you make the exact spiel. You know as well as I do, the paperwork is the same. This is nothing different. Just sign."

Rader's dark, Brioni suit jacket covered the back of the leather conference chair where he sat with his elbows propped on the over-sized, wooden table. His white, pressed, long-sleeved dress shirt displayed his gold cufflinks as he tapped his fists on his chin. Patience was not one of his virtues.

The balding, late middle-aged man regarded Rader and attempted a cold stare, failing with watering eyes. Sam glanced back at the papers in his hands. Rader noticed how pudgy the older man's fingers had become. Only a few years before, this guy had been the boss until a little incident where the wife returned home early to catch some extracurricular marital activity. Now, how she knew to go there at that particular moment, well it made Rader smile every time he thought about it. Amazing how an anonymous text can sway someone to react. The incident turned a once hard-charging, well kept, physically fit, and respected vice president into nothing more than a living, breathing waste of space. The whole affair had worked out better than Rader ever dreamed.

Because of the small indiscretion, Rader sped past Sam on the good ol' boy corporate ladder as the former mentor crashed. The man's life became a total dumpster fire. The event of Sam's release had been coming for more than two years, but the damned pandemic had put a wrench in kicking people out the door. His annual tradition of twenty-one employees let loose the week before Thanksgiving had been put on hold, and after two years, he finally had his day planned, a special one at that.

He hadn't sharpened the proverbial old ax for some twenty-one unlucky souls. No, today's action was a "just because he could" moment, and carried out under the guise of steel sharpens steel. One for shaping the organization for the upcoming year. And as of this Thursday, sixty-three heads were being brought forth to chop. It was Rader's version of Guillotine Day. At times like this, he wished he spoke French, so eloquent, insulting. Rader readied himself since daybreak to bask in the glory, but this spouse-cheating bastard, the first head of the morning, delayed the show by actually reviewing the paperwork.

"Really, Sam," Rader said with a low and firm tone, "no need to lose more hair over this. Sign the damn paper."

Sam didn't look up this time. "Jim, you are the epitome of a class act."

Rader smiled. He wrestled with the fact he once reported

to this pile of gassed up meat. Hell, for years, they often went out for happy hour. How in the world did he ever offer this weakness any respect? *Unbelievable.*

"It's Mr. Rader to you, but that doesn't matter now."

"Very true."

Sam grabbed a pen.

"Don't use that," Rader interrupted as he slid a blue ball-point towards Sam, where it rested untouched for a few seconds. Sam picked it up and signed on all four areas marked with yellow tape.

"Grace," Rader said, he had almost forgotten she sat adjacent to him, "make sure we only have blue pens."

"Blue pens," she responded with a nod and looked at Sam, "the packet contains all the standard information from pertinent documents regarding penalties about speaking ill of the company, to COBRA options, as well as other resources the corporation offers in assisting you in gaining your next employment."

Rader scowled at the packets. His thoughts centered around what a huge waste of money it was to print everything out. A simple link provided the same details.

"Thank you," Sam looked at Grace, "I can call for clarification?" he asked, pointing at the stack.

"Yes," she offered the slightest of smiles.

Rader motioned at the men on the other side of the glass walls. The lobby was known as the fishbowl and located in front of the conference room where Rader now sat. The only glass walls of the entire office were in the welcome area.

"No need for an escort," Sam said as a very large man entered wearing solid black slacks and a matching shirt accented with a maroon blazer.

"Policy," Rader interrupted and gestured to the standing

man, "Mr. Jansen will take you to your office so you can get your shit and go."

Sam stood to leave, and his attendant followed.

"Also, Sam, I apologize," Rader said. "We only had enough boxes for sixty-two people, so I put some garbage bags on your desk, which makes things easier don't you think?"

Rader maintained his slight grin though Sam didn't even bother to acknowledge him as the guard and guarded left the room. Leaving Rader and Grace alone.

"Grace. Is the asshole up?"

"Next is Jason David. Doree is escorting him to the room."

"Just say yes." He shook his head. "We should, under no circumstance, hire anyone with two first-names."

She did not move but from his peripheral vision, he saw her furrowed brows. He knew she disapproved of this day, and she had fought him for the past five months in preparation for his sixty-three termination spree. It pissed him off, the thought of her challenging him, but Human Resources had always been a pain in his ass. Nonetheless, he was the bigger burr in her saddle, and he reveled in it.

He recalled their argument several years ago when they hired the person about to be dismissed. She had pointed out he never wanted anyone in his division with two first names. The whole thing was childish, but every great leader had something quirky to be remembered by. He smirked at the very thought of him telling her he had never said such nonsense.

"Today is going to be a great day, Grace, so don't go stealing my joy."

"You take joy in this?"

"Of course not, don't mince my words."

Tired of waiting, he popped up from his seat, to the lobby, past the welcome desk, and through the main entrance doors.

This was going to take two days if Doree didn't deliver these people on time, including herself at the end of the day. He inhaled a deep breath knowing he needed to remove his anxiousness. Some entertainment helped in situations like this, one he played many times. He concocted this when trying to pass the time while feigning interest around those who were boring him to death. This little spice of entertainment was what he termed the "which one would it be" game. Simple, but effective.

The elevators faced the company entrance. All five were visible from the lobby. He didn't need to venture out to guess other than to tune into machinery. The whirr had a higher pitch when lifting, and the creep would be coming from two floors below. So one of the lifts carried his next victim. With a twenty percent chance of winning, he listened. Based on the noise, he decided. *Good 'ol number four, winner, winner.*

Along with a loud ding came the green light adjacent to the fourth one. Rader smiled, but let it fade as the metal hatch opened. These things were so slow. Man, he couldn't wait for humans to catch up with this technology. When the doors swished open and closed in under a second. No different than Star Trek or Star Wars. *No more dillydallying on an elevator.*

Doree exited, guiding Jason David. A man who worked out regularly, ate well and kept himself in nice, upscale clothes, from foot to neck or to be more precise, from Tom Ford Double Monk Leather Loafers to privately tailored slacks and dress shirts. The man was loved by all in the office. He was polite, completed his work on time. Went out of his way to help others. He was what everyone wanted, including Marissa Cavanaugh, and Rader hated him for getting caught.

They crossed through the glass entrance where the electric magnetic lock should have released during working hours. It did when he just went out. For some reason on their return, it stuck. Rader studied the framework at the top. The metal block mounted to the ceiling jiggled as he jostled the door. He kept an eye on it as all three of them walked through.

"Thank you, Doree," Rader said, "Jason we are meeting in the conference room." Rader stopped at the receptionist desk where it seemed someone different always sat, "Call maintenance and have them look at the door please. Specifically, that steel casing looks like it is going to fall." He pointed at the mechanism.

"Yes, sir," the woman said.

Rader turned to Jason and motioned for him to continue to the room where Grace held a slender packet, nowhere near as thick as the others. The younger man sat across from her.

"Jason," Rader started, then slid a file containing photographs in them, "take a look at these then you'll understand why we are letting you go."

Jason opened the folder and studied the contents within. He looked at both Rader and Grace, "No, I don't understand."

Rader moved forward in his chair and leaned with his head cocked very much like a dog's, "You think this," Rader pointed at the pictures, "is a viable office activity?"

"No, sir," Jason responded.

"Okay," Rader nodded, "then you know why we are dismissing you, and there is no unemployment as we already turned these pics over to them. In addition, for the policy violation, there is no layoff package."

"Is this some sort of joke?" Jason asked.

"No," Grace said, "it is against policy to have this type of relations with a coworker."

"And to have a go at it in your workspace," Rader added.

"I know," Jason said, "but that's not me in the pictures. I don't have a tattoo, and this guy has them down his arm and shoulder. I get he resembles me which makes this Nick Gearson, but not me."

Rader grabbed one of the photographs as Jason slid them toward him.

"I can take my shirt off to prove it," Jason said.

"Don't be tacky Jason, HR is in the room."

Rader was quiet as he slid the photo over to Grace who picked it up and squinted at the copy. Grace glanced back over at Rader with the shake of her head. Rader stared back at his hot seat employee and didn't say a word.

One thing for sure, Rader hated being wrong. His protocol on any mishap was to deny and point to the responsible team member which in this case would be someone from security or HR, and, after publicly humiliating the offender, he would accept responsibility for their poor results. Nothing ever landed directly on him and this two first named prick was getting a little too self righteous by absolving himself. *This is work not the justice system.*

"So, what now?" Jason asked, breaking the silence.

Your name grates on my nerves.

Rader waved at the glass door, and a mammoth of a man walked into the room.

"You can sign the papers or not," Rader said, "I don't care. Mr. Simpson here will show you out."

"What about Nick?" Jason asked.

"I don't know," Rader retorted, "why are you concerned? Hell, truth be told, he'll probably get promoted. If it is proven it is him in those stills then that is between him and us. One thing is for sure, no matter what, I will get all the cameras updated."

"I'm being fired over a mistaken identity?"

"What mistake?" Rader asked. "It's simple, Texas is a right to work state. Our right to terminate you. Mr. Simpson, please escort Jason from the premises."

"Can't I get my stuff?"

Rader turned to Grace who stared at the picture in front of her.

"Grace, stop looking at porn and answer Jason's question."

She held up the paper, "Not porn," she said addressing Rader. Then directed her attention at Jason. "Due to the sensitive nature of your position, at this time, you are only allowed to take your keys and phone."

"Mr. Simpson," Rader said, "do I really have to repeat myself?"

The muscle bound man motioned Jason toward the door and the two left. Leaving a very quiet conference room.

Grace broke the silence. "You ever try to embarrass me again, and I'll hurt you."

Rader squinted his eyes and slowly pursed his lips, "oof," he said, "and when do we start that?" He gave a quick wink.

"You won't like it."

He didn't care, and he damned sure wasn't going to let her kill what should be such a spectacular day.

"Who do we have next?" he asked.

"Laura Baker."

"She's from compliance, correct?"

"Yes, and a single mother of three."

Rader smiled a bit. He bet with himself about when she started to tear up all the way to outright crying in under a minute. He set a timer to see when she'd start crying, and the time caught his attention. An hour and a half had passed, and they had only done two.

"Again, a simple correct or yes will do, we don't need the personal details," he said, "and why are you going so damned slow on this."

"Because you wanted to do this one at a time."

"Does HR ever accept responsibility?" He peered over at Grace as if to stare her down. He hated how she ignored him by not looking at him even though they sat right next to each other. "There's not enough time for this shit. Pass me the list."

Doree appeared outside the glass conference doors with another woman. Rader recognized the following dismissal. His heart lifted. The obvious wide-eyed, doe expression along with raised eyebrow of concern gave away how important this job was to her. *She shouldn't be so damned needy.* He motioned for them to enter.

"Thank you, Doree," he said with a higher pitch and softened volume fabricating some pretense of giving a shit, "Please have a seat, Laura."

He waited for the woman to sit. Once settled, his steady gaze pierced into her eyes as if reaching into the depths of her soul. Rader grasped Laura's exit file and slid it over to her.

"Laura, we are letting you go," he said.

"Why?" She asked. "The company is making billions in profit."

"Very true," he responded, "but we are reorganizing and no longer need your position. As always, even in great times, we are looking to strengthen our organization through efficiency by streamlining roles and responsibilities. I mean the fewer people we pay, then the more we make for our shareholders as well as for ourselves." His lightened tone evaporated with every uttered word.

Water flowed down her cheeks as her lips quivered. Rader's spirit warmed as he smiled checking the time. She lasted fourteen seconds before it began. He hoped for outright bawling. *Come on, wail!* He pictured her leaning over the casket of a small child, losing her mind while clinging to the coffin holding something she loved. *Yeah, just like that.* So far, it was only the waterworks.

Grace slid a box of tissues to Laura. The tears continued like raindrop trails down a window. No wailing. No blubbering. And worst of all, no pleading. Rader began to slowly tap the table with his index finger. *Weak.* A total effort in attempting to hide his boredom and to be somewhat respectful. He only wished, he was able to hear what she would say to her friends. Maybe her ex. No, he vaguely recalled her husband had died in a car accident the year before Covid started. The insurance and lawsuits failed to measure up and after the litigation, she had little to show for it. He didn't need losers like this working for him. He was doing the right thing here. His conscience was one hundred percent clear.

"Laura," he said in an effort to get things moving, "do you have any questions about the paperwork?"

"No," she responded, "I'll sign whatever."

Rader choked back the bile starting to erupt due to his disbelief at what happened in front of him. They were letting her go, and she would have the audacity to simply trust what they gave her. *Damn. What a total disgrace. Have some gumption. Have something resembling a spine.*

"It's only an acknowledgement form of your understanding of the terms of separation and acceptance of the package you're receiving," Grace said and pointed at the first page of all the documentation.

As Laura signed, Rader motioned to one of the security goons. The man entered and towered over the signee.

"Mr. Johansson will escort you to your desk so you can gather your personal belongings," Rader said while standing as Laura was whisked away. His pleasant facade had completely dissolved.

"You don't have to sound so delighted," Grace said as she reached for the list.

"I'm not delighted," he said, "this breaks my heart, but the team has to continue to improve."

"How about training? There's plenty of improvement with a tad bit of effort."

"We hired them to do a job, and they should already know how to do it."

"And how do you explain the last name on this line-up? She's the best at her job and better than anyone else you have ever had."

"True, but it's a trust issue. She dropped the ball in the summer of '20."

Grace's eyes slanted and her nose flared, "she had fucking Covid."

"Language, Grace!" Rader paused, taking a slow breath, "It's a trust issue. And let's keep this professional. Otherwise, you'll find yourself on the other side of that table."

"Except, I don't report to you."

"Yet." He smirked and widened his arms. Grace shook her head and took notice of the list. "Listen, speed this up and call me for the last one when you get to it."

She nodded without making eye contact. He knew Grace was upset, but they had to remove the dead weight. Plus, he couldn't help if, deep down, it made his day. These people needed to look out for themselves instead of depending on someone else for their income. If he stopped working now, the only days he would miss were these, and not the dollars. He had plenty. Except, he did want to run the complete show; he deserved it. The position was so close it should have been offered years ago.

He left the conference room before Grace frustrated him further. He was convinced she was capable of stealing joy from Christmas. She was the Grim Reaper of fun. He smiled a bit when he realized she was his very own Angel of Death.

The main doors were jarred open, and a ladder was set up underneath the loose magnetic lock. At the top of the erected aluminum, Joe Essex worked. A man who Rader thought was borderline elderly, but turned out to only appear old. Instead of being near retirement age, the guy was only in his early forties. However, he was the embodiment of not only premature aging, but poor health as well. The man continued to smoke and drink as if he had no issues. Rader had heard Joe inhaled around four packs per day along with about two fifths before sundown.

Unbelievably, this cool cat was skinny as a rail, though he breathed like he had about half a lung. Seeing this man made it unthinkable for Rader to consider how this walking health violation managed to escape the culling. He had to make a mental note to stop forgetting about facilities.

Rader would have let Joe go several years ago, but figured the potential work entertainment of a mid-morning heart attack or some sort of health crisis was too much to give up on a layoff. Rader knew about Joe's medical issues, but the guy wasn't helping himself. So to save the company money he would get Joe next year. If the dumbass was still alive.

"Good job, Joe." Rader said as he checked out the mount.

"Thanks Mr. Rader."

Rader walked down the hall to his office. Inside, two televisions hung on the wall. They remained on at all times, one for regular news and the other for markets. Their volume muted, he only paid attention to the bottom scrolls and occasionally the subscripts.

CNN had a story about a plane crash. Something about a corporate jet. *Probably one of ours.* Rader hated to fly on theirs since the COO hadn't updated their fleet in over a decade. He understood about being frugal, but don't get cheap with the corporate toys. Especially when any error that high and fast ended in a ball of fire.

The typical brass thinking was to let things go past end-of-life and only replace when it broke. So, a cat cracker going way beyond the recommended life span and then goes boom, no one misses a few pipe-fitters. However when an executive plunges from thirty thousand feet, unacceptable comes to mind. *No one saves a buck on executives.* He was definitely worth more than being some mark in a field. Especially over lowering the budget. Besides, he had plans and none of them included being a memorial in the company lobby. One day his title would be CEO and his bank accounts in the billions.

He sat at his desk where everything represented something from the company except a three portrait picture frame filled with his kids. The pictures had not been updated since his wife left him twenty years earlier. He never wanted the little hellions, but she did. She carried the bullets so to speak. Her body, and she could use it her way. The bad side of having offspring was even though she still worked out, she wasn't as firm. The lack of tone was hard to miss after the final bake.

She still desired to work and have a full time nanny as well as completely disregarding his notion of not liking either option. He still provided the cash, yet the children were her responsibility. Bringing the urchins up to speed should not be outsourced, and since she wanted them, it was all on her. Eventually, once it was clear about the obligations, she said he couldn't say shit about how she brought them up. So, he went along with it.

Their discussion over the years was that she would pay for them. Otherwise, she could stay home and raise them. As soon as she made executive vice president at some tech company, she took off. Fine with him, as far as he was concerned she only needed to be the arm candy. She failed. So when she moved to California, hallelujah. He had all his weekends to himself.

As a result, he ended up paying child support. He swallowed that bitter pill and wouldn't ever make the mistake again. He paid for his pleasure and over the years he found self-gratification more satisfying. It was always the way he liked it. He didn't have to worry about making anyone else feel good.

A few years ago, his youngest graduated med school. He hadn't seen any of them in awhile, and they all acted strange when he showed up at the ceremony. It was all about his daughter. She accomplished a solid honor and was on her way to whatever residency which was great. Except no one seemed glad he went. His ex didn't acknowledge him as well as husband number two, and all three of the unappreciative jackanapes were awkward in every interaction. One of them had recently married, and he had never received a wedding invite. Hell, he paid for some of the youngest's school and a "thanks for showing up" didn't seem to be too much to ask. *The ingrates!*

Somehow, today wasn't going as planned. Things needed to start looking up. He opened his private file drawer and grabbed a phone along with a tablet. He connected the two and downloaded a particular bit of video that didn't display non-Jason David's tattoos, but a great shot of Cavanaugh.

He located a yellow sticky with a phone number on it under his keyboard. Then texted the recording to it. Of course, from where he sent it would show as unknown, then, as usual, he'd return the device to desktop support and be assigned another one. Well, in the very least, it should make for an interesting conversation at the David home. *Well, Mr. Two Names, how do you like me now?*

Rader needed some excitement and a couple of things might do the trick. One would be for Doree to have a total breakdown, and the other would be for him to receive a huge promotion in the same day. A knock interrupted his thoughts.

"Yes," he said.

"Mr. Rader," the voice came as the door opened. Doree was his admin, but the knocker was Cynthia. She was younger and incompetent which was why she never worked with him. "You probably haven't received the news regarding Mr. Fair, and I'm sorry for the interruption. However, Mr. Managold has sent a message saying he will reach out to you soon, so please be available. I think he plans to call your cell."

"Mr. Fair?"

"The plane crash."

"The one on CNN?"

"It was ours."

He needed a comeback and to make sure she realized he already knew. He had to maintain an illusion of knowledge and not be vulnerable.

"I didn't realize they had officially confirmed it."

"An official announcement is forthcoming and Mr. Managold plans on having a company meeting this afternoon. Also, Doree is preparing your lunch and will deliver it soon. I apologize for being late today."

The chicken on the chef's salad probably would be cold, and besides, he wasn't hungry. Good for Fair getting knocked out of the way, but unfortunately, there were two others in line before him.

"Understood. Thanks, Cynthia."

Rader searched for his personal phone on his desk. He verified the ringmaster hadn't called. Then wondered why the man would reach out to him and not anyone else on the executive team in New York.

Those guys were a mess, out of the twelve, nine were going through divorces. They had been home so much during the pandemic that their spouses could not endure being around them any further. Though Rader viewed several of them as weak, such as the recently departed Alan Fair, they all had no time for nonsense. Relaxing was never an option. If any of them were to die out of turn, then it made sense for it to be Alan.

The time on his phone caught his attention. If he was going

to eat then he needed to do it, but he didn't quite have the stomach for it. He daydreamed about using an actual guillotine for axing people instead of being forced to give a pay package to them for not working. The whole process made absolutely no sense. *They have unemployment. Why should they get anything else?*

Doree opened the door. Rader never understood her meekness. She had the potential to be twenty times the person she was in corporate life. Rather, she lacked confidence, and, though smart, she cowered at a shout, growing incompetent whenever someone watched her. Her skills with a spreadsheet were phenomenal. She was intuitive, creative, and thought through some of the most complex accounting problems, but she failed at the simplest of tasks when he stood over her shoulder. Sometimes he asked for a menial exercise and then proceeded to sit beside her to give him the opportunity to berate her on how she should know how to do her job.

He would miss that, but even if he let her stay, she would retire within a year. His preference for "goodbyes" was for them to be on his schedule and, therefore, his time would be better spent finding someone new.

"The chicken is still warm the way you like it," she said as she set the tray down on his desk.

"Appreciate it."

"And sorry to hear about Mr. Fair."

Sorry? I don't give a shit. "Thank you, Doree."

She left like a mouse scurrying back to its cubby. Yep, he couldn't take it any more. She was a goner. Too bad she wasn't going to max out her pension, she should have saved her money instead of sending kids to college and all that crap. Those brats of hers can care for her later in life. He bet they were just as sick of her weakness and most likely to leave her to rot in some senior living home.

He hoped to be around a bit longer to watch some of these things play out, but who knew in today's violent climate. He believed life's future cards would deal him into some active shooter event. His head had to be on a swivel at all times for real world violence. After he was in charge, he would hire personal bodyguards full time and not just at work. Those guys didn't think past the next minute, they only wanted an opportunity to kick ass.

Doree did awesome on the chicken, but the salad tasted like shit. Nothing had good flavor at this point. He hoped his weekend wasn't going to be ruined. Maybe letting Doree go by the day's close of business would salvage what was supposed to be a great day, but so far it was like a bad Patriots and Giants Super Bowl. *Come on Tom, it's fucking Eli.*

The mere thought of this becoming a sucky day pissed him off to no end. He should go check on the progress. It was in her best interest to be working and not doing something stupid like getting lunch.

Fair, and no telling who else, was dead. Rader knew this meant the phone call was to establish some executive stabilization with next in line succession. Senior management trained to be executives waiting for their chance. His time in line should have ended years ago. *Damnit Grace, hurry up and get to Doree.*

He stood to head her way. She should be through the list, any inefficiencies now were downright offensive. It didn't matter what he had asked for, she knew the end game and should be busting her ass to achieve it.

He checked the time. The day had flown by with it being almost two in the afternoon. He must have spaced out due to Fair going down, but all he cared about now was inflicting the max amount of pain. Doree's execution would save his day, and too much time had been wasted. Plus, she didn't deserve a full pension plus social security. She would have plenty in the long run, but not that extra comfort of a 100 percent of both. *Well, did she deserve it? No.* She worked as an assistant, or let's face it, a secretary. You either built your fortune in the first ten years, or you get nothing. He had made his, and everything since had been nothing but a bonus. Now he had to keep his name off lists, stay away from the latest hashtag fad, and he would be golden. If he didn't make it to the top soon, then his investments might draw some scrutinization. He didn't need noses snooping around in his security company, real estate transactions and how many downtown properties he owned. Especially, considering the current structure they rented was one of his. So far, the auditors hadn't asked him any questions, but certain details could make things spicy.

His replacement would find out about the expensive square footage, but the opportunity to misdirect existed by saying something about the property owners giving a better deal on the next go around. From there, the new contracts would indicate a moderate price schedule, then everything should be okay. Due to this being a three year agreement, no one would overtly question anything short term.

The amount wasn't too outrageous, but they did pay the second to highest rate for high rises. The company had been at a downtown location since the building was built forty years earlier. Around thirty-five years later and some sheer luck, the opportunity came up for him to acquire it. After figuring out the cost to move and the soft charges for the work disruptions of moving, he presented a manipulated case to the executives about how staying was cheaper. He had even convinced Fair that staying in the building would prevent the company from having to move to an older, less expensive dump.

Plus, he knew when a new agreement was due and banked on being the decision maker to agree to the deal. It went all as planned, and his present employer was paying off the loan. The current debt load was light compared to when he first started, and he continued to expand. One more year on this lease and it was all paid for. He had it made. By the time he did become the chief, he would also have a property management company valued well into ten figures, and it was all his.

He headed toward the abattoir where Grace conducted her reaping. No one else existed down the hallway. The closed doors shielded the remaining Senior Directors from any eye contact. In the open areas, everyone else sat at the desks, responding to emails or working on reports. No one chatted with idle banter, but they were possibly on Teams asking "who was left" and "how many gone." He made a mental note to have the discussion histories in his email by the end of the day. Those network nerds jumped whenever he called. He liked those guys. They worked.

As he entered the lobby, Rader's eyes focused on Joe's handiwork. The door was closed and all appeared normal. He thought about testing it out, but valued his ability to trust his workers. *Can't do everything.* Grace, however, needed guidance, she lacked the sense of urgency to get this done now, and they needed to jump to the last one in order for the day to end on a good note.

The receptionist was away. He recalled being told somebody should always be sitting at the desk. He would find the manager and chew their ass out. Grace sat alone in the conference room. He entered.

"What's wrong?" he asked.

"You mean other than the four coworkers that went down on the corporate jet today or firing sixty-two?"

"Sixty-two? So, Doree is next up?"

"I thought you came because I sent you a text."

"No," he ruffled through his pockets for a second and realized he left his phone on his desk. "I thought it was close to time for her anyway."

"Unfortunately, I'm efficient."

He sat for a quick moment to the right of Grace, then stood. He decided to wait in the lobby.

"You're leaving?" Grace asked.

"I'm waiting out there. The receptionist is away."

"I sent her to get Doree."

"I didn't see her going that way when I walked over here, and it's an office policy violation for no one to be watching the lobby."

"I know. I wrote the policy which is why I'm overseeing it. This whole front is made of glass. Plus, Doree was in the property break room."

"Oh. Why?"

"She's smart. That's why. She only had sixty-two names."

Rader's pissed-off meter shot straight up to red light high. There was no doubt in his mind, the warmth in his neck and face showed the coloration of his emotion.

"You told her."

"Don't blame me for you being a creature of habit. You let go twenty-one employees annually, and due to covid you have missed the past two years. So do the math."

He shook his head.

"We'll discuss this later," he said, "there's no way she'd figure that out. Besides, watch what I am doing now and all the companies will follow. Can't find good people my ass. You don't need them."

"You're saying, other businesses will out of the blue begin laying people off because of this. Nevermind, there are still open positions many corporation's can't locate quality people to fill?"

"You have no idea how this works. I bet a year's salary,

there will be a ton of layoff notices as early as January. If there is no fear of layoffs along with a bad economy, then we will have to pay higher salaries." *Come on Grace, get your head out of your ass, this is so basic.*

He shrugged and continued into the waiting area. The commotion at the office doors grabbed his attention. Those he expected had returned, but Doree's badge didn't work. The receptionist used her ID and the door released where she pulled the door. *They shouldn't have killed her access yet.*

Doree focused on Rader. Her wide eyes announced she knew. Her overall expression displayed the concern of her upcoming loss. *Oh, a great day indeed.*

As Doree crossed over the threshold there was a slight pop, and it echoed through the area. Rader didn't search for the sound as his eyes were entranced with Doree's. The budding panic of the upcoming execution was too ample for him to ignore, but something steel fell into his view.

Her escort gasped and froze whereas Doree maintained her vigil on Rader. Everything seemed to go into a slow motion as the metal came down where Doree made no further steps. She appeared to wait. The hesitation to go to the inevitable cost so much time.

Lady, push her! Not reacting, only staring as if she sat at a railroad crossing stuck in traffic watching the oncoming onslaught of a freight train heading right toward a fully loaded school bus of screaming kids.

Rader wanted to react, but nothing existed for him to do. Due to the distance between them, getting to her to push her out of the way was not an option. And how Doree didn't hear or how the receptionist behind her became a statue, not doing a damned thing, was beyond him. Some people were born to react and others were there to be victims. *A freaking redshirt receptionist.*

The steel block dropped slow, frame by frame, as if the events were recorded and paused between each shot. It hit with a hollow thud. Almost like when a ball hits awkwardly on a wooden bat and goes foul. Something wayward indeed, but the solid piece didn't bounce off. It sank slightly into her head and appeared like a lopsided hat.

Rader's gaze still held Doree's eyes. Only to visualize what once wore concern now glassed over. The pause of her step, the stutter and the topple to her knees leaving his line of sight as she sank on the other side of the lobby's welcome desk. *What in the hell just happened?*

The receptionist's first scream resonated loud and clear. *Weak.* The screaming woman turned and ran back to the elevators. *Well, here comes more company news.*

Her continued screams garbled when whatever salad she had for lunch coated the lift's door. Rader observed her jump on as it opened. The frantic woman disappeared.

No one had run out yet. He stared at Doree's corpse a second more before turning to Grace. He heard her now, she was on the phone requesting first responders. Finally, someone moved, and Rader realized he wasn't alone, but a few security guys were there. One knelt near Doree.

"No need, man," Johanson said, "Seen enough in my day to know what was once there is long gone."

The other guard appeared sad. Rader left the group and went down the short hall to his office. One of the directors came toward him.

"Assist Grace and push everyone else out of the area. Get help on the accounting side and keep people in their respective hallways either at their desks or in the executive break room."

It was all he said before entering his safe space. He paused, listening to Grace as she continued to direct the staff. Then shut the world off and went to his desk.

Did that just happen? He felt a void in the middle of his chest. A gigantic hole where he had hoped for an awesome day wrecked by the delays in getting people processed and out the door. The shit with Fair and now Doree. *Someone hates me.* If there was ever a time to eat a bullet, it was now.

Doree dying shattered everything. Today was meant to be a joyous day for him. Assert authority because he had it. Yet his well-planned day evaporated with an accident. His phone rang.

"Rader," he said.

"Hey Jim, it's Managold."

"Hello."

"I've got to keep this short. It's a real shit show here, but I told the board you will be appointed COO and my successor. Sorry for the crappy way I'm delivering the news, but we have to display a stable command. Besides, you would have been up here soon enough."

"Thank you, sir. It's a shame about Fair and the others."

"Yes it is, but Fair was a boy scout. You're the real deal."

"Thanks."

"Welcome."

The call ended with a beep. Rader fixated on it for a second. He had waited for this exact moment for quite a few years. If he didn't have so much of the stock, he would resign on principle. However, that was a lot of money to let it tank and then build back up. Besides, once he grabbed hold of the helm, he knew quadrupling the shares would be as elementary as breathing.

He would have this company trucking for another generation. Why? Because he kicked ass, that's why. Let everyone else feel empathy or compassion or whatever the hell they needed for their pathetic lives. No, Jim Rader was meant for corporate raiding and ending his days as the richest son of bitch to walk the Earth. Solomon's fortune would be a pittance compared to his final score.

Forward thinking separated him from the herd, especially on business decisions, relationships, vengeance, and even terminations. He calmed himself. Water filled his eyes as he paused his thoughts for the day. Doree's needless death robbed him.

A knock interrupted his reflection.

"Yes," he said.

The door opened and Grace stuck her solemn faced head in past the threshold. Her mascara had smeared around her eyes and down her cheeks. The dark stood out on her light brown skin.

"I'm handling the remaining paperwork; safety, legal, and insurance have all been notified," she said. "I know you know, but Doree is dead." She paused, taking a breath, "Too many deaths for one day."

"Very true. Thanks, Grace."

She nodded and disappeared behind the closing door. He had one goal and that was shot to shit. Joe's head needed to be served to him in a metal bucket full of nuts and bolts for killing Doree and stealing this day. Watching the panic build for missing out on a full pension was in his grasp. And completely not sorry; part of the joy of being the fat cat is tossing out others to shrivel away.

Now it was gone. Joe needed something disastrous to happen to him. Plotting time was needed for something devious and horrible to befall the idiot. Especially with being so far away and on top of Joe, ruin Grace for dragging her feet. Incompetent Joe would be an easy mark. Grace was a real professional, and it would be fun to tear her down. So he would need to promote her first.

Welcome to hell, Grace.

The happy thought brought a smile to his face.

PORTOBELLO

JUSTIN LOWE

T his is ostensibly a story written very much in the first person singular about me and what the daughter of a dynasty did to me after I had given her my all, or at least the best I could muster at the time. It is, in that respect, something of a cautionary tale, to those with opaque but vaunting ambitions to never try to marry into any situation unless you know precisely why you want in. And also what it's ultimately going to cost you to be there.

This is also an exemplar of the random and unsolicited kindness of strangers, even in a town as cold and forbidding as London in late November.

But let's get back to First Principles, shall we?

I had discovered a love of writing rather late and somewhat begrudgingly when I opened a book—Dostoevsky's *The Brothers Karamazov*—on a country campus and suddenly it all made sense to me, that people would live and die by and for words.

This was the same country campus, incidentally, where I met P- and where, subsequently, this whole story begins. Not the most original rite of passage, I'll grant you, but Fyodor fires those he touches with a strange compulsion.

He would touch P- the same way a few years later.

My options, at the time, were slim at best, but I had managed to land a job at a Sydney suburban paper with my own byline. The paper was owned by P-'s father, and I was happy enough to bide my time building up my dossier while I dated one of the daughters of what could be described as a local dynasty.

But, at the beginning of our relationship and of my journalist career, P- had one or two issues with her father. I won't go so far as to classify it as a complex, but you really had to earn her trust as a man. This was the eighties, I perhaps should have clarified before now, when the press was still very much a boy's club, the finance pages where she worked even moreso.

P- spent all her working hours (and they were long, believe me) sat amongst boys chasing quotes from boys so she could write about boys for the consumption of boys invested in their every little victory and defeat. After one impromptu visit, I was summarily barred from visiting her at work ever again, even from calling her, or leaving a note with old Roy at the front desk.

At the time I took it all on the chin because I loved the woman, or at least I thought I did. And I had gleaned from that one visit to her workplace what she was up against. Sad truth was, there could be no special man in her life, or the boys would clam up and make her job impossible. Simple as that. So I played along because I was the man she came home to, albeit late most nights and reeking of booze.

Well, I was the man she came home to wake up next to, anyway.

And so, things found their own equilibrium, their own round of seasons. Three days a week I would pen my copy for a suburban rag and slowly fatten my dossier, the other two I drove my father's cab and somehow managed to make more money than P-, despite her 90 hour weeks and her long liquid lunches with the movers and shakers of this emerald city.

Without ever really wanting to admit it to myself, I knew she had slept with one or two of them. It was the sudden flurry of questions about my day and the barrage of gifts that set the alarm bells ringing, but then they stopped as quickly as they started, and I returned to my factory setting of denial.

You see, like my late father, I am very much a creature of habit. Apart from the brief storm around the anniversary of my mother's leaving, my father preferred slow and steady like his only son. And like his only son, he had been drawn inexorably toward a smart, tempestuous woman.

I quit writing copy in the autumn of the year the Wall came down, not because I wasn't any good at it (in fact my editor offered me a week's paid leave to think it over), but because I could see what it was doing to P- and decided maybe it wasn't for me. Also because Dad needed my help with the cabs. He had three by then, and at 100 grand a plate that was quite a capital investment. He had been elected to the board for the third year running on the promise to make the government see sense on the price of plates, so his time was taken up.

And I was beginning to notice something was off with him. There were gaps. Not dreamy gaps like I was still prone to at the ripe old age of 25, but as though for a second or two all the words flew out of his head, and there was just a terrifying void. And anyway he was hardly driving at all by then.

He had played first grade rugby when he was fresh out of high school and the Japanese had finally laid down their swords. A stocky little winger who got his fair share of blows to the head. It took a while, but, finally, I convinced him to go see a doctor, and sure enough there was this weird kind of spiderweb shadow on the scans.

After dad's first seizure I started spending half my time at his place and half at P-'s. On weekends she would come over and play records with Dad and get hammered on his legendary gin and tonics. My father loved women, and they loved him and one time, so as I saw P- out to her cab, I wasn't surprised she was crying, the tears just rolling down her face.

"He's—"

But she couldn't finish, didn't need to.

So now we jump to a still evening after P- had been offered a transfer to the desk in London and had accepted it before even talking it over with me. She said it was one of those take-it-or-leave-it-right-now moments, and I had no choice but to believe her. I would ultimately decide to join her, but meanwhile, in her absence, I spent the evenings on Dad's back deck.

About four months later, that is where Dad and I were sitting, talking in snatches, mostly about my travel plans once I settled in London, found myself a job etc., and P- barely cropped up in the conversation. The moon was just waning and still so bright in the clear night sky you could see people walking their dogs down the steep hill to the water. But I don't think any of the situation sat well with Dad, even though he never said as much. P- had flown out in March, and I had been left treading water, looking after Dad and his cabs and wondering what I should do.

Then Barry came along and suddenly everything seemed easier. Barry started driving the night shift and was soon taking over my role as unofficial owner-operator of Dad's little fleet. Barry was easy to trust, and more to the point he and Dad had an easy way with each other that put me at ease. Dad told me it was time to go be with P-, even though there was gravel in his voice when he said it. My mind was made up for me. And so there we sat, gazing at the moon and listening to the crickets chirp in the clefts.

It was three days before I was due to fly out, and I was in that strange limbo before a long journey. Dad's neighbour, Gail, from two doors down and across, sang a greeting at the back gate which brought the painful silence to an end. I could just never quite make up my mind about Gail. After Mum had left us, Gail became a pretty regular visitor, even though she had a husband and family of her own. But, like I said before, Dad loved women and they loved him.

"Just thought I'd drop by and wish you *bon voyage*, Michael."

So it was real, I was really flying out to London. Until Gail had said those words it hadn't really sunk in. I looked at Dad and he looked at the beer in his hand, skimmed the beads off with his thumb and took a long sip.

Gail was a pleasant enough person I guess, but she always seemed to be looking for something. Waiting. Kind of lurking. Maybe she was just a naturally kind person waiting for an in. I was just never sure how much I should say around her in case I gave something away that I shouldn't have. Manners were invented for people like Gail. So I just played the host and offered her a drink knowing full well that she would refuse. In all the years I knew Gail, I never once saw her take a sip of anything stronger than a tonic and ice. And then the phone rang, and I skipped inside to get it, guessing by the time of night that it was either a cab broken down somewhere or P-.

It was P-.

The house had two phones—one in Dad's bedroom on what used to be Mum's bedside table, and the other mounted on a wall in the kitchen by the first of two Spanish arches above the cupboard where the whisky used to be kept. It had a long cord that reached all the way to the back step so Gail and Dad could at least get an echo of the conversation.

"P-?"

The operator interjected at this point to ask if I would accept reverse charges. The line pipped over what sounded like a party or a crowded pub full of very drunk people. I had to ask the operator to repeat herself twice. She had what I would soon learn was a thick Lancashire accent. She seemed a little underwhelmed by the whole experience. I told her yes without thinking. Dad would later be landed with a two hundred dollar trunk call charge that he would never mention, except to Gail.

"Em?"

"Hey, baby. Sounds like fun...."

Another thing I would soon learn about the English is that they produce a distinct murmur when gathered in one place like no other people in the world. It is its own kind of language somewhere between body and brain.

"Em?"

There was a male voice, close, English very English, barking *tell him! tell him!*

"You OK baby?"

"I had pleurisy...."

I had to pretend to know what pleurisy was and just cooed and awed.

"Em....god, go away, Lance! God, I wish we talked more...you were always working...."

"What's happened baby?"

"Em....I'm married! Please don't be cross—"

My father was already pretty short-sighted by then (one of the reasons he'd stopped taking the cab out at night), but Gail could see the news wasn't good and gave him a gentle tap on the arm as I gazed out speechless from the buttery light of the kitchen to the moon-silver light of the back deck where my father sat nursing his beer. I had heard P-'s voice and some male voice barking, *did you tell him?*, and suddenly Gail was there taking the phone out of my hand and passing it to my father. She never said a word, just sat on the deck with me, rubbing my back while my father seemed to spend a century with that phone pressed to his ear. I don't know how she knew, but she knew. She had met P- a couple of times and maybe saw something I didn't.

And then finally Dad lay the phone back gently in its cradle and it was done. With one simple gesture, like Gail's little sing-song *bon voyage* of barely half an hour ago, I was now being launched on a whole other journey.

You would assume an Australian would be accustomed to travelling long distances. Just driving a cab around Sydney could see me clocking up 400 kms in a night. But much like the Irish, Australians tend to fall into one of two camps. Either we are inveterate travellers or we are stolid homebodies. I guess, until I met P-, I was very much the latter. I had never flown before, never left the country before, and mine was a cheap flight that had to arc its weary way around the Russian-Afghan war and the uneasy truce along the Iran-Iraq border where a million corpses lay in shallow sandy graves around Basra and Khorramshahr. When we landed for the fifth time, in Romania, there were tanks lining each side of the runway. In all, I guess I spent upwards of 50 hours on that plane squeezed up by the window while two inexhaustibly sanguine Canadians made life hell for anyone within earshot with their relentless squealing inanities.

I had of course read about the patchwork fields of England, seen the rolling vivid green on TV, but seeing it for the first time as we broke through the dishwater clouds made me realise what a fatal mistake I had made. We circled in a loop for what seemed like an hour, actually coming in low over some islands at one point where I could see the tiny black dots of tractors in the fields and the toy houses all bunched up together in neat little rows. P- was down there somewhere waiting for me, a tiny little speck on this backdrop of green and rusty grey.

When we finally touched down at Heathrow, P- was there to meet me like she had promised Dad she would. She looked tired, but then I guess we both did. We hugged the longest hug since that last tear-stained hug in Dad's driveway. I was with Dad at the hospital after another midnight seizure the day she flew out squinting at scans that showed the spiderweb growing inexorably and some weird little dot at its centre that even had the neurologist scratching his head.

"Laurie hates me..."

"No, he doesn't."

She pushed me back clasping both my hands tightly and gave me a coquettish little pout that would have infuriated the P- I knew back in Sydney. Four months really is a long time when you're 25.

"He gave me a real talking to the other night...."

I just shrugged and snatched at my backpack before those two Canadians tripped over it, so blind were they to everything around them. I would actually encounter them again in a pub in Knightsbridge a few weeks later when I was at just about my lowest ebb. They were very kind and bought me dinner and put it in my head to go look for a job at Australia House, which I duly did. Embassy go-fer with a foreign posting supplement. In their own kind, feckless way those two girls saved me.

"You're too skinny for your height. How is he?"

"Dad?" I didn't want to tell her about the scans, didn't feel she had the right to know. It was petty of me, I know, but this was all torture by slow drip and I was busy constructing my shell. "He's OK. Playing a lot of golf."

"You need to eat more...."

"P-, you've been telling me that since our days back at college...."

She threw my hands away and pouted her angry pout. So that's what she had got out of England so far—a marriage and a pout.

"Oh...Em....don't!"

That greeting smile at Heathrow Airport was maybe the last smile I ever saw from P-. It would be all pouts and sneers from here on in.

I could tell at once she had been waiting for a while and that we were casting the same three shadows as back in Sydney. As we purred through west London in what turned out to be a very expensive black cab (no minicabs for P-), I marvelled at all the stone while P- simmered beside me. Even the stone pavements exuded a sense of permanence in stark contrast to the teetering world inside that cab. Acres and acres, miles and miles of stone. Where did they find all that granite and stone? Finally the cabbie felt the need, professional or personal, to break the silence.

"You two back from your honeymoon?"

Stone.

Stone.

Stone.

Black cabs back in those days played no radio unless you asked them to. I asked him to. Obviously, I wasn't familiar at the time with Radio GLR, but it didn't in any way help ease the tension. It just reminded me of the strange people I had landed amongst uninvited.

We got to her flat on Kings Road about four in the afternoon, but it was already dark. I was, of course, left to pay the fare while she disappeared inside and up a flight of stairs without a word. The cabbie offered me a wry empathic smile that in time I would grow accustomed to around the many watering holes of west London. I guess I have one of those faces.

When I finally found my way up the narrow stairs to her tiny apartment (after bursting into the stock room of a second hand clothes shop), I found P- on the phone. The strong scent of incense filtered up through the floorboards, and that combined with the damp stale air of the place brought on a fit of sneezing that only added to P-'s ugly mood. She pointed to a door which I assumed was where I'd be sleeping, but discovered was the bathroom. I could hear her yelling down the phone from in there.

"Well, there's no room for him here, Lance! I don't know, one of your drinking buddies? You've got enough of them. When are you leaving? Right now? Good. Look, I don't care, OK? It was your dumb idea..."

Or at least, that's what I thought I could hear. The bathroom door was heavy, black lacquered oak and there was jackhammering in the rear laneway. Maybe I imagined it all.

I lingered in there behind that solid oak door for a while looking at the spectre of myself in the shiny black lacquer. It was an inviting little space, despite the jackhammering. I felt like I could have spent the rest of my life in there, laying down on the cool checkerboard tiles and sniffing the incense from the downstairs shop. There was a bath, but no shower, which was a pity because when I flapped my shirt around a few times I realized I positively reeked after 50 hours on a plane. Maybe that was what had turned P- sour? She had always been very sensitive to sounds and smells.

When I finally mustered the courage to show myself again, P- was nowhere to be seen. The kitchen was so quiet I could hear the kitchen tap dripping between bursts of the jackhammer, but I could also hear faint rustling sounds from the bedroom that reminded me of all those nights when P- was dressing for some event and I wasn't allowed to peep until she was all dressed, and the cab was heavy on the horn downstairs. When I went to fill up a glass of water from that leaky tap I heard a faint impatient voice hissing at me not to.

"No-one drinks from the tap in London. God, haven't you read a book? There's some filtered water in the fridge."

I asked her if she was OK, but the only response was more rustling like someone turning over in bed. I found the jug of water and poured myself a small frosty glass. When she heard me rummaging around in my backpack for the duty-free malt I had bought back in Sydney, that tiny flat echoed with an unearthly shriek.

"Don't start unpacking Michael! God, this isn't fucking Earl's Court!"

When I told her what I was actually doing she let out a long groan and was soon slumped on the far end of the couch wrapped in one of the largest most ill-proportioned cable-knit sweaters I think I have ever seen, and holding out a rather cloudy glass.

We clinked glasses a little shakily like two characters at the end of a slasher movie who are yet to learn certain things aren't so easily put to sleep. I, of course, had travelled halfway across the world intent on keeping the thing alive. Even if it killed me. Which it very nearly did. P- rocked that cloudy glass back and forth under her nose and bunched her long legs under that enormous sweater as though waiting for a bomb to go off. Which it probably would have if I had lapsed into my usual habit of quoting Humphrey Bogart whenever we clinked.

"I got a postcard from Rose."

Rose was someone we both knew at college, but I got the sense very early on that Rose was a bit too straight-talking for

P-. That was what my father liked about Rose. No frills. None of that O'Shaughnessy verbiage. P- went and fetched the postcard off the top of the fridge. There was a stark white crease down the middle of it as though someone had folded it for the trash and then thought better of it. So Rose was in Thailand. She would be touching down at Heathrow on the 19th, two days away. I could feel P- watching me as I read it, running her whisky under her nose and her legs all hunched up under that sweater. Rose and I hadn't exactly parted on the best of terms because I couldn't make up my mind whether to go or stay. Our original plan was to travel together through Asia, but then Dad had his turn and I just couldn't commit. She had no idea about the mess she was flying into, unless she had rung Dad in the interim. Rose used to work as a radio operator for a rival company and she and Dad could bark radio codes back and forth at each other for what often seemed an eternity. Suddenly the idea of Rose being there in the same city lifted my spirits a little, and I guess in my exhaustion I forgot to hide it.

"I knew that would cheer you up."

I ignored the sardonic tone and asked P- how Rose knew her address. Part of me wanted Rose to already know the turn things had taken so I wouldn't have to explain the whole sordid saga to her. Or at least so I could get some idea how P- viewed her actions through a third party.

"Post Restante." She took a greedy gulp of whisky and grabbed at her knees like they were a couple of puppies trying to scatter a flock of pigeons. "God, you really are an innocent abroad. Good thing Rose is coming. You should get onto it if you guys plan to travel."

She held out her cloudy glass for a refill and chuckled darkly to herself. Actually, it was more like a yelp than a chuckle. She usually emitted it when she had said something she knew she shouldn't have. She rolled the whisky around on her tongue just like her father before he launched into one of his high-pitched diatribes. The tension was broken by the sound of a key arguing with the lock. It seemed to take forever to turn, and in the meantime P- managed to bestow this parting gift on me.

"God, we really need to get that lock fixed. Michael, you're just here because of that fucking ego of yours. Just to make my life as miserable as yours. You don't love me and you never did. You just had to have me. That's why you're here, because you think you own me and have every right to snatch me back. You're pathetic. You quit copy because you've got no balls and used your father as an excuse. My whole family thinks you're pathetic."

The door finally gave, and there stood Lance, all snaggle toothed and sad clown faced. He looked from P- to me and then back again and decided for some reason that it was safe to enter. P- offered a cheek, and he dutifully pecked it. I stood up to shake his hand but was soon wrapped in a long tight hug. The dimmer lights were low and Lance had what I would later learn were spastic retinas that made him seem a little manic when all he wanted to do was see. I wouldn't have blamed him in the circumstances. I hadn't considered Lance's feelings at all when I decided to throw caution to the wind and fly halfway across the world. But here I was, standing before the man who I should detest with every fibre of my being. He was dressed in a tailored three-piece pinstripe with a crisp white shirt and a pink tie, like a living breathing "welcome to London." P- snatched his bag and rummaged yet another single malt and a bottle of Veuve Cliquot. Lance eased the door gently shut like someone not quite sure how long they'd be staying. He had the most glorious Roman nose that seemed to lend a definitive tone to even the most trivial gesture. P- and I both watched with rapt attention as he curled his scarf over the hook on the back of the door, bowed theatrically to relieve P- of the Veuve, and then turned to utter the first of his many words to me.

"So.....two Australians in such a confined space....I must say, Michael, you are far the better behaved of the two...."

P- squealed that "school's out" squeal that was another thing I thought I owned. Lance had this habit of lapsing into Wildeian rhetoric when he was trying to read the room. It could prove a dangerous habit in mixed company, as I would later discover at the cost of a tooth.

"I see you brought whisky." The cork popped announcing a before and an after. "Islay.....you have taste, Michael..." He gave me a wink that P- seemed to feel drilling into the back of her skull.

"Really, Lance?"

I was worried if she bunched those legs up any tighter she would start depriving herself of oxygen. Lance presented P- and me with a crystal flue alive with bubbles.

"Here's to your safe arrival, Michael. I hear the flight is not for the faint-hearted. Chin, chin! Your first time in the old dart?"

I started explaining my theory on the two types of Australian, but P- rolled her eyes and hijacked the conversation in the cause of O'Shaughnessy brevity and the four-drink rule. They are a headstrong brood with no tolerance for heavy liquor. Her version didn't paint me in a very flattering light, but then I guess my explanation wouldn't have either. It was obvious even after a ten minute acquaintance that Lance had seen a good deal of the world and was keen to see a good deal more. He would find out soon enough that P- was very much cast from the same frumpish mould as yours truly, but I guess that's what comes of hasty marriages.

Lance held up a hand politely and steered the conversation away from me and onto the events of the day. Couple talk. I watched the bubbles dance and die in my glass. So this was how *after* felt; one eye at the keyhole. Lance confided a few hours later that he hadn't heard anything about me until after the wedding. He found P- crying in the women's toilet and coaxed it out of her. He should have been angry, but instead he laughed. He was as shocked by the sound of it as P- was, but the whole situation was so tragi-comic that he didn't know how else to react. He had no plans to be married, never had. In fact, he had a deep mistrust of the whole institution. And yet somehow here he was and here I was. The O'Shaughnessys can be a very persuasive bunch.

"I mean, how could you do that to someone?" he asked with those dancing eyes desperate to latch on to something. "I badgered her for an hour to call you. I was so bloody angry. For you, mainly, but for me too. I mean, who exactly had I married?"

This conversation took place a little later in a pub on Portobello Road after the whisky had begun to have its usual effect on P- and we both knew better than to hang around. Our hunt for dinner consisted of him shouting me a kebab. We both knew P- would be curled in bed already kicking angrily at the sheets. Once the food had soaked up some of the booze and put me back on something resembling an even keel, I told him I should never have come.

"I don't know what I was thinking."

"You're in love, Michael." His black eyes danced all over me as though I was casting two shadows. "Don't ever apologize for that."

The pub was a tiny hole in the wall with a small Jamaican restaurant out the back. It was pretty busy for a Tuesday night, but Lance was obviously a regular and the barman came right over.

"This him?"

Lance's smile twisted a little at the edges like someone struggling to loosen a rusty bolt.

"Daniel, this is Michael. Michael, Daniel."

Daniel held out a warm hand accompanied by a searching smile accentuated by a pair of the bluest eyes I think I have ever seen.

"Long flight?"

"Fifty hours."

"Jesus!"

"Daniel here is an actor. The real deal. West End mainly, but he'll be a big Hollywood star one of these days."

Daniel shrugged, tossed his towel over a broad shoulder.

"Usual?"

Lance gave me another searching look.

"You ever tried a Guinness? Daniel here pours the best Guinness in London. There's an art to it."

But Daniel had already started pouring two black creamy pints.

"Yeah...patience....sorry, but some of you Aussies pour it like a beer."

And so it came about that I was poured my first Guinness in London by the future James Bond.

While we let the pints settle, Lance gestured to someone watching us from the corner stool closest to the restaurant. Sat behind this mysterious figure was a gaggle of kids cackling in one of the booths. As he stood up in answer to Lance's coaxing, he turned to them and muttered something that had them all go quiet and look in my direction. He then swept around the corner of the bar in one graceful movement with a glint in his almond eyes that seemed to signal a job well done.

"Michael," Lance croaked, "I want you to meet Michael."

This other Michael waved his half-drunk pint in our direction and cast a wryly amused look at Lance.

"Fuck me, Lance! This him? You sure you didn't leave a bit of him behind somewhere?"

It would soon become the refrain of the evening, the autumn, the winter.

"Now, now, Michael. He's solid. He needs a place. You know of any?"

"Nice to meet you mate. Call me Micky. Micky Twoshoes."

I must have had the look of someone about to ask, but Micky simply pointed to his shoes—a pair of glorious olive-green leather and tan borders with matching laces.

"I got one or two ideas, Lancelot." He gestured over his shoulder at the sheepish ogling gaggle in the booth. It elicited an audible sigh from Daniel behind the bar. The crow's feet around Micky's eyes burst into a brief riot of mirth and mischief.

"Another, thanks, Daniel. Lance is paying. Still owe me for the fancy wheels, remember?"

"I gave you the money you asked on the night, Micky."

Daniel backed Lance up on this, although suddenly everyone looked a little uneasy at mention of "the night."

"It's OK guys." I felt the need to drag myself back out of the third person to the first. Third person, third wheel, it was beginning to wear.

"The guy's been through enough, Micky," Daniel said with a nod to me. "I'm happy to put him up for a day or two. Just leave them out of it."

Micky let this slide while he looked me up and down and his pint settled on the mat.

"See," Lance said. "He's solid. Knew it the moment I met him."

Daniel wandered off shaking his head to take an order through the restaurant hatch. Micky looked me up and down again and then gestured to one of the gaggle to get over here.

The kid hopped over on one foot for some reason and managed to bang his knee painfully on a stool. He was all baseball cap, dimple cheeks, and Nikes, and kept moving his weight from one leg to the other like a child on the verge of a tantrum. Micky looked him up and down with the same expression of wry amusement he'd aimed at me just a moment ago.

"What the fuck is wrong with you, Hassan?"

"Sorry, I really need to pee Micky..."

Micky shrugged at me and Lance and cast a dirty look at Daniel standing in the dark corner with his arms crossed.

"So...go, ya muppet....you know where it is...fuck me, the help these days!"

"This him?" Hassan asked. I swear I heard his teeth chattering.

"Hassan, Michael. Michael, Hassan."

Despite his obvious distress, Hassan took the time to proffer me a hand.

"Nice to meet you Michael. Sorry...."

I waved at him to go, for god's sake, and he was off in a flash elbowing some old guy out of the way in the process. For some reason that simple gesture was all Micky needed to trust Lance on this one. Micky didn't know much about Aussies back then, other than that they poured a shit Guiness and dressed like homeless people, but apparently, I intrigued him. I have known Micky Twoshoes for twenty years now and I count him as one of my oldest staunchest friends. But I suspect much of what he tells me is apocryphal about the effect I had on him that night. He calls me 'Em' just like P-used to before she stopped talking to me altogether. Hassan emerged from the toilet looking a bit more relaxed, but still jumpy.

"Here it comes! Fuck me, what you been doing in there?" Micky wanted to know. It was like watching a ventriloquist arguing with his dummy. "About to send in a fucking search party!"

Hassan sniffed and gave a guilty smile that lit up his dimple. Lance let out a loud guffaw and almost choked on the sip of Guinness he had just taken.

"Welcome to London, digger," he wheezed as I slapped him hard on the back.

For a while, probably since Micky had first turned around and given them all a talking to, I had been glancing over at the only girl in that booth. Admittedly, I hadn't really slept in two days, and I was more than a little tipsy by now, but to my jet-lagged eyes that girl was perhaps the most beautiful woman I had ever laid eyes on. She had already caught me looking at her over Micky's shoulder a couple of times, but now Hassan was back from the toilet, she decided enough was enough. She sprung up out of that booth and was at Hassan's side in a heartbeat, jutting her chin at me and slapping her empty pint down on the bar. Daniel let out another audible groan as he stacked the tray of dirty glasses in the washer and did his best to ignore her.

"You get a good eyeful, mate?"

Then she caught herself and cast a beautiful onyx eye over the gathering.

"Oh shit...oh fucking shit...this him?"

She toggled a perfectly manicured finger at me and asked once again.

"This him? Shit, I was expecting a fucking statchoo. He don't look like much, does he. Orright?"

Hassan looked her up and down much the same way Micky had done to him. There appeared to be some weird chain of command in operation.

"Yeah? And when was the last time you flew in from Australia, Yaz?"

She looked me up and down again. It must be a London thing, I remember thinking at the time.

"Australia? I thought you said he was from Tasmania or summink...."

She gave me a little knowing wink while everyone took a moment. I realized I just wasn't going to stop staring no matter how hard I tried. She was a one woman show, after all. So this is England, I thought, the patchwork fields already a distant memory. Lance straightened up with a groan out of his barfly slump. I had already forgotten he had his own problems, and yet, here he was, and here I was.

"Yasmin, meet Michael. Michael, Yasmin."

She proffered a cold hand, light as a sparrow's wing.

"Yasmin is studying at clown school. First in her class, apparently."

Her beautiful eyes lit up round and sad as a clown's.

"Yeah, fuck off Lance, fucking racist toff!" Another wink at me. "Anyway, where's my pint."

Hassan looked ever more uncomfortable. The dimple seemed to have gone back to its maker.

"Jesus, Yaz...."

The whole London *looking up and down thing* again as though I had landed in a city solely peopled by bespoke tailors.

"Helped him get into his car the other night, innit. Drunken toffs always losing their keys."

She shook her hand around so much her ring almost flew off her finger. Not a wedding ring, I noticed, and suddenly my mood darkened again. When Daniel set her pint down (splashed down may be a more accurate description) I went to reach into my pocket, but I may as well have been reaching for a gun.

"Hold on, hold on, hold on..." Micky said holding up a hand. "What you think you're doing?"

Lance gripped my shoulder and then mumbled something to Daniel who had soon poured a Guinness of his own and was watching this tragi-comedy like an actor taking notes. In my embarrassment I felt the need to ask how many people in this pub knew who I was.

"Skippy, the whole of Portobello Road knows who you are by now, mate. And I've gotta say, sorry don't take offence, but so far you're living up to the hype."

Yasmin picked up her pint with one hand and pinched her pierced nose with the other.

"Fuck, is he ever, Twoshoes! Gawd, mate! Don't you Tasmanians ever heard of barfs?"

Another wink. If you weren't looking for it, you would have missed it. She was just trying to bring me down from my broken heart, 50 hours in the air. *Men are dreamy fools, Skippy.*

"Yasmin," Lance felt the need to extrapolate from his tired slump, "the man has been two days in the air. I married the love of his life. Now, can you find him a place to sleep or not?"

"You fink I'm a fucking idiot, Lancelot? Planet ain't that big for a two-day flight. Racist fuck!" Then she cupped her hand to her mouth and leaned in close to me. I could smell her musk. "Only island state of the only island continent, right?"

I didn't realize you could stop a wink halfway through, but Yasmin managed it because of some look from me. I don't remember. I was so drunk and exhausted by then, but I guess I have one of those faces. For the first and last time, Yasmin laid a tender hand on me.

"You'll be alright mate....whatta you reckon, Hass? That Aussie's old flat? You mind climbing stairs, Michael?"

Lance felt the need to interject here, even though I swear I heard him snoring into his pint, and Daniel was hovering close.

"You're not talking about Westbourne Grove? 30 flights of stairs? In his condition?"

Yasmin thrust out her proud chin again.

"You're the only one with a condition, mate!"

Daniel quietly suggested that maybe it was time Lance thought about going home. I gave Lance a hug to coax him on his way, but he shrugged me off. I was on my second wind. He was married to my fiancée.

Later that night, or perhaps best described as the next sudsy November morning under grey skies whose ancient weight you can't imagine until you have woken under them, I found myself gazing down from the 16th floor of a council flat on a grey city blinking itself awake. It was a cold dank cavern with no electricity, no phone, and no real lock on the door. I lay there wrapped in my sleeping bag most of that first day listening to the hum of the city through the floor to ceiling glass, that same weird English hum I had heard over the phone that night P- broke the news. When was that? Three years ago? Three hundred? No, only four days and counting. I am still counting.

I got sick after a few days staring out that window. Suddenly I was wracked with fever and could barely stand up long enough to pee. Maybe it was all the stress, or those 50 hours on a plane, or simply the fact that I was too young to think about flu jabs back then and I had touched down in a cold dank London November with not enough clothes. So, I lay there on the scratchy patchwork matting smelling of some stranger's feet and willed myself to die while the London lights blinked back at me like Dad's hospital monitor. But it's a remarkable thing when you're lying prone like that in a cold council squat willing yourself to die, how quickly you become invested in all the little incidental sounds of the daily round. After three days, I think I learnt more about London than London has learnt about itself in 2000 years. But then, that's often the hollow boast of the rootless, loveless, and indigent, isn't it?

After a few days I woke to find a fresh pillow tucked under my head, another blanket over my sleeping bag, and a bowl of soup steaming right under my nose. I took a few greedy spoonful's and fell straight back to sleep. When I woke it was dark and there was another pillow under my head and another steaming bowl of soup. Chicken this time, although I was still too sick to taste it.

Then I remember gentle hands were lifting me and setting me down again on something soft, and when I woke the next time, it was light, and Rose was there with Yasmin laughing at my shock of hair while London blinked at me all grey and vast under leaden skies.

And the world so clear—so crystal clear.

AUTHOR BIOGRAPHIES

Brittany Bell is a middle school teacher who lives in Queens, New York with her husband and two tiny humans who call her mom. She holds a BA in English Literature from CUNY Queens College, an MA in Special Education from CUNY Hunter College, and is a proud Teach for America alumni. Brittany has been writing since childhood and currently belongs to two local writers groups, including one she moderates. You can usually find her reading, writing, playing outside with her kids, or snuggled up next to one of the family cats.

Jennifer Cinguina lives in New York. She has an MFA in Creative Writing from Fairfield University and a master's from The Medill School of Journalism at Northwestern University. Her writing can be found in *The New York Times* and various online literary magazines.

Vincent Czyz is the author of two collections of short fiction, the first of which won the 2016 Eric Hoffer Award for Best in Small Press, two novels, a novella, and an essay collection. He is the recipient of two fiction fellowships from the NJ Council on the Arts, the W. Faulkner-W. Wisdom Prize for Short Fiction, and the 2011 Capote Fellowship at Rutgers University. His stories have appeared in *Shenandoah, AGNI, The Massachusetts Review, Tin House, Copper Nickel,* and *Southern Indiana Review,* among other publications.

Morning. **Caroline Shannon Davenport** sits here half asleep. Needing coffee. She reads from her soon-to-be published novel, *Terror at the Sound of a Whistle,* and looks back through time. She considers her short story published in Anthology #7, "Perennials." She could dream up something else in this state of mind. Would it be too redundant? If not, she'll use it, otherwise she'll dream...and a cat strolls by.

Elizabeth Devecchi spent much of her youth in New England, setting out after high school to gather degrees and experiences, jumping from state to state, country to country. Author of the blog themoonthesunandlittleman.com, Elizabeth's short story, "The Hunt," appeared in Ariel Chart; and her essay, "A Moment in My Head," ran in Run Amok Book's The Growlery. Lately, she has delved into the world of horror, and her poem, "Oh, Brother" is included in the second installment of Black Spot Books' annual women in horror poetry showcase, UNDER HER EYE, released in November 2023. Her debut horror novel, A WHISPER IN THE DARK, is set for release by Wicked House Publishing in 2024 and her second novel, a thriller/horror, with a touch of the paranormal is being signed for release in early 2025. Elizabeth is an HWA and SCBWI member, and currently resides in Colorado with her family.

Beck Erixson writes about the beautifully awkward world of navigating the journey to happiness through friendships, love, and family—be it blood, found, or chosen. Her stories enhance the importance of positive interconnection, even when we feel lonely. She lives on the Jersey Shore and can often be found either writing by the river, or in it in some way.

Jon Fain has worked as a silk-screen printer, warehouse worker, resume writer, corporate documentation and training consultant, and freelance editor. He began publishing fiction in commercial and literary magazines in the 1980s, and later in some of the first online literary journals in the 2000s. He has close to 100 short fiction publications to date. His flash fiction chapbook, "Pass the Panpharmacon!" is available from Greying Ghost Press. He lives in Massachusetts.

Nathaniel Farcas was a 19-year-old award-winning short story author and had been writing poetry since the age of six. His poetry has been seen in the Southern Florida Poetry Journal (SoFloPoJo) as well as featured in New Words {press}. He was so very proud to be featured in the Running Wild & RIZE Annual Short Story Anthology. He left an enormous amount of stories, poems and two novels which are slowly being curated by his mother for continuing publication.

Ken Goldman, former Philadelphia teacher of English and Film Studies, is an Active member of the Horror Writers Association. He has homes on the Main Line in Pennsylvania and at the Jersey shore. His stories have appeared in over 970 independent press publications in the U.S., Canada, the UK, and Australia with over twenty due for publication in 2023-24. Ken's tales have received seven honorable mentions in The Year's Best Fantasy & Horror. He has written six books: three anthologies of short stories, YOU HAD ME AT ARRGH!!

(Sam's Dot Publishers), DONNY DOESN'T LIVE HERE ANYMORE (A/A Productions) and STAR-CROSSED (Vampires 2); and a novella, DESIREE, (Damnation Books). His first novel OF A FEATHER (Horrific Tales Publishing) was released in January 2014. SINKHOLE, his second novel, was published by Bloodshot Books August 2017.

Lauren Lang is a former broadcast journalist and current freelance photographer and videographer living in Denver, CO. In her spare time, she writes fiction, cooks, bakes, crochets hats for stuffed animals, gardens with the intent of taking pictures of the flowers should they live and terrorizes residents by pretending to be a wildlife photographer and running through area parks with her camera screaming, "Birds!" Occasionally, she does take a picture of a bird. More information about Lauren and her work can be found by visiting: https://www.facebook.com/AuthorLaurenLang/

Eric D. Lehman is the author or editor of twenty-two books, including *New England at 400, A History of Connecticut Food, Literary Connecticut,* and *Afoot in Connecticut: Journeys in Natural History,* nominated for the Pushcart Prize. His biography of Charles Stratton, *Becoming Tom Thumb,* won the Henry Russell Hitchcock Award from the Victorian Society of America, and was chosen as one of the American Library Association's outstanding university press books of the year. His revolutionary history *Homegrown Terror: Benedict Arnold and the Burning of New London* was a finalist in two categories of the Next Gen Indie Book Awards and was used in a question on *Jeopardy.* And his novella, *Shadows of Paris,* was the Novella of the Year from the Next Gen Indie Book Awards, a Silver Medal for Romance from the Foreword Review Indie Book Awards, and a finalist for the Connecticut

Book Award. In addition to teaching creative writing and literature at the University of Bridgeport, he is a regular contributor to Estuary and has been consulted on diverse subjects and quoted by *The Atlantic Monthly*, *USA Today*, the BBC, the History Channel, *Deutsche Presse-Agentur*, and *The Wall Street Journal*.

Justin Lowe lives in a house called *Doug* in the Blue Mountains west of Sydney where he edits international poetry blog, *Bluepepper*. "Portobello" comes from a work-in-progress comprising short stories, memoir and letters conceived while I waited on word from my publishers regarding my latest poetry collection (contracts are being drawn up as we speak).

Dalton Mire is a New York state native who has crisscrossed the United States and Canada. He worked for the Department of Defense Schools as a teacher and administrator in Japan, Korea, the Philippines, Germany, the United Kingdom, Panama, and Puerto Rico. He earned his Ph.D. at the University of Santo Tomas in Manila. He has won prizes in the Flash Fiction and Short Story genres in the Florida Writers Association competition, where he has also been a judge. He has published a variety of short stories and two novels: *Fracking Dinosaurs-The Cayuga Lake Disaster* and *Rafe-Lincoln's Samurai Agent*. Dalton now lives in Florida and can be reached at daltonmire@yahoo.com.

Jerry Purdon writes dark fantasy and horror stories. "Bloodlines" in Incurable: Stories from the World of CURE anthology appeared in Spring of 2025. Earlier works include "Beer in a Bar" and "Graveyard Game". His favorite thing in the world is to sit outdoors engrossed in a great book. He holds a B.A. in Literature from University of Houston - Clear Lake.

Jerry resides in Texas and is married to his ideal reader. You can find Jerry @ www.jerrypurdon.com

Kim Ransley lives in Tasmania, the small island at the bottom of Australia. She has a PhD in psychology and her stories often explore hallucination and altered states of mind. She has published poems and short stories in Australia and overseas and is currently working on her first novel. She has also published several non-fiction articles about the brain for news and science media around the world.

Mykyta Ryzhykh: Nominated for Pushcart Prize. Published many times in the journals Dzvin, Dnipro, Bukovinian magazine, Polutona, Tipton Poetry Journal, Stone Poetry Journal, Divot journal, dyst journal, Superpresent Magazine, Allegro Poetry Magazine, Alternate Route, Better Than Starbucks, Littoral Press, Book of Matches, TheNewVerse News, Acorn haiku Journal, The Wise Owl, Verse-Virtual, Scud, Fevers of the Mind, LiteraryYard, PLUM TREE TAVERN, ITERANT, Fleas on the Dog, The Tiger Moth Review, Lothlorien Poetry Journal, Angel Rust, Neologism Poetry Journal, Shot Glass Journal, QLRS, The Crank, Chronogram, The Antonym, Monterey Poetry Review, Five Fleas Itchy Poetry, Ranger magazine, PPP Ezine, Bending Genres Journal, Rat's Ass Review, Cajun Mutt Press, minor literatures, Audience Askew Literary Journal, Spirit Fire Review, The Gravity of the Thing, Ballast Journal, Star 82 Review, The BeZine, A Thin Slice of Anxiety, Synchronized Chaos, boats against the current, The Decadent Review, Corvus Review, American Diversity Report, Unlikely Stories, Triggerfish Critical Review, The Moth, Ripple Lit, Rock & Sling, Meniscus, Rabid Oak, ZiN Daily, Stone of Madness, The Cortland Standard, Quarter Press, Schredder, Wilderness House Literary Review, Poetry Porch,

Chewers & Masticadores, The Big Windows Review, Journal of Compressed Creative Arts, Third Wednesday, Cosmic Double, Dialogist, Consequence, Cool Beans Lit, Poets Choice, BarBar.

Joseph A. Schiller is a high school social studies teacher in Houston, TX USA, where he lives with his wife and three sons. Joseph has had several poems and short stories published along with a fantasy novel, Spanish translation of that novel, a non-fiction historical investigation, and an upcoming graphic novel.

Ibtisam Shahbaz is an emerging writer and poet based in Naarm. Her work is influenced by her childhood in Australia and Pakistani heritage. She has worked with Red Room Poetry, on their annual Poetry Month and Poem Forest projects. Her fiction has been published by outlets including Monash University Publishing, Old Water Rat Publishing and Hawkeye Publishing. She is currently the Poetry Editor at Be: longing Magazine. You can find more about her writing journey at www.ibtisamshahbaz.com.

Born and raised in Sioux Lookout, Ontario, ***John Tavares*** is the son of Portuguese immigrants from Sao Miguel, Azores. Having graduated from arts and science at Humber College and journalism at Centennial College, he more recently earned an Honors BA in English Literature from York University. His short fiction has been published in a variety of print and online journals and magazines, including anthologies and community radio and newspapers, in the US, Canada, and internationally. His many passions include journalism, literature, economics, photography, writing, and coffee, and he enjoys hiking and cycling.

Mark Williams's fiction has appeared or is forthcoming in Eclectica, The Baffler, Cleaver, The Main Street Rag, Bull: Men's Fiction, and Gargoyle. His poems have appeared in The Southern Review, Rattle, Nimrod, Beyond Words, and elsewhere. Kelsay Books published his poetry collection, Carrying On, in 2022. This is his third appearance in a Running Wild Press anthology. He lives in Evansville, Indiana.

By day, **Gary Zenker** is an award-winning marketer and copywriter, using his talents to help companies and nonprofits reach their audiences. By night, his particular madness is flash fiction, crossing genres to write stories revealing the highs and lows of the potential hidden inside people you might know.

He began his writing career in college, grammar-correcting bathroom stall graffiti (true story). He believes that prepared him for a long history of angry rejection and harsh critique of his writing. He is also the founder of two writers' groups (one of which he still runs after 15 years), is the primary instigator of Noir at a Bar which runs annual benefits for the Oxford PA public library and likes to write about himself in the third person, much to the annoyance of people around him. He has authored a handful of books and published two dozen more reprinting rock and roll artifacts. His flash fiction has appeared in a number of online publications and print anthologies including Chicken Soup For the Soul: Humor and two previous Running Wild Anthologies.

www.garyzenkerstoryteller.com.

EDITOR BIOGRAPHY

Ben White is an acquisitions editor for Running Wild Press who has worked with hundreds of authors, selecting titles for publication, polishing stories and novels, and putting together anthologies. His own work includes many poems published in various journals as well as a few full-length collections he finally got around to typing up and submitting: *Buddha Bastinado Blues, The Kill Gene, Conley Bottom: A Poemoir, The Recon Trilogy +1, Always Ready: Poems from a Life in the U. S. Coast Guard,* and *Say Their Names* (under Anonymous).

ABOUT RUNNING WILD PRESS

Running Wild Press publishes stories that cross genres with great stories and writing. RIZE publishes great genre stories written by people of color and by authors who identify with other marginalized groups. Our team consists of:

Lisa Diane Kastner, Founder and Executive Editor
Joelle Mitchell, Licensing and Strategy Lead
Cody Sisco, Acquisition Editor, RIZE
Benjamin White, Acquisition Editor, Running Wild
Peter A. Wright, Acquisition Editor, Running Wild
Resa Alboher, Editor
Angela Andrews, Editor
Sandra Bush, Editor
Ashley Crantas, Editor
Rebecca Dimyan, Editor
Abigail Efird, Editor
Aimee Hardy, Editor
Henry L. Herz, Editor
Cecilia Kennedy, Editor

Barbara Lockwood, Editor
Scott Schultz, Editor
Rod Gilley, Editor

Evangeline Estropia, Product Manager
Kimberly Ligutan, Product Manager
Pulp Art Studios, Cover Design
Standout Books, Interior Design
Polgarus Studios, Interior Design

Learn more about us and our stories at www.runningwild-press.com

Loved these stories and want more? Follow us at runningwildpublishing.com, www.facebook.com/runningwild-press, on Twitter @lisadkastner @RunWildBooks